GUNNER

WOLVES OF IRON VALOR MC BOOK 6

DEX HAVEN

UNDER A TEXAS SKY PRESS

DEDICATION

MEAN MAN

Thank you for believing in me even when I didn't.

EPIGRAPH

Desperado, why don't you come to your senses? Come down from your fences. Open the gate. It may be rainin', but there's a rainbow above you. You better let somebody love you. Before it's too late. -Don Henley & Glenn Frey

CONTENTS

Trigger Warnings

All of my books contain graphic intimacy, and likely some kind of physical violence (sometimes sexual)—but always with a triumph-centered resolution. Guaranteed HEA. I don't believe in giving away the journey before it begins, but I believe in honoring your peace. If you know certain topics are hard for you, I encourage you to trust your instincts and read with care.

That being said, I thought it was important to note that there are scenes in Gunner that include non-consensual sex (in dream sequences). It's also important to remind you that this is a paranormal series. There are creatures included that are not human and as such they may participate in non-human to human sexual contact. If these scenarios are triggering for you in any context, I do not recommend you continue.

A complete list of warnings can be found on my website: www.dexhavenauthor.com

CHAPTER 1

BRIE

Two weeks since County Line and my mirror still lied to me.

I sat at the thrifted white vanity in my bedroom, or let's call it what it was, a primary closet with delusions of grandeur. Two frosted bulbs flickered above the glass, one yellow, one blue-white, so my face split down the middle in a weird Monet-meets-crime-scene way. It suited me.

This morning, the reflection was extra brutal: my long inverted bob, which was longer in the front than back, refused to lay smooth, no matter how many times I'd used the flat iron. Purple smudges lay under both eyes because sleep and I were on a trial separation.

I ran the bullet-tip of my favorite eyeliner over my lower lashes, steady as a surgeon. Not because I was calm, but because if I didn't anchor my hand, I'd poke my eye out. My wolf—the animal part of me that should have made me fierce and untouchable; instead curled up somewhere between my ribs, watching and waiting for any sign of him.

Gunner. Even thinking of the name sent a glitch through my pulse. Finn "Gunner" Walsh, who'd first been so easy with me when he'd loaded my mother and me into his truck after we'd stepped off the plane when we'd been rescued from the nightmare in that Paris warehouse. That's where I'd seen my big sister, Harper, run a steel pipe through a man's neck and into his chest; killing him. Bronc had asked Gunner to drive us to the house Parker had generously provided for my mom and me to stay in while we tried to figure out what was next for us. He'd spoken so kindly to me then.

A couple of weeks later at the County Line Bar I didn't know he was there until a big, hulking creature had tried to back me up against him on the dance floor. He was all wrong, and I'd tried to pull away. But he was stronger and wouldn't allow it. Then Gunner happened. I hadn't seen him, but I heard his muffled voice, and the creature let go and backed away. Then his hands were on me. Gunner's hands—strong, calloused, and perfect—wrapped around my waist, then under my shirt until I felt them against my skin. It felt like electricity ran through my body. I had to try to play it off. There's no way I could let him see how he'd affected me. I just looked over my shoulder and teased him the way I knew he hated with an old cowboy reference. I called him 'Billy the Kid.' That's when he whispered in my ear that he wasn't an outlaw, but he wasn't the good guy either.

That was the last time he'd spoken to me. He acted like I was some kind of feral cat you lured with bits of leftover steak, then he'd said he didn't know if he should 'kiss me or strip my pants down and spank my naked ass red.' That had been his parting shot when he left me at the bar. He'd been grinding against my ass with his hand against my stomach, then he just left me there.

The moment had been surgical, precise. He'd leaned in, green eyes locked on mine. Every one of my internal alarms went off: scent of sweat and soap and leather, the ache in my belly, the stutter in my breath. My wolf uncurled, wild-eyed, tail up. He stopped just short of my lips—one centimeter—and let the entire universe pause on that knife edge.

I'd wanted it so bad I'd almost leaned in to bridge the gap.

Then he'd grinned and walked away, boots echoing on the sticky bar floor, not a backward glance. My wolf had howled, in the internal way you can't explain to normal people. Harper and Arsenal had arrived to pick me up like I was some kind of wayward child and not a goddamn 23-year-old woman. I was furious. So of course I ran after Gunner like a fool, yelling at him as I went.

'This isn't finished, cowboy! We're not done here!' Yep, I made a right fool of myself. And it was only made worse when he turned back to me and tipped his damn hat to me.

Then he said the words I wasn't sure I was happy to hear. 'You're goddamn right, little girl. We're not done here. Not by a long shot.'

I had just stood there until Harper took my arm and led me out to Arsenal's truck. I didn't say a word and thankfully, neither did she. She quietly dropped me off back at my house where I'd drown in a fit of pure self-loathing, drawn every curtain, flipped every mirror, and spent twenty-four hours watching reality TV and eating Ritz crackers in bed. Because I was a sophisticated woman, damn it. Because I did not want Gunner, or any man, to own me.

Except I did. And my wolf did. And no matter how many times I told myself that I'd grown out of needing—out of being needy—every cell in my body wanted to run after him and beg.

Avoiding my mother had been tricky, but she'd learned to keep her distance when I got like this.

I blinked. The makeup pencil slipped, leaving a jagged line at the outer corner. Good, I thought. Ugly fit better.

But the memory of him replayed on a loop, and my body responded with flawless recall. The flush started in my cheeks, hot enough to steam off the cheap primer, then swept down my throat, prickle and heat gathering behind my sternum. My hands wanted to do something: break the pencil, throw the compact, clutch at my own skin. Instead, I gripped the white laminate edge of the vanity so hard my fingers lost color. My legs pressed together, thighs as tight as a vise.

This wasn't new. I'd spent two weeks rerunning the scene, hoping it would fade or distort, that the real version was less humiliating than the one in my head. No such luck.

I dotted concealer under each eye, patted it in with the pad of my ring finger. Luc had said I looked pretty without it, but Luc lied about everything. Gunner wouldn't have. He would've told me I looked like shit, then kissed me anyway. Then done the other thing, probably.

The idea made my stomach do a little backflip.

"Get a grip," I whispered to my reflection. The mirror Brie sneered back, lips pale, eyebrows two different shapes. I tried to fix the left one and made it worse. My hand was definitely shaking.

Maybe it was chemical; could it be a mate bond? My sister Harper said it was ancient magic, as if that explained anything. I called bullshit, said we were mammals in heat, all biology and delusion. But Harper had accepted Arsenal and the bond that fate had clearly given them. They were sickly happy, so maybe I was the delusional one.

I pressed a knuckle into my sternum, hard, trying to root out the ache. My wolf flicked her tail and showed her teeth. The memory of Gunner's voice was stuck on replay, like a song with one sexy, humiliating line.

The scent of him was stuck, too, in my memory. Not cologne—Gunner wore soap, leather, the kind of sweat that came from actual labor. The opposite of Luc Renault and his expensive French aftershave and pressed shirts. Gunner wore snap-front plaid and jeans that had seen more action than I had. His hands looked like they could break me in half. I'd seen those hands pull on the reins of a wild bronco until the horse calmed under his touch. It was like magic.

I lined my lips, overdrawn, a little desperate. I wiped half of it away, then reapplied. Everything felt wrong. Too much. My throat was tight.

The problem was, I'd never wanted anyone before. Not really. I'd liked being wanted, had learned all the tricks: how to tilt my head, how to arch my back, how to look at a man and make him forget his own name. But with Gunner, none of those tricks mattered. He saw through it, stripped me bare with a look, and left me reeling.

My phone buzzed on the vanity. I flinched so hard my mascara wand hit my eyelid and left a black smudge. For a second, I let myself hope it was him. It wasn't. It never was. Just a group text from Harper, organizing "pack dinner" at the pack house.

I stared at the phone, at the message, at my own reflected disappointment. My wolf paced. I wiped the mascara off with a makeup wipe, furious at myself for the hope, for the need, for the visible evidence of both.

The mirror Brie looked back at me, smudged and haunted, her mouth set in a bitter line.

I shut the light off and let her disappear.

⁂

I flicked the lights back on, eventually. The mirror made a soft whine as it warmed, like it didn't want to see me either.

The second time around, I looked harder. I'd read somewhere that mirrors reveal the soul if you stare long enough, but all I got was a too-thin face and the beginnings of worry lines. Not what Paris promised. Not what I'd promised myself.

I pulled a silk scarf—blue with little golden fleurs-de-lis—from the jewelry tray and knotted it around my throat, too tight. The collar was a habit from France, where everything mattered more if you wore it with conviction. Here, in Texas, it just made me look like I had something to hide.

I was supposed to be sophisticated. That was the deal: Brie the cosmopolitan, the artist, the younger sister who never let a man define her. But if I peeled back even a square inch, all you'd see was failure. The charity case hiding behind MAC foundation and overpriced scarves. The girl who'd betrayed her sister, then tried to pretty up the truth.

Two weeks since the run-in with Gunner, I'd tried to be any place he might not be. I avoided the Compound, avoided Pearl's, I even avoided the goddamn grocery store, just in case his wolf senses would let him smell me down the freezer aisle. When Harper asked, I told her I was "reassessing." I didn't mention that every molecule of air in Dairyville had a Gunner flavor to it.

Why the hell was I like this? Why did it feel safer to believe I was too good for all this—too French, too damaged, too whatever—when the truth was I'd let Luc Renault fuck me up so bad I couldn't even want a good thing, let alone deserve it?

The flashbacks came in smells and colors. Wet grass, sugar smoke, the tinny reek of Champagne on Luc's breath when he whispered secrets in my ear. He was nothing like Gunner: Luc was sharp, polished, the kind of man who never needed to say he was dangerous because you knew by the way he watched you over his glass. He taught me how to drink absinthe, how to fake a Parisian accent, how to cut myself off from my wolf so I could be what he wanted—a human with a hint of extra. He called me "my little American," like I was a pet project. I liked it. No, I craved it. Attention was currency, and I needed to be rich.

He'd used me, of course. The whole time, he'd been working for Waylon Steiner, waiting for the right moment to hand me and Harper over. And I let him, because I liked feeling needed more than I liked feeling safe.

The shame of it burned hotter than Gunner's filthy words ever could. I dabbed highlighter on the tips of my cheekbones, trying to catch the light, but it only made the skin look harsher, more haunted.

I tried to meet my own eyes, but couldn't.

When Arsenal and his team finally busted into that warehouse, I was so relieved. I was so afraid Steiner was going to kill Harper. The way he was beating her was almost more than I could bear. I was responsible for that. My fucking stupidity caused her suffering, and the shame of that was something I didn't think I could ever get over. I knew Harper would forgive me, because Harper was built from forgiveness. Me? I'd never forgiven myself.

I'd gone straight from rescue to hiding out in Dairyville, refusing to let anyone see the cracks. Pearl said I was "healing," but I knew better. I was covering old wounds with new glitter.

I touched up my lipstick with the edge of my pinky finger. It was a shade called "Unimpressed," which made me laugh, but the sound came out thin and scratchy.

"Who are you kidding?" I made myself hold the gaze.

I remembered the way I'd talked to Harper in that cell. I was cruel to her. I told her she always thought she was better than me. What a bitch I'd been. And why? Harper was always kind to me. I was just jealous. Our parents fucking threw her away, and I chose to treat her badly because I couldn't believe Luc was using me. I believed a stranger over my flesh and blood. What did that say about me?

I wiped the lipstick off, then redid it, this time perfectly. My hands didn't shake anymore; they were frozen, numb. I added more blush, hoping for a healthy flush, but it looked painted and desperate.

I'd been a coward even with Gunner. I'd dodged him for two weeks, pretending like I had something better to do than sit at Pearl's and eat greasy fries while pretending not to look for him in the crowd. I told myself I didn't want a small-town cowboy, that I was meant for art and cities and maybe Paris again, someday. But the second he'd put his hand on my hip at County Line, my knees had gone soft and my wolf had bared her belly to him. I wanted that raw, brute thing he offered, and it disgusted me.

I caught myself hunching in the mirror, shoulders rounded, chin tucked like I was hiding from a fist. I straightened, forced my head up. The posture lasted half a second before I slumped again.

God, I hated this. I hated that Harper was so happy she glowed, that the pack had embraced her as if she'd never been away. I hated that even my own mother, brittle and vain as she was, had found peace somewhere in this town, drinking sweet tea on the porch and gossiping with Pearl like she'd been born here.

Me? I was the cautionary tale, the one who'd never fit. The one who could be bought for the right mix of praise and punishment.

A fly banged itself against the vanity bulb, desperate for the light. I almost envied it.

I scrolled through my phone, pretending to be busy, but every app was just a distraction from the panic gnawing at my insides. Every time the phone lit, I hoped it would be Gunner, then hated myself for hoping. He'd made it clear I was the one who needed to chase—he was never going to make it easy.

Maybe he knew what I was. Maybe he'd looked through my eyes and seen the rot underneath. Maybe that's why he'd left me stewing in my own humiliation, two weeks and counting.

I checked my reflection one last time, searching for a sign that the mask would hold. The blush was too harsh, the brows uneven, but the lips were a masterpiece. I forced a smile, all teeth. My wolf turned away, ashamed of me.

The worst part? I deserved it.

I must have sat there, staring at nothing, for ten whole minutes before I realized my hands had gone numb.

The makeup brush was still clutched in my right hand, the bristles smeared with the last of my "healthy glow." I set it down, deliberate, like the world might shatter if I moved too fast. It rolled off the edge and clattered to the floor, but I couldn't make myself care.

The room felt empty—vacuumed out, like after a storm. All the frantic energy was gone, replaced with something heavier and quieter. Maybe that was what resignation felt like. Or maybe it was just grief. For the girl I'd wanted to be. For the mess I'd made of things.

My wolf wouldn't even meet my gaze. She turned her back, tail between her legs, whimpering low in my chest. It hurt more than any insult Luc had ever thrown.

For a second, I just wanted to lie down and never get up again.

Instead, I remembered Juliet. The Luna. She'd tried weeks ago to reach me. It had been at one of those awkward "pack breakfasts," everyone pretending to be a family, passing scrambled eggs and homemade jam while ignoring the snide comments I let fly just to see who'd flinch.

Juliet had waited until Harper and Arsenal left the table, then leaned in with her signature calm, the way only someone who's survived hell and lived to tell about it could. "You know it's okay to ask for help, right?" Her voice was low and careful.

I'd snorted, rolled my eyes, said something about "therapy not working on feral animals." She hadn't blinked. Just handed me a business card—it had the name and number for the pack therapist. I'd tossed it in my purse for another time.

But now, as I sat there, head heavy in my hands, I remembered the card exactly: soft blue print, her name in neat serif, and a phone number that looked both friendly and official.

I'd saved the number in my phone just in case my coping skills reached rock bottom. I'd saved it as "Pack Shrink—Barf Emoji." Until now, spending time with my sister and my new friends had been filling that emotional gap for me. Harper wouldn't take no for an answer and forced me to speak to her about things, and I hated to admit it, but it had helped. I just hoped that this other emptiness inside would start to go away.

CHAPTER 2

GUNNER

Sunday morning church hit different after you'd spent the weekend pretending you didn't care about anything but cattle. Having your pack Alpha's angry blue-eyed stare burn clean through you, reminded you that ain't the case. I was third in today just behind Arsenal. That man always looked like he'd just had a fight or wanted to start one. Bronc was already seated at the head of the table in a white tee and his cut, and I wondered if our Alpha ever slept.

Wrecker bumped past me and plopped his massive frame into his chair. I paused at the doorway, took a slow inhale, let the smell of biscuit dough and black coffee burn off the last of my hangover. I'd been a son of a bitch lately, and everyone in this room knew why, even if they didn't say it out loud.

Pearl bustled past with a tray balanced one-handed, stacking it with enough sausage gravy and eggs to put down a goddamn grizzly. She gave me a hard side-eye, the kind that said she'd already heard about whatever trouble I was thinking of making, and I hadn't even done it yet. I nodded at her, careful not to smile. She'd have called me out.

"Morning, Gunner," Bronc's voice was flat. He tapped his index finger against his mug, rhythm precise, eyes never leaving my face. Arsenal just grunted and looked back down at his tablet. The man ran on military-grade caffeine and anxiety.

Big Papa and Doc filtered in. Everyone took their spots around the table; habit more than anything dictated our positions. Wrecker wore a TechNine henley under his cut and chewed his thumbnail his eyes on his phone. He hadn't shaved, and his scruff was getting on the shaggy side. I'm sure Parker didn't give a damn. He did no wrong in her eyes.

Pearl finished unloading the breakfast barrage and took her place at the head, even though she wasn't an officer per se. Everyone knew she was the one who'd keep the room from turning into a murder pit if things got heated. The noise dropped fast as Bronc lifted his hand. He never had to clear his throat or call the room to order.

He started with business. Always did. This week's work was running a dozen bikes to a dealership in Lubbock, fixing up a couple of custom orders, and doing a background check on some guy named Clyde who'd applied for a mechanic job and failed to mention three open warrants. The shop, he said, ran on trust, and even if you were hiding wolf ears and a tail, you didn't lie about the petty shit.

Then he looked right at me. Not subtle, not even close. "Gunner, you want to tell us why you've been so goddamn... distracted?"

I made a show of topping off my coffee. My hands were steady, but I could feel the burn behind my eyes. I'd always been the steady one—the guy who broke up fights instead of starting them, who stayed late to muck out the stables instead of sneaking off to get laid. I was always the comic relief; the one everyone counted on to bring the laughs. Now I could barely look my own crew in the eye.

"There a problem?" I asked, slow drawl intentional. The words felt thick in my mouth.

Arsenal let out a low snort. "You haven't answered your radio three times this week. Wrecker had to cover your Friday patrol. And you left the Friday perimeter log blank. What the fuck, Gunner?"

Wrecker shrugged, but even his usual devil-may-care act wasn't fooling anybody. "I get it, man. Shit's been weird since—" He caught himself and glanced at Pearl, then back to me. "Since Paris. But you gotta get your head on straight. We need you, man."

There it was, all laid out. I didn't even have to say her name. The whole room knew what was eating at me: Brie Lawson and her wolf, who had been flickering in my peripheral vision since the second I caught her scent. My problem was, I didn't know if the bond was real, or if I'd just spent too many years desperate to believe I had a mate out there at all. I was avoiding her and everyone else because I was afraid—actually afraid—of what might happen if I let myself want her.

Pearl set her mug down with a bang. "Let the boy eat his breakfast before you pick him apart," she said, voice syrup-sweet and dangerous. "He looks like he's running on dust." Pearl wasn't just Bronc's mama. She mothered all of us and wasn't happy if any of us were dealing with problems.

Bronc cracked a smile, but only for her. "Fair enough, Ma. Sorry, Gunner. Just want you at one hundred percent."

I nodded. "Understood, boss. Apologies. I'll get my shit together." I tried to eat, but the eggs tasted like cardboard. My jaw was almost too tight to chew.

They moved on to the next topic—security. Arsenal read off a list of threats, real and hypothetical. "Hollow Ridge pack has been quiet since the County Line run in. But I've got two sources saying there's a new beta rising up. Could mean a power play before fall. Keep all the patched ins heads on swivels." He paused, eyeing each man at the table. "We don't want some dick wannabe trying to make a name for himself like in times past. Everyone wants to get their hits in on Iron Valor to prove a point."

The room shivered a little at that. Last time someone tried to roll through our town with their chest out, it ended with me spending the night digging bullet fragments out of my left shoulder and the next two weeks pretending I couldn't feel the twinge every time I lifted hay bales.

"Wrecker, you're up," Bronc said.

Wrecker pushed aside his plate and pulled out his phone. "Got a ping off the Maltraz network—someone tried to hack the mainframe at two a.m. Think he's still trying to find a way in since Silas Drake failed. He's still pissed about last month, and likely hired new muscle from out-of-state." He gave an exasperated sigh. "I shut it down fast, and I went to work updating our firewalls."

Doc piped up. "If his people try to use a physical device—like at the shop—I've got an EM blanket we can install. We'll fry their laptop before they get in the door." He said it like he was reading off a prescription. Doc was good that way: calm, clinical, never flinched at blood or bullshit.

Wrecker gave a small laugh. "That's another reason I love you, Doc. You patch us up and still help protect our networks and shit."

Next came the pack health update, which was mostly Doc telling us the pups were healthy, nothing serious was going around, and that Juliet was "popping twins in just a couple months, and she's already tired of everyone telling her she's glowing."

"She's a saint for putting up with us," Big Papa's voice was gentle for a man whose hands looked like they could bend rebar. "And Gunner, you need anything, you let us know. We're your family. Aspen and Oscar, and I are always here. And hell, you'd for sure get one of her famous lemon tarts out of the deal."

I nodded, feeling something twist low in my belly. I wanted to say something; maybe thank you, maybe fuck off, I hadn't decided, but my tongue wouldn't cooperate.

Pearl poured more coffee, then touched my shoulder just long enough to make me flinch. "You look like hell, honey," she said, not unkind. "Don't let whatever's eating you keep you from your pack. They need you more than you think."

I forced a smile and lied through my teeth. "I'm good, Pearl. Just tired, is all."

The rest of the meeting passed in a blur: more talk about supply runs, who'd cover the perimeter, whether or not to upgrade the garage's security system. My mind wandered. I found myself tracing the wood grain of the table with my thumb, over and over, until my skin went numb.

They mentioned Brie only once, and it was Arsenal who did it. "Harper's sister's been quiet," he said. "Good. Less drama that way."

My face went hot. I stared at my hands, not trusting myself to look up.

"She's finding her place," Bronc said. "Or she will. Eventually." He gave me a quick look, then let it go.

When the official business wrapped, everyone stood and stretched. The sound of chairs scraping was deafening. I tried to bolt for the door, but Bronc caught my wrist.

"Walk with me," he said. It wasn't a request.

Outside, the wind was sharp and sweet, full of prairie grass and the faint musk of wolf. Bronc kept his hands in his pockets, walking slow, like he didn't want to spook me.

"You gonna tell me what's really going on, Gunner?" he asked.

I shrugged. "You already know."

"Say it."

I gritted my teeth. "I don't know if she's mine. I want her, but... I can't tell if it's real. Or if I'm just desperate. And she's so goddamn disagreeable most of the time. Makes it harder, you know? But I still want her smart ass. It's a fine damn ass. Does that make it real?"

He stopped and looked at me, face open for once. "Doesn't matter, in the end. Wanting her makes it real enough. Give it time."

I laughed, rough and ugly. "Don't have time. Not with everything else. I need to focus, Bronc. I can't keep screwing up."

He clapped my shoulder, hard. "You're not screwing up. You're just not used to being the one who needs help."

We stood in silence, just the wind and the distant hum of motorcycles. I wanted to say more, to ask for advice, but the words stuck.

"You'll figure it out," he said, turning to go. "And if you don't, I'll kick your ass until you do."

I watched him walk away, tall and solid and unbreakable. Then I went back inside, finished my cold coffee, and stared at the table until Pearl shooed me out.

I told myself I'd get over it. I was lying.

The next morning, sun not even cracked over the horizon, I was already shoveling feed into the stalls and wondering why the hell I was so tired. I'd only slept four hours, but that was normal, and the dark had been full of dreams I'd rather not remember. Mostly, I remembered Brie, and that pissed me off more than anything.

By eight a.m., it was time to face the officers again. Monday meant weekly review of anything not handled in the big church meeting, and I knew what was coming. Bronc liked to handle certain things in private, but with Arsenal, everything was a goddamn formation drill, "run it by the book," even if you didn't like what the book said.

I showed up ten minutes early, just in case. Wrecker was already there, elbows deep in a box of donuts and reading messages off three different screens at once. He shot me a look, smirked, then went back to his hackathon.

Bronc and Arsenal walked in together, talking quiet, like I wasn't supposed to hear. But my intuition was good enough to figure they'd decided on something about me.

Big Papa ambled in, folding his arms across his chest and surveying the room like he was waiting for someone to start a fight. Doc came in last, coffee already half-gone, phone out, not paying attention to anyone unless someone started bleeding.

Pearl was nowhere to be seen this time. There was coffee, but no food, which set the whole tone as less comfort, more confrontation.

Bronc called it in with a rap of his knuckles. "All right, Gunner, you're up."

I took my cue, nice and slow. "We got a dozen head ready to sell," I said. "Been a good year, so the stock's heavy. I need to cull the herd before the grass gets short. Figure it'll mean two runs, three days tops."

Arsenal didn't look at me. He was watching Bronc, who was watching me.

Bronc nodded. "You'll take Arsenal. Knock it out in one run. See how it shakes out."

My jaw went tight, and I forced myself not to let it show. "That really necessary?"

"Protocol," Bronc said, too quick. "Pair up, always. Besides, you know how the livestock haulers can get on auction days. Last thing we need is a hijack or a missing trailer."

I almost laughed. I'd gone solo for years—until now. Until Brie. The old bastard was making it obvious, but nobody else batted an eye.

Big Papa just smiled, slow and knowing. "Don't worry, Gunner. Arsenal doesn't snore."

"Can't say the same about you," Wrecker muttered.

Doc finally looked up. "You're in good shape, Gunner. Bloodwork last week showed clean. But you might want to ease up on the energy drinks."

I said nothing. There was nothing to say.

They wrapped up the rest of the meeting in record time, and everyone started to head out. Bronc hung back, pretending to look at his notes. Wrecker and Papa followed Doc, probably to go play chess or check on the new med supplies. That left me and Arsenal alone in the office.

He blocked the door, all six-foot-one of him, arms crossed, stare like a sniper scope.

"Say it," he ordered.

I met his gaze, refusing to blink. "What?"

"You're off. You've been off for weeks. You know what happens to enforcers who get soft, Gunner?"

I snorted. "You calling me soft, Arsenal?"

"I'm saying," he said, slow and flat, "if you want to pretend you're not fucked up over a girl, you'd better do it somewhere nobody can see."

I wanted to hit him. Not because he was wrong, but because he was right.

"Brie's not a problem," I said. "She's a distraction. And I don't want her."

Arsenal leaned in, inches away, and lowered his voice to a growl. "Bullshit. You want her so bad it's making the whole pack edgy. You stink of need, Gunner. Even the pups notice."

That landed like a punch. I took a step back, teeth gritted. "She's not mine," I said. "Maybe she *could* be. But she isn't."

Arsenal just stared. "You keep lying to yourself, or you just keep lying to me?"

I didn't answer. I couldn't.

He shook his head and dropped his arms. "Here's what I know. You think being alone makes you strong. It doesn't. It makes you stupid." He opened the door. "See you tomorrow, Gunner."

I walked out into the hallway, blinking hard. I didn't know if I wanted to fight Arsenal or buy him a beer. Both, probably.

Back at my truck, I threw myself behind the wheel and slammed the door, hard enough to rattle the old Ford's frame. My phone buzzed in my pocket. I checked the screen, hoping for a distraction. Instead, it was a text from Pearl: "Don't sulk. There's peach cobbler in the fridge."

I laughed, first time in days. It didn't fix anything, but it made the weight in my chest a little lighter.

Truth was, I hadn't gotten off since Brie moved in across the street. I tried, but it was like my body knew she was close, waiting to see who'd break first. Some nights I got close, but then her voice would float through my skull—usually some smartass quip or bitchy joke—and I'd lose it, limp as a dead rattler.

It made me want her more. It made me hate myself. It made me want to chase her down, drag her back, and make her admit she wanted it, too.

But mostly, it made me want to run.

I started the truck, engine growling under my hands, and tried to shake off the feeling. I had work to do—fences to check, stock to prep, a million little chores that didn't give a damn about my aching dick or my fucked-up head.

But as I drove away from the compound, I could feel Arsenal's words clinging to me, burrowing deep.

You keep lying to yourself, or you just keep lying to me?

Maybe it was both.

I gunned it down the dirt road, rooster-tailing dust behind me, and pretended I wasn't looking for Brie's car in the drive.

CHAPTER 3

BRIE

Monday morning found me in a small-town version of hell: brunch at Aspen Waters' bakery, pretending to be a functioning daughter and little sister while the stench of failure clung to me like stale perfume. I'd worn my favorite vintage scarf and three layers of highlighter, but it wasn't enough to hide the shadows under my eyes or the general air of a woman whose soul had been put through a meat grinder and left on simmer.

Aspen's morning rush had cleared out, so it was just us. A pitiful private party. Translation: Harper, Mom, and I sat alone, so I didn't have to worry about my dignity. Aspen had decked the place out with blue-and-white checkered tablecloths, with wildflowers in mason jars on every table. Sunlight spilled through the large storefront window and made the little glass cases gleam. The counter was overloaded with things that should have been illegal for anyone with a metabolism slower than a rabbit on Red Bull: lemon scones, apple turnovers, mini quiches with browned edges and tiny chives snipped on top.

The best part? No customers. It was just us, and Aspen's familiar, Oscar, who wore a little bowtie and plaid vest. He scuttled around refilling our tea as if he hadn't spent the last ten millennia plotting the downfall of all pastries everywhere. I couldn't help but find it cute, the way he held out a tray of strawberry tarts and called everyone "madam" or "milady."

I sat at the far end of the table, right next to the window, so I could escape with my eyeballs whenever the need arose.

Mom sat prim and proper; hair swept up in a perfect twist, her sweater set matching the silk of her skirt. She gave me the once-over, her gaze laser-focused on my roots, then my brows, then the scarf, which she'd once called "bohemian, in a kind of sad way." She smiled wide and brittle as though she hadn't seen me all morning. "You look... rested, darling. Dairyville must be doing something right."

Harper sat beside her, posture perfect, hair in an elegant ponytail, and still managed to look more relaxed than I'd ever seen her. Maybe that was the effect of pack life. Or maybe it was just Arsenal's wolf scent, which clung to her like an invisible blanket. She wore jeans and a white blouse and somehow made it look like a goddamn Ralph Lauren ad.

Aspen emerged from the kitchen, her skin somehow luminous in the bakery light, and sat down a three-tiered tray laden with finger sandwiches and petit fours. "Tea service for three, as requested," she said, and then to me, softer, "We did the lemon ginger; a personal favorite."

Oscar, not to be outdone, scampered up onto the table (God bless this pack and its unspoken rules for animal hygiene) and did a little bow. "May I tempt you with a scone, miss?" His British accent was so crisp it could've sliced bread.

I took the scone because defiance was exhausting and carbs were the only thing that didn't judge me. "Thank you, Oscar," I said, with genuine gratitude.

Mom immediately picked up a napkin and dabbed at her mouth, even though she hadn't touched a thing yet. "Isn't this delightful, girls? Harper dear, you must thank Aspen for going to all this trouble. It's so nice to see a young woman take such pride in her work. Brie, you could learn something from that."

Harper blushed and shot me an apologetic glance. "It's amazing, Aspen. Thank you so much. I'm dying for the apple turnover."

Aspen smiled and poured her a cup of tea, hands so steady it made me hate her a little. I tried to drink my tea, but it was still hot enough to scald the taste buds off a corpse. I set the cup down and focused on breaking the scone into precise, angry halves.

Mom was off to the races, commentary flying like buckshot. "Brie, I wish you'd have gone to that concert at the community center last weekend. I think you would have enjoyed it." She was giving me a look—subtle, but not subtle enough—because we all knew I wasn't interested in concerts at the community center.

"Well... I had some things to do at the house." Like wallowing in shame and staring at the ceiling.

She smiled as if I'd said something witty. "Well, you really should make an effort, darling. This is your home now, whether or not you like it. You have to assimilate." She pronounced the last word with extra syllables, as if maybe I'd forgotten how to do it.

Aspen piped up, quick, "Brie's helping me design the flyer for the new muffin menu." It was a lie, but I appreciated it.

"Of course she is," Mom said, saccharine smile. "Brie was always creative. I just wish you'd put it to more... social use. Why don't you sign up for the art class they offer at the senior center? It would do you good to be around people." She dabbed at her lips again, even though there was nothing there.

The tea was finally cool enough to drink, so I sipped and tried to let the warmth settle in my chest instead of the usual ache. For a second, nobody talked, and it felt like maybe we could just eat and enjoy being a family, even if it was the Discount Bin version.

Of course, that's when Mom started in again. "Harper, have you and Arsenal considered children?" She asked, casual as a hand grenade. "I read that it's easier if you start early, and..."

"Mom!" Harper's cheeks went pink, and she shot me an apologetic glance.

I nearly choked on the scone. "That's… wow, Mom. Even for you."

Mom was unfazed. "It's a reasonable question, darling. You're not getting any younger. None of us are." She smoothed a napkin over her knee, then looked straight at me. "Brie, is there someone special for you here? I notice you don't talk about anyone from France anymore."

My insides did a triple axel. I could feel the blood draining from my face.

Harper jumped in, voice gentle. "Brie's not really seeing anyone right now. She's focusing on herself."

Mom's lips pursed. "That's probably best. I always thought those French men were a little too… continental for you."

I snorted, bitter. "You have no idea."

She reached across the table and, for once, actually took my hand. Her grip was surprisingly strong. "You'll figure it out, darling. You always do."

I wished I could believe her. Or that the words didn't taste like lead in my mouth.

Oscar refilled our tea, and Aspen poured a little cream in each cup, her movements slow and soothing. She didn't say much, just let the clinking of spoons and the aroma of fresh pastry fill the spaces where conversation would have been.

Mom started talking about how long we'd be living in Parker's family home. I wasn't sure what she was even going to do for money. I think my father may have had a life insurance policy that was still good? Harper listened, nodded, even asked follow-up questions. I let the words wash over me, staring out the window at the empty street and the parked motorcycles gleaming in the sun. Out there, someone was living a real life, one not defined by brunches and whispered gossip.

I wondered if I'd ever get to be that person.

My phone vibrated; a text from an unknown number. I almost didn't check it, but curiosity won out.

It was a single sentence, no punctuation:

don't let them break you

I stared at the screen, heart pounding.

Was it Gunner? I didn't know if I wanted it to be.

I looked at Harper, her profile soft and sure in the morning light. Then at Mom, who was still talking about grout colors and the importance of a properly set table.

I excused myself, went to the restroom, and stood at the sink, hands shaking just enough to betray me if anyone looked too close.

I stared at my reflection. For once, the harsh overhead light felt honest.

"Don't let them break you," I whispered.

I wasn't sure who "them" meant anymore, or if it mattered.

Maybe I'd figure it out. Maybe I wouldn't.

I returned to the table, bracing myself for more maternal crossfire, but the dynamic had shifted. Harper's eyes were bright, her excitement tangible, and even Mom had the air of a woman who'd just arranged the world's neatest flower box. Aspen had retreated to the kitchen, probably to give us space, and Oscar was perched on the counter, nose twitching like he'd just detected a disturbance in the Force.

Harper jumped right in, as if she'd been waiting for me to come back. "So, actually, I wanted to talk to you both about something," Harper said, fingers lacing together on the table. "I'm thinking of opening a dance studio in Dairyville. There's an empty storefront across from the courthouse. The seller has agreed on an excellent sale price. I just need to get the contract signed and find a contractor and get the space prepped."

Mom was delighted. "That's wonderful! A proper business, Harper. You could teach children—maybe even adults. You could finally use your training." She actually reached across the table to squeeze Harper's hand, as if she'd just announced her candidacy for President.

"Here's the best part though," she said, leaning in. "The dance studio has two sides—one big, one a bit smaller. I only need the big one. The other space has great light and a storefront window. I thought... maybe you could do an art gallery. Or one of those paint-and-sip things. You know, with wine and acrylics and..." She stopped, grinning. "It could be fun, right?"

The suggestion hit me like a shot of espresso to the frontal cortex. For the first time in weeks, I felt my blood speed up for a reason other than panic. I could see it—rows of easels, the cheap, heady reek of dollar store acrylics, some group of loud Texans making bad jokes while I taught them how to draw cacti and wildflowers. Or maybe in the evenings, I could hang my own canvases in the window and let people judge them, the way they always had. Maybe I could turn it into an actual gallery.

The idea was stupid. It was small. It was so perfect I wanted to laugh and cry at the same time.

"You really want to do that with me?" I asked, voice coming out smaller than intended.

Harper beamed. "Of course. You could do private parties, girls' nights, whatever you wanted. Dairyville isn't exactly brimming with options, you know? People would line up."

Mom's hand went to her chest, nails clacking against her pearls. "That is a wonderful idea, girls. Brie, you could bring some... sophistication to the town. And Harper, you'd be the talk of Dairyville with your own studio."

I felt my posture change, back straightening, fingers tapping involuntarily against the edge of my teacup. "We could do bachelorette parties," I said, brain racing now. "Or birthday groups, or those weird team-building things where everyone paints the same bad landscape and pretends it's not a cult." My cheeks felt hot, but it was the good kind of flush—the kind that meant maybe, just maybe, I wasn't completely dead inside.

Harper caught my energy and amplified it. "We could cross-pro-mote—like, I'll teach them to dance, and you'll teach them to paint. They could do both in a weekend package." She looked at Mom, eyebrows up. "We'd be entrepreneurs, just like you always wanted."

Mom stared at me, a look of actual pride softening the lines at the corners of her eyes. "You see, darling? You only had to let people in. I'm so proud of you both." She reached for my hand, squeezing it gently, and I didn't even pull away.

For a minute, it was easy to imagine that we were a real family, that the last five years hadn't been a parade of disappointment and self-sabotage. Even Oscar looked approving, standing on his hind legs to set a miniature cupcake on my plate.

I felt lighter. Giddy. The urge to cry was still there, but it was from something other than misery.

That's when the bell over the bakery door jingled.

I didn't have to look up to know who it was. The air changed—the room got charged, like someone had slipped an electric eel into the espresso machine. My wolf snapped to attention, claws out, heart stuttering in my chest.

I kept my head down, staring at the little pink cupcake on my plate, but I could track every move by sound. The slow, boot-heavy footfalls. The scraping of a chair as it was pulled out. The low thump of something (probably a fist) hitting the tabletop.

Wrecker spoke first, voice cheerful and loud. "Hey, ladies! Hope we're not interrupting." He slid into the table behind us, clearly on his best behavior. Big Papa followed, settling next to him, his sheer size dwarfing the entire corner of the room.

But it was Gunner who caught my attention, even though he didn't say a word.

He just stood there, cowboy hat pulled down low, gaze scanning the table. He wore a button-down that probably cost as much as my entire outfit, sleeves rolled to show off forearms that looked like they could snap fence posts for fun. He didn't make eye contact—at least, not until I looked up.

Then he did.

For half a second, everything else went fuzzy. The room, the bakery, my own heartbeat—all muffled by the sudden, vivid clarity of his stare. It was the same as at County Line—predatory, amused, and so fucking certain of itself. He tipped his hat, subtle, and sat with his back to the wall, arms folded.

Oscar, unfazed, brought over a tray of cinnamon rolls. "For the gentlemen," he said, bowtie crisp, voice even crisper. "Would you care for coffee?"

"Black. Strong," Gunner said, not looking at me again. "Thanks, Oscar."

Mom clapped her hands, delighted at the company. "Isn't this fun, girls? I never tire of a full table. Brie, why don't you tell the boys about the new art studio?"

I wanted to melt into the floor. Instead, I managed a thin smile and looked at Wrecker, who was already halfway through a cinnamon roll. "It's not official yet," I said. "Just a maybe."

Wrecker grinned, mouth full. "You should do it. Dairyville needs something to liven it up. Maybe you'll get the tourists to come back."

Big Papa nodded, his voice gentle and deep. "A little color does wonders. You'd be surprised."

Gunner stayed quiet, but I could feel his eyes every time I moved. My wolf did a nervous circle, whining at the attention.

I tried to focus on Harper, but every hair on my body was standing up. "I'll just see you at the car," I said, scooping up my purse. "I've gotta check on that thing."

Harper looked at me, concerned. "You okay?"

"Yeah," I lied. "Just need to... you know."

Mom frowned, but she didn't protest. Maybe she'd finally learned it was better not to corner a wild animal.

I slid out from the table and made a beeline for the door, heart hammering so hard I could barely hear anything else.

As I pulled the door open, I glanced back once—just enough to see Wrecker punch Gunner hard in the arm, cinnamon roll flying out of his hand as he laughed.

Gunner's gaze caught mine, just for a split second, and his mouth twitched in something that might have been a smile.

I slammed the door a little too hard, the bell jangling like an alarm, and stepped into the blinding daylight.

Safe for now.

I kept walking, fast enough that my shoes made angry clacks against the sidewalk. I didn't even realize where I was going until I was halfway across the Dairyville town square, the bakery already two blocks behind me and fading into just another background hum of the morning.

The square was supposed to be peaceful. Trees, benches, a tiny fountain shaped like a cow (because of course it was), and a bandstand that hadn't seen a band since the Eisenhower administration. Most days, you'd see an old guy reading a newspaper, or kids running in circles with popsicles. Today, it was almost empty—a couple of women pushing strollers, one guy talking to himself near the library steps. It should have made me feel safe, but all it did was underline how exposed I was.

I collapsed onto the first empty bench I found, cradling my purse to my chest like it might deflect bullets. My heart was pounding so hard I thought I'd have an aneurysm. I pulled my scarf tighter around my throat, a stupid, useless gesture, but it felt better than nothing.

My wolf wasn't helping. She paced, restless, ears perked for footsteps that never came. I tried to breathe, in for four, out for four, the way I'd read on some website about how to calm yourself. But it was like I'd forgotten how to inhale without inhaling panic.

I dug my phone out, desperate for distraction, but the only thing on the screen was Harper's text:

you good?

I stared at it. Lied, as usual:

yeah. just needed some fresh air.

I couldn't bring myself to hit send.

I closed my eyes, but that was even worse. All I could see was Gunner's stare—green and gold, with the kind of certainty that made you want to both run and crawl into his lap at the same time. My body was betraying me, and I hated it, hated that no amount of logic or self-help or fuck-you-mom resolve could turn off the part of me that wanted to go back and finish what he'd started at County Line. My wolf whined, low, needy.

No. Not happening. I had a plan now. I had paint and parties and, if I was lucky, a new purpose that didn't involve getting bent over the hood of Gunner's truck.

I kept my eyes open, watching the square with the jittery energy of a lab rat waiting for the next shock. The flowers in the planters were too bright; the breeze too sharp. Every sound was amplified—the squeal of brakes, the far-off thud of a basketball, the faint grind of boots on pavement.

Someone was watching me. I could feel it.

I scanned the storefronts—nothing. The library, the post office, the empty windows of the courthouse. Every shadow was a threat, every passing car a loaded gun. I caught a flicker of movement in the alley behind the bakery, but it was probably just a cat.

Still, I couldn't shake the feeling that someone was hunting me. Not for violence, but for something worse. For the first time, I understood what prey felt like—why rabbits go into shock before the teeth even hit.

My phone buzzed again. This time, it was a number I didn't recognize again.

don't run, it's not as bad as you think

The message made my blood run cold, then hot. My hands shook. I wanted to laugh—maybe it was Gunner, maybe not. Maybe it was someone else entirely, but I doubted it. The wolf in me knew her own kind.

I forced myself to sit still, spine rigid, chin up. If someone wanted a show, I'd give them the front row.

The sensation built, the air getting thicker, the light sharper. Every part of me was tuned to the next move. It was almost a relief when it happened.

From the far side of the square, I heard boots. Slow, measured, heavy. They got closer, and I could feel my wolf shiver—first in fear, then in something almost like anticipation.

I gripped the edge of the bench until my knuckles ached, but I didn't move. I wouldn't give him, or anyone, the satisfaction.

Gunner didn't say anything. He just walked past, slow, his silhouette blocked by the sun, then stopped halfway to the bandstand. He didn't look at me. He didn't have to.

He just stood there, hands in his pockets, head tipped down, like he was listening to a secret only the pavement knew.

My wolf howled, silent and fierce, and I bit my lip to keep from joining her.

I didn't go to him. I didn't get up. I sat and watched, daring him to make the first move.

He didn't. Not yet.

But I could feel it—like thunder just before the lightning, like the split-second when you know you're about to fall and you can't stop yourself.

For the first time in months, I felt something other than shame or dread.

I felt alive.

I wasn't sure if that was better. But it was something.

My phone buzzed one last time:

just breathe, okay?

I had looked away. He had sent the texts. There was no question now.

I inhaled, slow, deep. The air tasted like clover and sweat and leather.

I held it in as long as I could and waited for the world to come crashing down.

CHAPTER 4

GUNNER

By the time the first streak of sun lit up the salt flats, my shirt was plastered to my back, and I'd run out of fucks to give about the smell. Branding day always drew the worst out of everyone, myself included—temper went quick as water in a cattle trough, patience burned up in the first hour. I pressed the last iron in, the sizzle and calf's scream loud enough to make my wolf flinch, and held it there 'til the hide hissed and lifted, black and raised. Then I let the calf go, and it shot through the chute with more dignity than I'd have if someone'd just melted my ass.

Four hours in, and already my arms ached to the bone. We'd started at five because that's the hour when only idiots and cattlemen are awake, and I'd wanted it done "before the real heat." It was already close to eighty and not even 9:30 yet, but I was the boss, and the boss man got what he wanted. Always.

I dropped the iron into the sand bucket, let my breath out slow, and rolled my head to work out the kink at the base of my neck. The air in the yard was thick with scorched hair, manure, and sweet alfalfa dust; the kind of Texas perfume that stuck to your skin for days. I wiped my face with my sleeve and turned to check the next calf in line.

But there was no next calf. Just a cloud of dust at the far end of the lane, the big black dually with IRON VALOR plates crawled through it like a battleship coming to port. Bronc liked to make an entrance, even when no one was watching.

The truck fishtailed, then straightened, rolling up to the corral where I stood like a schoolboy waiting for the principal. It was a new one—a 3500 with brush guard and enough engine to tow a house. You could smell the money on it, but Bronc drove like he was still back in Afghanistan, swerving every pothole like it hid a landmine.

He climbed out of the cab slow, assured that every man would wait. No cut today—just a faded tee, jeans, and aviators that turned his eyes into blue chips of ice. He was forty-three but built like a linebacker, his wolf just under the surface, always coiled.

"Mornin', Gunner," he called, like I hadn't just spent four hours doing the job of five men.

I spat into the dirt, watched it dry out in the space of a breath. "Alpha."

He walked up, boots silent on the packed clay, and leaned against the gate. His gaze flicked over the empty chute, the scorched brand, the way my hands shook just a little from the effort. He didn't miss much.

"Good work," he said, voice even. "Heard you did two pens yourself."

I shrugged. "Didn't want the pups slowing me down."

He nodded once, approving, then jerked his chin at the bottle of water sitting on the fence post. "Hydrate. We've got something else needs fixin'."

I drank mostly because it meant I didn't have to answer right away. Bronc had the patience of a saint with the stuff that mattered. For everything else, he moved at the speed of a cattle prod.

When I finished, he let the silence stretch out. Then, "Parker's old family place has another issue."

That house—faded blue, two stories, a porch that slouched like a drunk—had been empty for years until Nanette and her daughter moved in over a month ago. That house was filled with sad memories of what used to be a happy family. Parker's parents were killed when the bike they were on was sideswiped by an 18-wheeler some eight years ago. Parker and her piece of shit, traitor twin brother Axel lived there until after they graduated high school. Parker was sweet enough to offer it to Nanette and Brie.

"What is it this time?" I asked, cautious. "Seems like it's always something."

Bronc's mouth twitched, in a slight smile. "Everything needs work, Gunner. This is just a door, though. Nanette says it sticks. Can't get it to latch." He squinted at me over the aviators. "Thought you could take a look."

Of course he fucking did. And this was not a request. I waited for the punchline—the reason he needed me and not one of the other twenty hands on the ranch—but he just stood there, unreadable.

"Copy that," I said, hiding my annoyance. "When?"

He glanced at his watch. "She's home now. Brie, too. Finish your water and go."

That was Bronc: efficient, impossible, always two moves ahead. The heat rose up in me, not the kind from the sun, but the kind that made you want to hit something. I capped the bottle and set it on the rail.

"You want me to shower off first?" I said. "Or is the door gonna mind?"

He let out a dry laugh, just once. "Might as well go as you are. Don't need to impress anybody."

Except that's exactly what he wanted. He was hoping I'd run into Brie. He wanted me to, because he was an asshole and a matchmaker and believed in wolf-fated mates above all.

I couldn't say no, so I nodded and headed for the shop.

❦

I kept my work shirt on, sweat and all, and grabbed the toolbox from the tack room. My hands left gritty prints on the red plastic handle, but I didn't wipe them off. The less "presentable" I looked, the better.

The walk to Parker's old house was short—just across the road, through a windbreak of pecan trees and down a gravel drive lined with dandelions. The difference in atmosphere was immediate. The ranch vibrated with activity: calves bawling, diesel engines revving, the occasional bark from the kennel. Over here, you could almost forget there was a world beyond the drive.

The house itself was less impressive up close. The paint was flaking, the screen door had a rip near the bottom, and the porch swing leaned at an angle that dared you to sit. But someone had swept the steps, and a pot of pink geraniums sat on the rail, bravely defying the heat.

I stood on the lowest step and took a slow look around. Nanette's white car passed me as I made my way up the drive; her perfume didn't linger, but I could still pick up the faint signature of cold cream and Chanel on the front door. The other scent—lemon zest and flora—Brie.

I set the toolbox down with a thump and knocked once, hard.

No answer. I waited, fighting the urge to just leave. I tried again, and this time I heard the faint shuffle of bare feet on wood.

The door opened, and there she stood her face an accusation, deep turquoise blue eyes looking up at me, dark wavy hair, the blue streaked throughout.

"Finn."

I kept my hat on. "Brie. The Alpha sent me to fix one of your doors."

She eyed me like I was a wolf come to drag her back to the den. "Oh, yeah. Come on in."

She led me through the house to the back door. It was located off the kitchen. I was surprised at how remarkably neat and clean everything was. The kitchen was dated, with cabinets and fixtures that screamed early 2000s, but Nanette clearly had a flair for decor. She'd added attractive decor to the counters, not so much that they looked cluttered, just classically pretty with a mix of wood and metal. Several pieces of art adorned the walls; landscapes of Paris that I assumed Brie had painted. She was gifted; there was no question.

I immediately saw daylight coming in around the bottom corner of the door frame. I pointed at the gap where sunlight poured across the floor. "Doesn't shut all the way. It's definitely a safety issue."

She rolled her eyes. "Well, duh."

Fuck, she had a smart mouth. My eyes moved over her. She wore cut-off shorts and a tank she undoubtedly got from Parker that said: I LOOK BETTER BENT OVER A BOOK across the chest. She didn't even flinch when she caught me reading it.

I set my toolbox down, dropped to one knee and checked the hinges. They were loose; the wood splintered from years of slamming. I could fix it in five minutes, maybe less.

I fished a screwdriver from the box and tightened the top hinge. "You ever try to fix this yourself?"

She snorted. "I'm not allowed to touch the tools. Last time I tried, I stripped a screw and Nanette freaked out."

I grinned, couldn't help it. "You do that on purpose?"

She shrugged. "Maybe."

I finished the top hinge and then moved to the bottom. Her scent—lemon, with a wildflower edge—filled the air, and my wolf snapped to attention. I focused on the work.

"You doing okay here?" I asked, careful.

She hesitated. "I stay busy. There's not much reason to go to the pack house unless you're a joiner." She said the last word like it was a disease.

I nodded. "Understand that."

I tested the door; it swung smooth and easy. "All fixed."

She looked almost disappointed. "That's it? Bronc sends you to do all the hard jobs."

I wiped my hands on my jeans. "I'm the best there is. He knows it."

She rolled her eyes but didn't argue.

I picked up my toolbox, ready to leave, but she didn't move from her post at the counter. "You want a glass of water?" she asked, voice softer. "You look like you're about to pass out."

I did actually. The sweat had cooled to a sticky film on my skin, and my head pounded with leftover adrenaline.

"Sure," I said. "Thanks."

She pulled two glasses from the cupboard—real glass, not plastic—and filled them from the tap. She handed me one, cold and wet, and I drained it in two gulps.

"You always work this hard?" she asked.

I shrugged. "Only way I know how."

The silence dragged on for several seconds. I was done here.

"Well, try to keep the place standing." I grabbed my toolbox and tipped my hat and walked out the door.

I told myself I was done with her for now. Not forever, but she wasn't ready at this moment. I needed to keep my distance. But three hours later, patching barbed wire under the noon sun, her scent was still in my nose. Lemon and wildflower, the memory of her voice ringing in my ears. The way she'd watched me work, arms folded, eyes half-lidded and sharp. The way her tank top rode up when she reached for a glass, showing a strip of stomach so pale it made my mouth go dry. The words on her shirt—"I look better bent over a book"—crawled through my head, setting off a low, stubborn heat that wouldn't die.

It was nearly evening when Bronc called again.

"Door's still sticking," he said, not even bothering with hello. "Nanette says you didn't fix it right."

I gripped the phone so hard the casing creaked. "The fuck? Maybe she should try fixing it herself."

He chuckled, low and dark. "You know the drill. Get it done, Gunner."

The line clicked dead before I could answer.

I washed up this time. Changed into a fresh shirt, pulled my boots back on, and grabbed the toolbox. On the way across the road, I caught my reflection in the shop window. The circles under my eyes were darker, my hair wild, but my jaw looked set hard enough to crack stone. I didn't know how long I could keep this up.

When I got to the porch, the sun was dropping behind the pecans, painting the house gold and pink. The geraniums had wilted, and the screen door hung even lower than before. I knocked once, harder than necessary. Again, Nanette's car was not in the driveway.

This time, she opened up right away. The same shorts, the same tank, but now she wore a bandana tied around her head, blue and gold. There was a smear of graphite on one cheek, like she'd wiped sweat away with the back of her hand while sketching.

"Wyatt Earp," she said, voice deadpan. "Back for more?"

She did it on purpose, using a bullshit cowboy name. I felt the tick in my jaw, the pulse jump in my neck.

"Door still sticks," I said. "Alpha says to fix it. Don't understand what's happening here. It was fine when I left." I eyed her accusingly.

She grinned, slow and infuriating. "Well, come on in, Wyatt. I wouldn't want to get shot for insubordination."

"Enough of that. Earp wasn't a cowboy. Don't confuse him with me, sweetheart." I brushed past her to the back door.

The kitchen was brighter now, evening light slanting across the counter and turning the lemon glass on the windowsill to gold. The back door was closed, but I could see from ten feet away what the problem was: the wood frame had swollen with the humidity, bowed out so the latch didn't line up. It wasn't the kind of job you could fix with a screwdriver.

I'd need to shave the edge down, plane it, maybe even reset the whole hinge. Hell, the entire door frame might need to be replaced.

Brie was already in the next room, perched on the edge of the old upright piano bench, bare legs dangling. She held a sketchbook, but her eyes were on me, not the page.

I got to work, running my hand over the frame, feeling for the worst of the swell. I pulled a tape from the box and measured, made a mark with a carpenter's pencil, and then set the door loose from its hinges.

She watched, silent, for a minute. Then: "You always this... competent?"

"You have no idea, honey," I said, not looking up.

She made a little noise, part laugh, part huff. "Must be nice. Knowing what you're good at."

I took the door outside to the porch and laid it across two sawhorses. The house was quiet except for the creak of floorboards and the low hum of the old fridge. I ran a block plane down the high edge, the thin curls of wood falling in neat spirals onto the porch. The rhythm of the work calmed me, or maybe it just numbed everything else.

She came out after a minute, barefoot, still holding the sketchbook.

"You like working with your hands?" she asked, sitting cross-legged on the step.

I shrugged. "It's a living."

She studied me for a beat. "You don't talk much. Are you like that with everyone or just with me?"

"Guess it depends on my mood," I said.

She nodded, like she understood, and started to draw. I could hear the pencil scraping the page, the quick, nervous lines. I focused on the door, on the feel of the grain and the bite of the blade.

When I finished, I brushed the edge with my hand, checked the smoothness, then hefted the door up and set it against the wall. She watched me every step, not even pretending to sketch now.

"You're strong," she said. "Shit." She whispered to herself. "Guess you already knew that." She wasn't usually so awkward. It was kind of adorable.

I ignored her and went back inside, propped the door in the frame. It slid in easy now, perfect fit. I set the hinges, screwed them tight, and tested the swing.

It was good work. I took a step back, wiping sweat from my forehead, and realized she was right behind me, standing close enough that I could feel the heat off her skin.

"Barely even broke a sweat that time," she said, eyes locked on my hands.

I tried to move around her, but she didn't budge. "You're in the way."

She smirked. "What if I want to be?"

The air got thick, like a storm rolling in. My wolf paced, restless. I could smell her now—lemon, sweat, and something else. Hunger, maybe.

She set the sketchbook on the counter, arms folded. "So, why do you hate me, Finn Walsh?"

It hit me square in the chest. I stared at her, searching for a lie, but there wasn't one.

"I don't hate you," I said, flat.

She stepped closer, crowding my space. "You act like you do. Like I'm a problem to be fixed, or a job you got stuck with."

I let the toolbox drop to the floor, the clang loud in the quiet house. I stood my ground.

"You don't want the truth," I said. "Trust me."

She laughed, sharp. "I want *something*. Not sure what, but I want it."

I tried to look away, but she grabbed my wrist, fingers small but strong. "Say it. Whatever you're holding back. You're not scaring me."

I didn't say anything for a long moment. Then, slow, like dragging a confession out of a stubborn dog, I said:

"You're not ready. You think you are, but you're not. You act tough, but you're just a little girl playing grown-up, and I don't have the patience to break you in."

She jerked her hand back as if I'd slapped her. Her eyes flashed, teal-blue and wet with rage. "Fuck you."

I nodded once. "Yeah. That's about what I expected."

I turned to go, but she moved faster than I thought possible, darting in front of me and blocking the hall. "Don't you dare walk out. Not after that."

"Move," I said, voice low.

She shook her head, and the bandana slid out of her hair, causing it to fall wild around her face. "No. Make me."

I could've walked around her, could've shoved her aside, but my hands wouldn't move. My body felt like it was filled with static, every nerve on fire.

She stared me down, daring me. "Go on, cowboy. Fix it. Or fuck it up. But stop running."

Something in me snapped. Maybe it was the weeks of wanting, the nights of not sleeping, the way she kept worming into my head even when I tried to drown her out. Maybe it was my wolf's incessant chanting, "*Mate, mate, mate.*"

I grabbed her by the arms, hard enough to leave marks, and pushed her back against the wall. She gasped, not in fear, but in something closer to excitement.

I leaned in, mouth at her ear. "You want to know why I can't stand you, Maverick?"

She looked hurt for a fleeting moment, then laughed, breathless. "Enlighten me."

I tossed my hat off and kissed her, all teeth and anger, and she bit back just as hard. Her legs locked around my hips, her arms pulling me closer. I could feel every part of her, soft and tense and wanting.

She dropped her legs and clawed at my shirt, tearing it loose from my waistband, her hands hot on my back. I shoved her harder against the wall, lips on her throat, her jaw, her mouth. She didn't shy away. She met every move, fierce and wild.

I could taste salt and sweat and the sharp tang of lemon from her skin. She dug her nails into my waist, drawing blood, and I growled low, animal. I owned every inch of her mouth, my tongue memorizing every taste. There was no other sound in the room, just the sound of breath and skin and the occasional tap of her head against the drywall when I pinned her too hard.

When I pulled away, we stood there, chest to chest, hearts hammering.

She was the first to speak, voice rough. "Still think I'm not ready?"

She might have kissed like a fucking woman on fire, but when I looked at her, I saw a spoiled brat.

I pulled back, looked her in the eyes. "You're trouble, Maverick. That's what you are. You're reckless and have no discipline. You think everything is a game, and you're the one moving the pieces across the board. I got news for you darlin', this isn't a game I'm interested in playing."

She grinned, lips swollen, still thinking she was in control. "What does that mean?"

I let her go, put my hat back on, and picked up my toolbox. She watched, smug and triumphant.

"It means you're still not ready, little girl."

I left, the sound of her confused gasp following me home.

CHAPTER 5

BRIE

The door shut so hard it rattled the glass in the windows, and I just stood there, back pressed to the cool, flaking paint, half expecting Gunner to storm back in and finish the job; yell at me, or fuck me, or both. Instead, the only sound was the distant crunch of gravel under his boots and the useless pounding of my own heart.

He'd called me "trouble," Maverick, a "little girl playing grown-up," and it was worse than any slap. Worse than the way he'd kissed me, so hard I was certain my mouth was bleeding; worse than the way he'd looked at me just before he let go, as if he pitied me for not being enough. I could still taste him—salt, coffee. It was all over my lips, my tongue, my teeth.

I sagged to the kitchen floor, knees knocking together, arms wrapped tight around my ribs like I could maybe hold the rest of me together. The leftover adrenaline made my teeth chatter. I pressed my forehead to the hardwood floor and let myself breathe, just breathe, in and out until the rush of blood slowed and the dizzy part of my brain stopped screaming.

He was right, obviously. I was a mess. A spoiled brat, a fuckup, a "project" no one would ever finish. I told myself I didn't care, but every molecule in my body was vibrating with humiliation and hunger, and it was all for him. I hated him for it. I hated myself more.

The thing was, I'd never wanted someone to want me this badly. I was good at making people notice me—could bat eyelashes, flash a smile, lean just so over the pastry case and score a free almond croissant without even trying. At university, I'd won a barista's entire week's tips just for giving him my number, which I never answered. It was easy. It was a game.

But Gunner didn't play games. At least, not with me.

He played them with everyone else. I'd seen him at Pearl's, in the smoky warmth of the bar, laughing and trading stories, high-fiving the other wolves and ruffling the hair of the MC's newest kid like an affectionate big brother. He was golden, unbothered, the center of every joke. But the minute I walked into the room, the humor dried up, and he'd stare at me with this complicated look—half disgust, half ache.

Why did he go cold with me? Was I so broken?

I picked myself up and paced to my bedroom, slamming the door behind me, then locking it for good measure. The walk through the house was automatic; I'd memorized every creak in the floorboards, every spot where the paint peeled, every place the light hit wrong and made the whole place look haunted. Sometimes I felt like the house was an extension of me—pretty enough from a distance, all cracks and holes if you looked too close.

I flopped onto the bed, barely missing the sketchbook I'd left open on the comforter. My latest drawing was a half-finished self-portrait, but it didn't look like me; it looked like someone who didn't care what happened next. I tossed the book across the room and buried my face in the pillows.

My wolf had nothing to offer. She was curled up in the corner of my brain, licking her wounds. "You're trouble, Maverick," Gunner had said, voice so low and final it vibrated right down to my bones.

For a split second, I hated him. Then, as the minutes crawled past, the hate slipped into a sticky sort of longing, so familiar it made me want to cry. He was probably already back at his barn, tossing hay and pretending he'd never even set foot in this house. I wondered if his hands were still shaking. Mine were.

I squeezed my eyes shut and tried to pretend this was all a bad TV show, and that next week I'd be a whole new Brie—one who never got nervous, never let a man make her feel like this. But I'd seen enough to know that even the best pilots got canceled before the season ended. I was already on reruns.

I should have felt angry, but all I could manage was tired.

I didn't realize I was crying until I felt the warm, stinging wetness on my wrist. Not the pretty, cinematic tears you dab away with a monogrammed handkerchief, but the ugly kind; snuffling, hiccupy, making the skin under your nose raw. I swiped at my face with the sleeve of my favorite cardigan, blue and gold, the one Luc had always said made me look "très chic."

I wanted to throw it out the window.

The worst part was, for a second in that kitchen, I'd really believed Gunner was going to fuck me. Not just because I wanted it, but because it would prove I wasn't just a broken toy—prove that I could make him lose control. I'd almost kissed him first, and the fact that he beat me to it, and then stopped, made the humiliation burn hotter.

I wasn't even good enough for a quick lay. Not for him.

I remembered the first time I ever made a man look at me like I was the last glass of water in the desert. It was at a high school party back in Houston, where I'd borrowed my sister's lipstick and wore a dress that showed off my young curves. I was sixteen, and I knew I was hot, and I'd made a varsity quarterback trip over his own feet. It was stupid, but for five minutes I'd felt untouchable.

I'd spent the last seven years chasing that feeling, and every year it got a little harder to catch.

Luc Renault had seen right through me. He'd called me a "little rabbit," but the way he said it had made me feel elegant, fragile, impossible to catch. He'd treated me like a secret, something precious, but I knew now that I'd only ever been a tool to him. A disposable one. It's hard to trust yourself when you allowed a man to use you; whose goal it was to traffic you.

Gunner was the first man to see every crack and still want to break me down further. He didn't lie, didn't even try. That scared me more than anything.

I wanted to text Harper, or even Parker, and tell them what an absolute asshole Gunner was. But I didn't. I didn't want them to see how much it hurt.

My phone buzzed on the bedside table—a notification from some art account I followed, nothing important. I left it unread.

The tears had mostly dried by the time I heard the sound of tires crunching the gravel outside. My mother's car. She was home early, probably to make some casserole or reorganize the pantry or, God forbid, check on me.

I scrambled to the bathroom, splashed cold water on my face, then studied myself in the mirror. The skin under my eyes was puffy, but I could fix that with makeup. I could always fix it. I ran the flat iron through the front two chunks of my hair, slicked on some concealer, and practiced a smile.

It looked wrong.

I locked my bedroom door and tried to ignore the sound of her heels on the hardwood, the cheerful "Brie? Darling? Are you home?" echoing down the hall. She'd come looking if I didn't answer. I tucked myself under the covers, pretending to sleep.

It only took two minutes for her to knock. Three sharp raps, just like when I was a kid, and she wanted to quiz me on state capitals or what fork went with the fish course.

"Brie?" The knob rattled. "Are you alright?"

I willed her to go away, but she was nothing if not persistent.

"Brie, I made us some tea. Why don't you come join me in the kitchen?"

She always made it sound like an invitation, never an order. But it *was* an order.

Nanette was a dead ringer for a lady on a cruise commercial—pearl earrings, hair just-so, and an apron as if she'd ever dirtied herself baking. She stood at the stove, arranging two mugs on a tray with thin, perfect lemon slices balanced on the rim, like she expected Martha Stewart to rate her form. Her movements were so deliberate I almost laughed, but my throat was sandpaper. I hovered in the doorway, damp with humiliation and wanting to retreat, but that would mean losing the only neutral zone in this house.

She didn't turn around. "I hope you don't mind chamomile. The black tea keeps me up." The way she said it, you'd think sleep was a leisure activity, not an Olympic event. Then, as she set the sugar bowl just so: "Rough night?"

My lip started to tremble, and I bit down on the inside so hard I tasted iron. I tried to play it off. "You could say that." I gripped the edge of the counter, fingers pressed so hard to the cool stone they turned white. The silence in the kitchen was louder than the whirr of the fridge, the tick of the clock, louder than every accusation I'd leveled at myself in the last hour.

Nanette finally faced me, and her eyes were clinical—first scanning my hair, then my smudged eyeliner, then the cut-off shorts I'd worn two days running. "Sit," she said, voice gentle but absolute, the way only women raised in the South can pull off.

I slid onto the stool at the counter, hands in my lap. She poured tea, her hands steady even when she set the cup in front of me. Then she just looked at me, that calm, implacable stare.

I broke first. "He hates me."

Nanette blinked, and if she'd been anyone else, I might have detected a smirk. But this was my mother: if she found my drama entertaining, she'd never let on. "Is that so?"

"I know it," I said, the words spilling out, ugly and wet. "You should have heard what he called me. Spoiled, a brat, not ready for anything. That I act like everything is a game and I don't know how to be a grown-up."

She folded her hands, interlaced them, and rested her chin on the nest of knuckles. "Is any of that... wrong?"

It felt like a slap, but not the cruel kind. The kind you need to reset your vision. I blinked, tears threatening to tip over, but I didn't want to cry in front of her. "It's all wrong. Or it's all true. I don't know. He thinks I can't handle myself, that I'm just... I don't know, a project."

Nanette reached over, and for the first time in months, touched my hand. Her skin was dry and smooth, the pressure soft but unyielding. "Brie, darling, you are not a project. You're a person. A complicated, beautiful, difficult person." She paused, then added, "You get that from both sides."

The heat behind my eyes turned sharp, and I shook my head. "No, Mom. That's bullshit. I'm not complicated; I'm just broken. He saw it the second he met me. I act tough, but I'm just... pathetic. I can't even talk to him without losing my mind."

She smiled, but it was sad around the edges. "You've always been intense. Even as a baby. Never satisfied with just being held, you wanted to be flying. You wanted everything at once, and when you couldn't have it, you'd scream the house down."

I let myself smile at that, just a little. "Sounds about right."

She poured herself a cup, stirred in exactly one spoonful of sugar, and went on. "I know I didn't make it easier for you. Your father... well, he wasn't much for boundaries. He loved you, both of you girls, but he wanted you to shine so badly that he never let you learn the dark parts. And he thought Harper could handle everything. He was the worst of fathers and I wasn't much better at being a mother. I should have done more for both of you girls." She looked away, and the admission hung in the air like a bruise.

It wasn't what I expected. I reached for my own cup, hands shaking, and sipped the too-hot tea just to have something to do. "I'm sorry, Mom," I said, voice tiny. "I know I'm a nightmare sometimes."

Her eyes snapped back to me, fierce. "Don't ever say that. You are not a nightmare. You are a storm, and the world needs storms, even if they don't always know what to do with them." She leaned in, conspiratorial. "You know, when you were ten, you locked yourself in your room for three days after your father forgot your ballet recital. When I finally coaxed you out, you told me that you'd figured it out: if you pretended you didn't care, it wouldn't hurt as much." She sipped her tea. "I never forgot that."

I let the silence stretch, because what do you even say to that? It hurt in a new way, not the old self-loathing, but something softer. Regret, maybe. Or longing.

I tried to meet her halfway. "I don't want to be like this. I want to be... normal. I want to let people in without scaring them away or making everything so fucking hard."

Nanette's smile was pure forgiveness. "Then try again. With Finn. Or with anyone. But don't give up because you made one mess. Lord knows I've made plenty."

I snorted, surprised into a real laugh. "You? You're like, the queen of not messing up."

She set her cup down, both hands around it. "You have no idea, darling." The words were so low I almost missed them.

I wanted to ask, but something in her eyes made me stop. Instead, I reached for her hand again, and this time she let me hold it for a long moment. I could feel her pulse, steady and slow, as if nothing in the world could shake her. I envied that. I wondered if I'd ever feel that kind of peace, even for a minute.

I squeezed. "Thanks, Mom."

She squeezed back. "You're welcome. And Brie?"

"Yeah?"

"Don't ever believe you're not worthy of a good man. Or that you're too much. The right man will love you for exactly that."

I nodded, but didn't trust myself to answer.

She stood, smoothed her skirt, and started cleaning up the tray. "Why don't you get ready for bed? Tomorrow's another chance to try again."

I watched her stack the cups, move so efficiently, so self-contained. It struck me that maybe she was just as scared of showing the cracks as I was.

"I love you, Mom," I said, voice stronger now.

She turned, her smile breaking wide and true. "I love you, too, Brie. Always."

I left the kitchen, the scent of lemon and chamomile trailing after me like a benediction. For the first time in forever, I didn't feel alone in the house.

I walked to my bedroom, steps light, heart heavy but buoyed by hope. Maybe she was right. Maybe tomorrow, or the next day, I could try again.

Anything good was worth fighting for. I'd remember that.

My room was just as I'd left it—a crime scene of watercolors, laundry, and half-finished Amazon boxes. But tonight I wanted the white noise of the bathroom, the only room in the house with a lock that worked. I went straight for the Jack-and-Jill, flicking on the row of frosted vanity bulbs until the entire room glowed like a department store at midnight. It was the only way I could stomach my own reflection.

I closed the door and leaned against it, staring into the mirror, hoping maybe the version of me looking back would offer up some kind of secret code. She didn't. She looked tired. But something was different, and not just the new blue highlights or the mascara stains under both eyes. I studied the outline of my jaw, the angle of my shoulders, the curve at my hip where my shorts cut in. My boobs, never my best asset; actually filled out the tank top now, and I hadn't had to add a new belt hole in weeks. I pressed a palm to my ribcage, expecting the same sharp edge of bone I'd hated all through France, but found soft muscle instead. My legs looked less like toothpicks, more like legs.

It was embarrassing, almost. To admit how much it meant. To see yourself coming back to life, molecule by molecule, just because you weren't constantly being hollowed out by fear. I ran my fingers through my hair, which had grown half an inch since we moved here, and let myself smile a little. I still felt like a mess—emotionally, mentally, soulfully—but physically? I was no longer the girl in the warehouse, or the one cowering in Luc's penthouse waiting for the next blow to fall. I was myself again.

Which made it all the more infuriating that I was so, so obsessed with Gunner.

I tried to shake the memory of his hands on my waist, his voice in my ear. It was pointless; every nerve ending in my body seemed tuned to a frequency only he broadcast. I rolled my shoulders, tried to will away the feeling, but it only pulsed deeper. The ache at the base of my spine, the throb between my legs, the rush of blood every time I replayed the kiss. I was in trouble. Real trouble.

I turned on the tap, letting the water run scalding, and yanked my tank top over my head and let it land on the floor. I kicked off my shorts, then hesitated, glancing over my shoulder as if I might catch someone spying through the frosted window. No one would. It was just my own shame crawling along the floor behind me.

I set my phone on the little wooden bench by the tub, then went to the pantry to dig out the fancy bath salts Harper had given me as a "congrats for surviving" present. I dumped a full scoop into the hot water, watching the pink clouds dissolve. It looked almost radioactive, but it smelled like a lavender bomb. I reached for the bottle of drugstore bubble bath I'd stolen from Parker's bathroom and squeezed in enough to make a small mountain of foam. The tub filled fast, steam curling up to fog the mirrors.

I made a playlist. Soft, old stuff—Norah Jones, a little Ray LaMontagne, even some acoustic Taylor Swift, because why not? I set the iPad on the closed toilet and hit play, the sound muffled but familiar.

I braced myself on the edge of the tub, dipped a toe, and hissed. The water was perfect—hot enough to sting, hotter than I deserved. I lowered myself in slowly, like a queen being lowered into a ceremonial grave, and let the heat lap at my skin. The bubbles came up to my neck. For the first time all day, I let myself breathe.

My body reacted instantly. The ache, the need, all of it sharpened as I relaxed. My thighs clenched, my hands gripped the rim. I closed my eyes, head tipped back, and tried to focus on anything other than Gunner's mouth, but it was like trying not to think of pink elephants. The harder I fought, the more present he became. The taste of him, the scratch of his stubble, the way he'd bitten my lip and left a perfect, bruised imprint.

I let my right hand drift over my stomach, tracing lazy circles just below the waterline. I could feel my own heartbeat, hard and frantic. I squeezed my eyes tighter, letting the music and the memory swirl together.

I wondered what it would feel like to call him. Just to hear his voice, to know he was somewhere on the other end of the world. Maybe he'd answer with a "Hey, Maverick." Maybe he'd ignore it. Either way, it was safer than sitting here pretending I didn't want to die for him.

I reached for the phone, hands slick and pruney, and hovered over his contact. Gunner. I hadn't changed it, hadn't dared. I stared at the picture—just the blank circle with a G, because he didn't do selfies and I'd never managed to snap one without him catching me.

What would I even say? Hey, remember when you kissed me so hard I forgot my name? Or: I can't sleep unless I pretend you're here, holding me down so I don't float away? Or maybe just: I'm sorry. I'm so fucking sorry.

I set the phone back down, face-up, and let it idle. Maybe in a few minutes, when the water started to cool, I'd have the nerve. For now, I just soaked.

The song changed to something slow and sad, and I rolled onto my side, bubbles slopping over the porcelain. The motion jarred the little bench, and my phone teetered, then slid to the tile floor with a crack. I groaned, wiped my hand on a towel, and fished it up and set it back on the bench and sank back into the feeling of the hot water against my skin.

CHAPTER 6

GUNNER

By ten o'clock, I'd showered the cattle stench off my skin, trimmed my beard with the precision of a surgeon, and was down to nothing but a threadbare towel, drying off in the dark of my bedroom. My phone was charging on the window ledge, blinking with a blue notification. I figured it was a calendar reminder about the livestock auction at the stockyards, but when I checked, it was an incoming call, not a text.

Brie.

My thumb hovered over the answer button, suspicious. Was she calling to try to lure me back to her house for some phantom repair, hoping for a part two of what happened earlier? I waited out the first ring, debating, but the stubborn part of me wanted to hear what kind of shitstorm she was about to unleash.

I answered on the third ring, said nothing, and held the phone to my ear.

At first, I heard only the slosh of water and the faint click of a playlist—something soft and sad, Ray LaMontagne or someone similar. The music was soft drowned out by the steady pulse of water. She must have dialed me by accident. I waited just to be sure, and that's when I caught the little gasp.

It wasn't a pain noise. I'd heard enough of those in my line of work to know the difference. This was more like the sound a woman makes when she's alone, the world kept at bay by a locked door and several inches of bathwater.

I froze, towel halfway to my thigh. The right thing to do would have been to hang up, pretend I never heard a thing. But the second moan hit, soft and real, and the right thing went straight out the window. My body reacted before my brain caught up. My cock, barely calmed from the shower, surged to life, straining under the terrycloth.

I set the phone by the bed and clicked speaker, the hiss of water and the low drone of her breathing filling the room. I sat on the edge of the mattress, legs spread, towel tenting in the middle. I could picture her, knees drawn up, brunette and blue hair curling at her neck, body pale and half-lost in a mountain of bubbles.

She must have shifted in the tub, because there was a slosh and a high, shaky intake of breath. Then she muttered, almost too low for the mic: "Damn you, Gunner. Why are you so fucking sexy?"

That's when I lost whatever moral ground I'd had. I slipped the towel off, let it hit the floor, and lay back, wrapping my hand around the base of my cock, squeezing just enough to ease the ache. I stroked slow, matching her rhythm. The slick sound of water on skin was clear through the speaker.

She whimpered, a broken little plea, and my balls drew tight. I'd have mocked myself if it weren't so goddamn perfect.

I closed my eyes and let her voice carry me: "Finn. Oh, god. I want you—" She cut herself off with another gasp. "Please, yes, just—"

I picked up the phone, brought it close, just to hear every little sound. I wanted to say her name, let her know I was listening, but something told me she needed this, needed to believe she was still alone. That she was safe.

Her moans built, climbing from soft whimpers to something sharper, rough with need. She didn't bother hiding it. Each time she cried out, the urge to answer her, to tell her what she did to me, got harder to fight.

I smeared some lotion I kept on the nightstand on my hand to ease the friction of my hand.

"Fuck," she breathed, voice raw. "I want you. I want your mouth, your hands—oh, oh, God—"

I couldn't take it anymore. I pumped faster, fist slick with the small amount of lubricant the lotion gave. My hips jerked up, chasing release.

Then she said it, her voice breaking on the words: "I promise I'll try to be better for you. So you'll want me."

That nearly undid me. I wanted to tell her she didn't have to change, that I wanted her exactly as she was—bratty, reckless, broken. But the only answer I could manage was a guttural groan.

Her breathing quickened, stuttering. "I know I belong to you, Finn. I want you so much. Yes, please..."

We came at the same time. Her cry, muffled and sharp, told me she'd bitten her lip to keep from alerting her mother. I growled her name, low and rough, away from the phone so she wouldn't hear me.

The line went quiet, save for her ragged breaths and the drip of water from the tap. I listened, spent and shaky, as she sank back in the tub, the water lapping gently at her sides. I imagined her skin pink and splotched, her hair floating around her face, her heart racing as fast as mine.

I waited until her breathing evened out, then ended the call before she realized. I knew she'd see the 40-minute call eventually, but that was a problem for future Finn.

Right now, I let myself lie back on the bed, arm flung over my eyes, and just smiled. I hadn't felt this light in months, maybe years. I hoped I'd see her in the morning before I left for the cattle auction. Maybe I'd pull her aside and tell her, flat out, that she didn't need to try for me. That I was already hers.

Sleep came easy, then. When I drifted off, the last thing I saw behind my eyelids was the streak of blue in her hair, bright as a Texas wildflower.

Auction day never started late, and the only men more punctual than cowboys with a deadline were Marines on parade. The morning air was sharp as broken glass, still carrying a little bite from the night. The sky was a washed-out navy, horizon just going pale. I'd barely had time for a granola bar and a thermos of Pearl's percolator mud before Arsenal showed up, full camo and all, double-checking the load lists and the paperwork.

We had eight head to move—three Black Angus Steers, two calves, three heifers, all fat as state fair champions and twice as ornery. I was scheduled to drive the lead truck; Arsenal would run tail. Each truck had a wrangler riding shotgun in case of trouble, and three ranch hands had already shown up to help funnel the cows down the chute and into the trailers.

I took a moment on the loading dock, watching the sky catch fire to the east. My hands smelled like saddle soap and coffee. The barn cats stalked mice through the hay bales, their little shapes black against the brightening yard.

Arsenal was already in the back pen, clipboard in one hand and a short coil of rope in the other, barking orders at two farmhands and a college kid I'd known his whole life. Arsenal ran the operation like a prison break, and it took about ten minutes for everyone to get in line.

I did a final check on the trailer locks, the thick bars and the safety chains. Last time we'd done this, one of the cows kicked a latch open and took off down State Route 60. Bronc nearly had a stroke. I'd have been more worried if I didn't secretly like the chaos. He wouldn't make the run with us today with Juliet being pregnant and all. He barely left her side these days. It was damn cute the way he acted like he wanted to carry her everywhere.

We had both rigs loaded by the time the sun topped the tree line. That's when I saw a familiar Lexus creeping up the drive, dust pluming behind it. Harper was coming to tell Arsenal goodbye, Brie in tow.

The boys lined up on the rail to watch, predictable as sunrise. I could practically hear them wagering on what would come out of the car this time.

Harper climbed out first. She wore skinny jeans, a white tee with a print of a ballet dancer, and a dusty pair of Ariats. Arsenal's posture went from combat-ready to parade rest, and his eyes went soft, just for her. She waved, looking more at home than I'd ever seen her, even in a barnyard full of wolves.

Then Brie got out.

The effect was instant. The air changed. I'd say she glowed, but that was too easy. It was more like she soaked up every eye in the county and didn't mind one bit. She wore cutoff shorts, a faded Def Leppard shirt that tied at her waist, and a pair of Old Gringos that almost hit her knees. Her hair was all wild waves that framed her face, blue streaks peaking through the brunette strands. She looked like she'd been styled for a Texas fashion shoot, except I knew damn well she'd just rolled out of bed and thrown on what she liked.

Five of the hands, grown men, two of them twice my age, literally climbed the fence to get a better view.

Brie didn't even look at them. She kept her eyes on the gravel, chin down, a little blush high on her cheeks. But I saw her glance up once, quick, in my direction, and her wolf peeked out through the lashes.

Territorial, possessive, primal: my own wolf bristled up. I dropped my wrench and stalked over to the fence.

"You boys want a picture, or you wanna keep your jobs?" My voice left no doubt about whose territory they were gawking at.

The youngest, a kid from Tulia with a neck tattoo, tried to look contrite. "Uh, sorry, Gunner." He scrambled down like the rail was electrified. The rest slithered off, back to the chutes and the hay bales.

Harper sauntered over, beaming. "Mornin' boys." You'd think she was queen of the operation.

Brie hung back, arms wrapped around her middle, doing her best not to meet my eyes. I wasn't about to let her off that easy.

"Maverick!" I looked Brie's direction. "You're up early."

She looked at me then, the same way a cat does—curious, wary, daring you to reach for her. I grinned, knowing she'd see it for what it was: I heard you last night.

The flush on her face deepened, but she held her ground. "Wanted to tell you bye, and to be safe." Her voice was soft, careful, her cheeks pink. She didn't dare look below my chin. I had no doubt she'd noticed that she'd accidentally made that call last night, and I'd listened to her touch herself while thinking of me.

Arsenal strolled up behind, smiling with all the warmth of a gun barrel. "We'll be back tomorrow, barring an ambush or a tornado." He was only half joking.

"Good luck at the sale." Harper hugged Arsenal with so tight I thought she'd crack a rib. He bent down and whispered something in her ear, and she actually giggled. I'd have called him whipped, but he wore the look too well. Couldn't say I didn't envy him.

I turned back to Brie, who was shuffling her feet in the gravel, tracing circles with her toe. She finally looked up, her eyes bright, blue streaks catching the sun.

"Thanks for coming out." I told her. "Means a lot."

She rolled her eyes, but there was a softness to it. "I know you'll be back tomorrow, and it's not like you're going off to war or anything. But..."

"Feels like it sometimes. Never know when a stray cow or a drunk teamster is gonna end you."

She flashed me a smile. "Well, don't die. I'd be pissed if I had to do the next load myself."

Fuck, she was so beautiful. The urge to touch her was strong. I wanted to reach out, push the hair from her face, kiss the sarcasm right off her mouth. But I settled for stepping in close, until her scent hit me; lemon and honeysuckle, clean and sharp.

"You can text me, if you want." Her voice suddenly small. "Let me know you made it there safe."

I leaned down, speaking just to her. "I plan on it. You sleep good last night?"

Her eyes snapped to mine, wide and scandalized. Then she smirked, too smart to let me have the upper hand. "Sure did, cowboy."

She started to walk away, hips swaying just a little. I caught her wrist, gentle. "Brie."

She turned back, hair in her eyes.

I said, "I'll see you soon," and let her go.

As I climbed up into the cab of the dually, Arsenal was already starting the engine in the chase truck. The ranch hands scattered, the day's work just beginning.

In the side mirror, I saw Brie standing at the fence, arms folded, watching me with a look I hadn't seen before—soft, almost hopeful, with her sharp edges I didn't want her to lose still evident.

I grinned at her, tipped my hat, and threw the truck in gear.

Right before I pulled away, I rolled down the window and yelled, "Hey, Maverick!"

She looked up, startled. I hollered, "Try not to drop your phone when you're in the bath next time."

Her jaw dropped. Then she laughed, loud and wild, head thrown back.

I hit the road, feeling like I'd finally won something worth winning.

CHAPTER 7

BRIE

By the time Harper and I reached her car, Gunner's dually was nothing but a sun-silver glint on the flat Texas road, followed by a comet-tail of cattle dust. I watched his truck disappear, the pit in my stomach growing instead of going away, like the calories of a single powdered donut I was already planning to eat for breakfast. I clutched my scarf tighter and tried to play it cool, but Harper saw everything.

"You know you're allowed to have a crush, right?" She said, unlocking the Lexus with a chirp. "It's not a federal crime."

I snorted and flopped into the passenger seat, staring straight ahead as she buckled up. "It's not a crush," I said too fast. "It's more like a chronic illness."

She laughed, a light, bell-like sound that didn't match the rest of her—she was all long limbs and neat muscle, hair back in a no-nonsense braid. She was annoyingly beautiful, but even more annoying, she wasn't even trying. "There are worse things," she said, putting the car in reverse. "At least he's easy on the eyes. And great personality too, apparently."

The drive from the ranch into Dairyville was all empty, pale blue and yellow, telephone poles leaning like drunk frat boys, the only traffic the occasional feed truck or a flock of buzzards circling above. I rolled down the window and let the wind slap my cheeks awake, sucking in the scent of sweet grass and something else—smoke, maybe, or the ghost of a prairie fire. It was better than perfume. It felt clean, or at least honest.

Harper drummed her fingers on the wheel, humming along to the radio, which was playing a song I hated from a band I'd never admit I liked. I watched the world slide by, counting the fences and the miles.

We hit Dairyville's Main Street in under fifteen minutes. The town was literally a square of connected streets dotted with two-story connected buildings: a hardware store, antique shops, children's clothing stores, a hair salon, boutiques, and even a furniture store. It was like a scene from a Hallmark movie. And slap-dab in the middle of one of the blocks, Buttercream & Blessings.

Aspen's bakery was painted the color of sunshine with a yellow and white awning, and white trim. There were hand-painted signs in the window advertising things like "SALTED CARAMEL CREAM PUFFS" and "PEACH COBBLER DONUTS." The glass was always streaked from the morning rush. A four feet tall likeness of Oscar stood outside with his little paw pointing toward the door. His other paw held a "welcome" sign that displayed their hours. I cracked up laughing at that. He no doubt conjured that little piece of art, and it was perfect.

Inside, the bakery was wall-to-wall warmth and the smell of sugar and cinnamon. The air was humid with yeast and flour, and sunlight poured in through the front window, turning the glass display into a jewelry case for pastries. I spotted Juliet right away—her blonde hair was silky and healthy looking; probably from the prenatal vitamins. Her stomach had officially crossed the line from "maybe she just likes bread" to "yep, that's a baby in there (or in her case, *two* babies)." She wore a floaty, cream-colored dress and sat at the largest table, fending off a tray of lemon bars from Maddie and Parker.

I got the sense that Aspen had already been through and orchestrated everything. There were matching mugs at every seat, flowers in a pretty little thrifted vase. That little witch put a comfy touch on everything.

Harper pulled up a chair, and I let myself be dragged into their orbit. The table was round, which made it impossible to ignore anyone, and within thirty seconds I had a cup of coffee in my hand and a lemon scone the size of my fist on my plate.

"Brie! Darling!" Juliet reached for my hand, squeezing it with more strength than I thought a pregnant woman could muster. "You look... radiant. Am I seeing some color in your cheeks?"

Maddie, who wore a tie-dye hoodie and had recently decided to dye her own hair pink, leaned over and said, "Don't be weird, Jules. She looks exactly the same as yesterday. Except maybe more murder-y?"

I snorted, a crumb flying onto my scarf. "Wow, thanks for the compliment, Maddie. I've been working on my serial killer aesthetic. Trying to stay ahead of the trends."

Parker, who looked like she hadn't slept in three days, just grinned at me over the rim of her mug. "Honestly, I respect that. If I had a face like yours; all sweet and cute, I'd be mean as hell too. Keeps people on their toes." Man, I loved Parker. I hoped her lack of sleep was because her monster of a mate, Wrecker, was wearing her out in the sack and not because she's tracking bad guys.

The banter ping-ponged around the table, with Harper reining it in when it threatened to go too far off the rails. It was easy, almost cozy, and for a few minutes I felt like maybe I'd landed somewhere safe, even if only temporarily.

The conversation turned, as it inevitably would, to men.

"So, Gunner," Juliet said, slicing a lemon bar with a plastic fork. "How's that working out? You two seemed... close at the pens today."

I choked on a sip of coffee, nearly spraying it onto the table. Parker pounded my back, not gently. "Wow, subtle," I wheezed. "I see where this is going."

Maddie waggled her eyebrows, being silly. "Was he lookin' hot? Or just like, Gunner cute? There's a difference."

Harper, for her part, pretended to study the donut in front of her, but I could see the way her eyes crinkled at the edges. "I think they're asking how your home improvement project went," she said.

I wiped my mouth and looked at the ceiling, buying time. "First of all, Juliet, I didn't see you at the pens this morning."

She smiled. "Well, Bronc has eyes everywhere, honey. And if *he* does, I do too."

I just nodded. "And as far as Gunner. He fixed the door yesterday. Very competently. And then he accused me of being a brat and a project, and then he left."

Juliet winced, and her hand found mine again, thumb rubbing circles. "Oof. That's harsh, even for Finn."

Parker snorted. "Not really. He's been in a shit mood for weeks. You should've seen him at last month's poker night. He barely spoke and almost broke a chair over Eli's head."

"That was Eli," Maddie said, deadpan. "He could have deserved it."

I shrugged, trying to seem unfazed. "Maybe I did too. He's not wrong. I'm not exactly low-maintenance."

Juliet's voice dropped, all the air of a therapist with a thousand hours under her belt. "You're allowed to be complicated, Brie. Trauma isn't something you just walk away from." She squeezed my fingers, and this time I didn't pull away.

For a split second, the urge to spill everything—to tell them about the bath, the accidental call, all of it. But I swallowed it hard and tried to smile.

"It's fine. Honestly. He's just..." I gestured helplessly, searching for the right word. "He's Gunner. I don't know how else to put it."

Juliet nodded, her expression soft. "He's the pack's enforcer for a reason. I'm just glad you're not scared of him."

I opened my mouth to correct her, but stopped. Was I scared of Gunner? Not exactly. I was scared of what he made me feel, which was worse.

The others had already moved on, Parker telling a story about a malfunctioning security system and Maddie one-upping it with a tale about a raccoon that broke into the motorcycle shop. I let their voices wash over me, picking at my scone until it crumbled to dust.

That was when I felt it—a sudden, sharp tingling at the base of my neck, like a static shock from inside my own skin. For a split second, the bakery went blurry around the edges. I looked up, expecting to see someone watching through the window, but all I saw was the empty street, the post office across the way, the Oscar statue outside the door.

I rubbed my neck, trying to chase the feeling away. "You guys ever get that thing," I said, as casually as I could manage, "where it feels like someone's thinking about you so hard it burns?"

Maddie nodded, solemn. "It's called anxiety, babe. Welcome to the club."

Juliet caught my eye, and for a moment, I wondered if she saw more than I meant to give away. "Sometimes it means a storm's coming," she said, voice dreamy. "Or maybe you just have a new pack. Takes a while to adjust."

I tried to laugh, but it came out thin. "Maybe that's it."

The tingling faded, but the unease lingered, sticky and cold under my skin. I tried to shake it off, but couldn't. I sat there, surrounded by women who'd survived worse than I ever had, and still felt like the only person in the room.

A shadow passed over the front window, just for a second, but when I looked up, there was nothing there.

The moment snapped, the laughter picked up again, and the spell broke. But I couldn't shake the feeling that something was coming for me, fast as a pickup on an empty Texas road.

Harper and I walked the two blocks from Buttercream & Blessings to our new space, shoes crunching lightly tapping on the sidewalk, the sun a strobe between clouds and power lines. Dairyville's main drag looked like a diorama of "Old America" you'd see in a Norman Rockwell painting: flags on every pole, window displays of antique furniture, little mannequins modeling tiny dresses, shop owners sweeping the same three feet of curb for the thousandth time. We came upon our storefront, and I tried to imagine how my gallery windows might look one day.

Harper unlocked the door with a flourish, giving me a look that said, "You better be excited about this." I was. I truly was.

Inside, the air was cool, stale, and thick with the must of old wood floors and dust. The front room was huge, its bones visible in the cracks of lath and the warping of the once beautiful ceiling tiles. Light came in through a grid of mismatched glass, painting strange shapes on the floorboards. It was at best, a haunted mansion for bored ghosts; at worst, a condemned structure waiting for a legal reason to collapse.

But Harper beamed, and for a second, I could almost see it: the echo of music and movement, a large mirror along one wall, barre attached. The blank walls blooming with color. Through an opening, another large space opened up. It mirrored the other side. Twin doors to Main Street with the panes of the window lights painted over took up one wall. I could imagine the others covered in my art and the art of other Texas artists. My pulse thumped in my throat, the earlier weirdness replaced by something like nervous hope.

"Think anyone else could do this?" she said, spinning in a slow, arms out circle. "Dance studio in Dairyville, Texas. Art gallery. Us, together."

I shrugged, trying to play it cool. "There's probably a reason no one's done it before. We're either brilliant or doomed."

She laughed, and the sound rebounded off every wall, loud and exuberant. "I'll take both. I spent my entire childhood dreaming of something bigger. That wound up buying me years of essentially prison time. Now, I think small sounds pretty damn good. If the bitch pack will let me..." She stopped, then started again. "You know they tried their damnedest to keep bringing up the fact that I danced in that goddamn club. Made it out that I liked it; that I wasn't worthy to be in this pack or being Jess's mate."

That sent my anger nuclear. "You just show me who it was, Harper. I'll personally rip their throats out. Consequences be damned. You're the best fucking person I know. Who are they to judge you or anyone for that matter?"

She walked up to me and put her hands on my shoulders, eyes shining with unshed tears. "Thank you, little sis. But there is no need for you to do anything. Our Luna tore each one of them new assholes. She called in their husbands also. And if they didn't have a husband, she called in their fathers. Let them all know under no uncertain circumstances that if any of them were ever heard saying one sideways thing about me, she'd personally escort them off of Iron Valor pack territory."

I could not believe that. "Holy shit!"

"Rest easy, Brie Bear. Our Luna has our backs." She stood confidently in saying those words.

"So you're good now? Everyone plays nice with you?"

"God, no," she said, snorting. "But... they're not so bad now. Or maybe I just don't care anymore." She looked at me, serious for a second. "I think you belong here too."

I didn't answer. The truth was, I didn't know yet if I *did* belong here, or anywhere. But it seemed I'd found my little tribe. Parker, Maddie, and Aspen all seemed to truly care about me. I know I'd fight for them. And Juliet was a Luna who, while only a few years older than me, seemed so much wiser. I had no doubt she had my back. I had more than enough reasons to want to stay, not even counting Finn.

Before I could change the subject, the door creaked behind us. In walked who I assumed was the architect, Chantel, straight from Amarillo. She was tall, model-thin, with shiny strawberry blonde hair and green eyes that missed nothing. Her suit looked expensive, and her face looked like it had never broken a sweat. She carried a leather portfolio under one arm and didn't bother with a handshake.

"You must be Brie and Harper," she said, nodding once. "I'm Chantel from Frost & Cook. I'm early, hope that's okay."

Her gaze slid over us, noting every frayed edge and boot scuff. I felt my cheeks flush, but Harper just smiled and motioned her inside.

Chantel was a wolf from the Rose Valley pack. Bronc said her reputation was great, but he wasn't familiar with her. She was all business and got right to it. She opened the portfolio and spread blueprints over a card table, weighing down the corners with paint chips and a stack of granite samples. "I've sketched out three options for the dance floor. Floating laminate's cheapest, but the sprung floor is best for the ankles." She tapped each drawing, rapid-fire. "We'll need to reinforce the mirrors on this wall—support's terrible, and you don't want glass shrapnel with kids around. For the gallery, I recommend track lighting, and we can do movable panels to maximize hanging space."

She was efficient, impersonal, and even I had to admit her ideas made sense. She clearly had done her research as well. I'd never even heard of a sprung floor. She talked about color theory like it was a branch of military science, and every time Harper mentioned a hope or worry, Chantel had an answer before the thought was finished.

We spent an hour pacing the floor, measuring windows, squinting at paint swatches. Harper was all energy, bouncing from detail to detail, while I hung back, watching Chantel work. She was completely unflappable, and after a while, I started to find her confidence reassuring, almost soothing. It was like having a dictator for a decorator.

As she finished, Chantel snapped her folder shut and gave us a look, clinical but not unkind. "You're both very different. That's a good thing, for a business. You'll need each other."

It sounded like a threat, but I knew she meant it as advice.

Harper thanked her, and they set up a follow-up appointment for next week. As soon as the door shut behind Chantel, we both dissolved into snorts.

"She is terrifying," I said, clutching my stomach. "I thought she was going to have me sandblasted."

"She's perfect," Harper said, giddy. "She's like a general, but for art supplies."

I slumped onto the dusty floor, letting the sunlight draw patterns over my shorts. "She looked at us like we were trailer trash. Maybe she thinks that about our pack too. If only she knew, we Iron Valor wolves rubbed elbows with kings."

Harper grinned, her eyes bright. "She will eventually."

I looked at her, at the empty room, the blueprints, the possibilities. For the first time in months, I wanted something—a future, a place that belonged to me; and sharing it with my sister seemed pretty perfect.

"We'll make it work," I said, and almost believed it.

Harper sat down beside me, thigh to thigh, and we watched the dust dance in the beams of afternoon light, quietly taking it all in.

By the time darkness washed Dairyville into silence, I'd showered, gone through two face masks, and watched exactly forty-six minutes of a French murder drama without reading a single subtitle. The house was quiet—Mom had gone to bed early, and even the air conditioner gave up its rattle and settled into a low, satisfied hum. I sprawled on my bed in a tangle of sheets, feeling vaguely hollow and more than a little sorry for myself.

That was when my phone buzzed.

It was a text, not a call, and my pulse kicked at the familiar number: Gunner.

I stared at the screen, debating, then opened it with the reckless hope of a woman who has nothing left to lose. The message was a single line:

You make the prettiest sounds when you think you're alone.

My cheeks flared red so fast I actually gasped. I sat up; the phone clutched in my sweating palm, staring at the words like they might sprout claws and drag me through the glass.

Another buzz almost immediately:

I could listen all night, Maverick. But I'd rather you made those sounds for me in person.

I dropped the phone on the comforter, breathing fast, hands pressed to my face. I knew he'd had to hear me last night. I'd seen that I'd accidentally dialed his number. When I'd checked further, I saw the call had lasted forty minutes. He'd stayed on the line and listened to me. He'd heard me whining his name. I knew that's what he'd referenced this morning, and I actually thought it was funny. So what? He heard me getting myself off. Good for me.

My wolf stirred, rolled belly-up and whined for more.

I typed back, rapid-fire, thumbs shaking:

You didn't have to perv. You could have hung up.

Three seconds later:

I could have. But I didn't. You really wouldn't have wanted me to.

I bit down on a yelp, then thumbed back:

Dream on, cowboy.

His reply came so fast I knew he'd already written it.

If I did, I'd still wake up hard as a fence post thinking about you.

I snorted. It was such a Gunner thing to say. The laughter, raw and a little wild, made my stomach flutter.

A pause, then:

Tell me what you're wearing right now, Maverick.

I looked down at myself: bralette, ragged blue shorts, bare legs tangled in a quilt. My skin flushed, but the idea of telling him made something inside me spark.

Nothing you'd like, I wrote. Boring old pajamas.

I'd like you better out of them. I know you're not shy.

A moment, then:

Prove it. Show me.

My heart galloped in my chest. Was he kidding? Was I? I debated, then—fuck it—I snapped a quick shot of my legs, knees up, one foot bare, the rest artfully out of frame.

You're not getting more than that, I sent.

He replied with a single word:

Liar.

Before I could respond, another message landed:

Are you wet, Brie?

I nearly dropped the phone. I'd never had a man ask me that, not so directly. My thighs pressed together of their own accord, the heat starting to build. I hesitated, then typed:

Maybe.

His answer was instant, hungry:

Go to your drawer. I know you have a toy.

I stared at the screen, jaw slack. How did he...?

His next message came before I could even blush:

Don't play innocent. You came on the phone for me last night, didn't you?

I squeezed my eyes shut, mortified and wildly turned on. My hand slid under the pillow, found the small pink vibrator I'd shoved there last night after my shame bath. I thumbed the power on just to feel the vibration in my palm.

I thumbed back:

You're an animal.

He didn't deny it:

You love it.

Tell me exactly what you're doing.

I exhaled, slow, the room suddenly too warm. My fingers found the hem of my shorts, slipped inside, and my body jerked at the touch. My skin felt fever-hot; my nipples hardened under the thin cotton bralette.

I let the toy hover over my clit, the vibration just enough to make my knees buckle inward. My head went fuzzy. I typed, one-handed:

It's on low. I'm teasing myself. Is that what you want to hear?

He replied:

No, I want you to do it right. Push those shorts down. Open your legs for me. Pretend I'm there, watching you.

I did. God help me, I did. The sheets were soft under my thighs, the air cold against my flushed skin. The vibrator pressed against me, and I nearly bucked off the bed.

I whimpered just once, then went with text dictation:

I'm spread wide. It feels good. Are you hard for me, Finn?

His answer:

I'm always hard for you, Maverick. Keep going.

I set the phone on my nightstand and circled the toy over my clit, a slow, aching rhythm that made my breath hitch every time. I pinched a nipple through the bralette, rolling it until the nerves sparked.

I wanted to tell him everything, so I did.

I'm dripping. I'm sure the sheet is wet. I wish it were your tongue.

His reply:

It will be. I want you to think about me between your legs. I want you to fuck yourself for me, Brie. I want that toy inside your sweet pussy just like I will be soon.

I shoved the toy inside me, the shock of sensation almost too much. I gasped his name—out loud, not just in my head.

My body arched, every nerve ending tuned to that pulse, the heat in my belly coiling and tightening. I rocked my hips, grinding down, chasing it.

Tell me you want me, Maverick.

I wanted to fight him, to make a joke, but all I could manage was the truth:

I do. I want you so fucking bad.

Now I want you to come for me, Brie. I want my name on your lips when you do.

The orgasm hit hard, blinding and fierce, ripping the air out of my lungs. I writhed against the sheets, biting down on a moan so loud I worried Mom would hear. My hand clutched the phone, white-knuckled, and I managed to dictate my message, mid-shudder:

Oh, fuck, Finn. I'm coming.

The aftershocks lasted forever, or maybe just a few seconds. My skin tingled, my eyes watered, and the phone nearly slipped out of my hands. I curled into a ball, giggling and weeping and more alive than I'd felt in years.

Good girl. It will be my tongue and my cock making you come next time.

I smiled at the screen, dizzy and satisfied.

I like it when I can be good for you, Finn. I don't always want to make you crazy. But I'm not gonna lie. I kinda like it when I make you crazy too.

That's my bratty girl.

CHAPTER 8

GUNNER

Stockyards Station looked like hell had upchucked its best and brightest onto Exchange Avenue and told them to buy some calves while they were at it. The smell hit first: smoke, cow shit, and cheap beer, all churning under the gold sunrise that made every tin roof shine like the gates of heaven. You could hear the boots before you saw them, a thumping rhythm of impatience and bad knees as the old hands herded themselves toward the auction barn. I fit right in, boots scuffed, hat low, the only thing clean about me the white of my teeth when I grinned at someone I wanted to irritate.

Inside the café, the air was already thick with sweat and fryer oil. You had to fight to get a table, but Arsenal was already there, two plates and a pot of coffee in front of him, scanning the room like someone might try to take his bacon hostage. He wore his Iron Valor cut, but the shirt underneath was pressed and the jeans dark—always the extra effort with him. I sat across, folding my arms and letting the chair rock back on two legs.

"Didn't know you woke up before six if no one was yelling at you," I said.

Arsenal didn't look up from his coffee. "Didn't know you could find a shirt without a stain on it." He took a sip and then set the cup down with military precision. "You sleep at all?"

I shrugged, pouring cream into my mug until it went from black to the color of river mud. "Enough." I didn't mention the two hours of restless tossing, or the way my body had burned after that last text from Brie. My wolf hadn't shut up since.

A waitress with blonde hair that definitely came from a bottle dropped off a plate the size of a tractor tire: eggs, hash browns, and a chicken-fried steak the size of my head. "Anything else, sugar?" She asked, eyes flicking to Arsenal, who didn't notice. I tapped her wrist before she left.

"You got any honey for the biscuits?" I asked.

"Course." She winked and walked off, hips working overtime.

Arsenal smirked, finally meeting my eye. "You ever eat like a normal person?"

"Normal's not my brand," I said, slicing off half the steak and shoveling in a forkful. The taste lit up every cell. God, I loved simple food. "You want some, Marine?"

"I'll stick to my own protein." He forked up a big bite of omelet and chewed, slow, like he was timing it to a metronome.

"What do you think beef is?" I asked, mouth full of steak and gravy.

He raised an eyebrow. "I prefer my protein minus heart attack inducing extras."

I continued to saw off pieces of chicken-fried steak. "I'm nothin' if not full of extras."

"Uh huh."

We finished our meal in silence, the way men do when there's actual business to be handled. The auction barn outside was already starting to fill. I could see the new crop of buyers through the window, city cowboys in pressed shirts and polished boots, trying to look like they belonged. They didn't. You can't buy the kind of ugly it takes to work cattle for thirty years.

"Cattle made the trip okay," I finally said, breaking the silence. "None got antsy, none jumped. That's a first."

Arsenal set down his fork and wiped his mouth. "Means you did your job." Then, softer: "Or you're distracted enough you didn't care enough to notice."

I grunted. "I got this."

He leaned back, arms crossed, assessing. "I'm not the one you have to convince."

"You gonna bring it up or just stare holes through my skull?" I asked, but I already knew. He was going to make me say it.

He waited a second, then nodded toward the window, like he didn't want to embarrass me in public. "You hear from her?"

I let a grin slip. Couldn't help it. "She's fine."

Arsenal smiled, small and private, then shook his head. "You ever gonna admit you like her?"

I stabbed a last chunk of steak. "I admitted it to myself. That's enough."

"Not for her, probably," he said. "Some women like to hear it." He poured more coffee, watching the stream. "You know, you don't have to fight everything that feels good. Even Big Papa lets himself have a donut now and then."

I scoffed. "That's not the same. He's got Jesus. I got an art major with unresolved trauma and a renegade heart."

Arsenal's brow furrowed. "You saying you'd rather have Jesus?"

I looked at my hands. "I'm saying I don't know what to do with her."

He waited, patient as death. Then: "You don't have to know. You just have to not fuck it up."

I barked a laugh. "Well, shit. Why didn't anyone tell me sooner?"

He let that hang, taking another bite of omelet.

The door slammed behind us, and a knot of buyers came in, loud and obnoxious. The noise level spiked, and for a while, all you could do was listen to the clatter of plates and the auctioneer's early-morning warmups rolling through the open windows. It was almost peaceful if you liked chaos.

I ate until I couldn't, then sat back, letting the fullness settle in.

"You ever wonder why we haven't heard from Maltraz?" I asked, voice low.

Arsenal's face went flat. "Every day."

"It's not right," I said, pushing my plate away. "That demon bastard doesn't go silent unless he's plotting."

Arsenal nodded, gaze flicking to every face in the diner. "He's not the type to just walk away after we humiliated him. He'll wait, then he'll hit back."

"We need to talk to Bronc," I said. "Soon as we get back."

"Agreed," Arsenal said, eyes never stopping. "You think he's coming after the pack, or after Brie?"

"Both, if he can manage it. But I bet he comes for the weakest link first."

Arsenal set his cup down, then leaned in, elbows on the table. "That puts you in the crosshairs, buddy."

I wanted to argue, but he wasn't wrong.

I rolled my shoulders, trying to shake it off. "I'll be ready."

He gave me a hard look. "I believe it. Just don't let your dick override your instincts. You're better than that."

"Thanks, coach," I said. "Now eat your protein and let's go make some money."

He grinned, just a little, and we finished breakfast like we always did: fast, focused, and ready for whatever kind of trouble waited outside.

The sun was all the way up when we walked out, the heat building off the asphalt. The crowd had doubled, maybe tripled, and the smell of burnt coffee was almost drowned out by the diesel and old leather.

Arsenal clapped me on the back, hard enough to rattle my teeth. "Let's go," he said.

I looked over my shoulder once, searching for something I wasn't sure was there. A sign, maybe, or just a reason to hope.

All I saw was a sky so blue it almost hurt.

They say you never forget your first auction—the press of bodies, the perfume of hot steel and parched earth, the way men's voices cut through the din like they were sharpening knives on hope. Most of the world figured stockyards belonged in another century, but step into the Exchange and you'd see: Texas ran on the blood and sweat that soaked these old planks, and the men who called it home never grew tired, just grew meaner.

The barn was a cathedral of noise and dust. Cowboys stacked five deep around the gates, arguing the merits of Brangus versus Hereford, and every other hand held a Styrofoam cup of coffee or a can of cheap domestic that nobody was old enough to admit to drinking. The auctioneer stood on a dais that looked salvaged from a failed high school musical, microphone cord coiled around his fist like a bullwhip. His voice rolled through the rafters, rising and falling, a river of numbers and nonsense that carried every man with it.

Arsenal kept to my shoulder, quiet, scanning for threats but not expecting any. This wasn't our kind of war, just a marketplace with higher stakes. The only real violence here was the way men's egos bruised when they lost a bid.

We drove the trailer up just after seven, in line with three other rigs. Two belonged to outfits from the Hill Country, fancy names and fancier paint jobs, a third was from outside of Waco. Arsenal caught the name—R.

Ponderosa—and gave me a nod, like he'd already clocked the whole family tree.

I walked the pens with him, checking every head, fingers trailing along hides slick as blacktop. My steers looked good. Better than good. They were cut glass, all muscle and low mean eyes cool as pond water. I caught two buyers watching from the catwalk, trying to look casual. They wore city boots, probably out of Dallas, and one already had his phone out to snap a photo of my lead steer. I winked at them, just to see if they'd blush. One did.

Arsenal grunted. "Told you, Walsh. You breed 'em mean, people notice."

I shrugged, but the pride buzzed warm in my gut. "Mean's all they know."

He started to say something else, but that's when the auctioneer's call rolled out, and the barn went dead quiet. First lot up was a run of Charolais—decent, but not mine. I watched the action anyway, paying attention to which hands went up and who had the deep pockets. You learn quick in this business that most men are cheap, but when they want to win, the checkbook opens faster than a lawyer's zipper.

They got to my steers just before ten. The auctioneer read off the notes—"Champion stock, Iron Valor breeding, guaranteed weight and vaccinated up the wazoo." The pen gate swung open, and my boys swaggered out, hooves clicking like they owned the place. The crowd shifted, interested.

"Who'll start me at fifteen?" the auctioneer barked, and three paddles went up at once. He didn't even pause, just rolled right into the chant, numbers flowing like water off a tin roof.

I didn't watch the bidders; I watched the cattle. They paced the ring slow, tails flicking, ears alert, sizing up the men as much as the men sized them. My wolf bristled with satisfaction. This was our territory, even here.

"Twenty-two hundred!" someone called, and the crowd murmured. That was higher than I'd dreamed, and it wasn't even noon.

"Twenty-two, now twenty-three, do I hear three?" The auctioneer's voice could've cut through a tornado.

A hand from the Hill Country crew went up. "Twenty-three!"

Another, from the city boys. "Twenty-four!"

It ping-ponged like that, back and forth, the numbers rising faster than the dust. By the end of it, the top steer went for twenty-six fifty, and the rest followed just behind.

When the gavel came down, I felt it like a punch to the chest. Arsenal clapped me on the shoulder, harder than needed, and I let myself grin. It was a damn good haul.

We moved on to the heifers, and the action didn't slow. The calves got more attention than I expected—good genetics always paid off, but it was something else, the way buyers argued in low voices about my breeding line. I caught the words 'Iron Valor' more than once. By the end, we'd cleared nearly twenty thousand for the whole run.

It should have felt like a victory, and in a way, it did. But every time the auctioneer called my name, every time someone mentioned the Walsh bloodline, my mind skipped like a stone, bouncing from the barn to Brie's last message, the sly way she'd said "maybe" when I asked if she was wet.

I wondered what she was doing now. Painting, probably, or arguing with her mother over the merits of American breakfast food. I pictured her at the little table in Aspen's bakery, hunched over a sketchbook with paint on her fingers and hair falling in her eyes. The image made my cock twitch, which was as inappropriate as it was inevitable.

Arsenal noticed. Of course, he did. He was a predator, too.

"Gunner, you with me?" he said, voice low, nudging me back to reality.

"Always," I said, but my own voice sounded far-off.

He smirked, but didn't press. "Good. Because if those Waco boys get rowdy, I'm not bailing your ass out of jail. Not this time."

"They wouldn't dare," I said, but I kept one eye on the edge of the barn, where the Waco crew was clustered. They watched me, but it was more curiosity than threat. We'd kicked enough teeth in enough times to keep them nervous, at least for now.

We loaded out the remaining calves, Arsenal doing most of the heavy work while I handled the paperwork and smiled at buyers who wanted to shake my hand. I hated the politeness of it, the way men pretended to care about you when it was really just about the next transaction. But I played the game, because that's what you did.

By two, we were done. I signed off the last bill of sale and let Arsenal lead the way to the trucks.

Our hands joined us, respectively, and the ride was quiet. The road back to Dairyville was long and mostly empty, fields stretching out on both sides, every fence post and cow skull glowing in the late sun.

I watched the road, letting my mind drift.

The memory of Brie came back stronger now. The way she'd looked at me that morning, chin up but eyes wide, like she wanted to run and stay at the same time. The way she'd said my name, just once, soft as a confession. I could smell her on my skin, even through the sweat and dust of the auction barn.

Somewhere near Amarillo, my phone buzzed. I checked it without thinking. It was a photo from Brie: her hand, paint-smudged, holding a coffee cup with a smiley face in Sharpie on the side. Underneath, she'd written: "Try not to start a fight. I want to see you with both eyebrows intact."

I smiled, despite myself. I thought about replying but didn't want to seem too eager. But I knew I was already doomed.

The sun dipped low, turning every ditch and fence into a silhouette. We made Dairyville by dusk, the town so still you'd think nothing ever happened here.

But I knew better. Trouble never left for long.

As we pulled up to the Iron Valor clubhouse, I saw the lights were on. Bronc was waiting. I squared my shoulders, forcing my mind to focus.

Tonight, I'd eat, catch up on my sleep. I'd wait until tomorrow to see Brie. I'd force myself to send her one quick text:

Made it home safe. Gonna shower and hit the hay. We'll talk tomorrow. Night Maverick.

Saw three dots. Then nothing. I'm sure she was pissed. I really didn't want to piss her off. I was exhausted. Maybe this could be lesson one in little Brie not getting her way.

I got out of the shower to a terse message waiting. Oh yeah. She didn't like the fact that I hadn't made time for her. She didn't even consider how long I'd been on the road or how little sleep I'd gotten the night before. She didn't say something like, *glad you're home safe.* Or, *I can't wait to see you tomorrow.* Nope. Not my little brat. This is the message I got:

"Fine."

Which, when a woman says, *fine,* that generally means it's anything but.

Pearl ran the kitchen like it were the bridge of a warship, and every man who crossed her threshold was either a soldier, a stowaway, or on KP duty until further notice. The main table in the Iron Valor clubhouse was packed: Bronc at the head, his Alpha presence undeniable even in a t-shirt and tattered jeans, Arsenal at his right, Wrecker left, and Big Papa squeezed next to Arsenal with a gravity that pulled all conversation his way. Doc sat in his usual seat next to Wrecker, and I took the last seat on the other side of Papa.

The food was classic Texas: biscuits dripping butter, sausage gravy laced with red pepper, scrambled eggs fluffy as whipped clouds, and bacon thick enough that you could use them as treads on a sled. Pearl set each plate down herself, dishing them up with a smile that dared you to criticize the seasoning.

"Eat up, boys," she said. "You look like you've been living on caffeine and regret."

Papa snorted. "Ain't that the Iron Valor food pyramid?"

Arsenal, already halfway through his second helping, just nodded and kept eating.

I'd barely made it to my seat before Bronc's gaze zeroed in on me. "Report."

It wasn't a question. The room went quiet, except for the scrape of forks on plates.

I gave him the numbers first, because that's what he wanted. "Cleared just under twenty thousand net, and there's already talk about booking next year's calves in advance. Buyers came from as far as Galveston and Oklahoma City. I heard two say our stock is better than half the legacy lines in the state."

Arsenal backed me up. "He's not exaggerating. Men were taking pictures of our steers for their social media. It's getting to be a brand."

Bronc's mouth twitched up at the corners, a rare public display of pride. "Good work. Both of you."

Pearl topped off Bronc's mug, then circled around to Papa. "Anything to add, sweetheart?"

Papa shook his head. "Not unless you want to hear about the time Gunner tried to break a longhorn with a piece of licorice and a strip of duct tape."

Arsenal leaned in, voice deadpan. "He got thrown so far, his boots landed before he did."

I grinned, let the room enjoy the joke. "Yeah, and I still made it to breakfast. Unlike some people."

Pearl bopped me with a towel. "That's enough, boys. Let's talk business."

Bronc shifted, and the room tensed like a coiled spring. "We've had eyes on Maltraz since he went underground, but the trail's colder than a witch's tit in January. No hits, no chatter, not even a whisper from the local packs."

Arsenal put down his fork, posture going rigid. "He's not the type to just run. He tried to drain our accounts, poisoned half our pack, and his demons nearly killed Papa." He gave a tight nod to Big Papa, who just shrugged like getting possessed and bled out by demons was all in a day's work.

"We know he's still trafficking women," Wrecker said, voice low. "Word from the coast is, he's paying good money for supernatural girls. Human, too. The jobs go through burner phones and third parties, but it's all Maltraz." His words made my head hurt.

Papa wiped his mouth, slow and deliberate. "I'd pay a month's wages to rip his spine out myself."

Bronc's eyes narrowed, blue as an arctic lake. "The Council's supposedly aware. The very demon king who's running the operation sits on the goddamn Council, and they're *aware*."

Arsenal's laugh was all frost. "They're aware. Ya *think*? And they're gonna do fuck all about it. Until they take someone who belongs to the Council, they are gonna ignore the issue."

Bronc looked around the table, weighing the mood. "I need to know. Are we gonna take this fight to him? Or do we sit and wait for him to bring it back to our doorstep, because he damn sure will bring it back? And Gunner, when he does, he's gonna have both barrels aimed right at your girl."

All eyes at the table were suddenly focused on me. Not everyone was aware that Brie was my mate. Hell, *she* wasn't even aware.

"Guess *that* fucking cat just got yanked right out of the bag. I haven't even had this talk with Brie yet, but she's my mate."

After a series of whoops and 'bout times, it got quiet again.

"And I know that Maltraz likely will target her since she got away in Paris. I don't know if I like her being a sitting duck." I caught all the eyes in the room when I told them that.

Papa raised his gigantic hand. "Maybe we could bait him. Put the word out that Iron Valor's got a line on a rare blood witch. Maltraz can't resist a flex."

I met Bronc's gaze. "Or we do it the old way. Call in a favor from King Rafe. Tell him the demon king's running girls through his territory. Rafe'll be pissed enough to use his own dogs."

Bronc rubbed his jaw, frown deepening. "Both of those have merit. But we have to be smart. Maltraz has eyes everywhere. We show our hand too early, we lose."

Papa grinned, wide and sharp. "Then we don't show our hand. We show our teeth."

The table went silent, every man chewing on the words.

Pearl started to clear plates but paused at my shoulder. "You all need to remember who you are. Iron Valor built a legacy by outsmarting the bastards, not just by out-muscling them." She patted my back, gentle. "Use your head, Gunner. You've got a good one."

I swallowed, the compliment landing harder than I expected. "Yes, ma'am."

Bronc finally spoke. "Wrecker, start tracing the buyers on those girls. Quietly. Papa, see if the witches in Amarillo have heard anything—no one talks to strangers, but they'll talk to you and Aspen." He turned to me. "Gunner, you're on recon. If Maltraz is baiting the pack, I want you to be the one he sniffs out first."

I straightened, pulse pounding. "Copy."

Pearl started to laugh, but it was soft and secret. "My boys, all grown up and ready to start another war."

Papa reached for another lemon bar. "We're getting damn good at it."

We finished breakfast without another word about Maltraz. The next hour was for strategizing, mapping out contacts, figuring who would run interference and who would play decoy. Bronc stayed at the head, but his eyes were on me more than usual, like he was waiting for me to crack.

I didn't, not this time.

When the room emptied, Pearl caught me alone. She fixed my collar, like I was a child again, then leaned in close. "Be careful with that girl, Finn. She's got more power than you think."

I nodded. "I know."

She kissed my cheek, then went back to her kitchen, leaving me in the doorway with the smell of roses and coffee and the faintest touch of her perfume.

Outside, the sun was already burning off the morning haze. I saw Arsenal and Papa heading out. Bronc stood on the porch, arms folded, watching the road.

For the first time in weeks, I felt settled. Not calm—never that—but settled.

I knew I needed to go pick Brie up. We needed to talk, but not at her house. She was coming over to my place this time.

CHAPTER 9

BRIE

If I'd known that being a grown-up meant waking up disappointed before you'd even opened your eyes, I might have stayed fifteen forever. The morning after Gunner got home from his trip to Fort Worth tasted like old lipstick and defeat, even though I'd done everything right. I'd soaked in the best bathwater, shaved what wasn't already lasered, and softened my skin with the best lotions thinking that after the way he sexted me, he'd want to get his hands on me when he got home. And after all that? Nothing. He'd texted "night, Maverick" and then vanished like a magician with a double major in emotional ghosting.

For a full twenty minutes, I debated throwing my phone at the wall or, better, marching across the dirt road and demanding satisfaction, old-school duel style. But how did I handle it? Text book response. I replied with:

"Fine."

I lay there, staring at the faint water ring on the ceiling (French apartment, move over—this was the new aesthetic), listening to my mother clatter around in the kitchen like she was auditioning for a Foley gig. I refused to let anyone see I cared, so I spent an extra five minutes perfecting my eyeliner, then another ten getting my hair into a "messy bun" that looked less like I'd slept in it and more like I'd fought a wild animal for the right to exist.

That's when I called Maddie. If anyone could salvage a day from the quicksand of mediocrity, it was her.

She answered on the first ring, voice husky with sleep or a hangover. "Tell me you're bringing coffee."

"If you bring the car, I'll bring the promise of coffee and maybe a pastry from Aspen's after lunch."

Her exhale sounded like a dragon dying. "Deal. Where are we going?"

"Pearl's, then the shops. I need..." I paused, staring at my open closet, which contained exactly three wearable outfits and one dress I was pretty sure belonged to my sister. "Everything. I need everything."

"Say no more, queen," she said. "Be there in ten."

By the time I heard the familiar crunch of tires of Maddie's pickup, I'd lined my lips twice and pulled on my cowboy boots. My mother was perched at the dining table, wearing a powder-blue tracksuit and a cloud of Chanel, the local paper folded to the crossword.

She looked up, one eyebrow already mid-arch. "Plans for the day, darling?"

"Lunch. Shopping. Therapy by way of retail."

She hummed, unimpressed. "Be careful out there, sweetheart. And pick out something pretty."

"Of course, Mom. I'll find some pretty things to wear." I blew a kiss and sprinted for the door, grabbing my faded blue tote (it said Musée d'Orsay on it, just so everyone would know I was cultured).

Maddie's truck idled, AC cranked up. She was as pretty as ever with her freshly dyed pink hair in one long braid over her shoulder. She'd gone light on the makeup with only dark eyeliner and hot pink lip gloss on her pouty lips. She had on jeans and boots and a Morgan Wallen t-shirt. The girl was effortlessly beautiful. I loved her.

She sized me up. "You look good. You expecting to see someone?"

"Is it that obvious?" I groaned.

"Honestly, yeah. You look like a woman with a secret."

I slumped into the seat, letting the icy air hit my face. "If by secret you mean an untreated attachment disorder, then yes. I've got it in spades."

She smirked, pulling out onto the street. "Who are we ignoring today? Your mom or Gunner?"

I closed my eyes, dramatic. "Both. And also myself."

She howled, thumping the wheel. "I have missed this."

Pearl's was already packed when we rolled up, but since her mother owned the place, the hostess waved us in like we were celebrities. There was a table free by the window, sun glinting off the little vases of wildflowers that Pearl swapped out every morning. I wanted to live in that kind of confidence—every surface curated, every detail soft and inviting.

The menu was classic: chicken-fried everything, two whole pages devoted to pie, and a coffee so strong it could be used to strip paint. We ordered two lunch specials, which turned out to be BLTs with extra B.

"So," Maddie said, propping her chin on her hand. "What's the plan after we buy you all the clothes?"

"Not sure yet. Maybe I'll join a cult."

She grinned. "Girl, we're Iron Valor. That's about as much of a cult as you can get. And my big brother is the guru."

I let myself smile. "True. Also, I'm suddenly flush, so I want to spend money irresponsibly."

Maddie's eyes lit up. "You finally broke the trust?"

"I did," I said. "Harper handled all the legal crap, and Mom can't say no anymore. I am an heiress with absolutely no plan and even less self-restraint."

"Fuck yes, Brie. Blow it all on shoes. Or, better yet, invest in crypto. Make it a zero-sum game."

I shuddered. "Nope. I want things I can touch. Like a pair of jeans that doesn't scream 'lost in time.' Or maybe a jacket."

Maddie sipped her coffee. "Or you could buy a horse. Gunner could keep him for you."

My stomach did a weird little lurch. "He could be my stable boy?"

She cackled. "You wish."

The food arrived, and we ate like wolves, hands greasy and hearts lighter. The talk moved on to the dance studio, the local politics, a rumor about the council president's son being caught with a prostitute (news: he was the prostitute). We made a plan to hit at least three shops before heading to the feed store, where Maddie said she needed to buy Parker's little dog Rocket a new toy.

It was on the way back to the house that I saw him.

Not Parker's dog, but Gunner. He was across the road, in the big corral behind his house. At first, I didn't realize it was him; all I saw was the horse, jet black and furious, slamming its head up and down with a wild, terrified beauty that made me want to both run away and paint it forever. There were a couple of ranch hands on the rails, but Gunner was alone in the ring, boots braced, hands steady on the rope. He looked exactly like every cowboy fantasy you could buy at a gas station in Texas, except this was real, and it was dangerous.

Maddie noticed me staring. "That's Gunner's job, you know. He doesn't just look hot in plaid for Instagram. He tames them. Breaks them in."

I blinked, still watching as the horse spun, its hind legs kicking at air. Gunner stood firm, all muscle and patience, not moving until the animal tired itself out.

"What do you mean, his job?" I asked genuinely puzzled. "I thought he was a cattleman."

She looked at me like I'd grown a second head. "Well, he's that too. He's a rancher. He owns the ranch, so he does it all. That's how he makes his living. It's just like when the men you're used to put on a suit and go to the office. He puts on his jeans, boots, and hat, and breaks horses some days."

I flushed, embarrassed. "Sorry, it's just... I thought he worked for the ranch. Like, as a manager or something. I didn't realize..."

"He owns it, but he also works it." Maddie sounded proud. "The ranch has been in his family for generations. Gunner owns this part of it. He provides for the pack, though. Basically keeps the entire pack's cattle in line also, plus any wild stock that gets brought in. This is what he's good at."

I tried to process the idea of someone liking their job or even being good at it. The only "work" I'd ever done was the odd gallery internship, where my most crucial skill was not spilling kombucha on the prints. The rest were high school performances for a disinterested audience of teachers.

We'd gotten out and made our way over to the fence. I leaned on the railing closer than I should have, mesmerized. Gunner was talking to the horse now, voice low and calm. The animal's wildness dialed down, a slow wave of respect radiating out from the man to the beast. There was something almost holy about it—the way he could take violence and turn it into something cooperative.

Maddie nudged me. "You okay? You're staring."

I shrugged, voice gone small. "I've never seen anything like it."

She laughed. "You're from Texas, babe. You just never saw this side of it."

Gunner didn't even look up. For a second, I was pissed. Was it possible to be this obsessed with someone who couldn't be bothered to make eye contact? Then I realized he was probably just trying not to get trampled. Still, a girl could hope for a glance.

The horse finally stopped fighting. Gunner let it circle, then leaned over, stroking its neck with slow, sure hands. The animal shivered, sweat running in rivers down its sides, but it let him. When he slid out of the saddle, it lowered its head, letting him pat the soft spot between its ears. The ranch hands started clapping, and even Maddie joined in.

"He's good," she said, almost reverent.

"He is," I echoed, not sure if I meant Gunner or the horse.

He lingered in the corral, wiping his hands on his jeans, talking to the others. I watched the muscles in his arms tense and relax, the way he threw his head back when he laughed, the way every motion seemed completely unselfconscious. There was a power in it I'd never known before, a sense of purpose that made my own life feel cartoonish by comparison.

The wild horse wandered over to where I stood, nuzzling the fence with its wet nose. I reached out, tentative, and it let me touch the velvet skin. Its breath was hot and sharp, full of grass and wind.

I stroked the horse's nose, glancing back at Gunner, who was still all business with his men.

Maddie said, "You want to go over there, don't you?"

Yes. "No."

She arched her brow. "Liar. Go say hi."

I hesitated. Then, "What if he doesn't want to see me?"

She leaned in, voice fierce. "You're Brie fucking Lawson. He should be so lucky."

I snorted, but the words stuck in my head. I gave the horse one last scratch, then let myself stare at Gunner just one beat longer. He still didn't look over.

That was fine. I could wait.

The horse came back around slow, hooves slicing twin furrows through the red dirt, then stopped just out of reach, nostrils flared. There was something familiar in the way it assessed me, a challenge, maybe, or a test. I stuck out my hand, palm open, and waited.

Again, the animal didn't shy away. It nosed my fingers, hot breath dampening my skin. I let out a shaky laugh because I couldn't believe this was actually happening.

Maddie took a photo. "You look like Snow White, but more..." she squinted at the camera, "...Texas."

I petted the horse's nose, feeling the buzz of energy under its velvet skin. It was still wild, but not angry; more like it wanted to be understood.

"I used to ride, you know," I said, voice just loud enough for Maddie to hear. "High school. English saddle mostly, but we did some jumping. I was pretty good."

She looked at me, skeptical. "Not the same as that," she said, gesturing at the horse. "That thing would eat you for breakfast."

I scoffed. "It's just a horse."

Maddie leaned closer. "You are not going in there."

I glanced at Gunner, who was still engrossed in conversation. "He said it's tamed."

"Yeah, by him. And even then, barely."

I looked at my boots—tan, ostrich leather, stupidly expensive and barely broken in. My jeans hugged my thighs just right, and the shirt I wore was plain but flattering. For the first time since Paris, I felt almost like I belonged somewhere. It was intoxicating, and maybe a little reckless.

"Watch this," I said, swinging a leg over the bottom rail.

"Brie, no!" Maddie hissed, but I was already inside the pen.

The ground was soft and uneven, and I nearly twisted my ankle before I even reached the horse. I walked slow, hands out, making those soft "shhh" sounds I'd heard Finn making. The animal eyed me, but didn't spook.

I touched its neck, ran my hand up to the mane. It shivered but didn't move away. My heart was pounding so hard I could barely think, but all I wanted in that moment was to do something—anything—that would make Gunner notice.

Maddie's voice came through the rails, panicked but low: "If you die, I'm not giving your eulogy. You know that, right?"

I grinned, almost giddy. "I'll be fine."

The horse turned its head, massive black eyes staring me down. I patted its withers, then, before I could chicken out, reached for the saddle horn and pulled myself up.

It happened fast. One second I was airborne, jeans creaking, boots braced in the stirrups. The next, the horse exploded, bucking with a violence that made the entire world go sideways.

I screamed, a sound that was part terror, part exhilaration. The animal whipped its head, slamming me into the saddle so hard my teeth clacked. My hands slipped on the reins, and I grabbed for the mane, holding on for dear life as the beast twisted and launched itself across the pen.

I heard Maddie shouting, "Brie, get off! Get off!" But it was too late. The horse was in charge now, and I was just along for the ride.

We made it halfway around the ring before my grip gave out. The horse jerked left; I went right, and the rest was physics.

I hit the dirt ass-first; the impact knocking the wind clean out of me. My right shoulder caught next, a dull, hot pain shooting up my hip and down my arm. I rolled onto my back, gasping, staring up at the bright Texas sky. Tears were already pouring down my face.

The horse skittered to a stop, shook itself, and trotted away like it hadn't just tried to murder me. The ranch hands were already running over, but it was Gunner who reached me first.

He knelt down, grabbed my hand, and hauled me to sitting. "You okay, Maverick?" His face was unreadable, equal parts worry and fury.

I wheezed, still trying to breathe through my tears. "Did I look cool?"

He grumbled a laugh, then shook his head. "You're a goddamn lunatic."

Maddie arrived, pale and wild-eyed. "You almost died!" she shrieked.

I shrugged, then immediately regretted it but couldn't speak.

Gunner put one hand under my upper back and the other under my knees as he picked me up.

I leaned into his chest with a sob. "Hurts."

He looked over at Maddie and uttered three words that brooked no argument.

"Madison, go home."

He didn't say another word to me as he carried me across the yard, pulling me tight to his chest. His front door came into view in just minutes. The heat between us had an edge, the kind that could burn or cauterize depending on the day, and I had no idea which way today was going to break.

Inside, the place smelled like leather, old cologne, and something darker—maybe the weight of a life that didn't leave much space for knick-knacks or sentimental crap. I noticed a bookshelf that sat along one wall in the great room that held tons of books. Gunner hauled me down the hallway, past the living room filled with leather-clad furniture and straight into a bedroom with a bed the size of a small country. I tried to memorize everything—the rough wood dresser, the muddy boots lined up by the wall, the single photograph of a smiling boy and a German Shepherd on the nightstand. I was so busy collecting details that I almost forgot the pain radiating up my side.

He sat me on the edge of the bed and crouched down, putting his face level with mine. "Where does it hurt, Maverick?"

I considered lying, but the concern in his eyes was like a cattle prod to my ego. "My butt. And my shoulder, I guess. Maybe my pride."

He snorted. "Pride'll heal. Lemme see the rest."

He gripped my knee, warm and certain, then tugged on my boots. It was the least sexy undressing of my life—awkward, dusty, and over in seconds—but my skin burned with embarrassment, anyway. He yanked them off, tossing them aside, and then reached for the button on my jeans.

I slapped at his hands, half-hearted. "What do you think you're doing?"

He met my eyes, expression dead serious. He pushed my shoulders back, so I was lying across the bed. "You don't get to ask questions right now. I'm in charge." His fingers found the zipper and pulled it down, then gripped the ankles of my jeans and gave a sharp tug. The jeans peeled away, dragging a layer of dirt and dignity with them. Underneath, my ass was already bruising on the right side—a deep, red flush radiating out like a target. I winced just looking at it.

He rolled me slightly to my side and ran a hand over the bruise, testing for tenderness. "You landed hard."

I tried to sound tough. "I've had worse."

He pulled on my arms, sitting me up, then started on my top, deftly undoing the buttons one by one. The fabric hung open, stained with sweat and a streak of red clay. I was still in my bralette—purple lace, because I'd hoped for a different kind of undressing today—and the way his eyes lingered made my heart start sprinting again.

He peeled the shirt away, then gently pressed my shoulder. I hissed, more from surprise than pain.

"Not broken," he said, relief softening his jaw. "But will likely leave a bruise."

He lay me back, hands moving slow and careful. "Roll over, Maverick."

I obeyed, face burning. The bedspread was soft against my cheek, and I tried to focus on the thread count instead of the fact that my ass was basically on parade.

He ran his fingers over the bruise, pressing at the edges, and I nearly jumped off the mattress. "Jesus, Finn—"

"Hold still," he ordered. His voice was calm, but there was a roughness underneath it that made me shiver. He traced the bruise from the top of my hip down to where the skin was less angry, then worked his way up my thigh. Each touch was electric—half pain, half something else.

He leaned in close, his breath warm against my neck. "You could've broken your damn tailbone, Brie. What were you thinking?"

I muttered into the pillow. "Wanted to get your attention I guess.."

He went quiet, then said, "Fucking hell of a way to do it little girl."

I almost laughed. "You say that, but you didn't see the way the ranch hands were looking at me. Like I was some dumb city girl."

He gripped my thigh, squeezing just hard enough to sting. "You don't care about them. You care about what *I* think."

It wasn't a question, but I answered anyway. "Yeah. I do."

He let go, but not before running his hand over the bruise one last time. "Well, what I think is that you're fucking crazy. And stubborn. And you never do what I tell you."

I craned my neck to glare at him. "Then stop telling me what to do."

He grinned, wolfish and wide. "Not happening."

He left for a second, came back with an ice pack wrapped in a towel, and pressed it to my ass with zero warning. I yelped, more at the shock than the cold.

"See? You need me to keep you in line," he said, smirking.

I tried to flip onto my back, but he held me there, one hand on my hip. The weight of him was grounding—equal parts restraint and comfort. He held the ice in place with one hand, using the other to gently stroke my hair. I hated how much I loved it.

We sat there in silence, the only sound the whirr of the ceiling fan and the thunder in my chest. After a while, he set the ice pack aside and lay down next to me, propping himself up on one elbow.

"What am I gonna do with you?" he asked, voice low.

I couldn't think of a single smart thing to say. For once, my mouth failed me.

He leaned in, lips brushing my ear. "Answer me, Maverick."

I swallowed, heart in my throat. "Anything you want," I whispered.

"Well, sweetheart. You're not gonna like my first idea."

CHAPTER 10

GUNNER

"Well, sweetheart. You're not gonna like my first idea."

Her eyes met mine, blue-green flashing a challenge through the lingering water of her tears. She didn't move, didn't flinch, even with my hand still planted on the round of her bruised hip. I gave it a squeeze, enough to make her jump, and then used the leverage to roll her all the way onto her belly. Her arms scrambled under her, fingers knotting into the bedspread. She looked so small against the wide expanse of my mattress, her hair a mess around her face, the backs of her thighs smeared with dirt and indignity.

I sat beside her, my own anger simmering in my chest. If she'd landed wrong, she could have broken her neck. If that horse had kicked... My wolf howled inside my chest. But none of it mattered now. I was the one with her in my bed, so I was the one responsible for fixing her. For reminding her she didn't have to wreck herself to be seen.

"Lie still, Maverick." My voice was gentler this time, but she obeyed, all defiance melted into compliance. She tucked her hands under her chin, elbows sharp on the sheets. The bruise on her hip had already deepened to an angry plum; she'd landed so hard.

I let my hand follow the line of the bruise, slow, careful. She shivered. I traced down to her thigh, over the curve of muscle, then up, dragging my rough palm across her ribs and back. I wanted to be gentle, but she needed to know what happened when she lost her mind in my orbit.

She twisted to glare at me. "If you're going to yell, just do it. I'm a big girl."

I snorted. "No, you're not. Not yet." I paused, thumb pressing a circle into her side, feeling the heat rise under her skin. "But you want to be; and you *should* be. And that's what gets you in trouble, Maverick."

I got up just long enough to grab the leather strap I kept on a hook behind the door. Her eyes tracked me, widening as she recognized it—a thick, broad old saddle strap, smooth and heavy in the hand.

"No." Her voice was small. "You don't mean to use that."

I laid the strap on the nightstand, just within her field of vision. Then I went back to the bed, sat so my hip touched hers, and put my hand on her back. "I haven't decided yet. But you're going to take your punishment, Brie. You know you deserve it. You need it. Every goddamn thing you did today screamed for it. I'm going to show you that someone cares enough about you to punish you when you do something that puts your life in danger."

She didn't answer. But the way her breath went ragged told me I'd called the shots.

I leaned in, lips at her ear. "Do you trust me?"

She closed her eyes, lashes dark against her cheek. "Mmm hmm," she whispered.

"Say it."

"I trust you, Finn."

"Good." I set her upright and placed her on my lap. "There are rules Maverick."

She looked confused, then understanding flickered across her face. "You mean... like, sex rules?" Her cheeks went bright pink.

"Yeah. Consent rules. You ever done anything like this before?"

She shook her head, a little mortified but more curious than scared.

I took her hands, sandwiched them between mine. "I'm not the Alpha of this pack. But in this house, I am the man in charge. That makes me the Alpha of this house. And when you give me control, that means I take on the responsibility to keep you safe. Understand?"

She nodded, biting her lip.

"Here's what's gonna happen." My voice was steady even though my wolf was pacing like a madman inside. "Anytime we do anything that involves me taking control of your body, you're gonna call me 'Sir.' That's a reminder to both of us who's calling the shots, and who's letting go." I let that sit, watching her reaction.

She flushed. "Sir," she whispered, trying it on for size.

"Good girl," I said, and felt her shiver. "If anything I'm doing to you is too much, or you want to stop, you say 'red.' Be certain you want whatever I'm doing to you to stop. Once it stops, we will not go back to it. If you're feeling uncomfortable or are reaching the point that you need to slow down the activity, you say 'yellow.' If you're good, if you want more, your word is 'green.' Got it?"

She swallowed. "Yes, Sir."

The words made my cock throb, but I kept my face blank.

"And I'm gonna check in with you often. If you ever feel lost, I need you to tell me. Don't just tough it out. That's not what this is about, Maverick."

She nodded again, eager, her eyes big and shining.

"You ready to keep going?"

She hesitated, then: "Yes, Sir."

I reached for her face, brushed her hair back. "You're a natural at this," I murmured, before I even meant to say it. "You're doing so fucking good, Brie. I want you to feel proud of that."

Her mouth parted, and I could tell she wanted to say something—maybe a joke, maybe a protest. I kissed her instead, deep, so she'd know she was safe.

When I broke away, I shifted her, so she lay across my lap. She went willingly, arms dangling, hands reaching my ankles, legs draped down to the floor. I slid my hand inside the waistband of her lace panties and slid them down her legs.

"I told you that your ass would be bare for this. Now, here's what's going to happen next." I made every syllable count. "You're gonna get ten swats. They're gonna hurt; it's punishment. Because you asked for it when you ran into that pen, and because I know you want it, too. You want to be handled. Don't you, Maverick?"

She was so still I wondered if she'd fallen out of her own body. But her hips shifted, and I saw the need run through her. "Yes, Sir. I want it."

"Good girl. You're gonna count them out, one by one. And you'll say 'Sir' after each number."

She closed her eyes, braced herself. "Yes, Sir."

I palmed her ass, feeling the heat already there, the bruised muscle shining on her hip. I wanted to go gentle, but I knew she needed the opposite.

"Ready?"

She nodded, then remembered: "Yes, Sir."

I raised my hand, paused for just a second, and then brought it down with a sharp, clean slap. Her body jerked, a whimper caught in her throat.

"One, Sir," she gasped, voice clear.

I let my hand rest, just for a second, then did it again. A perfect echo, the sound ricocheting off the walls.

"Two, Sir," she managed.

By the third, I could feel her body melt into me, surrendering all that stubborn energy and letting me have it. It was breathtaking, watching her let go.

"Three, Sir."

I rubbed her between each smack, gentle with the aftermath but never letting her drift. I kept the rhythm, building her until she was lost in it.

"Four, Sir."

With every number, she sounded more sure, more desperate for the next. I could smell her, sweet and sharp, and knew she was falling into the pain.

"Five, Sir."

I checked in: "You okay, baby?"

She twisted, hair wild, tears in her eyes, and gave me the faintest smile. "Green, Sir." Her head flopped back down over my legs.

That was all I needed.

I continued, savoring the way she shuddered after each, the way her hands clenched my calf.

"Six, Sir." She bit out the words, tears starting to fall.

"Seven, Sir." The breath was gone from her voice, but she got it out.

"Eight, Sir."

I ran my hand between her legs again, and this time she moaned, loud and needy.

"Nine, Sir."

I drew out the last one, palm poised, feeling her body coil in anticipation.

I brought it down with a flourish, the sound and heat rolling through her at once.

"Ten, Sir," she almost sobbed, going completely limp over my knees.

I gathered her up, holding her tight, her face pressed to my chest. I stroked her hair, her spine, until she calmed.

"You did so good," I murmured, voice thick. "You're such a brave girl."

Her voice was small and shaky. "Thank you, sir."

I pulled her up, kissed her deep, slow, then set her gently on her knees, facing me.

The thing about horses—about breaking them in, anyway—is that the real work starts after they stop fighting. That's when you find out what they're made of. If you're lucky, the wildness isn't gone; it just lets you touch it, shape it, make something new out of the chaos. That's what it felt like with Brie. She wasn't a girl who folded easily, not for anyone. But right now, on her knees in front of me, she was wide open and waiting for what came next.

I stood over her, jeans open, my cock straining against the fabric. Her eyes stayed glued to it, hungry and a little scared, but not enough to back down. I let her stare for a moment, then pushed her back onto the bed, belly down. Her knees folded under her, and her ass arched up, still hot and marked from before. I took my time smoothing my hand over her, letting the heat bloom under my palm.

"We're not quite done here, Maverick. What you did was so fucking reckless and dangerous you need a punishment fitting the transgression. I don't want you ever to think of doing something like that again. It could cost your life next time, and that is something I cannot let happen. So we're going to go ten more, sweetheart. You remember your job?" I asked, voice thick.

She nodded and looked like she wanted to protest. But the way she squirmed told me she wanted my hands on her body more desperately than she wanted to argue with me. She braced herself on her elbows and looked at me over her shoulder. "Count to ten, Sir."

"Good girl. Color?"

She took a deep breath. "Green, Sir."

Before she had time to think about the situation, I brought my hand down, not as a warning but as a promise. The slap echoed, the sound sharper than the sting. She gasped, whole body tightening under me.

"One, Sir." The words tumbled out of her.

I ran my fingers between her thighs, then pressed two against her slick center. She was dripping, soaked and ready for me. I dipped a finger inside, curled it, gave it a twist that made her knees pull to her center.

She whimpered, but when I pulled out, she arched for more.

I landed the next swat a little higher, let my fingers slide back into her, this time holding them there a second longer. She squirmed, caught between the pain and the pleasure.

"Two, Sir." Her voice was less certain, but her body was more honest than her mouth ever was.

Another, then another. I continued to finger-fuck her, stretching her, filling her up. She was quickly clutching the blanket, face pressed into the mattress.

"Green," she moaned, when I paused to check in.

I let myself smile. "You're a greedy little thing, aren't you?"

She managed a shaky laugh. "Yes, Sir."

I kept going, changing the rhythm, never letting her guess which would hurt more—the slap or the way my fingers fucked her after. By eight, I wet my thumb, circled it around her asshole, watching the way she tensed.

"You ever had a man play with your ass, Brie?"

She hesitated, then: "No, Sir."

"Do you want me to?"

A shaky breath. "I'm not sure, Sir."

I pressed my thumb against her, not forcing, just coaxing. She flinched, but then relaxed, letting me in. It was almost too much for her, but she took it, every inch.

"Your ass will always be part of your punishment," I said, working my thumb deeper. "But it can be for pleasure, too, if you let it. You need to relax sweetheart, or it will hurt more going in the first few times." She relaxed as my thumb passed the first ring of muscle.

Her moan was low, more animal than girl.

I gave her one last hard swat.

"Ten, Sir," she cried, her whole body bucking as the last swat landed. My fingers worked her cunt, and my thumb stayed buried in her ass, and when I brushed her clit everything ignited. She shook and cried out as she fell apart with a massive shudder against my fingers and thumb. The combination of pain and pleasure overwhelmed her senses, and the relief of her release showed on her tear-stained face. I continued to stroke her as the aftershocks rocked her little body. When I pulled my hands away, she collapsed in a heap.

I wiped my hands on a towel I'd laid on the bed and pulled her up, turned her in my arms, and gathered her to my chest. I kissed the top of her head, her cheeks, even the tears that streaked down her face. I held her until she was quiet again, just breathing hard, her heart hammering like a fist.

"I'm so proud of you, Brie," I whispered. "You took every bit of that. You're so much stronger than you know."

She buried her face in my neck, hands clinging to my shirt. "Thank you, Sir."

"I think you know how badly you needed that." I cradled her, letting her come down easy. "And you also need to know that every punishment doesn't end with you being allowed to come. Since it was your first time and things have been so stressful for you; I allowed it this time."

She looked up at me, glassy-eyed. I knew she wanted to tell me that wasn't fair, but she didn't, and that was progress.

I was a man at the end of my patience. My dick was still rock hard for her body and tonight I would take my fill

When she had recovered, I laid her back on the bed. She remained only in a pretty purple lace bra, and she allowed me to peel that away, slow and reverent. I wanted to see all of her, every inch. Her body was lithe, soft in all the places I loved, but toned from a lifetime of running toward or away from trouble.

I stripped off my shirt and then pulled off my jeans, and her eyes widened when my cock sprang free, hard and aching for her. I fisted it, moving my hand up and down its length.

"You look worried, Maverick." I teased.

Her cheeks flamed, but she didn't look away. "I don't know, Sir. It seems... big. I don't see how that's ever going to fit."

I bent to kiss her, nipping her bottom lip. "Sweet girl, trust me. Your pussy was made for me. It will fit perfectly. I promise." I pressed her back into the pillow, then I knelt between her thighs and ran my hand down her belly. When I reached her pussy, I spread her open with my fingers. The sight of her—wet, pink, quivering—damn near made me come just looking.

I sobered for a moment, the realization that she was my mate hitting home.

"You need to know that I'm not going to fuck you and run, Brie. If that's what you want, this stops right now."

She propped herself up on her elbows so she could look at my face that was all but diving into her sweet cunt.

"Finn Walsh, you're it for me. No man has ever made me feel the things that you do. I know I'm not what I need to be for you, but you're the first person who has ever made me want to be more than I am right now."

"Fuck, little girl. That's beautiful. I want to make things so good for you that it won't even seem like an effort for either of us. And I'm going to start right now by taking my fill of every drop of the slick you've made for me. My tongue is going to lick and taste every part of your cunt, inside and around."

Her moans as I dove in were the greatest reward I could have received. I spread her labia with my fingers, revealing her pink pussy walls and giving my tongue the invitation to dive right in. I lapped at her juices as she threw her head back in ecstasy. Then, I plunged two fingers in, twisting them and curving them as I moved my tongue up to her swollen clit. Her hips rose to meet my mouth, rocking up and down as she fucked my face.

I pulled back a bit. "That's it, Maverick. Fuck my hand and mouth. Keep pumping your hips into my face and tongue. You look so goddamn sexy chasing your release."

I kept licking and sucking, taking my fill of her. I pressed my tongue, so it was flat against her clit then brought it to a harder point, keeping her on edge until she was writhing and bucking against my face.

"Oh, shit, cowboy! I can't...it's just...ahh!"

She screamed her release and suddenly my mouth filled with her essence, her hips quivering with her climax. She panted and tried to catch her breath.

She looked shocked. "Holy shit! What was that?"

"That was all you little girl. Never saw anything more amazing than you coming all over my mouth and tongue."

Her face told me she'd never experienced that type of orgasm before. Her head hit the pillow like she thought we were done for the night.

"Oh, Maverick, we're not close to being finished."

She looked at me in surprise.

"Finn, I don't think I can!"

"Little girl, you have more orgasms in there for your *Sir*." I gave her the gentle reminder with a soft swat to her thigh.

"Sorry, sir." She gasped.

I took my cock back in my hand and got on my knees before her. I bent her legs and opened her wide for me. I ran my finger through her wetness and then gave her clit a couple of love taps, and she tried to close her legs.

I hesitated for a moment.

"Color, Brie."

Her turquoise eyes met mine. She realized what she'd done. "Green, Sir."

A grin snaked its way across my face as I rubbed the head of my cock against her clit and watched the way her body arched to chase it. I laughed.

"That's what I thought. Naughty girl."

I rubbed my dick back and forth across her pussy, gathering the wetness there. Then, I leaned over her, caging her in with my arms. I reached down and lined up with her entrance and eased the tip inside, holding her gaze the whole time.

She gasped, nails digging into my biceps, as I slid into her, letting her stretch around me. Inch by inch, I filled her, giving her time to adjust, to want more.

"You feel so goddamn good," I groaned, fighting to keep control. "So fucking tight."

She whimpered, legs wrapping around my waist, pulling me deeper still. I bottomed out, hips flush against her ass, and held there, letting her feel how perfect the fit really was.

I started to move as I fucked her slow, deep, every thrust deliberate. I wanted to brand her from the inside out, make her remember this for the rest of her life. With every stroke, she got louder; the moans turning to pleas, then to screams.

The feel of her wrapped around my cock was like nothing I'd ever felt before. I'd had my dick in my fair share of pussies, but this—this was different. It felt right. Every thrust was heaven. Her scent filled my nose—lemon and flowers, sunshine and happiness. Goddess; this was what it felt like to make love to my mate. I wanted to bite; to knot, to claim, but I refrained. I needed more time. Right now, I'd just feel. I pounded into her over and over; and she raised her hips to meet mine thrust for thrust.

When I sensed her start to break, I reached between us, found her clit, and rubbed it in circles, fast and light. She'd been so close to the edge she almost immediately shattered, body clamping down so hard on my cock I saw stars. She sobbed my name, lost in the pleasure, and I was right behind her. I foolishly hadn't used a condom, so I pulled out right before and shot ropes of cum from her stomach to her throat. I came so hard it was almost painful. I felt like my entire life had culminated in this moment. Like I'd been chasing something that I'd finally had in my grasp.

I collapsed beside her, grabbing the towel from the nightstand. I carefully cleaned my cum from her belly and chest while she caught her breath.

I pulled her close to me and leaned against the headboard and opened the bottle of water I'd set next to the towel. She wanted to protest, but I insisted she drink it all; that her hydration was important after such intense physical activity. After a while, I rolled us onto our sides, keeping her tucked against my chest. I brushed the hair from her face and kissed her eyelids.

"You okay?" I asked, needing to be sure she'd not gone beyond any boundaries she'd wanted.

She opened her eyes, dazed but clear. "Yeah. I'm... so good."

I smiled, pride and relief mixing in my chest. "That was incredible."

She kissed me, her affection clear, then tucked her head under my chin. "I like this," she mumbled. "Being yours."

I held her tighter. "You were always meant to be, Maverick. Even when we didn't know it."

We lay like that, tangled in sheets and sweat, until the world faded out and nothing was left but the quiet, the afterglow, and the promise that tomorrow we'd do it all again—only better.

Tomorrow we'd talk about being mates and what that means. Hell, I only hoped she felt the call of the mate bond the same way I did.

CHAPTER 11

BRIE

When I woke, the world was all haze and slight muscle ache, like I'd run a triathlon in my sleep and finished last in every event. The sun through Gunner's bedroom window was already up and aiming for my eyes, so I rolled away from it, straight into the dent in the mattress his body had left. The sheets still held the ghost of last night: sweat, heat, a little dried blood where his stubble had abraded my thighs raw. I stretched and immediately regretted it—my ass was still bruised, my thighs sore in ways that told a story without words. My wolf healing made it better than it might have been had I been human. Boy. That said something.

I felt wrecked and reborn. I felt... content.

The first thing I noticed was the emptiness. The space beside me was cooling, his scent fading into cotton and air. I clutched the sheets, half expecting to find a note pinned to my chest saying, "Thanks, but this was a one-time special." Instead, there was a literal note on the nightstand, written in neat, slanting blue ink:

Church with officers at 7. You looked too perfect to wake. Help yourself to food and coffee. Clothes in the hall.

Be back soon. -FW

I stared at it, the F and W mashed together in the signature like he was trying to economize his handwriting for speed. I ran my finger over the edge of the paper. It felt heavier than it should.

Underneath, there was a pen and a single Advil gel cap, left for me like a communion wafer. I popped it without water and pushed myself upright, letting the blanket fall. My skin was a disaster—fresh bruises mapped out on my thighs, the sweep of my ribs, and yes, that special bullseye on my right cheek. My wolf purred at the sight, smug and possessive.

I wrapped the sheet around myself and padded out of the room, heart hammering for no reason at all. The hallway was painted a warm, lived-in tan, with family photos hung in a lopsided trail leading to the kitchen. The faces in the frames were all Gunner—taller and skinnier at first, then with the stubborn edge to his jaw fully set by college. A high school graduation photo with a brother and sister at his side, both younger, both with that same wild Irish smile. His mother, holding a pie. His father, enormous and craggy, wearing a black hat and a grin you could see from Mars. There were no women, no ex-girlfriends, no ghosts. I checked.

In the kitchen, the light was soft and gold, slanting through the window and glancing off the clean lines of the countertops. The place was tidy but not precious. There was a note on the counter—Aspen's handwriting, curly and looping:

Eat, or I will know.

Beside it, a white box tied with pretty blue and white twine. Inside the still-warm cinnamon rolls she'd made famous. The smell hit me like a home invasion—sugar, butter, a hint of citrus. The coffee maker held a carafe of still-hot coffee, next to a mug with "World's Okayest Rancher" on the side.

I laughed. I couldn't help it. I tore into a cinnamon roll with my hands, and let the frosting paint my lips. The caffeine sizzled through my system. By the time I finished the first roll, I felt almost human.

I slunk back to Gunner's room, found the duffel bag in the hall, and dug out the clothes he'd left: a pair of gray joggers, two sizes too big, and a t-shirt with the logo for the Amarillo Livestock Auction stretched across the chest. I held the shirt up to my nose and inhaled. It was pure Gunner—sun, leather, the memory of him holding me down and making me call him Sir. I shivered.

As I got dressed, my wolf started up again, low and insistent: *Mate. Mate. Mate.*

Last night, I'd let myself believe it was just sex—epic, world-ending, rewrite-the-dictionary sex, but still just sex. Now, the word "mate" was stamped in every cell. My body recognized him before my mind did. The bond pulsed behind my sternum, not just a string but a steel cable, a lifeline and a shackle all at once.

I tried to slow my breathing. This was what I wanted. Right? To be claimed, needed, possessed by someone who made me feel strong and small at the same time. But the finality of it pressed against my ribs, a weight I wasn't sure I could lift. What if I weren't enough? What if he saw the cracks and changed his mind? What if being "mate" meant being perfect, and I was still the mess I'd always been?

I tugged the waistband of the joggers up over my hips. They were soft and well-worn. The shirt hung to my mid-thigh. I looked ridiculous. I looked...right.

I stood in front of his bedroom mirror, squinting at myself in the daylight. My hair was a tangle, the blue tips standing out like war paint. My face was splotchy but alive, lips still red from biting. I brushed my fingers over the bruises, then touched the skin above my heart, where it hurt most.

We're going to be okay, I told my wolf. We just have to try.

The wolf licked its paw and settled in, smug and at peace for the first time since Paris.

I went back to the kitchen, made another cup of coffee, and sat at the table to wait. I didn't know what the day would bring, or what Gunner would say when he got home. But for the first time in a long time, I didn't feel like I was running. I felt claimed, and it was the best kind of terrifying.

I finished the second cinnamon roll, licking sugar off my fingers, and looked out the window. The ranch stretched forever, fields and fences and a line of pecan trees dark against the sky. I tried to picture myself here—a gallery in town, dinners at this table, a life that felt rooted instead of borrowed.

It seemed impossible. But I wanted it.

That was the beginning.

Downtown Dairyville was five blocks of nostalgia posing as progress, and our new building was smack in the middle—a two-story brick-and-mortar leftover from the days when people did their shopping on foot and not by algorithm. I parked the Lexus (Harper's, but she'd let me drive today) in front of the curb, next to a battered feed truck and a golf cart loaded with someone's groceries. The fresh paint on the facade gleamed in the Texas sun, a kind of midnight blue that made the old brick pop like a before-and-after shot on a reality show. The awning above the front windows read "Tierney-Davenport Building" in chunky serif, and I made a note to one day swap it out for something less geriatric.

The architect Chantel was pulling away just as I'd pulled in. She'd been more hands-on than I'd thought she'd be, regularly checking on the construction crews. She wanted to be sure her designs and blueprints were being followed to the letter. It had been a few weeks, and things had really started to take shape.

Harper was already inside, talking to the construction foreman. I could hear her laugh through the glass, bright and insistent, even over the whine of a power saw. She wore high-waisted jeans, a sleeveless blouse, and a pair of Blundstones—her "I'm not here to mess around" outfit. Her hair was up in a bun, but stray pieces fell out, framing her face in the kind of deliberate chaos you'd pay $200 for at a salon. She saw me through the window and waved, then pointed to her watch in a way that said "you're late, but I forgive you."

I hustled across the sidewalk, ducking past a pair of construction guys in matching orange t-shirts, and let myself into the cool, echoey space. The ground floor was already gutted to the bones, dust swirling in sunbeams. Rows of bare bulbs hung from the rafters, and the smell of fresh paint and sawdust was so thick you could taste it. There were two ladders, three folding tables covered in blueprints, and a stack of drywall leaned against the far wall like dominoes waiting to fall.

Harper called out, "You're here! You brought coffee, right?"

I handed her the drink carrier—Aspen's again; I'd grabbed extra cinnamon rolls for the crew. "You're lucky I didn't eat all of these on the way over." I tossed her one, nearly missing her head. She caught it one-handed, then gave me a squinty, up-and-down look, noticing my small wince.

"Gunner the cause of that?" She asked, eyebrows up.

I flushed. "Combo situation. I started it. He finished it."

She just grinned. "Oh girl, there's a story there that is dying to be told. When you're ready, I'll be ready to listen."

We walked together to the back, where the new dividing wall was going up—metal studs already set, insulation peeking out like pink cotton candy. The forewoman, a short woman with inked arms and a permanent scowl, met us there.

She gestured to the wall that would divide our spaces. "We'll have this up by Thursday. Drywall done in a couple of days. Office doors after that. Your side's got the better light, by the way."

Harper smirked. "Told you."

We did a walk-through of the space. The ground floor was divided into two large sections. On one side, the future studio for Harper's dance classes; on the other, my gallery, with an open floor plan, a reception area and small office at the back. The ceilings were high; the ductwork painted matte black; and the floors were original hardwood, sanded and sealed. Upstairs, a catwalk circled the open atrium, leading to my office and a storage room.

I stood in what would be my gallery, picturing it full of paintings and sculptures and people who didn't see Dairyville as a dead end. "It's perfect," I whispered.

Harper nudged me. "You're going to crush it here. You know that, right?"

I let myself believe her for a second. "I want to. I want to do something...big." I looked out through the unfinished windows at Main Street, where the only movement was a dog sleeping in a patch of shade. "I don't want to just sell art. I want to bring something real here. Get people talking."

Harper's gaze softened. "You're already doing that. You're the only person I know who could turn a boarded-up furniture store into a dream in just weeks."

I shrugged, embarrassed. "You did tons of the heavy lifting, harassing contractors and consulting with the architect. I just made mood boards and picked colors."

"That's called being a visionary, babe. Plus, let's face it, our trust fund did most of the heavy lifting."

She wasn't wrong about that. Money talked.

The forewoman's walkie crackled, and she excused herself. Harper and I wandered up to the mezzanine, where the UV-coated glass windows had just been installed. The sunlight came through in cool sheets, turning the floors blue and gold.

"This is your office," Harper said, pulling me up to the unfinished room. It was barely framed in, just a suggestion of walls, but the view was incredible. You could see the entire gallery below, every inch of future space.

I looked down at the unfinished gallery below, imagining opening-night crowds, wine glasses, the hum of people who actually cared about beauty. "It's insane," I said. "How did we even get here?"

She leaned against the frame, arms folded. "We survived. We did what we had to do. And now we get to do what we want." Her tone was matter-of-fact, but the emotion was there, coiled tight.

For a long moment, neither of us said anything. We just stood looking out over our half-built empire, letting ourselves believe it might actually work.

Eventually, Harper broke the silence. "You think Gunner will show up to opening night?"

I laughed. "Only if I promise him there'll be whiskey and chicken wings."

She grinned. "He's good for you, you know."

"Is he?"

"You're smiling more. Even if you don't know it."

I glanced down at my hands, not sure what to do with the praise. "It's weird. I feel...lighter. Not less sad, just...like I can breathe."

"That's called healing, babe."

"Yeah, I think it is." I said behind a smile.

We circled back to the main floor, stopping to check out the progress on the windows. The new glass was thick and flawless, the kind you saw in high-end boutiques in Dallas. My name was already stenciled on the door, "Wildbrush Gallery," in matte silver. Seeing it there made my chest ache, but in a good way.

"I want to get local artists on the roster," I said, thinking out loud. "Young ones, especially. There's so much talent out there, and most of them don't have a place to show."

Harper nodded. "You'll make it happen."

"I hope so."

She cocked her head. "Have you told Mom?"

"About the gallery? Yeah. About last night? *Hell* no."

She snorted. "One crisis at a time."

I wanted to ask her about how things were with Arsenal, if she'd finally told him about the nightmares, the panic attacks, all the stuff we never admitted in daylight. But I let it go, for now. Today was about hope, not history.

As we made our way out, the foreman flagged us down and handed over a binder of paperwork—permits, paint samples, the works. I tucked it under my arm, feeling official and, for the first time, maybe even a little grown up.

Harper slung her arm around my shoulders. "Ready to take on the world, Wildbrush?"

I nodded, savoring the feel of her weight, the warmth of her confidence. "Past ready."

My office was temporarily set up on our kitchen table. I'd rather be working at the gallery, but the construction noise wasn't conducive to conducting any real business yet. I had my new over the top plush office chair delivered here so I could at least work in comfort and style. My mother had thankfully, promised to stay clear during work hours.

My laptop sat in front of me along with a wide-screen monitor that was filled with several examples of Wildbrush Gallery logos I'd mocked up. I had finally settled on one that would work for a signature on my email. The paintbrush bristles were made to look like a bunch of wildflowers, and the stylized lettering was layered over it. It was simple and refined. I'd used that signature on the emails that I'd sent to several artist agencies earlier this week, hoping I could snag a young up-and-coming artist hungry enough to want to have an exhibition in the middle of nowhere Texas. I had a legal pad on my desk on which I'd scrawled in Sharpie: "Wildbrush Gallery: Opening Show." The rest of the pad was a fever-dream of sticky notes, color schemes, and wild guesses about how I was supposed to launch a business.

I had thirty unread emails and the kind of nervous energy that made it impossible to focus on any one thing for more than three minutes. I bounced between spam, overdue invoices, and promo blasts until a subject line caught my eye:

WBG: Exhibition Proposal — Lysander Hale, Hale & Marrow Arts Management

My breath hitched. I recognized the business name as one of the agencies I'd contacted in my email blast. They mostly handled blue-chip galleries and the occasional Midwestern upstart. I clicked the message, heart thumping.

Hi Brie,

Congratulations on the new space! Your email indicated that you're opening with a focus on regional artists. I'm currently working with a young landscape painter, just out of RISD, who's doing remarkable stuff with Texas and the Southwest. She's exactly the kind of energy I think you want for your inaugural show. I've attached a couple of images, plus her CV.

Would love to Zoom when you can and talk about a possible solo exhibition for your launch. Let me know your availability!

Best,

Lysander Hale

I scrolled to the attachments. The first image was of a massive, impossible sky—watercolor on canvas, with the colors blown out to near-electric, clouds like bruises and sun flares. The second was a bleached desert with a single dead tree, the kind of painting that made you feel dry in the throat just looking at it. The CV said the artist's name was Inez Chavez, age 24, a Santa Fe native.

My head buzzed. This was it. This was the kind of stuff I'd hoped to show, the kind of painter that made Dairyville more than a punchline.

I set up a Zoom for noon, then scurried to the bathroom to check my face. I'd showered this morning, but my hair was a tangle and the blue streaks had lost their luster. I did the best I could with a little water, then redid my eyeliner with the trembling precision of a surgeon in an earthquake. The mirror made me look tired but determined. I stuck out my tongue at it, just to prove I wasn't scared.

Back at my makeshift desk, I rehearsed my lines. "Thank you so much for reaching out. I'm obsessed with Inez's work. We'd love to host her. I'm open to your ideas for the show." I tried to say "curatorial direction" without wanting to die. I opened and closed the Zoom window three times, just to be sure my camera worked.

At 11:59, the screen went black, then flickered to life. Lysander appeared, perfectly lit in some fancy Boston office, the kind of guy who looked more like a catalog model than a human being. He was early thirties, with slicked-back platinum hair, a perfect jawline, and a smile that made you want to simultaneously impress him and punch him in the face. He wore a tailored blue dress shirt, no tie, sleeves rolled just so. When he said "hi," his accent came through in sharp consonants and vowels that stretched out like taffy.

"Brie Lawson!" he said, grinning. "I feel like I'm talking to royalty."

I laughed. "I promise, I'm barely local gentry."

He winked. "Well, the grapevine says otherwise. I'm familiar with your work. I know you haven't hit it big. You seem to have been absent from the art scene for a bit. But, I think the new gallery's going to blow up well beyond little Dairyville, Texas."

I tried to act casual and play down my time away from the art world. "Thanks Lysander. And yeah. I unfortunately had to step back for a couple of years. Damn life just got right in the way of me doing what I was born to do." I laughed. "But this gallery is my passion. Right now it's more of a blank canvas, but we're getting there."

He leaned in, elbows on his desk. "I'm going to cut to the chase. I think you're exactly the person to launch Inez Chavez. She's a prodigy, but she's got zero market presence. She needs someone with vision and guts. Doing what you're doing tells me you've got both."

It took everything I had not to blush. "Based on the work you sent me, I believe you're right. It's...stunning. I want to see it in person."

"Easy fix," Lysander said. "She's an easy flight from Santa Fe. I can bring her by next week."

I almost spit out my coffee. "You're coming to Texas?"

He laughed, flashing teeth. "My boyfriend says I need to get out of New England or I'll never lose this accent! You know, where's the keys to my cah, I need to drive to the store and all that." His laughter was infectious. "Plus, I want to see the space."

Something in me relaxed, knowing he was spoken for. The pressure to impress without flirting was instantly gone.

"Bring him," I said. "There's a great steakhouse down the block, if you're not a vegetarian."

Lysander's eyes sparkled. "I'll hold you to that." He leaned back, then cocked his head. "Can I ask a personal question, Brie?"

"Uh, sure?"

"Why there? Why Dairyville, when you could be running a gallery in Austin or even New York?"

I hadn't expected the question. I hesitated, then shrugged. "I think there's beauty in starting over. In making something out of nothing. I want to prove that you don't have to be born to it. That you can be a little messy, a little weird, and still make it. And I guess I believe in family. My mom and sister are here, and that's where I want to be."

He nodded, looking genuinely impressed. "You're going to be great at this. And if you ever want to get out of Dairyville, let me know. Hale & Marrow always has room for rebels."

The rest of the call was logistics—shipping schedules, marketing ideas, possible dates for the opening. Lysander was a fountain of advice, and by the time we hung up, my notebook was a battlefield of scribbles and exclamation points.

When the call ended, I closed the laptop and let my heart settle. This was happening. I had a show; I had a gallery, and in a week, a man who I hoped would become a good friend was flying out to validate my existence.

I felt a swell of pride. I'd done this. I was doing it.

I checked my phone. There was a text from Gunner:

Home tonight after 7. Let me know if you want dinner. Or dessert.

I grinned, typing back:

How about both? I've got a lot to celebrate.

I set the phone down and stared out the window at the backyard with the pretty lemon tree and thought about the gallery. I pictured it filled with light and color, laughter and art.

This was my world now, and I was ready for it.

CHAPTER 12

GUNNER

The last thing I wanted was to leave her.

Brie slept on her stomach, star-fished across my sheets, cheek mashed flat and wild hair haloed in every direction like she'd lost a fight with a tornado made of blue paint. My shirt was up around her armpits, the rest of her bare as sunrise, the bruises I'd left fading from plum to a defiant lavender. Her leg twitched every few minutes, like even in sleep she was daring someone to try her. Sunlight crawled across the foot of the bed, inching up toward her toes.

I wanted to wake her up with my mouth, pull her into my lap and spend the next hour proving that last night hadn't been a fever dream. Instead, I wrote a note.

I left it on the nightstand, then stood in the hallway for a solid minute just watching her breathe, hating that I had to go. But Bronc's text was clear as the gospel: Officer's meeting at seven. Pack threat level Orange. Do not be late. That meant all hands, uniforms, and extra caffeine. So I closed the door soft behind me, laced up my boots, and forced myself out into the world.

The ranch was blue and gold, dew burning off the grass, the last stars fading as I cranked my dually down the drive. I passed the corral, where the black horse was already up and shaking out its mane, watched over by two sleepy hands who looked like they'd spent the night in the barn. I saluted them and drove on, radio turned low.

The Iron Valor clubhouse looked exactly as it always did: square-shouldered, defiant, and welcoming all at once, the American flag snapped out front, and the faded IRON VALOR MC sign catching the sun just right. There were three bikes and four trucks in the lot, plus Bronc's silver F-350 with the custom plates. Inside, the air was humid with the smell of yeast rolls and sausage gravy.

Pearl had the kitchen hopping; everyone knew their jobs and did them exactly the way she'd ordered. She wore a yellow apron and lipstick brighter than most road flares, and she was already pouring coffee for Wrecker when I walked in.

"Mornin', Finn," she said, voice smooth as butter. "You hungry or too worked up to eat?"

"Yes, ma'am," I said. "Wait... I'm hungry and a little worked up I guess."

She arched a silver eyebrow. "You look like you haven't slept. That girl keep you up all night?"

I couldn't tell if it was a question or a threat. "Not all night, ma'am," I said. "I had to save a little for today."

Wrecker heard that and choked on his biscuit. "Liar," he said, wiping crumbs off his cut. "That girl's been sending up fireworks since she moved in. Pretty sure you two were trending on Nextdoor."

Pearl smirked, then pointed at the hallway. "Go wash up, Finn. And if you see Doc, tell him to stop pretending he's not already here. I saw his car."

"Yes, ma'am," I said again, then slipped out before she could interrogate me further.

The bathroom mirror confirmed it: my hair looked like shit, and there was a faint scratch on my collarbone that wasn't there last night. I scrubbed my hands and tried to make myself presentable, but I mostly just looked tired and mean. Good enough for government work.

Back in the meeting room, the officer's table was already loaded for bear: Bronc at the head, everyone else in their usual spots. There was a platter of biscuits the size of small mammals, two trays of bacon, scrambled eggs heaped in a bowl, and enough hash browns to dam the Red River.

I sat next to Arsenal, who slid a mug of coffee my way. "You look rough," he said, not unkind.

"Yeah," I said. "You should see the other guy."

Papa snorted. "The girl or the horse?"

"Both," I said. "But at least Brie survived the landing."

Big Papa grinned, cheeks red from laughing. "Heard about that stunt. Girl's got more balls than half the men I know."

"That's because she dated men with none," Wrecker said. "Present company excepted, of course."

I ignored them and loaded a plate, stacking bacon between two biscuits like a sandwich. For a while, the only sounds were chewing and the scrape of forks. Pearl refilled everyone's mug before they were even half empty. Wrecker had four sugars in his, which is why he never shut up.

Pearl came back in from the pantry, drying her hands. "Finn," she said, "Maddie called this morning. Said she's worried about Brie, what with the tumble she took. You boys keep an eye on that girl."

I nodded. "She's tough. Learned her lesson."

Doc leaned in. "You teach it to her personally, cowboy?"

"Yeah, you spank her pretty or just bark orders?" Wrecker asked.

They all started howling, like a bunch of teenagers. I flipped them off and took a bite of biscuit.

Arsenal, who was the only one with any class, said, "Brie's fine. She's more wolf than most wolves I know. She'll bounce back."

Bronc, who'd been silent, finally looked up. "You sure she's ready for what comes next?" His eyes were blue and sharp as fresh-cut ice.

I knew what he meant. I nodded. "She's ready. She just doesn't know it yet."

Papa grinned, teeth flashing. "So when's the big moment? You gonna claim her tonight or drag it out for another week?"

Wrecker raised his mug. "Twenty says he does it before midnight."

"I'm not betting against the man," said Arsenal. "I've seen that look on his face. He's already halfway gone."

Doc threw in another two cents' worth. "You know she's gonna talk circles around him, right? That girl's brain is like a steel trap lined with glitter and venom."

I shrugged. "She can try. But I'm not so easy to break."

Papa wiped his hands on a napkin. "Heard her say yesterday you were the best thing that's happened to her."

That quieted the table. Even Bronc looked impressed.

I didn't know what to say to that, so I just shoveled more food into my mouth. After a while, the subject changed to pack business, the latest from the territory, who'd moved in or out, how the drought could eventually affect beef sales. But the whole time, Wrecker kept side-eyeing me like he was just waiting for the right moment to bring it back to Brie.

When the food was gone, and the plates cleared, Pearl came by to collect the dishes. "Finn," she said, "You do things on your own time. Don't let these bullies bother you."

"I know, ma'am," I said.

She nodded, satisfied, then turned to Bronc. "You boys handle your business. I'll bring out pie in an hour."

As soon as she left, Bronc straightened his back, and the entire table went quiet. "Here's what we know," he said. "Maltraz has been silent, but there's movement off the coast. Wrecker?"

Wrecker sat up, his bullshit persona replaced by the soldier. "We're seeing the old demon's signature on some of the West Coast traffic. Small packs, usually female wolves, but a couple of witches, too. Someone's buying them up and moving them through the port."

"Who's buying?" Arsenal asked.

"That's the thing," said Wrecker. "Most of the transactions are through shell companies or dead drops. But the last two were bought by a known affiliate of that damn Varic Otero."

Arsenal whistled. "The fuck do vamps need with wolves?"

"Same reason they need anything," said Bronc. "Power. Leverage."

Big Papa nodded. "Or maybe they're just bored."

Doc put down his phone. "I'm guessing if Maltraz is moving women, it's not for the joy of it. There's a bigger play."

Bronc leaned in. "Menace reports that Maltraz is above reproach. He's on his best behavior at Council, looks clean. But off-book, we can't prove shit. Every time we get close, the trail goes cold."

Wrecker said, "There's chatter that he's building a new house in Tijuana. If we can get a man inside—"

Bronc raised a hand. "We don't send anyone in until we're sure. Maltraz basically killed Papa last time. We don't take that risk unless there's payoff."

Papa rumbled, "I'll go. Man needs to learn I don't die easy."

Bronc smiled, just a little. "You'll get your shot."

Arsenal, who'd been thinking, said, "If Maltraz is trafficking girls, he's not doing it alone. He's never been a people person. Who's he partnered with?"

Wrecker shrugged. "No one worth mentioning yet. But I'll keep digging."

Bronc nodded. "Good. We stay sharp; we watch each other's backs. If Maltraz makes a move, we respond as a pack. No more lone-wolf shit. Understood?"

Everyone nodded.

Bronc turned to me. "And you. You keep an eye on your girl. If she's the weak link, he'll exploit it."

"Understood," I said. "And I've been trying to prep her for anything. Been teaching her to shoot and shit. She's getting pretty good with a 9mm; at least against wild hogs."

That got approval and a few laughs.

The meeting broke up with the scraping of chairs and the rumble of boots on the tile. I caught Arsenal's arm on the way out.

"You really think I can manage a claim with her?" I asked.

He grinned. "Don't see why not."

I shook my head. "I hope so."

He clapped me on the back. "Go easy on her, cowboy. Some girls are fire, but she's lightning."

I watched the others drift out—Papa to the back porch, Doc to the clinic. Wrecker stayed behind, picking at the last scraps of bacon.

"You got something to say?" I asked.

He looked up, eyes silver in the light. "Just this: If you don't lock that down, you'll regret it forever."

I smiled. "Who says I haven't already?"

Wrecker shrugged. "Not my business. But you deserve something good, Gunner. Even if you don't think you're up to the job."

He left, and I stood in the empty room, letting the smell of biscuits and coffee settle over me.

I headed for the exit, but Bronc caught my arm.

"Walk with me, Finn."

He led me out onto the back porch, where the air was still cool, and the lawn stretched out in a neat stripe to the treeline. Bronc shoved his hands in his pockets and stood in silence for a minute. I could hear a lawnmower in the distance, and the clang of metal from the garage where the prospects were working.

"I need to ask you something," Bronc said, not looking at me.

"Sure."

He was quiet, then: "This thing with Brie."

Here we go. "Yes, sir?"

"You know I like her. You know I want you happy. But..." He hesitated, the word hanging like a weight.

"But?"

He sighed. "I've seen the way you look at her. Seen the way you look at a lot of women, but this is different. You're more...intense."

I snorted. "Didn't think I had a softer setting."

He smiled, then turned serious again. "I've been to Kazimir's place in Philly. I know what you're into. Hell, I know you got a taste for control, for the leash. But I don't know if Brie has it in her."

My skin prickled. "You think I'll break her?"

He held up a hand. "No. That's not it. I just... I've seen wolves break over less. Some girls need time to grow into it. You ever see what happens to a wild horse if you bridle it too soon?"

"Yeah," I said. "But you also know sometimes the wild ones need a hard hand. Or they run themselves off a cliff."

Bronc took a deep breath. "You're right. Sometimes. But you care about this one, so I'm telling you—don't go too fast. Don't give her more than she can handle. She's strong, but not invincible."

I looked him in the eye. "We have rules, Bronc. Safewords. Boundaries. She's not just my sub—she's my partner. My mate; fated to be so. She's fucking amazing at it."

He watched me for a long second. Then he nodded and clapped me on the shoulder.

"I believe you. Just promise me you'll talk to her. Not at her."

"I will," I said. "Tonight, actually."

He grinned. "That's my boy."

I started to go, but he called after me. "One more thing, Gunner. If she says red, you stop. No matter what."

He was starting to piss me off. I'm a fucking good Dom. I don't need another one questioning me.

"Due respect, Alpha. Don't question my ability to be a good Dom to my sub. I'm impeccable when it comes to her safety and well-being. If I ever feel like I'm out of control or need a refresher; you'll be the first one I come to."

He nodded, satisfied. "Apologies. Go get her, son."

I left Bronc on the porch and headed for my truck, the sun already burning off the last of the dew. I had a night to get ready for, and a girl to win over for good. Bronc's words continued to tumble in my head. My mate and I weren't playing at Kazimir's club. This was real life.

I didn't plan on losing.

Brie arrived early, in a dress this time, blue and soft as a spring sky. She wore boots, but the rest of her was pure trouble: legs bare, hair loosely tousled with blue-streaked brunette waves falling to her shoulders. And I fucking swear she had on a lipstick that God help me was as pink as her pussy. She carried a tiny bakery box from Aspen's place and a bottle of wine that looked expensive enough to require an owner's manual.

"You're early," I said, trying not to stare.

She grinned, eyes dancing. "You said seven, but I was starving, so—"

"Come on in," I said, opening the door all the way. "Food's hot. And you look…" I trailed off, lost for words.

She gave me a once-over, taking in my shirt (a white pearl snap, ironed to hell), jeans, and the boots I'd polished for the first time since last Christmas. "You clean up nice, cowboy."

I flushed. "Yeah, well, when I got a woman who looks like you, I had to try to keep up."

She followed me to the kitchen, set her stuff on the counter, and immediately started poking through the grocery bags. "You got the cake," she gasped, pulling out the Buttercream & Blessings box. "Italian creme?"

"Best in the county," I said. "Maybe in the world."

She popped the lid and ran her finger through the icing and dragged it across her tongue. "You know the way to a woman's heart is through cake, right?" She groaned around her finger, and I thought my cock would bust my zipper.

I arched a brow. "Dammit, that's all it took? I could have saved myself a fuck ton of trouble."

She laughed, pure and bright, then caught my eye. "What else did you get?"

I got my raging dick under control and started unpacking. "Ribeye steaks. Creamy mashed potatoes. Carrots in something sweet and orange; don't ask me what. And the sprouts are for me, so don't feel pressured."

She eyed the spread, then me. "You're feeding an army."

"You eat like a bird," I said, "so I had to make up the difference."

She hip-checked me. "Maybe I'm just polite."

I set two plates on the table, while Brie grabbed the silverware.

"Look at us. Just like a real couple. I like it." She paused, then grinned. "Sir."

I grabbed her around the waist and kissed her. Hard. "Keep that up little girl, and this meal will wind up getting cold."

"I thought we had things to discuss." She said in a whisper as she quickly turned away.

The tension in my chest cracked. I watched her pour the wine, watched her fold the napkins like we were at a five-star joint, watched her set the table with the care of someone who wanted everything perfect but not too perfect. It was like watching a storm organize itself into something beautiful.

I pulled out her chair and waved my hand for her to sit. I followed her, sitting at the head of the table.

"You okay?" I asked. "After last night, I mean."

She looked at me, eyes wide. "I'm more than okay. I—" She hesitated, looking down at her plate. "I've been thinking about it all day."

"Thinking *good*, or thinking you want to press charges?"

She snorted. "Good, Finn, Jesus. I just... I have a lot of questions."

"Ask," I said. "That's what tonight's for."

She took a sip of wine. "You really want honesty?"

"That's *all* I want. I insist on it."

She set her glass down and took a breath. "I'd never felt like that with anyone. Not even close. It was like every nerve in my body lit up at once, and I just wanted—" She broke off, looking down at her hands. "I just wanted to be good for you. I still do. Is that...normal?"

The words punched through my chest, sharp and sweet. "Yeah, little girl. That's normal. For you, for me. I've never wanted anything more than to see you like that."

She looked up, and there was something fierce behind her shyness. "Does that make me a sub?"

I leaned back, smiling. "Makes you mine, is what it makes you. But yeah, that's what the word means. If you want it."

She nodded fast. "I do. But I also want to know... why is it like this? Why does it feel so big? Is it just the sex, or is it... the mate thing?"

My fork stilled on the way to my mouth. There it was. *The* question I'd been waiting for.

"So you've felt it too. The mate bond. That's what this is," I said quietly. "I knew it the first time I saw you. There is no denying we're mates; fated by the Goddess."

Her face softened. "I felt it too. Not right away, but... I knew something was different. I think my trauma kept me so out of tune with things. But my wolf kept pushing me at you, even when I was being impossible."

I grinned. "You *are* impossible. But that's one of the things that makes you, you."

She threw a carrot at me. "Butthead."

I caught it and ate it, never breaking eye contact.

She looked down again. "So last night... why didn't you... finish it?"

I frowned. "What do you mean?"

She bit her lip. "You know. The bite. The knot. The... whole mating process."

My face went hot. "You want the truth?"

She nodded.

"Because I wanted you to know what you were getting into first. Because I wanted *you* to choose me, not just your wolf. But what you got, that's all me. The entire package, Maverick. I'm a man, a wolf, and a Dom. I need your submission. It feeds the need inside of me to protect you and yes, to be in charge of your pleasure and your pain. That is one hundred percent true in the bedroom and to an extent in our everyday life. I don't want a slave. I want a partner. I will always respect you, your opinions, your wants, and concerns. But my hope is that your trust will extend beyond the bedroom to the other areas of our lives as well."

She was quiet for a long moment. "I can do that. I love the idea of being strong enough to take care of myself, but I also revel in the idea of being taken care of. Does that make sense? I'm all for women having the power of their own agency. And if that means they choose this, then that can be celebrated also."

I set my fork down. "Then you'll get both. But you have to be sure."

She looked at me, eyes shining. "I am. I don't think I've ever been more sure of anything."

We stared at each other; the food forgotten.

"You want to be mine?" I asked, voice rough.

She smiled. "More than anything."

My hands trembled. I reached across the table, took her hand in mine, and held it like it was the only thing anchoring me to the earth.

"Say it," I whispered.

She squeezed my hand, nails digging into my palm.

"I'm your mate, Finn Walsh. Now and forever. I want your bite. I want you to claim me."

The words settled around us, heavy and perfect.

I stood up, circled the table, and pulled her up out of the chair. She jumped into my arms, her legs wrapping around my waist, her arms around my neck. She fit against me like we'd been made for this. Her face buried in my neck as tears ran down her face with emotion. I could feel her heart beating against mine, frantic and steady all at once.

She looked up, eyes wet but unafraid. "So what happens now?"

"Now let's eat some cake," I said, because anything else would make me lose my mind.

She laughed, a real, unfiltered sound. "FINN!"

I kissed her hard and fast until she was kissing back.

We didn't eat cake. I'd hauled her down the hall to my bedroom in minutes. I had changed the sheets from the mess we'd made last night, knowing that we were about to wreck them once more.

"I'm not going to go slow, Maverick. I want you too bad."

I slammed the bedroom door shut with my foot; the sound echoed through the room like a gunshot. Brie was still clinging to me, her legs wrapped around my waist, her breath hot against my neck. Her dress was bunched up around her hips, and I could feel the heat of her pussy pressing against the hard ridge of my cock. Fuck, she was already dripping for me, her wetness soaking through the fabric of her panties and onto my jeans.

"Take it off," I growled, my voice rough with need.

She hesitated for a split second, her eyes wide and dark with desire, then she nodded and started to wiggle out of the dress. I didn't wait for her to finish. I grabbed the hem and yanked it up over her head, tossing it to the floor in a crumpled heap. She was left standing there in nothing but a pair of lace panties and her boots, her skin flushed and her chest heaving.

"Those too," I ordered, nodding at her panties and boots.

She bit her lip, her cheeks flushing even darker, but she didn't argue. She hooked her thumbs into the waistband and slid them down her legs, stepping out of them and kicking them aside. Her pussy was glistening, swollen and dripping with arousal. I could smell her from here, the sweet, musky scent of her desire hitting me like a punch to the gut.

"On the bed," I said, my voice low and commanding. "Now."

She didn't need to be told twice. She scrambled onto the bed and knelt in the center, her hands on her thighs. She was trembling, her breath coming in short, shallow gasps, but she didn't look away. Her eyes were locked on mine, dark and hungry, and I could see the excitement in them, the raw, primal need that mirrored my own.

I started stripping out of my clothes; the snaps popping quickly as I ripped off my shirt. I didn't care about being slow, about savoring the moment. I was too fucking wound up, too desperate to be inside her, to feel her tight, wet cunt wrapped around my cock. I tossed my shirt aside, then unbuckled my belt and shoved my jeans and boxers down my legs in one swift motion.

My cock sprang free, hard and throbbing, the tip already slick with pre-cum. I kicked my boots off and stepped out of my clothes, then climbed onto the bed. I turned her body so she was ass high, her pussy on full display, and I couldn't resist reaching out and running my fingers through her wetness, spreading her wide. I reached around and teased her clit.

She gasped, her body jerking at the touch, and I gripped her hips to hold her still. "Stay," I growled, my voice rough with authority.

She nodded, her breath hitching, and I took my time, sliding my fingers through her slickness, teasing her entrance before pushing two fingers deep inside her. She was tight, her walls clenching around me, and I groaned at the feel of her, fucking her with my fingers, and then curling them just right to hit that spot inside her that made her cry out.

"Sir," she moaned, her voice trembling, and I could feel her thighs shaking, her body on the edge.

"Not yet," I said, pulling my fingers out and smearing her wetness over her clit. "You're gonna come when I'm inside you, when I'm knotted in your cunt and biting your neck. You understand?"

She nodded frantically, her breath coming in short, desperate gasps. I flipped her over onto her back and spread her legs wide. Then I lined up my cock at her entrance, the tip pressing against the opening of her dripping cunt. I didn't hesitate. I grabbed her hips and thrust into her in one smooth stroke, burying myself all the way. The warmth of her pussy welcomed my cock as it wrapped me up tight. Goddamn, the feeling was heaven.

She cried out, her body arching, and I groaned at the feel of her, her walls clamping down around me like a vice. Fuck, she felt incredible, her pussy hot and wet and so fucking tight, and I couldn't stop myself from fucking her hard and fast, the sound of our bodies slapping together filling the room. I had both of her legs spread wide for me as I looked down at where we were joined. Her tiny body opening up to accept my dick was fascinating.

"Sir," she moaned, her voice trembling, and I could feel her tightening around me, her body shaking with the force of her orgasm. "Sir! I can't hold it!"

I slapped her clit. "Don't you dare come little girl! Not yet. You'll come when I bite you. Hold on."

"Yes, Sir."

"Such a good, good girl for me."

I could see how much my praise affected her. Her face was bliss at my words.

"You're mine," I growled, my voice low and rough. "Mine. And I'm so proud sweetheart."

I continued to pound into her tight pussy until I was about to erupt, and I knew she couldn't hold it another moment. I leaned over her body and kissed her one last time before I moved to her neck licking, sucking and tasting savoring everything about her. The lemon and floral scent filled my nose. My canine teeth elongated, and I sank my teeth into her neck, just above her collarbone, and she cried out, her body arching and trembling with her release. Her fingernails raked across my back. I could taste her blood on my tongue, hot and coppery, and I groaned, my cock pulsing inside her as I came, my knot swelling and locking us together.

She came again, her body shuddering, her pussy clenching around me, and I kissed her neck, licking the bite mark and soothing the sting. She was panting, her chest heaving, and I pulled back just enough to look into her eyes.

"Bite me," I said, my voice rough with need. "Claim me."

She hesitated for just a second, then she leaned up as her own canine teeth grew and sank her teeth into my shoulder, her bite sharp and sure. I groaned, my cock throbbing even more inside her as I felt the bond snap into place. Our bodies locked tight together until my knot solidified our mating.

When she finally pulled back, her teeth stained with my blood, she looked up at me, her eyes wide and dark with desire. "I feel you everywhere," she whispered, her voice trembling. "It's like you're a part of me." She was awed by the power of the bond.

I nodded, my chest heaving, and I kissed her again, hard and possessive. "That's because we *are* a part of each other now. Our bond is forever, sweetheart. Goddess blessed." I agreed.

We stayed like that for a long time, our bodies locked together, our hearts pounding in sync. And when my knot finally went down, I pulled out of her and gathered her in my arms, holding her close. I eventually went into the bathroom and dipped a washcloth in steaming hot water. I came back to her and cleaned her bite area and wiped between her legs, soothing her. I crawled into bed beside her, feeling a contentment I'd never felt before wash over me as we both drifted off to sleep, our bond sealed and our hearts finally whole.

CHAPTER 13

BRIE

By the time Lysander and Inez were due to arrive, I'd circled the gallery space at least a hundred times. I checked the clock on my phone; the time blinking back at me like an accusation: 9:12 am. They weren't due for another eighteen minutes, but the to-do list in my head was already whiplashing through possibilities. I'd run my thumb over every inch of exposed brick, flicked dust bunnies from the baseboards, and even tried to realign the potted snake plant by the front window for maximum Instagram appeal. The new polish on the wood floors was still curing, which meant I could smell the lemony bite of cleaning fluid everywhere I walked, a little dizzying in the best way.

The gallery wasn't even open, but it already looked like the place had a life of its own: steel and glass, hardwood and hope. The ceiling soared, raw beams and black-painted ductwork overhead like the skeleton of some giant prehistoric bird. I'd hung the industrial pendant lights in a precise, alternating pattern, the bulbs soft enough not to scream "fluorescent middle school," but bright enough for artwork. There were still ladders leaning against the north wall, blue tape Xs stuck at regular intervals for the future install. The back room, AKA my office, was stacked with paint cans, leftover tiles, and a curling extension cord that snaked across the threshold like a lazy python.

I paced, then retreated to the plate-glass windows, glancing up and down Main. A single FedEx van idled in front of the children's clothing store across the street; otherwise, nothing but wind and shoppers. I told myself it was "peaceful," but the silence just pressed on my ribcage, making me jump every time a car zipped by.

By 9:28 I heard the engine: a muted European purr, absolutely foreign to Dairyville's normal decibel range of mufflers and tractors. It was a silver sedan with out-of-state plates and a rental sticker still peeling from the bumper. The doors opened with synchronized precision—first Lysander, then Inez, each one an argument for the world outside of Texas.

Lysander Hale looked exactly as I'd imagined from his Zoom call, but taller, with a kind of long-limbed angular grace you'd expect from a ballet dancer or a professional saboteur. He wore black jeans, a white shirt crisp enough to have its own social media presence, and a tan trench coat that would've been laughable anywhere south of Oklahoma, but here somehow made him look like the most important person within a fifty-mile radius. Inez was shorter, maybe my height, but with the kind of posture that made you stand up straighter just by looking at her. She had dark, sharp eyes and wore silky black hair pulled back and tied off with a long scarf. Her jacket was leather, probably vegan, and her boots looked more expensive than my last apartment rent.

They didn't just enter—they *arrived*. Lysander held the door, then swept in, his voice preempting anything I might have said: "You, my dear, are a goddess of transformation. Look at this!" He spun, arms open, like he was about to attempt a jeté across the concrete. "It's stunning. I knew you had taste, Brie, but this is…"

He trailed off, letting his hand do a lazy circle around the room. Inez, meanwhile, stalked the perimeter, touching the bare walls like she was inspecting a crime scene.

I tried to channel confidence, but my palms were already sweating. "Welcome to Wildbrush. Or, the closest thing I have to it until the dry-wallers finish and I can afford a sign that doesn't look like an Etsy fail."

Lysander grinned and gave me a dramatic hug, almost spinning me off the ground. "This is so much better than I hoped. You look radiant, by the way. Love that lipstick!"

I rolled my eyes. "I ordered it from Macy's just in case of emergencies."

He gave me a withering look. "Darling, everything you do is an emergency," and then turned to call over his shoulder: "Inez, thoughts?"

Inez ran a finger over the brick, leaving a faint line in the dust. "It's authentic. And not too precious." She flashed me the barest flicker of a smile. "Good bones."

"Good bones," Lysander repeated. "Did you hear that, Brie? Inez Chavez only says that about places she actually likes." He dropped his voice to a faux whisper. "She once called a Chelsea gallery 'an overpriced mausoleum' to the owner's face."

Inez didn't argue.

I laughed, the tension draining a bit. "Well, as long as it's not a mausoleum, we're winning."

We started the walk-through. Lysander and I flanked Inez like we were security detail, though it was clear who was leading the parade. I pointed out the tall windows and explained my plan to use the front wall for her largest canvases. "The natural light in the morning is basically made for your color palette. It's like—here, look—" I dragged them to the tape marks by the window and pulled up the mockup on my tablet, then superimposed it against the blank wall.

Inez squinted at the screen, then at the wall. She nodded, just once. "Yes. The lavender in *Drowned Plains* will glow in this light."

Lysander patted my arm, then stepped aside to let us have our moment. I led Inez down the corridor to the secondary gallery, describing how I'd rotate in her smaller pieces as part of a seasonal display. "And I want to hang my own landscapes in the permanent section here—" I pointed to a stretch of wall that still had two exposed junction boxes and a scribbled note from the electrician: "NO POWER UNTIL INSPECTED."

Inez examined the space, then said, "Your work is very different from mine. But I think the contrast will be good." She fixed me with those hawk eyes. "You are not afraid of bright colors."

I grinned. "I am afraid of mediocrity. Color is easier to fix than boring."

She smiled for real then, and it was like sunlight catching a mountain ridge.

We finished the circuit, past the unfinished bathroom (tile laid, no mirror yet) and to the back into what would become my future assistant's office. Lysander was already there, leaning on the cheap folding table I'd pressed into service as a desk. He held up a finger: "Before I forget, your caterer is a genius. These little cranberry-fig goat cheese crostinis?" He bit one in half. "Michelin-star level."

I looked at the spread I'd set out—Aspen's best, the stuff that made even contractors pause mid-cursing. There were canapés with shrimp tarts, bacon-wrapped dates, and a cheese platter that looked like it belonged at a wedding. Inez reached for a pastry, then motioned at the walls. "When do you open?"

"Soft launch is in three weeks, if the building inspector isn't a total bastard. I want your work up by then. Your exhibition *will* be the grand opening."

I waited for a sign of worry, but Inez just said, "You will need the lighting finished by next Thursday. The colors need warm white. Not blue." She glanced at the fixtures overhead. "Those are very..." She fished for a word.

"Warehouse?" I offered.

She nodded. "Yes. Warehouse."

"There will be lighting tracks installed that can be adjusted per the artist's instructions." I told her.

Lysander shrugged out of his coat and perched on the edge of the table. "I'm so happy with this, Brie, honestly. You're a natural." He crossed his legs, balancing his phone on his knee. "I've already told four buyers that you're the real deal. No pressure, but Inez's whole career might ride on whether Dairyville's premier gallery has a successful opening."

I tried to laugh, but the words landed with real weight. "No pressure at all," I echoed. "Just the fate of the Southwest's best new artist and the future of my entire adult life."

Lysander grinned. "You're going to crush it. I can tell. I'm not supposed to play favorites, but you are my favorite."

I looked at Inez, who was now moving paintings out of their crates, holding them up to the walls one at a time, making tiny hand gestures like she was already arranging the whole show in her mind.

I found myself smiling, not just polite but with real, honest-to-god joy. "Thank you," I said, and it felt too small, but I meant it.

We spent the next hour plotting layouts, talking through everything from price points to which day of the week would attract the most visitors. Lysander had all these spreadsheets and color-coded documents, but he was surprisingly chill about letting me take the lead on curation. Inez was more interested in the details—"Will there be security at night?" and "Do you want artist statements in English or Spanish?"—but even she was clearly energized by the prospect of showing here.

Every once in a while, I caught Lysander just looking at me, an inscrutable little smile on his face. At one point, he pulled me aside while Inez was busy measuring the west wall.

"You know," he said, voice low and serious, "I could see you doing this in L.A. Or New York. Maybe Berlin, if you wanted to be really insufferable."

I rolled my eyes. "Not happening. I like it here."

He grinned, then his voice went soft. "You belong here, don't you? That's rare."

I wanted to argue, but I didn't. "Maybe I do," I said. "Or maybe I just want to prove to everyone who ever doubted me that I can make something out of nothing."

As if wanting to lighten the atmosphere, he spouted, "Marketing. I know you have your Instagram, and I can do a push through our agency, but have you considered collaborating with local businesses? You know, cross-promote. Aspen could make a Wildbrush pastry, the dance studio could do a pop-up performance during the opening, stuff like that."

I nodded, scribbling notes. "I love it. I want the opening to feel like an event, not just a gallery show. Maybe live music? Or a mural in the alley?"

Lysander clapped. "Yes! This is the energy. It'll be a party."

We went around and around—website banners, print ads for the Amarillo paper and Dallas/Fort Worth area advertising, Facebook event, even a possible write-up in the university arts magazine. I let myself imagine what it would look like: the space packed with people, voices echoing against the brick, every wall humming with art and ambition.

At one point, Lysander looked at his phone, then locked eyes with me. "So, the real reason I'm here..." He trailed off, tapping his nails on the glass. "I want to stay through the opening. See it through, you know?"

I blinked. "You want to stay in Dairyville for three weeks? What about your boyfriend? Won't you miss him terribly?"

He laughed a little too loud. "Well, I would have if I hadn't seen a pic of him wrapped around a hulking Spaniard at an out of the way club. I'm just thankful I had friends there who recognized him or he might still be fooling me."

"Oh no, Lysander, I'm so sorry that happened. That little cunt!"

He laughed. "Oh yes, just more ammo for my Mother who had warned me about him. So I've given her no grandchildren and no prospects since I can't seem to choose the right person to settle down with. And her lack of faith in me extends to the company. She thinks I'll mess this up, or get bored and fly home early. I need this to be perfect. I need you to know I have your back." His eyes were suddenly softer, less glossy and more real. "I've already booked a room at the Victorian house on the edge of town. The one with the wraparound porch. I want to help."

Something about the way he said it made my chest hurt. Not in a bad way, but in the way that happens when someone is unexpectedly on your side.

I reached over and touched his arm, just above the wrist. "Thank you, Lysander, really. I couldn't do this without you."

He glanced down at my hand, then back up, smiling for real. "Well, let's make it legendary, darling."

Inez finished her water, then looked at her phone. "We should leave soon. My flight is at two."

Lysander perked up. "Let's get going." He stood, smoothing his shirt. "Brie, you're amazing. I'll see you tomorrow?" He offered his hand, and I shook it, trying not to feel like a fangirl.

After they left, I lingered in the echo of their voices and the citrusy-smoke smell of lunch. I gathered the plates and set them in the tiny gallery sink, then stood at the window for a long minute, just watching the light move over the floor.

I'd been so sure I'd mess this up, or that no one would take me seriously. But today felt different. It felt like I was building something that mattered, that had roots. Like maybe, for once, I wasn't just passing through my own life.

I swept the crumbs off the table, tucked my notes under my arm, and started planning the mural for the alley wall, because why the hell not?

This was the beginning, and I wasn't going to blink first.

Lysander met me at the gallery in the late morning. We immediately continued planning where we'd left off yesterday. We had to be precise when it came to the placement of certain paintings. We chatted comfortably as we looked at mock-ups of the gallery on my tablet; our heads close together as we huddled around the folding table.

It was almost lunchtime when Finn showed up. I heard the heavy tread of boots on the fresh concrete, and even before I looked up, I knew it was him: the way the sound settled in my gut, the way the air felt suddenly tighter. He stood in the front doorway, backlit by the Texas sun, arms folded across his chest, eyes locked on me.

He'd worn a clean plaid shirt that stretched across his substantial chest. It was tucked into Wrangler jeans that fit his muscled thighs just right. His cowboy hat sat low on his head with his auburn curls peaking around almost to his shoulders. Damn, he looked good enough to eat. He took two steps in, then paused, scanning the room. His gaze caught on Lysander, who was standing next to me, holding a tape measure across my shoulders to show how wide I wanted the spacing. Lysander was close, not in an "I'm hitting on you" way, just the efficient, European "I do not care about personal space" way. Still, I saw Finn's jaw go tight.

Lysander noticed him and broke into a wide, effortless grin. "You must be Finn!" He stuck out his hand, and Finn took it after a millisecond's hesitation.

"Lysander," the man said, "Hale and Marrow Arts Management. I've heard so much about you."

Finn's grip was probably painful, but Lysander didn't flinch. "Brie's told me you're a legend around here," Lysander went on, eyes twinkling. "The stories! I've been dying to meet you."

Finn looked at me, then back at Lysander. "Yeah? What stories?"

I stepped in. "Don't believe half of what he says."

Lysander laughed. "Oh, I'll never tell." He patted Finn on the arm, then went back to laying out the measuring tape.

I tried to shake off the tension, but it clung to me like the last sticky note on a refrigerator.

Inez was just here for the day and had arrived a bit after Lysander this morning. I was glad for her help. She looked up from her end of the table. "We're finalizing display spacing. Is this your partner?" She said it deadpan, as if the idea of me having a partner was as unremarkable as ordering lunch.

I shook my head. "He's—uh—he's Finn, my boyfriend." It was the first time I'd officially introduced him as that, but I couldn't very well call him my "mate" in front of humans. That might sound a bit odd to them. Thankfully, Finn rescued me from my awkward introduction.

Finn cut in. "What are you planning with the lighting?" His tone seemed interested, but I could hear the edge underneath.

Lysander explained, going into detail about the fixtures and color temperature, and even though Finn clearly didn't care, he nodded along, every so often glancing at me as if to say, "You sure you want to trust this guy?"

We moved around the gallery, checking the height of the spotlights and talking about traffic flow for opening night. I was acutely aware of every gesture, every word: the way Lysander would lean in, almost conspiratorial, to ask my opinion, the way Finn trailed after us, a step behind, arms crossed, lips pressed into a line.

Eventually, Lysander had to take a call. "Sorry—New York. I'll be ten," he said, slipping outside with a practiced smile. Inez went to check on her pieces in the car, leaving Finn and me in the middle of the gallery, surrounded by silence and half-finished work.

He waited a second, then raised a brow at me. "That guy always this... friendly?"

I rolled my eyes. "He's an agent, Finn. He's paid to be friendly."

Finn grunted, glancing at the door where Lysander had disappeared. "Seems like he's paid to do more than that."

I bristled, folding my arms. "What's that supposed to mean?"

He looked at me, eyes searching. "Just want to make sure you're not getting played. You barely know him."

I let out a shaky laugh. "I barely know anyone in this town. Lysander's literally the only person besides you, Harper, and the girls who gives a damn about my future."

Finn didn't say anything, just watched me with that dark, unreadable look. The kind that made me want to squirm and scream at the same time.

"He's gay, Finn." I added, voice rising. "You're going to ruin the one friendship I've built since I got back from Paris. Is that really what you want?"

He exhaled, the air going out of him all at once. "No," he said, voice low. "That's not what I want."

We stood there, both breathing hard, both refusing to look away.

I changed the subject. "Can you help me move the ladder? We need to tape off the wall before the paint crew finishes."

He nodded, walking over to the far corner where the big aluminum ladder stood. I watched him go, wondering how a person could be so strong and still seem so fragile.

The contractors started disassembling a tall scaffolding near the back wall, metal pipes clanking as they loosened bolts. I was setting out fresh blue tape strips, careful to keep the line straight, when a sudden metallic screech ripped the air. I spun around.

One of the workers had stepped back, wrench in hand, as the upper tier of the scaffold shivered, then started to tilt forward. The whole frame began to collapse, slow at first but gathering speed. I was directly in its path.

For a second, I couldn't move. My mind registered the weight, the height, the probability of broken bones, but my body was rooted. Maybe I was tired. Maybe I thought I deserved to get hit. All I knew was I stood there, mouth open, as the scaffold lurched closer.

I heard Finn shout my name, but the sound was drowned out by the clatter of falling metal. And then, just as the top rung clipped the air inches from my head, someone crashed into me from the side, shoving me hard to the ground. The scaffold hit with a sound like thunder, pipes ringing off the concrete, sparks flying as the frame buckled and twisted.

I hit the floor, wind knocked out of me, arms tangled with someone else's. I looked up. Lysander was on top of me, breathing fast, blood running down the side of his face.

He blinked, dazed, then smiled. "Darling, you have the worst luck." Then he rolled off, clutching his forehead.

Finn was there in seconds, hauling me upright, checking my arms, my neck, my skull. "Are you okay? Are you hurt?" His hands moved over me, rough and desperate, voice barely controlled.

"I'm fine," I whispered. My ears were ringing. I tried to stand, and my legs almost buckled. "I'm okay," I repeated, and then looked for Lysander.

He was already sitting up, propped against the wall, blood streaking his temple and the front of his jacket. Finn grabbed the hem of his own shirt, tore it, and pressed it to Lysander's head.

"You saved her life." Finn's voice was raw. He looked Lysander in the eye, and for a second there was something almost like respect on his face.

Lysander grinned, wincing as Finn pressed the cloth to his skin. "Wouldn't be the first time I'd played the hero. But it usually gets me better press."

Finn let out a laugh, sudden and unexpected. "You're a tough bastard, aren't you?"

Lysander winked. "I survived art school. And my mother. This is nothing."

Finn shook his head, and for a moment, the two of them were just men, breathing in the shock and aftermath, sweat and blood and relief pooling around them.

I tried to thank Lysander, but the words got lost. My hands wouldn't stop shaking, and my heart thudded so loud I could barely hear myself think.

I heard Inez's boots on the concrete, then saw her rush over, face pale. "What happened?" she demanded.

"Brie almost got pancaked," Lysander said, gesturing at the mess. "I was her knight in shining armor."

Inez didn't smile. She reached into her bag and pulled out a gauze pack, then knelt and started to clean the cut. Finn stepped back, still watching me.

"You okay?" His voice was softer this time.

I nodded. "Yeah, yeah, I am."

He brushed my hair away from my face, fingers lingering on my cheek. "You scared the shit out of me."

I wanted to say, "Me too," but all I could do was grab his hand and hold on.

The contractors were already picking up the fallen pipes, muttering apologies and checking the damage. Lysander was laughing with Inez, even as she scolded him for being reckless. Finn wrapped his arms around my shoulders, holding me until I stopped shaking.

For a moment, everything else—jealousy, anger, fear—just vanished. We stood there in the middle of the chaos, the three of us tied together by the near-miss, the adrenaline, and the fact that sometimes the world keeps spinning even when you think it should stop.

I realized, as Finn kissed the side of my head and Lysander flashed me a bloody, triumphant smile, that this was my life now: complicated, messy, never exactly safe, but so much more real than anything I'd ever had before.

It was terrifying, and I loved it.

CHAPTER 14

GUNNER

When the dust settled, I stood there like my boots were bolted to the gallery floor. Everything else was in motion—contractors moving the twisted scaffold, Lysander pressing a blood-soaked napkin to his head, Brie hugging herself and refusing to meet my eyes—but I couldn't get my brain to fire a single coherent thought except, Don't let her be hurt. Don't let her be hurt. Don't let her be...

She wasn't. That was the insane part. She was upright, eyes wide and wild, hair full of drywall dust but her bones all in the right places. Lysander's arm was around her shoulders, holding her steady, and the sight of it made my jaw clench so hard my teeth nearly splintered. Some chunk of me wanted to rip him off her, throw him through the gallery window, but the smarter part—the part that remembered I'd have been too slow to save her—wanted to thank him with every goddamn word I knew.

I settled for doing neither. I just watched.

Brie tried to joke about it, about her "trend of narrowly avoiding tragic, lawsuit-worthy death," but her voice kept catching. She was trembling, the aftershocks still working through her, and the more she tried to act like it was nothing, the more obvious it became that it was everything.

Lysander didn't look so hot himself. The blood running down the side of his face had slowed, but a goose egg was blooming above his left eyebrow, already purple at the edges. Inez appeared from the back of the building and zeroed in on him, ignoring everyone else as she checked his pupils, asked if he could count to ten in reverse Spanish, then barked at the construction staff to bring ice. Lysander shrugged her off, eyes never leaving Brie.

"I'm fine, darling." He had a napkin pressed to his head. "But you, Brie—you have to stop being such a disaster magnet. Some of us are not built for heroics."

Brie tried to smile. "You did okay."

He squeezed her shoulder, and I felt my hands curl into fists. It was worse because she let him. She didn't lean away, didn't make a joke, just let him hold her while she got her bearings. It made my skin itch.

I stepped forward, maybe too fast, because Lysander tensed. For a second, I thought we were gonna square up like a couple of dogs over a dropped steak, but then he caught my eye and did this little nod—like a bow, almost. A white flag. He got what I was, what she was to me. He wasn't here to fight. He was here to keep her alive, same as me. Fuck, he wasn't even into women, and I *knew* that.

That nod cooled something ugly in my chest. I'd torn off a corner of my shirt for the cut on his head. He took it gratefully.

I went to Brie, held her by the arms, and checked her over like I'd never seen her before. I ran my hands up her forearms, brushed drywall out of her hair, looked in her eyes for a sign of concussion or shock. She shivered, and I caught her, pulled her in close.

"You're okay." I buried my face in her neck. "You're okay."

She nodded into my chest. "You're crushing me, Finn."

I loosened my hold, just a fraction. "Sorry."

"I'm fine." I could hear the quiver of fear in her voice. "But thanks for checking."

She didn't let go, though. Not for a long minute. I knew she was waiting for her heart rate to slow, for the adrenaline to bleed off. It felt good; her holding onto me. It felt necessary. I wanted to be the person she sought for safety and comfort.

Lysander dabbed at his head, then tried to laugh it off. "So much for a soft launch. The only thing soft is my skull now." He eyed me with a strange kind of respect, like we were both members of some club neither of us had asked to join.

Inez insisted on hauling him to the Victorian Inn, muttering about ice packs and Tylenol and the inability of men to properly care for their own bodies. Lysander let her, but before he left, he turned to Brie.

"See if you can get this one to give lessons on how a man is supposed to take care of the one he loves." Nodding at me, "because *mine* sure missed the mark."

Brie gave him a sad sort of look. "Aww, honey. I'm sorry. You'll find a guy who'll treat you right. You're too precious not to."

He gave her a small smile. "You're probably right."

She hugged him, careful not to touch the wound. He hugged her back, tight and quick, then handed her off to me like he was passing a baton in a relay. I hated that it made sense.

I reached out and shook his hand. It was stupid, but it felt important. His grip was cold and a little damp, but strong.

"Thank you."

He just looked at me, eyes a little watery from the impact, but also sharp and clear. "Don't let her out of your sight." It seemed like a warning.

"Never planned to." It was a promise as much to myself as to him.

He nodded again, then let Inez lead him away.

When they were gone, it felt like the world went quiet. The contractors continued to mumble apologies and clear away the mess. And then it was just me and Brie in the echo of all that nearly was.

I wrapped my arms around her, maybe too tight again, but she didn't complain this time. Her face pressed to my chest, and I could feel her breath even out, slow and sure. I stroked her back, up and down, until the trembling stopped.

I gave her hand a gentle pull. "Let's get out of here. You've had enough art for one day."

She nodded, silent.

We walked to my truck; her tucked under my arm. I helped her up into the seat, careful of her head, her knees, every inch of her. It was all I could do to still my hands enough to get her fastened into her seatbelt.

She noticed, of course. She always did.

"You okay, cowboy?" Her voice went back to its regular setting.

I looked at her—really looked at her—and felt the tight band around my chest start to loosen. I gave her a quick kiss on her forehead. "I am now."

She touched my face, soft and gentle. "You're such a mess, Finn Walsh."

I laughed, low and rough. "Yeah," I said. "But I'm your mess."

She smiled, and the world made sense again.

I shut the door, circled to the driver's side, and got us the hell out of there.

By the time we made it back to the house, the late sun had already started to turn the porch posts gold and set the shadows sharp across the gravel drive. I killed the ignition, then sat there a second, just holding the steering wheel and listening to her breathe. It felt like if I took my eyes off her for even a minute, the universe might pull some fresh stunt, and this time I might not get so lucky.

Brie reached over and poked my shoulder. "Are you going to carry me inside, too?"

I played along. "Would if you asked."

She rolled her eyes but smiled, and the sight of it let me finally unclench.

Inside, the house felt different than it ever had—it belonged to both of us now. Her scent drifted everywhere; lemon and paint and that wild sweetness only *I* could really smell. There were a pair of her boots in the hall, a half-read book on the arm of the couch, and her tote bag slouched against the wall, half its contents spilling out. Even this house knew she belonged here.

"Go shower, Maverick." My voice was gruff and low. "Get that dust off you."

She hesitated, scanning my face for some hidden meaning, then shrugged and headed for the back bathroom. I watched her go, memorizing every step.

While she was gone, I turned to dinner. The slow cooker had been going all day, and the smell of stew hit me the second I cracked the lid—rich and spicy, beef falling to pieces, carrots so soft they didn't even need a knife. I gave it a stir, then tore open the loaf of French bread I'd picked up from Aspen's bakery. I cut thick slices, arranged them in the basket, and set the table with the real bowls. It felt important, doing things right tonight.

Every minute or so I glanced down the hall, half expecting her to call for help, or to need something, or to just vanish. I caught myself doing it and tried to stop, but it was like my body wouldn't cooperate.

Brie took her time in the shower, which was out of character. When she finally came out, she was wrapped in her silky robe, hair wrapped in a towel turban. She looked pink and scrubbed, like all the day's terror had finally been washed away.

She leaned in the kitchen doorway, watching me work.

"You going to let me help, or just be your trophy wife tonight?"

I pretended to weigh the question. She wasn't officially my wife yet. I had every intention of remedying that. "Sit. You've had a hell of a day."

She grinned, and for once, she did as she was told without an argument. She curled up at the head of the table, folding one leg underneath her, and watched as I ladled out the stew. I made sure to give her the best pieces—the ones with the fat melting off and the big hunks of carrot. I set the bowl in front of her and poured her a glass of tea.

"Smells like heaven." She breathed in the aroma with her eyes closed. "You'd make someone a damn fine wife."

"Look who has jokes." Fuck, she made me happy.

She laughed, and my world brightened at the sound.

I sat beside her, just watching her. She dug in, bread in one hand, spoon in the other, and for a while the only sound was her eating. Every time she looked up, I was staring.

She caught me at it, finally. "What? Do I have pepper in my teeth or something?"

"Just making sure you're still here."

She went quiet, then reached across and took my hand.

"I'm not going anywhere, Finn. Not tonight. Not ever."

I swallowed, then nodded. "Good."

We ate the rest in an easy rhythm; her telling me about the gallery plans, how Lysander wanted to hang the biggest canvas right in the window, how he'd gotten her to agree to paint a mural on the alley wall. Her hands moved as she talked, animated and alive, her eyes bright in a way that I'd never seen.

"You're really doing it." I wanted to heap all the praise I felt she'd deserved on her. I wanted her to realize how big this was.

She shrugged, but the pride was obvious. "I guess I am."

"You still have doubts?"

She hesitated, then shook her head. "Not when you're around," she said. "You make me feel... possible."

I didn't have a word for what that did to me. Maybe there wasn't one.

"When I look at you Maverick, I see magic just stored up waiting to be unleashed. You only needed someone to believe in you. You only needed to believe in yourself."

Her eyes shone with unshed tears. "To think the love of a good man could make all the difference."

"I think it was just good love that made the difference."

I kissed her on her cheek and picked up her empty bowl. She tried to help, but I waved her off, made her stay seated while I loaded the dishwasher and put the leftovers away. She wanted to argue, but I shook my head.

"You've done enough for today, Maverick. Let me take care of you."

She watched me, head cocked, like she were seeing something new.

I wiped down the counters, rinsed my hands, and dried them on the old towel. The house was still and quiet, the only sound the hum of the fridge and the clatter of dishes as I set them in the racks.

When I finished, I came back to the table and found her still watching me. She got up and took my hand and led me to our bedroom like she was worried I might vanish if she let me wander. She kept her hand wrapped around mine, thumb stroking the scar at my knuckle. When we made it past the doorway, she stopped and looked up at me, eyes steady. I thought she might say something wise or philosophical about survival, about how lucky we were to still be here, but she just reached up and dropped the towel from her hair and untied her robe, letting it fall open.

She shrugged it off her shoulders, and it drifted down her back, pooling on the carpet. She stood gloriously naked before me. But I stood stock still, hands clenched into tight fists at my side. I wanted to see what she would do. This was her show for now. But the sight of her standing there, bare and wild-haired, punched the air out of me.

I didn't even get a word out before she hooked her fingers into the waistband of my jeans and started walking backward until she was close to the bed. She started to undress me, beginning at the collar of my shirt. One snap and then the next. She was precise; methodical. When they were all undone; her small hands moved inside to push the shirt off my shoulders, caressing my skin with the movement. She laid small kisses to my nipples my abs, my navel, until she reached the waistband of my jeans.

"You're so fucking perfect," she whispered against my skin, voice gone rough and needy.

I tried to answer, but her hands had already moved to my belt buckle, undoing it then popping the button and pulling down the zipper. Luckily, I had removed my boots when I came through the door, so there would be nothing stopping her from taking my jeans to the floor.

She roughly tugged my jeans and boxers down my hips in one not-so practiced motion. My cock sprang free, hard and already leaking, and her turquoise eyes sparkled with hunger as they met mine.

She stroked me once, then twice. "You always take such good care of me." She dropped to her knees on the rug. "Sir?" Her voice slightly trembled as she looked up at me. "May I...?" Her hand loosely wrapped around my raging hard-on.

The air was thick with the smell of her desperation and my dominance, a fucking cocktail of lust that made my cock twitch against her lips before she even touched it. She was on her knees, like she'd been born to serve, her gorgeous eyes locked on mine, begging for permission.

I didn't even answer with words—just a sharp nod, my hand tangling in her hair, yanking her head forward until her hot little mouth was wrapped around my dick. She moaned around me; the vibrations made my knees weak, and I throbbed against her tongue, already leaking pre-cum like a faucet.

Her mouth was a goddamn vice, tight and wet, her tongue working the underside of my shaft like she'd spent her whole life practicing for this moment. Her small hands weren't idle either—they gripped the base of my cock, jerking me in rhythm with her mouth, her fingers sliding over my balls, teasing them like she wanted to milk every fucking drop out of me.

"That's it, my filthy girl," I growled, my voice low and rough, "take what I give you."

She obeyed, hollowing her cheeks and sinking down until her nose was pressed against my pelvis, her throat stretching around me. I could feel her gagging, but she didn't stop, didn't pull back, just took every fucking inch like the good girl she was.

"You're such a good girl," I muttered, my hips rolling forward, fucking her face now, her throat making these wet, slurping sounds that drove me fucking wild. Her eyes watered, tears streaking her cheeks, and she looked up at me like I was her god, her lips stretched obscenely around my cock. Pride showed on her face.

I could feel the pressure building in my balls, my thighs tightening as I got closer, and I warned her, "I'm gonna come, Maverick."

But she didn't pull away. She fucking shook her head no, her eyes locked on mine, and I lost it. My cock pulsed, shooting ropes of cum straight down her throat, and she swallowed every fucking drop, her tongue lapping at my tip like she couldn't get enough.

When I was done, I pulled out slowly, my dick slick with her spit and my cum, and I grabbed her chin, forcing her to look at me. "Clean it," I ordered, my voice harsh, and she didn't hesitate. Her tongue flicked out, licking my shaft from base to tip, her lips closing around me to suck off every last trace as spit ran down her chin.

Finally, I pulled her up, her body pressed against mine, her lips swollen and wet. I kissed her deeply, my tongue fucking her mouth, tasting myself on her, and I didn't give a shit. She was mine, my filthy little mate, and I was so fucking proud of her.

"Good girl." My hands slid down to grip her ass, squeezing hard. "You're my naughty, dirty girl."

"You need to come, Maverick?"

"Yes, Sir. Please, I need it."

I pulled her over to the bed as I wasn't nearly finished with her. She was still gasping, her chest heaving, her skin glistening with sweat and spit, when I bent her over the edge, her ass high in the air, her pussy glistening and begging for me.

"You ready for me, baby? This isn't going to be gentle." I growled, my voice thick and dark, and she whimpered, her thighs trembling as I ran my hand down the curve of her spine, feeling the heat of her skin beneath my palm. My fingers traced lower, slipping between her ass cheeks, and she shivered, her breath hitching as I found her slick, dripping cunt. I shoved two fingers inside her without warning, her tight little hole clenching around me like a vice. I curled my fingers, fucking her hard and fast, her body jerking as she cried out, her hips bucking against my hand.

"Color," I demanded, my cock already throbbing, ready to claim her again.

"Green, Sir!" she screamed, her voice breaking, and that was all the permission I needed. I pulled my fingers out, slick with her juices, and lined my cock up with her entrance. She was so fucking tight, her pussy fluttering around the tip of my dick as I pushed inside her. There was no gentleness here—no slow, sweet fucking. I slammed into her, burying myself all the way in one brutal thrust, and she arched her back, her nails clawing at the sheets as she screamed my name.

Her cunt was a furnace, hot and wet and perfect, and I fucked her hard, every thrust driving her closer to the edge. I could feel her clenching around me, her body trembling as I hit that sweet spot deep inside her, but I wasn't going to let her come—not yet. I reached around, rubbing her clit with rough, uneven strokes, teasing her until she was whimpering, begging for release. But I denied her, pulling my hand away just as she was about to tip over the edge, leaving her gasping and desperate.

I slapped her clit, not hard, just enough to make her jolt. "You gonna come for me, or do I need to work harder?"

She sobbed, desperate. "Please, Sir, I'll do anything—"

My knot was already starting to form, swelling at the base of my cock, and I paused for a moment, just to watch her pussy stretch to accommodate me. It was fucking mesmerizing—the way her tight little hole swallowed my cock, her body adjusting to take every inch of me. I started moving again, small, shallow thrusts that had her moaning and writhing beneath me. I could feel her clit throbbing, her pussy pulsing around me, and I knew she was close—so fucking close.

"You like being my doll, filthy girl? You like being fucked until you don't even know your name?"

"Yes, Sir. Please, please!"

I gathered her wetness on my fingers, slick with her juices, and rubbed her clit hard and fast, watching as her body jerked, her back arching as she finally came undone. Her pussy clenched around me, milking my cock as I followed her over the edge, my knot locking us together as I came hard, filling her up with every last drop of my cum. She was screaming, her body shaking with the force of her orgasm.

"I love how you take what I give you, baby. I love how you trust me to take care of you. So fucking proud of you." I was almost as breathless as she was.

I leaned over her, my breath hot against her ear as I whispered, "So glad you're mine."

We stayed like that for what felt like forever, her body draped over the edge of the bed, my knot still buried inside her, until it finally started to deflate. But even then, I wasn't ready to let her go. We were one animal, one heart. Forever.

CHAPTER 15

BRIE

*I*t started as heat.

Not the gentle, sleepy warmth of Gunner's arms. Not the way his chest radiated safety, or the furnace of our joined bodies beneath the quilt. This was a different fire—darker, raw, and so real it singed the inside of my skull.

I was on my knees, naked and sweat-slick, pressed against the flat stone floor of a room that looked like our bedroom but wasn't. The air pulsed orange and red. The walls were built of rough, uneven blocks, mortared together by some tarry blackness that wept in rivulets down to the ground. There was no window, no door, just a low ceiling and the knowledge that if I looked up, I'd find nothing but infinite darkness staring back at me.

But I wasn't alone. He was behind me—my wolf, my cowboy, my Gunner. He'd wrapped his arms around my middle and his chest was at my back, and he was talking to me, but the words dripped like hot wax in my ears. They burned, but I wanted them. Needed them.

I felt him move, the blunt weight of his cock hard between my thighs. His hand knotted in my hair, and he pulled me backward, making me arch. My mouth fell open, ready for whatever he gave me. I was hungry, desperate; I wanted to please him.

I turned, and Gunner's face was in shadow. His voice rumbled through me: "You gonna be a good girl for me, Maverick?"

"Yes, Sir," I said, but my voice didn't sound like my own. It was smaller. More afraid.

He laughed—a thunderclap, rattling the stones under my knees. He reached forward and pushed my head down, bending me over until my cheek scraped the grit of the floor.

And then it changed.

I was still kneeling, but now the room throbbed with a low, red light, the air thick with sulfur and rot. The hands on my hips weren't Gunner's anymore—too long, too tight, with curved, digging claws that pierced my skin but didn't bleed. I tried to move, to crawl away, but my legs were locked in place.

I heard a tail, the lazy thwack-thwack of something heavy on the stone, and I realized I was salivating, drooling down my chin as I strained to breathe. I looked back, expecting Gunner's lean hips, the tan line I'd kissed a hundred times, but instead there was a mass of muscle and dark, glossy skin, glistening with heat. A tail the width of my wrist coiled around my thigh, squeezing, forcing my legs open wider.

I opened my mouth to scream, but something thick and slick was already between my lips, pushing in, filling my throat. I gagged, but the hand on the back of my skull held me in place, forcing my face down, grinding it into the grit. My eyes watered. The taste was acid and smoke and sex. I tried to bite, but my teeth didn't work; I could only suck and swallow and sob.

Behind me, the tail slid higher, curling between my ass cheeks and up to my pussy. It was slimy, hot, alive. I felt it probe, circling my entrance, then slam inside in a single, punishing stroke. I screamed—soundless, airless—but the hand never let go. The tail fucked me, in and out, making my whole body rock and jolt. Every time I tried to pull free, the claws dug deeper into my hips, scraping bone.

And then, through the haze, I saw the wall in front of me shift and melt, revealing a mirror. In the reflection, I was still myself, but my eyes glowed bright gold, and my mouth stretched wide around a cock that was not human—ribbed, black, and leaking something pale and sticky that dripped down my chin. The tail inside my pussy thrashed until I came even though I tried not to, then pulled free, spraying a splatter of viscous fluid onto my back.

I looked up. It wasn't Gunner.

The face was Maltraz's—demon king, skin the color of iron, with rows of gleaming white teeth, eyes burning like open wounds. His mouth twisted in a smile, and he grunted, "Swallow, girl," in a voice that shook the world.

I tried to spit, but the thing in my mouth jerked and spasmed, pumping heat and poison down my throat. My stomach clenched. I started to gag, to retch, to vomit, but the hand just held me down, suffocating me in the filth.

"Swallow," the demon hissed again. "You're made for this, aren't you, slut?"

He slammed my face into the floor once, twice, and I heard something crunch in my jaw. I choked, vision flickering to black, but I still couldn't escape. I was so tired. So full. So scared.

The scene repeated, over and over, cycling through Gunner's face and Maltraz's, the room growing smaller and hotter each time. Sometimes there were others, shadows watching from the edges, tongues flicking, claws scraping stone. Sometimes there was just me and the hands and the tail and the voice, always the voice, always telling me what I was meant for.

It built and built, until I felt my skin splitting, my insides unraveling, and I started to scream—not just in the dream, but out loud, a ripping animal noise that tore through my throat.

Then hands, real hands, grabbed my shoulders, shaking me.

"Brie. Brie! Wake up. Wake up, baby. I'm here."

I came to on a wave of cold sweat, my mouth open and howling. My entire body spasmed against the sheets, limbs flailing, and I thought for one awful second I'd pissed myself or worse. I was tangled in the blankets, suffocating, but Gunner's arms closed around me and pulled me up, rocking me, shushing me, his voice a lifeline in the dark.

"It's okay. It's okay, I've got you. You're here, you're safe, Maverick."

My chest heaved. I clawed at his arms, desperate to prove he was real, to feel something solid. The taste in my mouth was sour, the back of my throat raw. My whole body trembled, but I couldn't stop crying, couldn't even slow it down. I felt like my bones had been hollowed out and filled with liquid terror.

"Don't let him take me," I sobbed, the words breaking apart in my mouth. "Don't let him...don't... please..."

Gunner just held me tighter, lips pressed to my hair. "No one's taking you, Maverick. I swear. You're with me. You're safe."

The world swam back into focus, a little at a time. The familiar geometry of the bedroom—my painting over the dresser, his boots by the door, the ugly old lamp he'd said was "classy in a Western way." It was still night, the digital clock pulsing 3:08 in blue numbers. The only sound was my own ragged breathing and Gunner's heartbeat under my ear.

I clung to him, feeling the panic recede by millimeters. My hands shook so badly I couldn't unclench them from his shirt.

"Fuck, baby, you're freezing," he said, tucking the blanket up around my shoulders. "I'm right here. I'm not letting you go."

I shook my head, wiped at my face, tried to find words. But the dream was already leaking away—faces, sounds, the oily feel of not-blood. I wanted to tell him what had happened, what I'd seen, but all I could say was, "It was bad. Really, really bad."

He nodded, rocking me a little. "Do you want to talk about it?"

I tried. I really did. But when I searched for the memory, all I could find was the feeling; a cold, sick dread, the kind that sinks under your skin and refuses to budge. The specifics were gone, washed out by fear and shame.

"Can't remember," I whispered. "Just that I was scared. And darkness."

Gunner's arms went rigid for a second, then softened. "You're safe now. I won't let anything hurt you."

I wanted to believe it, but my wolf didn't. She curled up in the tightest ball, tail over her nose, and shivered. There was something wrong, something unfinished, but I couldn't touch it.

I pressed my face into Gunner's neck, inhaling the deep, honest smell of him; leather, earth. It grounded me, pulled me out of the dream's gravity well. For a long time, he just held me, whispering soft things I didn't need to understand. I cried until my head pounded, until my sinuses ached and my chest hurt, but it helped. A little.

At some point, he eased me back onto the pillow, curled around me like a shield. "I'm right here," he said again. "Sleep, Maverick. I've got you."

And somehow, I did. I drifted off; the sweat drying on my skin, the ache in my body dulling to a manageable hum. The dream didn't come back, not for the rest of the night. But I woke with the sunrise, head splitting, sheets twisted around my ankles, and a sour, metallic taste in my mouth.

Gunner was already awake, perched on the edge of the bed, watching me with worry so thick it nearly had mass.

"Mornin'," I croaked.

He smoothed my hair. "Hey, wildcat. You slept through, after..."

I nodded, not wanting to finish the sentence.

He studied my face, like he was waiting for me to shatter again. "You sure you're okay?"

I wanted to say yes, but the word stuck. Instead, I shrugged, reaching for his hand.

"I will be. Just... hold me a minute, okay?"

He did. He pulled me close, rubbed my back until the last tremors faded.

I still couldn't remember the nightmare, not really, but the dread lingered, like a bad flavor you can't scrub off your tongue.

I knew deep in my gut that it hadn't been just a dream.

But if there was anything worse out there than what I'd just survived, I didn't want to know about it.

The gallery was so close to finished I could taste the drywall dust in my coffee.

Every morning brought some new evidence of near-completion: the glass-walled mezzanine now gleamed above the main floor, the last of the blue tape was gone from the windows, and the HVAC guys had finally stopped turning the whole building into a wind tunnel. The second floor was my domain, the office and conference nook framed out in matte-black steel and sound-insulating panels, so you could look down into the open gallery without actually hearing the contractors curse below. Lysander called it "The Penthouse," which made me snort Diet Coke out my nose the first time he said it.

I was curled up in my new office chair—floral, overpriced, worth every penny—staring down at a spreadsheet of RSVPs for Inez Chavez's show. Lysander was sprawled on the couch opposite, laptop balanced on his knee and a bagel slowly dissolving in his mouth.

"You know," he said, "If you squint at the RSVP list, you can see the three people who matter and the thirty who wish they mattered." He shot me a wink. "But that's gallery business, darling. Half the crowd just wants to be seen."

I muttered, "Then they can be seen from the sidewalk. Let's just put all the beautiful people out there and make them stare at the real art through the window."

He laughed, then clicked his tongue at the screen. "God, I love you. You're so much meaner than you look."

It was our fourth day in the new office, and I felt like a raccoon in a luxury hotel: twitchy, caffeinated, terrified someone would discover I had no idea what I was doing. The desk was already a wreck—sticky notes, color swatches, a sketchbook open to three separate disasters-in-progress, and a mug of hours-old coffee that had a design of old creamer swirled on the top. Outside, the sound of drills and hammers echoed up the stairwell.

I checked the RSVP numbers for the third time, then set the laptop aside. "Do we really need to have the wall labels done by Monday? I'm still waiting for Inez to send half her titles."

"Deadlines, honey," Lysander said, not looking up from his own spreadsheet. "Nothing like the threat of public humiliation to move an artist's ass."

I snorted, then felt the heat of embarrassment flare up my cheeks. My insides still shook from the nightmare last night—a cold, crawling dread that had left me gasping awake at 3 a.m., Gunner's arms squeezing me so tight I'd nearly passed out again. The dream itself was gone by morning, but the sick, hollow feeling hadn't left.

Lysander must have noticed, because he set aside his laptop and gave me the kind of look reserved for animals about to chew off their own legs.

"Are you okay, Brie?" he asked, voice gentle. "You seem...haunted today."

I opened my mouth, then snapped it shut, then opened it again. "I had a nightmare last night. Bad one. But I don't remember a damn thing about it. Just the panic." I tried to smile, but it came out twisted.

He nodded, crossing one leg over the other. "I had night terrors as a kid. Woke up screaming every night for a year. My mother said I was possessed by a goblin." He paused. "She wasn't entirely wrong, but that's for another day."

The words made me laugh, which I needed. "How'd you get them to stop?"

He grinned. "They don't. I just learned to weaponize my insomnia." He looked at me over the rim of his mug. "It's probably just nerves, sweet thing. You're launching the gallery, the show's a couple of weeks out, and you're trying to keep a relationship going with a man who could bench-press a tractor. I'd be shocked if you weren't having night sweats."

"Maybe," I said, but it didn't feel like just stress. Still, Lysander's smile was so disarming it was easy to let him talk me down.

He closed his laptop, stood, and circled behind my chair, draping his arms over my shoulders. "You need to find something to remedy this. Can't have you losing sleep on the regular."

I snorted. "In my life, that's a tall order."

He ruffled my hair, then leaned in. "Don't you Southerners make some kind of hot toddy or something to help you sleep?"

"Maybe. I'll check with Aspen. She's originally from Georgia. If anyone can figure something out, it would be her." Of course I was thinking of the fact that she's a witch and might be able to whip up a spelled drink for me.

We spent the next hour locked in logistics—printing checklists, double-checking guest lists, arguing over whether Aspen's vegan canapé platter would go over better than the baby quiches. Lysander was a tornado of efficiency and dark humor; by the end of the morning, we'd crossed off more than half the to-do list. I started to feel almost normal.

At eleven sharp, Harper arrived, a little windblown and a lot frazzled, arms loaded with binders and a fresh bouquet of wildflowers from the nursery. Her own dance studio was nearly done—just a floor left to varnish and a sound system to install. She looked up at the glass office and waved, then bounded up the stairs in long-legged steps.

"Wow," she breathed, setting down her things. "It's so bright up here. I love it."

"Better be," I said. "We're paying more for the view than the square footage."

She set the flowers in a water cup, then plopped on the couch next to Lysander. "What are we doing?"

"Finalizing the guest list for Inez's show. And panicking about wall labels," I said, gesturing to the mess.

Harper made a face. "I'd rather be up here with y'all than trying to convince the plumber to show up before Monday. He canceled again."

Lysander looked up from his laptop and said, "Brie's sister, the ultimate contractor whisperer. Maybe the plumber's intimidated by your muscles."

Harper rolled her eyes, but it was clear she liked the attention. "Not likely," she said. "He's just an ass."

I grinned. "Tell him the grand opening is in three weeks, and if he doesn't have the pipes done by then, you'll hex him."

Harper arched a brow. "Do I look like a witch?"

"Honestly? A little," Lysander said, and she snorted.

The mood stayed light until Lysander left to grab lunch. He offered to bring back poke bowls for everyone, but I asked for a plain bagel and cream cheese, blaming my "fragile constitution." Once he was gone, Harper went quiet, picking at the edge of her sleeve.

I glanced over, caught her biting her lip. "What's up, Harp?"

She looked down, then forced a smile. "It's nothing. Just...I heard some of the pack women talking at the market. They're...they're saying things about me. About the studio."

The anger snapped awake in me, sharp and sudden. "What things?"

She looked even smaller. "They said I shouldn't be teaching little girls to dance. That I'm a bad influence. Because of...you know...what happened in Houston. How I was a stripper and all. That it's not appropriate. That I'm ruined."

My hands balled into fists on the desktop. "That's bullshit. Every one of them knows what happened wasn't your fault. Dad put you in that club, not you. You did what you had to do to keep us safe."

Harper shrugged, eyes wet. "Doesn't matter. Once a rumor starts, it spreads. I'm afraid the mothers are gonna pull their kids from my class."

I couldn't breathe for a second. The old, helpless shame curled in my gut, but this time I didn't let it win. I reached over and grabbed her hand. "You have to tell Juliet."

Harper looked up, startled. "I hate to stress her with her pregnancy and all."

"She's in charge of the pack, just like Bronc, right? It's her job to stop this kind of shit." I squeezed her hand. "She's a badass, Harper. She's not going to let them treat you like this."

Harper shook her head. "I don't want to cause trouble. I just want them to leave me alone."

I wanted to scream. Instead, I leaned in. "You're not causing trouble. You're standing up for yourself. You're the best person I know, Harper. The strongest. If you want me to go to Juliet for you, I will. Or I'll take it to Arsenal. If he handles it, there won't be anyone left standing."

She smiled, watery but real. "Maybe you're right. If he gets wind of this, nobody is safe. Juliet is my best bet. Thanks, Brie."

We sat for a while, just holding hands, until the door opened and Lysander swept back in, arms loaded with takeout and his phone clamped between his ear and shoulder.

"Lunch, and drama," he said, dropping poke bowls on the desk. "I just had to take a call from Mother. That's always a delight."

He winked at Harper, who wiped her eyes and smiled. "You okay, darling?" he asked.

She nodded, and I felt the simmering rage settle to a slow boil. Lysander set out food, regaled us with stories about his mother's mafia-level negotiation skills, and the moment passed.

But I didn't forget.

By the time Harper left to check on her own studio, I'd already drafted a mental letter to Juliet. I wasn't going to let anyone bully my big sister.

Harper was a survivor.

And I was going to make sure she stayed that way.

I spent the next hour pretending to work, but I was really just stewing over what those pack women had said about Harper. Every time I tried to focus on the guest list, my brain kept replaying the look on her face—shock first, then resignation, then that awful, brittle little smile as she tried to wave away the hurt. It made my hands shake so bad I nearly cracked the handle off my coffee mug.

Lysander was an ace at reading a room. When Harper left, he set aside his phone, came to perch on the edge of my desk, and asked, "You want to talk about it, or just plot revenge in silence?"

I gave him a grateful smile. "How do you do that?"

"Years of fending off New York galleristas, darling. I can spot a mood shift at fifty paces." He reached over and squeezed my shoulder—a nothing gesture, but it sent a bolt of relief through me. "You know you're not responsible for her sadness, right?"

I tried to believe it, but the guilt was baked too deep. "She's my sister. I'm supposed to protect her."

Lysander leaned over my desk, taking my hand. "Then do. Use the tools you have. Slander works both ways, and I can be very, very mean."

I laughed, the sound coming out raw. "You're dangerous, Lys."

He grinned. "That's why you like me."

The gallery's front door buzzed—a sound no one else would notice, but which sent a flicker up my spine.

From my office, I could look right down onto the main floor. Gunner stepped through the vestibule, boots echoing on the new hardwood, head swiveling with the laser focus of a man on patrol. His hair was a little wild, his jaw stubbled with red-gold, and his eyes were so dark with purpose they looked black from up here.

I caught my breath.

Lysander quickly let go of my hands. "And there's your man."

I nodded. "He doesn't like surprises."

Gunner paused beneath the glassed-in mezzanine, looking up at me. I raised a hand in a tiny wave; he didn't smile, but he did tip his head, just enough for me to know he'd seen me. Then he scanned the rest of the gallery, a perimeter check worthy of a Secret Service agent. When he was satisfied, he started up the stairs.

Lysander, ever the strategist, gathered his stuff and said, "I'll go check on the lighting downstairs. You two need a minute."

He slipped out just as Gunner arrived at the door. I braced myself for a scene, but he only looked at me—hard, hungry, and with something else, too: a worry so sharp it almost hurt to meet his gaze.

He didn't say anything at first. Just pulled me into his arms and kissed me, long and thorough, like we were both starving. I clung to him, fingers twisted in his shirt, the world shrinking down to the feel of his body against mine and the taste of coffee and salt on his lips.

When he pulled back, he rested his forehead against mine. "You okay, Maverick?"

The nickname made me melt. "Yeah," I said, voice small. "Just...rough day."

He nodded, thumb brushing my cheekbone. "Saw his hand on you." His tone was even, but I caught the flare of jealousy in the line of his jaw.

I sighed. "Lysander's not a threat, Finn. He's gay, you *know* this. For another, he's my friend."

Gunner's lips twitched, almost a smile. "He touched you."

I couldn't help but laugh. "He's a toucher, apparently. It's all platonic, I swear."

He wrapped me tighter, like he could squeeze the doubt out of both of us. "You're mine, Brie. I don't share what belongs to me. Don't forget that."

I buried my face in his neck. "I won't. Sometimes I wish I could crawl into your skin and just stay there."

He shivered, then lifted my chin, so I had to meet his eyes. "That's a dangerous thing to say to a man like me."

"Good. I like your dangerousness. And I love you."

He kissed me again, slower this time. When he broke away, he cupped my face in both hands. "You tell me if anyone bothers you. I mean it."

"I will. Promise."

He seemed satisfied, but he gave the office a quick scan anyway. "You're safe here?"

"Safest place in the world," I said, only halfway believing it.

He grunted, then kissed me once more, just a quick press of lips, and headed back down the stairs. I watched him do a full sweep of the gallery, pausing to test the locks and eye every shadow. When he was done, he returned to the base of the stairs and called up, "I'll be back at six, Maverick. Be ready to eat."

"You got it, cowboy."

He left, the air buzzing in his wake.

I flopped into my comfy chair, heart racing. Lysander poked his head in a minute later, eyebrow arched.

"Everything good?"

"Yeah," I said. "Just security detail."

He laughed. "You're lucky. Some of us have to hire men that hot by the hour."

I snorted, then looked back at the guest list. For once, the numbers didn't matter. I could only count the hours until dinner at Pearl's, and then—if I was lucky—another night tangled up with Gunner, safe from everything except my own craving.

This was my life now: work, worry, hunger, heat.

I wouldn't have traded it for the world.

CHAPTER 16

GUNNER

I tried to play it cool all the way to Pearl's, but the truth was, my nerves were shot to hell. Most of that came down to Lysander—the smooth-talking, platinum-haired gallery rep who'd nearly bled out on the floor for Brie. I'd spent the better part of twenty-four hours trying to get my head around why that made me want to snap something in half. The man wasn't even competition, not by any stretch of the imagination. Lysander was gay—like, museum-grade gay. He was the kind of guy where he'd see a shirtless man and ask what moisturizer he uses. The kind where he'd walk into a biker bar and immediately rearrange the barstools because the spacing "felt emotionally off."

And even if he weren't gay, he'd have to be clinically insane to want to tangle with my mate. But logic had never been my strong suit when it came to women, and jealousy was a bastard that crept in like kudzu. It didn't matter if it was rational—it was mine, and I owned it.

Brie was in high spirits, all things considered. She'd thrown herself into her work, which for her meant a flurry of emails, last-minute vendor calls, and frantic sketches on the legal pad she clutched like a lifeline. By the time we parked out front, she was still halfway through a conversation with her own reflection in the visor mirror, reciting what sounded like her entire gallery opening speech under her breath.

"D'you want to finish that before we go in?" I asked, watching her lip the words "innovative" and "accessible" like they'd been loaded into a shotgun.

She snapped the mirror up, clicked her pen closed. "No, I want to drown it in bourbon and fried food like the goddess intended."

I grinned. "Pearl's probably got your usual table ready."

She side-eyed me. "You always act like we're on a date, cowboy."

"That's because we are," I said. "Anytime I'm out with you is a special occasion."

We walked in arm-in-arm, which always felt less like a statement and more like mutual reinforcement against the Dairyville gauntlet. Pearl's was already humming—two guys from the bank at the bar, a family of five on their way to a wedding reception in the side room, and in the back, a knot of Iron Valor cuts holding down the corner booth. The place smelled like heaven: frying oil, sweet onions, cigarette smoke that still clung to the curtains from the days when that was allowed.

Pearl herself intercepted us before we hit the hostess stand, looping a towel over her shoulder and hugging us both at once. She was built tall and broad and had the kind of presence that could stop a bar fight with a look.

"Well, if it isn't my favorite trouble magnet and the best thing to ever happen to him," she boomed, squeezing Brie so hard I heard a vertebra pop.

Brie laughed. "Hi, Mama Pearl. Any chance you've got something with extra carbs and zero guilt?"

"Honey, the only thing I don't have is guilt. Sit yourselves down. I'll bring you the sampler and a couple of specials. Finn, you want a double?"

"Always," I said. "Thank you, ma'am."

Brie plopped into the booth and immediately started laying out her notepad, phone, and a stack of Post-Its like she might have to take depositions mid-meal. I watched her for a minute, just absorbing the kinetic energy that seemed to buzz off her skin, her hands never still. Even after everything she'd survived, she could still turn a room electric.

I hated to bring it up, but the thoughts of last night had me twisted into knots. That dream was like a storm rolling through the room. The way she'd kicked, thrashed, and screamed words that made little sense was unsettling. She'd bitten my bicep so hard she'd left a bruise the size of an egg. And the fact that she'd remembered none of the dream at all seemed so strange.

I took a swig of water, then tried to keep my tone casual. "So. Did you have flashes of the dream you had last night today?"

She paused from looking at her phone her brow furrowed. "I didn't. It's so weird. I remember feeling terrified, but nothing else. Guess it was no big deal, or I'd have remembered it."

I leaned forward, elbows on the table. "You were screaming, Brie."

That stopped her. She set the phone down, hands pressed flat on either side of the legal pad. "I don't remember, okay? I woke up. I was in bed; you were there; it was fine. I have shit to do. I can't afford to get sidetracked by a bad dream."

The words came out sharp, but I didn't let it bother me. "I'm not saying you can't handle it, Maverick. I just don't like waking up to you in a cold sweat, is all."

She exhaled, pinched the bridge of her nose. "I'm sorry. I just... every time I think about it, it slips away. Like, the more I try to remember, the less there is. It's just this feeling. Like something terrible happened in that dream that my mind doesn't want me to remember. So I figure I'm better off not trying so hard to remember it, ya know?"

I reached across and squeezed her wrist. "That makes sense sweetheart. I don't want you to think about it if it could cause you more pain. That's the last thing I want for you. I want to carry all the things you can't carry; that's all."

She smiled, the first real smile since we'd sat down. "I know. That's why I haven't lost my mind yet."

Pearl appeared with drinks and two plates the size of hubcaps. The sampler was a pile of hushpuppies, fried pickles, and something that might once have been a jalapeno, battered and deep-fried to oblivion.

"You're a saint," Brie said, popping a hushpuppy in her mouth.

"I'm an enabler, darling," Pearl said, then fixed her gaze on me. "You keeping this one out of trouble?"

I shrugged. "She's a tornado unto herself ma'am. I just try to build a fence around it."

Pearl snorted. "Just don't let her talk you into one of her 'health kicks.' I've heard she tried to sub out the mashed potatoes for kale; I had to stage an intervention."

"Never again," Brie vowed, solemn as a priest.

Pearl leaned in, voice dropping to a whisper. "I see you two've been on the rumor circuit. Harper says your gallery's all but ready for the big time."

Brie flushed, then tucked a piece of hair behind her ear. "I don't know about that. But it's nice to finally be doing something that matters."

Pearl nodded, then added. "Well darlin', getting yourself mated to the most eligible man this side of the Red River was a pretty big get if you ask me." She slapped Brie on her shoulder and sauntered off to the next table to terrorize another patron.

"Well, she's got me there," Brie said, and I laughed.

"I'm the one who won the prize in that deal," I said. "You improved my standing by about a hundred percent." I squeezed her hand.

We ate for a while in silence, just listening to the hum of the bar, the low twang of a country ballad on the jukebox, the rattle of ice in the cheap plastic glasses. I felt the tension start to drain out of me, replaced by the warmth of being somewhere I belonged.

After a minute, Brie wiped her fingers on a napkin and said, "Hey, Finn?"

"Yeah?"

"Do you think I should try medication? For the sleep thing?"

I weighed my answer. "If you want. But I think you just need to let your mind go a little. Maybe less caffeine after three p.m."

She laughed, but it didn't quite reach her eyes. "I can try."

She looked around the bar, then leaned in. "My mom used to make this thing—hot toddy, but with, like, every herb in the cabinet. You ever hear of that?"

"Sure," I said. "Pearl probably has a family recipe. Want me to ask?"

Brie nodded. "I think I'd rather drink witch's brew than pop pills."

I flagged Pearl down as she walked by with a tray of chicken-fried steaks. "Ma'am, you got a hot toddy recipe? Something strong enough to put down a wolf?"

Pearl grinned, wiped her hands on her apron. "Honey, I got a recipe that'll put a full-grown Alpha in a coma. Gimme five minutes, I'll have you a to-go jar."

Brie lit up, more at the idea of a homemade remedy than any actual belief in its efficacy. I think it was the gesture, the continuity—someone from here helping her feel like she belonged.

While we waited, she rattled off more plans for the opening. Who was coming, who wasn't, which reporter from Amarillo would try to make her gallery look like a "meth den with a taste for abstract." I watched her, listened, let myself be hypnotized by the way her hands moved, the cadence of her voice.

Pearl returned with a Mason jar filled with golden liquid. She unscrewed the lid, added a lemon wedge, then tightened it back up. "Thirty seconds in the microwave before bed. Sip it slow. Don't call me if you end up howling at the moon."

Brie took the jar with reverence, cradling it in her hands. "Thank you, Pearl. You're an angel."

"Just don't tell the local priest," Pearl said. "He might make you confess to being a liar."

As we got up to leave, I paid the tab and threw a ten in the tip jar. Brie grabbed my hand, the warmth of her palm a promise.

"You know I love you, right?" She said, voice low.

I looked her dead in the eye. "I know. But I like hearing it, anyway."

We walked out into the night, the jar of hot toddy gleaming like a lantern in her grip. I helped her into the truck, then slid behind the wheel, feeling for the first time all week like maybe, just maybe, things were going to be alright.

But then I glanced at Brie, and saw the way she clutched that jar, white-knuckled, like it was the last thing keeping her together.

And I wondered how long we could keep pretending that love was enough to save us from whatever was waiting in the dark.

Back home, I did everything in my power to keep Brie from unraveling. The minute we crossed the threshold, I insisted she go straight to the bedroom and get out of her day clothes. I hung up her jacket, collected the mason jar toddy, and told her I'd holler when the bath was ready. I wanted to fuck her so bad it made my teeth hurt, but I'd made her a promise: tonight was about rest, not ravaging.

I ran the tub long and hot, pouring in half a bottle of the artisanal bath soak I'd picked up from the farmers' market last Saturday—smelled like cedar and bluebonnet honey, the kind of scent that clung to skin for hours after. I flicked the switch on the little Bluetooth speaker we kept by the sink. Out poured the sound of distant thunderstorms, heavy on the rain, just enough bass in the thunder to trick your heartbeat into slowing down.

I set out a towel for her, extra thick and plush, and lit one of the candles from her stash—a white, jar thing that smelled like exotic flowers.

She appeared in the doorway, hair twisted up, face scrubbed bare. There was something so naked about her in that moment, not just the way she was wearing my old t-shirt and nothing else, but the way she looked at me like I was the only thing holding her together. She took in the scene, the effort, and said, "You are absolutely precious, Finn Walsh."

"I'm a man of many talents," I said, and kissed her on the forehead. "Now get in before I toss you in."

She grinned, dropped the shirt, and slid into the bath. She hissed at the heat for a second, then leaned back, eyes going heavy-lidded. "Feels like a crime to be this spoiled."

"It's called being loved," I told her, as I handed her the toddy already the perfect temp, and shut the door, giving her the privacy she claimed she needed but never actually wanted.

While she soaked, I stripped the bed and put on the "hotel sheets"—the Egyptian cotton ones she'd insisted we buy after one night in a Dallas Four Seasons. I even remembered to turn on the electric blanket, so the bed would be warm when she crawled into it. By the time she came out, wrapped in a towel with the ends of her hair still wet, I was sitting on the edge of the mattress waiting for her.

She crawled in next to me, still smelling of honey and rain, and nudged my thigh with her foot. "Are you gonna give me a massage, or do I have to beg?"

I smiled. "Babe, you never have to beg. But it's more fun when you do."

She rolled her eyes, then sprawled belly-down on the sheets, arms folded under her head. I warmed my hands by rubbing them together, then started at her shoulders, working my thumbs into the knots that always built up just below her neck. Her skin was warm and damp, and she hummed with every hard press, the sound somewhere between a purr and a sigh.

I worked my way down her back, slow and methodical, focusing on each muscle like it owed me money. When I reached her lower back, she arched, shifting her hips and making it impossible not to notice the swell of her ass, the way her thighs parted ever so slightly in invitation. I dug my thumbs into the tops of her glutes, working the tension loose.

I kept kneading her, working my way down her legs, kneading her calves, then circling back up to start again. The second time I made it to her ass, I slipped my hand between her legs, cupping her mound and feeling the heat radiate off her.

She pressed her hips into the mattress, moaning softly. "Mmm, Finn."

"Just making sure you're relaxed," I teased, but my cock was so hard it was an act of God not to climb on top of her and take her right there.

Instead, I kept my word to myself. I focused on her, on the way her body responded to every touch, every press. When I couldn't take it anymore, I rolled her onto her back, spreading her legs and settling between them. She looked up at me, eyes glazed, lips parted, and for a second all I could do was stare at her—this beautiful, broken, perfect woman who'd let me be the one to put her back together.

I bent down, kissing her belly, her hips, the insides of her thighs. She was already wet, slick and hot and eager for me, and I licked her slowly, savoring every taste. She bucked against my mouth, hands tangled in my hair, her moans getting louder, more desperate. I kept her on the edge for what felt like an eternity, then finally let her come, her whole body tensing under my tongue.

I didn't stop. I licked and sucked, pushing her through a second orgasm, this one leaving her limp and panting, her hands falling away from my head. When she was done, I cleaned her up with a warm cloth, then pulled her into my arms and tucked the blanket around us both.

She fell asleep almost instantly, her head on my chest, her breath warm and even. I lay there, staring at the ceiling, feeling the last of the tension slip away. For the first time in days, I let myself relax.

I must have dozed off, because the next thing I knew, it was deep night—the kind of dark that made the world feel hollowed out and abandoned. The clock read 2:37. Brie was still asleep, breathing steady, but something was wrong. I could smell it before I heard it.

There was a tang in the air, sharp and metallic, like a fresh cut or a struck match. It didn't belong. I sat up, sniffed the air, but couldn't place it. A second later, Brie started to whimper.

It began as a low moan, barely audible, then built into a soft, desperate chant. "No, no, no. You won't take him from me. You won't—" Her voice broke on the last word, and she started to sob, fists clenched tight in the sheets.

I shook her gently. "Brie. Babe. You're dreaming."

She gasped awake, eyes wild, and for a second she didn't recognize me. Then she slumped against my chest, shaking. "It was... it was so real."

"What happened?"

She shook her head, wiped at her face. "Can't remember. Just... darkness. And then I thought I'd lost you."

I held her close, stroking her hair, whispering nonsense until the trembling stopped. After a minute, she drifted off again, her breath ragged but settling.

But I didn't sleep. I lay there, staring into the dark, the smell of blood and steel still hanging in the air. I'd never heard of a wolf who could bring a scent back from their dreams.

Whatever it was, it wasn't done with us.

And I'd be damned if I let it take her away.

The next morning, I got Brie up and out the door before the sun had fully risen. She'd barely touched her toast and was in a foul mood, not her usual

"I hate mornings, kill me now" routine, but the tight-lipped, no-jokes kind of bad. I left her at the gallery with a kiss and a promise to pick her up at five. She gave me a look that said she wasn't sure she'd last until noon.

I went home and did what any rational, not-at-all-paranoid man would do: I spent an hour crawling around the baseboards and HVAC vents of our house, sniffing for gas leaks or anything metallic, checking the circuit breaker for shorts, running every tap and drain just in case. Nothing. The place was clean, almost aggressively so. The only thing I found was the lingering scent of her on the sheets, mixed with cedar and a memory of sweat.

After exhausting every possible home hazard, I gave up and went out to the pasture. A section of barbed wire was down along the west fence, probably knocked over by one of our idiot steers trying to reach the greener grass on the other side. I loaded the tools into the bed of the truck and set out, knowing the job would take half the day at least.

The labor was pure, simple, and honest. The only things that mattered were the heft of the post driver, the way the wire bit my palms through the gloves, and the burn in my shoulders with each swing. I let my mind go blank, except for the occasional intrusive thought about last night: the sharp tang of metal, the panic in Brie's voice as she fought her invisible enemy.

It made no sense, any of it. But sense was a luxury. I'd spent most of my life making do with the scraps of logic fate tossed my way.

The job took longer than it should have, mostly because I kept stopping to watch the clouds roll in. There was a storm on the horizon, a thick blue wall with the promise of lightning in the air. My wolf always got restless before a storm, and today was no exception. I could feel the hair on my arms standing up, taste the ozone on my tongue.

I hammered the last post into place and wiped the sweat off my face with a bandana. My hands were raw, my shirt soaked through, but I didn't care. I'd take honest pain over the ache in my head any day.

On the drive back, I turned the problem over and over: Was I going to tell Bronc? The man was my Alpha, and my friend, but there were things you just didn't share. Especially when it made you sound weak. No one ever said that out loud, but it was the rule. If you couldn't handle your mate's nightmares, you didn't deserve her.

But then I thought about what Pearl had said. How Brie wasn't like the others. How she needed more than just a strong arm or a quick tongue. She needed someone who'd stand between her and the whole damn world, even if the fight was inside her own head.

I resolved right then that if tonight was anything like last night, I'd go to Bronc. I'd ask for help. I didn't care if it made me look soft. I cared about her.

By the time I got back to the house, I had just enough time for a quick shower and a change of clothes before heading to the gallery. I didn't want to show up looking like I'd been chewed on by the ranch, but I also didn't want to be late. Brie hated waiting.

I parked across the street, took a deep breath, and walked in. The gallery was a hive of activity—two workers were painting the trim along the east wall, another was setting up tables in the back for the opening. And there, at the far end of the main room, was Brie.

She was perched halfway up a stepladder, adjusting a massive land-scape painting on the wall. Lysander was at the foot of the ladder, hands on her hips to steady her as she leaned out, tacking a label into place.

I saw red.

It was irrational; I knew that. The man was harmless. But there was something about the way his fingers dug into her waist, the way he looked up at her with that easy, practiced smile. I wanted to rip him off the ladder and toss him through the plate-glass window.

Lysander noticed me first. He gave a little wave, then said something to Brie, who looked down and beamed.

She scrambled down the ladder, dropped the hammer onto the table, and hurried over. "You're early," she said, eyes bright.

I shrugged. "Missed you. And I wanted to see the progress."

She looped an arm through mine, guiding me toward the back office. Lysander trailed after, all grace and detachment, but his eyes never left us.

Once we were in private, Brie hugged me hard, burying her face in my chest. I held her, breathing her in, the jealousy already fading.

"Everything okay?" I asked.

She nodded against me. "Better now." Then, quietly: "Thank you. For last night. And for not making a big deal out of it."

I squeezed her. "You don't have to thank me. It's what we do."

She pulled back, smiling. "Lysander wants us to come to dinner tonight. Celebratory, he says. Are you okay with that?"

I considered it. The smart move would be to decline, plead exhaustion or an early morning. But the thought of leaving her alone with him made my skin crawl. So I nodded.

"Yeah," I said. "Let's do it."

She grinned, then stood on tiptoes to kiss me. "You're the best."

As we left the office, Lysander was waiting by the door. He smiled at Brie, then shot me a look—something like respect, something like a challenge.

I matched it.

We walked out together, the three of us, into the late afternoon sun. The storm was closer now; the wind picking up, electricity crawling over the skin of my arms.

I didn't know what was coming. But whatever it was, I'd face it head-on. For her.

Even if it killed me.

CHAPTER 17

BRIE

There's something about Dairyville's "authentic" Tex-Mex that always made me feel like I was participating in a low-budget reality show. Maybe it was the way the chairs wobbled, or how the chili-lime air clung to every inch of exposed skin. Maybe it was that the restaurant—a converted car wash—was just loud enough to drown out most attempts at eavesdropping, but not so loud that I couldn't feel every conversational power play reverberate through the Formica table.

Gunner and I walked in a few steps behind Lysander, who was still dressed in what he'd worn to work at the gallery; a linen shirt, tan straight-leg slacks, and loafers without socks. The hostess, who doubled as the bartender, did a little double take at his accent, which Lysander immediately cranked to eleven as he requested "the table with the best view, darling, preferably near a mural." He threw in a wink that almost upended her tray. She led us to a booth under the painted eyes of a Dia de los Muertos mask where the bench cushions were sun-bleached and squeaked when you sat.

Gunner took the outside seat, arm slung over the backrest, exuding a calm that felt more like the stillness before a tornado. I slid in next to him, with Lysander opposite. He immediately started fussing with the menu, then set it down with a sigh. "You know what? I'll just ask them to bring whatever the chef recommends. That's the only way to truly experience the local cuisine."

He flagged down the waitress, who, to her credit, did not roll her eyes, and ordered enough appetizers to feed a football team: besides the chips and salsa, which were already on the table; he ordered three kinds of queso, and "as much guacamole as you can legally serve." He added, "and a pitcher of the house margarita—unless you boys can't handle your tequila?"

Gunner's smile didn't reach his eyes. "I'll stick to beer. Got work in the morning."

"A man of responsibility," Lysander purred, nodding with mock solemnity. "I admire that."

The chips were light, salty, and crispy. Lysander dipped a chip, crunched it, and closed his eyes in theatrical ecstasy. "Heaven. Actual heaven. I've been in Texas a couple of weeks, and I'm already addicted to this stuff. No wonder you people all look like you could wrestle a bear."

"I've wrestled worse," Gunner said, voice low.

"Now, now, let's not flex at the dinner table," I said, nudging Gunner's thigh under the table.

Lysander grinned, flicked his gaze to me, and then, as if he'd just remembered why we were here, produced a folder from his slim bag and slid it across. "First things first, business. I've made a schedule for the install and previewed the press packet. You're going to die when you see the Amarillo Reporter's write-up. I think they called you a 'provocateur.' Are you prepared for local stardom, Brie?"

"Am I prepared?" I spread my hands. "I've had years of being ignored and/or mocked. Stardom would be a nice change of pace."

He poured some salsa into a little bowl, then said, "They really do adore you. Inez is terrified, by the way. She thinks you'll outshine her at her own show."

I cracked up. "Inez is my new painting idol. She could outshine the sun."

Gunner tapped the folder, then opened it, flipping through the pages. "You got numbers for head count? The lot behind the gallery's not big, but I can get us overflow at the pharmacy."

Lysander's eyebrow shot up. "See? This is why you're the brains of the operation. I'd forgotten about parking. Maybe a valet?"

"Probably better to block off the street, if the city'll let us." Gunner looked to me. "You want me to call the Chief?"

I nodded, surprised he'd even think of that. "Yes, please. If we have anyone important coming, the last thing we need is a parking war outside."

"I got prospects who can valet for you." Gunner told us.

Lysander's eyes got as big as saucers. He'd never seen Gunner in his cut. "You're in a motorcycle gang?"

Gunner rolled his eyes. "It's actually a club, not a gang. You don't wanna catch anybody in that club hearing you call us a gang either. You might get your pretty teeth rearranged."

Lysander swallowed hard. "Of course, sir. I'd not want to offend anyone."

"Anyway. Whoever we'd use to valet would be dressed in appropriate attire for a high-toned event like Brie's gallery opening."

Lysander nodded. Then he leaned in, and for a second his entire persona sharpened. "You have no idea how much I appreciate your logistical genius, Finn. Most of my clients just throw me to the wolves." He giggled. He had no idea how close he *was* to wolves.

Gunner didn't laugh, but he didn't growl, either. Progress.

The queso arrived. Lysander dunked a chip and held it up. "If I gain ten pounds this week, I'll die happy." He turned to me. "You know, you could easily be doing this in Houston, or Santa Fe. Why stay here?"

I didn't want to look at Gunner when I answered. "Because this is my home."

Lysander smiled. "That's the best answer. I hope you don't mind, but I've already set up a call with a couple of buyers. One is coming from Santa Fe, actually, just for your opening."

I choked on a chip. "What? Why didn't you..."

He raised a hand. "Surprise! It's more fun this way. And if you sell out opening night, you'll have to start painting more things for me to sell!"

The waitress arrived with our entrees—enchiladas swimming in red sauce, a carne asada plate, and a salad for Lysander "because I'm civilized, darling." She refilled our drinks and vanished before Gunner could object to the pile of peppers he hadn't ordered.

We ate in relative silence for a while, except for Lysander, who never stopped talking. He told stories about art school in Berlin ("It was like being in a cult, but everyone was prettier"), about his mother's insane collection of Italian glassware, about how he once met Damien Hirst and found him "shockingly dull, like a tax accountant who got lost on his way to the Tate Modern." I laughed at every one, because it was impossible not to. Gunner only smiled when directly addressed, and even then it looked like the effort might break his jaw in half.

Eventually, Lysander turned to me and said, "So, are you ready for the big night? Do you have an outfit? A statement piece?"

"I have a dress," I said, "and the world's most boring pair of heels. And I thought my 'statement piece' was supposed to be the art."

He rolled his eyes. "Darling, the dress is the art. The rest is just context."

He launched into a monologue about the necessity of fashion as emotional armor, and for once I felt like maybe I'd been missing out by never having a gay best friend. He suggested a "scarlet lip, but not too matte," and told Gunner, "you should try a blazer, or at least iron your shirt, for God's sake." I thought Gunner might combust, but he only grunted, kept eating. He had no idea how much Gunner was worth. Money just wasn't the be-all, end-all for him.

The check came. Lysander swept it up before anyone else could move. "It's a tax write-off," he insisted. "If I'm going to play gallery daddy, I'm going to do it right."

Gunner tried to protest, but Lysander silenced him with a wave. "Besides, if I let you pay, you'll ruin my reputation. People expect me to be a little insufferable."

We stood to leave, Lysander carrying the folder, me with a takeout box, and Gunner—ever the gentleman—holding the door. Outside, the storm had moved in, thunder rumbling over the flat blacktop.

At the curb, Lysander turned to Gunner, extended a hand. "Thank you for coming, and for not killing me. I like you, Finn. You're not nearly as scary as you look."

Gunner shook his hand a little too firmly, but managed a "You're alright, Lysander."

Then Lysander turned to me, and without hesitation, leaned in and air-kissed both my cheeks. "You are a star, Brie. Never let anyone tell you different. I won't be at the gallery tomorrow. Sadly, Mother insists I fly into Boston for a family event. But I'll be back Sunday morning."

He stepped into his waiting Uber—a Prius with a pride flag decal—and vanished into the rain.

Gunner stared after him for a second, then looked down at me, jaw working side to side. "Do people actually do that? The kiss thing?"

I shrugged. "I guess they do. Maybe it's an East Coast thing."

He muttered something under his breath, then took my hand. His grip was tight, grounding, as if he was anchoring me to this moment, this place, this small-town reality where nothing was ever just what it seemed.

"I like *you* better," I said, voice small.

He grunted. "Good. Because I'm not learning that cheek-kiss bullshit."

We walked to the truck, thunder rolling in the distance, the rain spitting sideways across the hood. Gunner opened the passenger door, waited for me to climb in, then circled to the driver's side.

As we pulled out of the lot, I looked back at the restaurant, its neon sign flickering in the storm, and thought: this is my life now. Art, awkward dinners, storms that never quite break, and a man beside me who'd burn down the world to keep me safe.

I wouldn't have it any other way.

The drive home was a whole geography of silence.

Gunner kept one hand locked at twelve o'clock on the steering wheel, knuckles white as pickled onions. The other hand hovered between the shifter and the radio dial, but he never touched either. The roads outside town were long, low, and black—striped with reflective paint that caught the high beams in eerie slashes. Every fence post was a blur of rain-lacquered silver, the fields beyond shivering with the first wind of a coming storm.

He didn't say much, not at first. He let the engine do the talking; the faint rattle of loose gravel, the heavy thunk of a tire meeting a pothole. The air in the cab was thick with the ghost of Lysander's cologne, or maybe just the aftertaste of all those unsaid words. I wanted to break the silence, but the only thing I could think to say was, "You okay?" and I was pretty sure he'd lie.

So instead I watched the lightning stutter along the far horizon, counting the seconds between each white-hot strike and the slow roll of thunder behind it. I curled my fingers in my lap and tried not to fidget. Gunner never took his eyes off the road.

When he finally spoke, it was almost a relief. "You got a lot on your plate, Maverick. I just want to make sure you're not burnin' out."

I let out a shaky breath. "I'm not. I mean, I am, but not in a way that's going to break me. I'm... okay. Or I will be."

He nodded, jaw working. "You ever wish you could just turn it all off? The work, the planning, the people?"

I didn't even have to think. "Not really. It's the nothing that scares me." I stared out the window at the endless fields. "If I'm not moving, I start to feel like I'm disappearing. Like I was never really here at all."

He digested that, the way he did with every hard truth I handed him. "Guess we're opposites, then," he said, voice soft. "I could sit in the same patch of dirt for a hundred years and never get bored."

I smiled, reaching for his hand. I found it, squeezed. He squeezed back, and for a second, it was enough.

The rest of the drive passed in that hush. The storm crept closer; the old truck rocked in the wind. At some point, he started humming along to the radio—a low, familiar country ballad—and the sound smoothed out the sharp edges in my chest.

When we got home, the world felt wrapped in cotton. Rain tapped the porch roof, steady and slow, and the lights inside glowed yellow against the night. Gunner killed the engine, the cut through the silence. "You coming in, or you want to sit a while?"

I thought about it. "I want to be where you are." Because it was was the first thing that came to mind, and because it was true.

He smiled, just a little. "That's easy, then."

We walked in together, shoulders brushing, the comfort of routine slotting over us like a soft quilt. I dropped my bag by the door and toed off my boots. Gunner hung his hat on the hook and grabbed me by the wrist, spinning me into a gentle hug.

I buried my face in his chest. I could smell the leather of his belt, the soap he used (always the same, always the cheap kind), and underneath it all, the clean spice of his skin. He held me there, arms around my waist, chin resting on top of my head. For a long moment, there was nothing but the sound of our breathing, in and out, the perfect rhythm of two animals content to be alive.

We changed for bed in the low-watt bathroom light. I watched him move, the solid lines of his back, the way he took care with the buttons on his shirt, how he folded his jeans before setting them aside. I pulled on one of his old t-shirts and brushed my teeth with the high-quality toothpaste he always bought; you only get one set of teeth after all. I caught a glimpse of myself in the mirror, hair wild, face pale and splotched, but my eyes—my eyes looked brighter than they had in years.

He met me in the bedroom, already under the covers, reading from a dog-eared paperback he kept on the nightstand. He set it aside when I climbed in, pulled me close, and tucked the blanket around my shoulders. The wind rattled the windowpanes; the rain had picked up, drumming a slow rhythm against the siding.

I curled into his chest, soaking up the warmth. He traced lazy circles on my back, fingertips rough and calloused, but gentle as rain. I closed my eyes, let the comfort of him wash away the last clinging shreds of doubt.

It was in that soft darkness, with his heart thumping steady under my ear, that I started thinking about all the ways he cared for me. Not the big, loud gestures—though he had those, too—but the tiny, invisible kindnesses. How there was always coffee waiting for me in the morning, just the way I liked it, even if he had to set an alarm to get up before me. How the fridge was always stocked with my favorite drinks, the lemon seltzer and the weird green juice I'd become addicted to in college. How he'd started bringing home fresh flowers—wild ones from the ranch, or the occasional grocery store bouquet—and set them in an old glass jar on the kitchen table, because he knew I liked color in the house. And how he'd noticed, without ever being told, that I was almost out of shampoo, and had driven all the way to Amarillo to buy the brand I used because the store in town never carried it.

The realization hit me so hard it made my throat ache. For the first time in my life, I felt completely, stupidly safe. Cared for. Loved in a way that didn't require me to perform or impress or become someone else. Just loved.

The tears came out of nowhere—hot and silent and embarrassing as hell.

He must have felt me shaking, because he rolled onto his side, cradling my face in his big, warm hand. "Hey." His thumb brushed my cheek. "Talk to me."

I tried to laugh, but it came out a wet, hiccupy mess. "I'm sorry. I'm not sad. I just…" I broke off, wiped my eyes with the back of my hand. "I just can't believe this is my life. That I get to have this. You. Us. I didn't think it was possible."

He looked at me like I'd told him the secret to immortality. "You deserve all of it, Brie. More than anyone I know."

I shook my head. "You don't get it. I was always the fuck-up. Even when I was doing everything right, I felt like I was always one step away from blowing it all up. I thought that's just who I was. But with you, it's like—like the world finally makes sense."

He kissed the corner of my mouth, the salt of my tears. "You're my mate, Maverick. There's nothing you could do to fuck this up. Even if you tried. You show the world the fighter you've always thought you had to be. And yes, you can be that bratty little girl that I love. But I see the tenderness beneath it all. I see it in the beauty of your art. That's what is in your soul. Two things can be true at the same time. "

I laughed, because I knew he meant it. "I'll try to balance those two better."

He grinned, pulling me closer. "I'm serious. I thank the Goddess every damn day that she gave you to me. Even if I don't say it."

I buried my face in his neck, breathing him in. The mate bond pulsed between us—warmth, light, something that felt almost holy. For the first time in a long time, I let myself lean into it, let it hold me up instead of fighting to carry it alone.

"I love you," I whispered, soft as the storm outside.

He pressed his lips to my hair, my forehead, my cheek. "I love you, too, little girl. More than anything."

And just like that, I was whole.

I drifted off to sleep, the thunder a lullaby, his arms a fortress. For a few precious hours, the world outside could do whatever it wanted. In here, I was exactly where I belonged.

The sound of rain on the skylights was a relentless white noise that started in the ears and ended in the bones. It was the kind of Saturday where the hours dissolved, where the storm pinned everything in place and all you could do was survive the deluge. The gallery had become a mausoleum of unfinished dreams and the smell of wet paint.

I wandered through the main floor, arms folded tight across my chest. The temporary walls were only half-built, metal braces sticking out like broken ribs, protective mats on the ground squelching under every step. Every surface was covered in fine drywall dust; even the exit signs looked like they were losing a slow fight with time. The humidity made the air taste like soggy cotton.

I didn't know why I insisted on working today. Maybe because there was no one to talk to, no one to ask me how I was, no one to notice if I stood in the middle of the gallery and screamed until my voice cracked. I'd sent the contractor crew home at noon because they were all but finished with everything. Lysander was in Boston. Gunner had gone with Wrecker's help on a short cattle haul; he texted that he'd be home by six.

So it was just me, the storm, and the unholy pile of paperwork that refused to shrink no matter how many hours I fed it.

I took the long way up to the office—through the darkened lobby, past the wall of still-unhung canvases, up the metal stairs where each footstep echoed like a hammer blow. The glass-walled "penthouse" looked out over the whole gallery, every window streaked and rattling with the rain. From up here, the world outside was just a blur of gray and motion.

I slumped into the cushioned office chair and pulled the laptop toward me. The spreadsheet glared back on my large screen monitor, full of notes and reminders and cells highlighted in angry, anxious colors. I rubbed my eyes, scrolled through the numbers, and tried not to think about how I couldn't remember entering half of them. My body felt like it was made of old bread; every joint was stiff, every breath sticky in my lungs.

I rolled my shoulders, cracked my neck, tried to blink the fatigue away. I'd been fighting it all day—the slow pull of sleep, the leaden sense that the real world was a few feet behind me and catching up fast. I couldn't keep my focus; the numbers on the screen squirmed, doubling and then snapping back into place.

The HVAC kicked on. The hum was deeper than usual, more of a shudder. It vibrated through the glass walls, rattling the pens in their cup, making the shadows twitch. Thunder rolled overhead, low and predatory.

My wolf stirred in my gut, uneasy.

I looked up, half expecting to see someone standing in the gallery below. Empty, except for the shifting shapes the rain made on the polished floors. I exhaled, looked back at the spreadsheet, and tried to concentrate.

But then the air changed.

The temperature dropped, sharp as sleet. Something in the pressure—an old, animal sense—told me I was being watched. The hair on the back of my neck stood up. I could feel it: the weight of eyes, the steady, hungry gaze of something that did not belong here.

I reached for my coffee mug, hand shaking a little, and the spreadsheet flickered. The pixels rippled, like a rock had been thrown into the digital pond. For a split second, the cursor moved by itself—skittered from cell to cell, then stopped dead center on my name. I stared, willing myself to laugh, but the sound stuck in my throat.

A breath touched the back of my neck. Not a breeze, not the hiss of the vent—an actual, unmistakable exhale. Warm. Human, almost. Then a low, distant chuckle. Like a radio tuned to a dead channel, but the voice came through, anyway.

I whipped around so fast my chair nearly toppled. Nothing. Just the office, empty except for me and the hum of the storm. I stood, fists balled at my sides, and scanned every inch of glass, every reflection. My heart was going so hard I thought it might shake itself apart.

Then, as I turned back to the monitor, I saw it: a reflection in the corner of the darkened screen. Just for a second—a dropped frame, a glitch—there was a tall, sharp figure at the office door. It was gone before I could fully register it. I whipped my gaze to the doorway. No one.

But the sense of wrongness only grew.

I pressed my palm to the glass wall, peered down at the gallery below. At first, I saw nothing. But then a shape moved—subtle, a smudge of deeper black drifting between the unfinished walls. It was walking. It stopped by a canvas, leaned in as if to study the work, then melted into the gloom.

"Fuck this," I whispered and started for the stairs.

But as I reached the top step, the voice came again, right behind my ear. This time, it was perfectly clear.

"Soon."

I turned, heart in my throat, and for a second I thought I saw a shadow stretched against the glass wall. Not a person, not a thing—but the absence of both. My stomach cramped. My wolf shrank into the smallest, coldest place inside me.

I stumbled down the stairs, every step jarring my teeth. The gallery was empty, silent except for the wild percussion of rain on the roof. I forced myself to walk the perimeter, check every exit, every room, every broom closet. Nothing. Not even a hint of footprints on the mats.

When I got back to the office, I realized I'd left my phone behind. I grabbed it off the desk, and as I did, I caught sight of my forearm—streaked with a black smear, like soot or ash. I wiped it on my shirt, and it disappeared. For a moment, I wondered if I'd imagined it, if this was all just a side effect of too much caffeine and not enough sleep.

But the terror wouldn't leave.

I sat back down, breathing slow, trying to steady my pulse. The rain outside sounded like it was trying to carve its way into the building. My hands shook as I checked the laptop—everything normal, no sign of the flicker, no weird cursor movement. The spreadsheet was right where I'd left it, my name highlighted in calm, professional blue.

I looked out the glass wall again. The gallery was as it should be. Empty. Still.

But I knew I wasn't alone.

My first instinct was to call Gunner, to hear his voice, to let it anchor me back to reality. But I couldn't bear the thought of him hearing the fear in mine.

Instead, I typed out a text: *You coming soon?*

A minute later, he replied: *Wasn't planning to come for a couple hours. You okay?*

I looked at the empty gallery, the storm outside, the glass that could shatter with the right pressure.

I typed: *I just miss you.*

He sent back a heart emoji, then: *I'll head over now. Lock the doors. Don't open for anyone but me.*

I watched the dots pulse in the reply field, his presence almost a force in itself. My wolf uncurled a little, enough for me to breathe.

I shut the laptop, wiped my hands on my jeans, and turned on every light in the gallery.

Outside, the thunder came closer, rolling in like a tide.

Whatever was out there, I knew it would find me.

But not tonight.

Not if I could help it.

Chapter 18

Gunner

The tech cave was the back room of Wrecker's ranch-style house. He had a wall of server racks that hummed like angry bees. If Dairyville had a missile command center, this was it. The room smelled like gourmet coffee, dirty novels, and genius-level intrigue. If you didn't know better, you'd assume he and Parker lived in there. And with the exception of their playroom in the basement; you'd be right.

I'd followed Wrecker back here after he helped with a short cattle run to a small ranch on the other side of pack territory. Now he was at his desk, hunched over three screens, two of which displayed enough scrolling code to induce an epileptic seizure. The third screen showed the live feed from the ranch's outer perimeter, which at this hour was just a vulture squabbling with a crow over some dead varmint. He didn't even look up.

"Got time to do some snoopin'?" I asked, dropping onto the battered rolling chair that creaked like a dying goat.

"Always," he grunted.

The dude never slept, I swear. "You up all night again?"

"Yup," he said. "Had to push out a firmware update for the Council's tracker nodes. They can't find their own dicks without my code." He finally looked at me, those glacier-gray eyes as cold and flat as always. "Brie's okay?"

"She's thriving. Got her hands full with the gallery grand opening. Thanks for asking."

He snorted. "You never ask for help unless you're really fucked."

I grunted, because he wasn't wrong.

Parker popped her head through the doorway, hair still wet from a shower. She wore yoga pants, a tank top that said "NOT YOUR BABY GIRL." Her wild pink and brunette hair made her look both smarter and more dangerous than any human had a right to. She carried two mugs—both black, both filled with the kind of coffee that you get in those fancy-schmancy coffee shops.

She set one down in front of me, the other in front of Wrecker, then curled up on an overstuffed couch under the window. "Afternoon, Finn," she said, voice sleepy like she had just woken up from an afternoon nap.

"Thanks, Wren," I said. She grinned at the nickname.

Wrecker sipped his coffee and, without even a glance at Parker, said, "You need me to run that check?"

I nodded. "Yeah. I want everything we can get on Lysander Hale. And don't skimp."

He typed one-handed, without looking. The man could probably write code in his sleep.

Parker, ever the gossip, perked up. "Who's Lysander Hale? That's an amazing name. Is he a vampire?"

I laughed. "He wishes."

Wrecker didn't smile, but his fingers danced faster. "Art dealer. Out of Boston. Works with Brie's gallery. Clean as a goddamn whistle, but let's see what's under the surface."

Parker made a face. "You know, I once dated a guy who was obsessed with those murder podcasts. Always convinced that every new person was a serial killer."

"That's not far off," I said. "Except y'all can actually find out if they are."

She grinned. "If you want to know my criminal history, just ask."

Wrecker, not looking up, said, "Already did. You should be in jail."

"Fuck off," she said, but she was smiling. There was a weird tenderness between those two, like a pair of feral dogs who'd decided to share a bone. Speaking of dogs, about that time I heard the pet door flap crash open and the ugliest dog west of the Mississippi came bounding into the room.

Parker's voice immediately went into pet baby talk when she picked him up to cuddle him. "There's my good boy. So precious. Look! Finn's here!"

I swear the pooch winked at me. Made me grin.

I sipped the coffee. It was scalding and bitter and perfect and turned back to Wrecker. "So, what's the verdict on Hale?"

He shrugged. "Born in Foxboro. Trust fund baby, but smart enough not to piss it away. Degree in Art History from Princeton. Interned with Sotheby's. Partied like a motherfucker in college—there are pictures—but nothing nasty. Came out his sophomore year, parents were fine with it, big donors to every charity you can think of. After college, moved to Paris for a couple years, then went to work for his mommy's firm, Hale & Marrow in Boston. Company's clean. Personal life is boring as hell. Looks like his mom is overbearing, but not in a criminal way. Had several boyfriends, nothing serious."

Parker was scrolling through her phone. "He's really pretty," she said. "Like, almost too pretty."

Wrecker growled—a real, guttural thing. She looked up at him, grinned wider, and said, "Easy, big guy. I'm not going to run off with a pretty boy who likes boys from Boston."

He didn't answer, but I could feel the tension leak out of his frame. He was as territorial as any man I'd ever met, and twice as bad about hiding it.

I set my mug down. "So he's just a normal, overachieving, ex-frat bro with good skin and rich parents."

"Yep," Wrecker said. "Not a threat."

Parker smirked. "You're jealous. Admit it."

I shot her a look. "I'm not jealous of that guy. I just don't trust people who don't have any dirt."

She stretched, toes pointed like a ballet dancer's, and said, "Maybe he's just really good at hiding it."

Wrecker snorted. "Nobody's that good."

Parker glanced at me. "What's he doing in Dairyville, then? Slumming it?"

"Reppin' Brie's first artist for her opening exhibit." I felt the edge in my voice and tried to smooth it out. "I just want to make sure he's not going to make trouble."

Wrecker tapped on his keyboard, then turned the screen so I could see. It was a profile pic of Lysander, dressed in a tailored suit, hair perfect, smile so white it hurt the eyes. The dude looked like a Disney prince who'd just snorted the Kingdom's GDP. There was a photo of him arm-in-arm with a big foreign-looking guy, both holding champagne.

"See?" Parker said. "He's cute."

I leveled a finger at her. "Don't rile up the monster, Wren."

She held up both hands in mock surrender. "Just saying. I'm Team Gunner, anyway."

Wrecker shot me a sideways glance. "You want me to dig deeper? Could have some dirt off-books."

I shook my head. "Nah. If he's clean, he's clean. I just..." I trailed off, because the next words were going to sound petty as hell, but I said them anyway. "I just don't want him getting in Brie's head. She's been through enough."

Parker's expression softened. "She really loves you, you know."

"I know." I said. "I'd walk through fire for her."

I finished my coffee, stood, stretched. "Thanks for the recon. I owe you one."

Wrecker just nodded, already back in the code.

Parker hopped off the couch, followed me to the door. "Hey, Finn?"

"Yeah?"

She hesitated, then said, "If you need anything... like, if you need to talk, you can come to me. I know I'm not your usual type for that stuff, but I can listen."

I smiled, genuinely. "Thanks, Wren. I'll keep it in mind."

I was almost out the door when my phone buzzed. I fished it out, thumbed the screen. Text from Brie: *you coming soon?*

I started typing a reply when the mate bond shivered under my skin—a weird, electric unease, like the air right before a tornado drops. My heart rate spiked. The world went sharp-edged for a second. I re-read the text. On the surface, nothing alarming. But underneath, I could feel her—tight, anxious, scared. I typed: *Everything alright? You sound off.*

There was a pause. Then: *I just miss you.*

It was a lie. She was scared.

I pocketed the phone and forced a calm I didn't feel. "I better get going."

Parker nodded, reading the situation perfectly. "Tell her I said hi."

On the drive over, I had a death grip on the wheel. Every few seconds, I checked my phone in its dash cradle, waiting for Brie to reply with something that made sense. She didn't. The mate bond still vibrated in my head, a tuning fork stuck on anxious. My pulse wouldn't slow.

Ten miles out from Dairyville, my phone buzzed. Not a text, but a call. Bronc's name flashed on the screen, all-caps, no bullshit. I considered letting it roll to voicemail. But he'd know I saw it. And you didn't ghost the Alpha, not unless you wanted him at your front door with coffee and an awkward lecture about pack accountability.

I thumbed the speaker button, kept my eyes on the long, empty road. "Hey, Bronc."

He was in full leader mode, not wasting time. "You okay, Gunner? You been quiet since that little talk we had."

I grinned tight. "Just working. Brie's gallery opening is in a few days. She's running on caffeine and fumes. I'm wrangling cattle and playing support."

"Hell of a support job, son. I heard about the incident with the scaffold." Bronc's voice was like old whiskey—burned on the way down, but left you warmer for it. "I'm glad she's okay."

"Yeah." I let the word linger, the way you did when there was something else underneath.

Bronc wasn't fooled. "You wanna tell me what's eating you?"

I flexed my hands on the wheel, watched the town's water tower loom up through the drizzle. "Brie's been having nightmares. Bad ones. Couple nights ago it got damn bad."

"Post-trauma?" he asked.

I hesitated. "Don't know. At first, I thought it was just nerves. But it's more than that now. I can feel her fear through the bond." I left out the metallic smell. That part sounded crazy even to me.

Bronc was quiet for a beat. "She ever had nightmares before?"

"Not that I'm aware. The damnedest fucking thing is that she can't remember anything about them after she's awake. Which based on how she wakes up screaming and thrashing like hell itself is on her tail; I guess it's a good thing."

"Shit." He exhaled slow. "Listen. Opening night, there'll be a dozen of us in the crowd, not to mention extra security. Even Menace and Savannah are flying down for it. You got a full-court press on your side. And if it gets out of hand, you call me or Juliet. We'll sort it out."

I bit my cheek. "Juliet's coming? Even this close to...?"

He snorted. "She's seven months pregnant, Finn. Not dead. She bought some kind of fancy sequined maternity evening gown. And I'll be dressed up like a dignified Alpha. You gonna let me outshine you?"

I laughed finally. "Maybe I'll find a bolo tie and make you look under-dressed."

"Now you're talking." He paused, the mood lightening. "You and Brie need anything, you call. Day or night."

I meant to say thanks. Instead I blurted, "Bronc?"

"Yeah?"

"Did this happen to you? I mean the mate bond going off like a fire alarm?"

Bronc didn't answer right away. "When she disappeared last year. After I got her back and re-established our bond, one night she came up missing." He paused as though the memory had assaulted him. "She'd wandered out into the woods behind the house. She was still so fucking traumatized she got turned around and had no idea where she was. I felt her fear like a bolt of lightning through the bond and took off, letting that feeling guide me." He gave a small laugh. "She wasn't far from the house, but I'd never been so goddamn glad to see anyone when I saw her small frame sitting on a log bawling her eyes out. If you're feeling Brie's anxiety, it's because she needs you; and you'll be there for her too."

That hit deep, the way good advice does.

We hung up with a promise to see each other at the opening, and I turned onto Main. The gallery was the only building for three blocks lit up like a UFO landing. The entire town was dark—power outages were common in Dairyville when the rain got biblical—but Brie wisely had a backup generator installed just in case, and the place blazed with every bulb on the circuit.

I parked half on the curb and jogged to the front door. I used my key and opened the door. Inside, the warmth and light were almost enough to make me forget why I'd rushed over.

Almost.

Brie stood in the entryway, arms crossed over her chest, pacing a rut into the rain-protected hardwoods. Her eyes were red-rimmed, mascara smudged from earlier tears. The minute she saw me, she ran straight into my arms, burrowing her face in my chest.

"Hey, hey," I murmured. "You're okay. I'm here."

She shook, and it took her a while to steady enough to speak. "I—I saw something, Finn. I know it sounds stupid, but I think there's something wrong here."

I held her tighter. "Tell me what happened."

She pulled back, wiped her face, and started talking. Her words came fast, jagged. "I was in the office, doing RSVP stuff. I must have dozed off. But it wasn't sleep. I felt...watched. Like something was in the room with me, behind the glass. I looked up, and there was this—this shadow. And then it was gone, but I heard a voice. Right next to my ear. It said, 'Soon.'"

She shuddered, then looked up at me, eyes so wide and blue I felt it in my bones. "When I got up, I checked the gallery, but nothing. I even checked the doors, the bathroom, everywhere. It was just me. I locked myself in, turned on every light. But I keep feeling it. The air is wrong."

I smoothed her hair. "Maybe it was a dream. You said you were exhausted."

"I know what dreams are, Finn." The words came out sharp, brittle. "This wasn't that. I was awake. Or at least I thought I was."

I wanted to say something comforting. Something that would make sense of it. But the truth was, the last few days had knocked every certainty sideways. I'd never seen my mate so raw, so convinced she'd been touched by something she couldn't see. And my wolf was pacing the length of my chest, ears pricked for danger.

"Alright, sweet girl," I said, holding her at arm's length. "Here's what we're gonna do. We're gonna check every inch of this place together. But before we do, I'm gonna give the guys a call and see if they wanna meet at

Pearl's for dinner. Then we're gonna go have a sit-down with everyone and eat some good food and enjoy good company. How does that sound?"

She nodded, mouth set. "Anything sounds better than having to be alone in this building."

"You won't have to," I promised. I kissed her head and sent her to the restroom to clean her face and get herself ready to go.

I did a lap of the gallery, office, and back rooms. I checked the roof access, the stairwell, even the alley behind the dumpsters. Nothing. Not a single sign that anyone but us had been in the building.

Back in the main room, Brie watched the storm through the front windows, her hands jammed deep in her hoodie pockets. "You think I'm going nuts."

"Not even a little," I said. I pulled her into my arms, kissing her temple. "If you feel something's wrong, that's all I need to know."

She softened against me. "It's just... I wanted this to be my thing. My gallery. But now I'm afraid to be alone in it."

I didn't know what to say. I'd never believed in ghosts or things that go bump in the night. But I'd seen the way the world changed when you weren't looking—how easy it was for bad things to sneak in. And I wasn't going to let Brie face anything alone.

"Come on," I said. "Let's lock up, go to Pearl's, and eat something unhealthy."

She managed a smile, but it didn't reach her eyes.

We turned out all but the security lights, set the alarm, and headed for the truck. As we left, I glanced back at the big plate-glass windows. For half a second, I thought I saw a shadow flicker along the wall behind us. But it was gone so fast, I almost convinced myself it was just a trick of the storm.

Almost.

As we drove to Pearl's, I rested my hand on her thigh, thumb tracing small circles just to remind her I was there.

But my mind kept spinning. If there was something stalking my mate—something more than nightmares—I'd burn Dairyville to ash to stop it.

Whatever it was, it was real.

And I would find it.

Pearl's was packed, the noise level set to "barn raising." We claimed the long table at the back, near the jukebox and under a bank of Christmas lights that never came down. The smell of frying oil and pecan pie was so thick you could taste it in the air.

The girls—Aspen, Parker, Harper, and even Juliet, who looked radiant and almost ready to pop—clustered at one end, chattering about the upcoming gallery opening, baby names, and the latest pack drama. Aspen's eyes sparkled when she talked about her bakery's custom cake for opening night, and Parker cackled every time Harper told a story about the bitchy pack moms trying to slow her down. Even Juliet was laughing, one hand perpetually resting on her belly as if she could barely keep the twins from busting out early.

Brie fit right in. The tightness in her shoulders melted, her voice clear and wicked, her laughter bright enough to make people at other tables turn and stare. Every once in a while, her eyes would dart my way, and she'd grin like we shared a secret no one else could see.

At the other end, the men had already settled into the familiar rhythm of "who can eat the most," "who can bullshit the hardest," and "whose life is the most tragic." Arsenal ran point, as always, dissecting the best routes for parking at the gallery and which local cops to bribe for crowd control. Papa watched it all with the serene patience of a man who'd lived through a few wars and still thought nothing beat a good pot roast.

Wrecker sat beside me, clean shirt and all, glowering at a plate piled two feet high with fried pickles. He jabbed one in my direction. "So, you need me to do a sweep of the gallery?"

"Yeah," I said. "Just wanna be sure there's nothing underhanded happening there. Brie was sure she saw something, but shit, she's been working herself to pieces. Plus, she doesn't sleep but a couple of hours each night. She's runnin' on fumes, man."

He chewed, contemplative. "Could be a stress hallucination. People get them before big events all the time."

"You sound like you've had experience," I said.

Wrecker shrugged. "You know my past. Been in high stress, life or death scenarios... Seen worse. Keep an eye on her, though."

I nodded. "I'll keep two on her." Then I glanced down the table. Brie was animated, cheeks pink, hands slicing the air as she debated with Harper about the best Instagram filter for baby pictures.

She caught me looking, held my gaze for a long moment, then mouthed "thank you."

I gave her a wink, heart thumping. Fuck, even stretched to the breaking point; she was the most alluring thing I'd ever seen.

The food arrived in waves, like an edible apocalypse. Pearl herself delivered two platters of her famous chicken-fried steak, mashed potatoes, and gravy so thick you could patch drywall with it. The whole table dug in, forks and knives a blur.

Halfway through the meal, Bronc raised his glass. "To the opening night of Wildbrush Gallery. May it bring as much chaos as it does culture." The pack howled and clapped, even the human regulars getting in on it.

Brie beamed, radiant, the shadows gone for the first time in days. Fuck if I wasn't proud to be her mate.

After dessert (bread pudding, sweet enough to stop a heart), we lingered until the place emptied out. The girls hugged goodnight, promises flying about outfits and carpooling. The men did their usual slap-on-the-back routine, then drifted into the night, bellies full and spirits higher than they'd been all week.

I drove Brie home in silence, her head resting on my shoulder, her hand warm in mine.

That night, after she brushed her teeth and washed her face, she stood next to me at our big bathroom double sink, hair damp and face clean of makeup. She looked up at me, eyes clear and full of something fierce.

"Do you want me, Finn?"

The question nearly broke me. I didn't answer with words. I gathered her up, lifted her onto the edge of the counter, and kissed her until her lips were bruised and she was breathless.

She laughed, soft and wild, as I peeled off her shirt and bared her skin. She slid her hands under my shirt, fingers tracing the lines of my back. I pulled off the rest of my clothes and carried her into the shower, turned the water hot, and let it cascade over us both.

I took my time, washing her hair with slow, careful strokes, running my hands over every inch of her. She pressed herself against me, wet and slippery, her nipples hard against my chest.

When I knelt in front of her, she tangled her hands in my hair and moaned as I licked her open, tasting her, loving the way she trembled under my tongue. It wasn't long before she came hard, thighs clamped around my ears, her whole body shuddering.

I stood, kissed her mouth, and lifted her up to wrap her legs around my waist.

"No knot this time," I growled, voice rough. "I need it hard and fast."

She bit my shoulder, giggling. "Yes, Sir."

I turned her around, pressed her hands against the shower tile, and drove into her. She gasped, clenching around me, her ass slick and perfect in my hands.

"Fuck, you feel so good," I said, thrusting harder, faster, until I felt the pressure build and explode, both of us crying out as we came together.

When it was over, I held her there, both of us shaking, the water washing away everything except the need to be close.

I dried her off with the soft, fluffy towel, tucked her into my shirt, and carried her to bed. She was asleep before her head hit the pillow, face peaceful for the first time in weeks.

I stayed up a little longer, watching her, listening to the storm roll away.

Tomorrow would bring whatever it brought.

But tonight, my mate was safe.

The air in our bedroom was thick with that scent again. Not Brie, not me, not even the trace of cedar from my freshly laundered t-shirt on her skin. This was metallic—so heavy it made my gums tingle, so sharp it sliced through sleep like a razor through silk. I tried to move, to shake it off, but my limbs were heavy, lashed down by some invisible gravity.

It was pitch black. The clock on the dresser read 2:34, its red digits bleeding into the dark. Brie was next to me, tangled in the sheets, her body thrashing as if she were running in her sleep. I reached for her, but my hand wouldn't budge. It was like being held under ice—aware, but unable to break the surface.

I forced my eyes wider. The darkness was wrong. Thicker than it should be, like tar, it dripped down the walls and pooled at the corners of the room. And then, just for a heartbeat, the black shimmered, peeled back, and I wasn't in our bedroom anymore.

The floor was stone, cold and pitted beneath my knees. My wrists were chained, thick iron links bolted to the ground. The air was still, hot and suffocating, lit from above by a sickly yellow light that pulsed like a heartbeat.

Brie was there, naked, sweat slicking every inch of her body. She was kneeling, head bowed, hands clasped behind her back. A shadow stood in front of her—a figure I recognized at once, even before he spoke.

"Is this what you crave, little wolf?" The voice was mine, but layered with something darker, richer, more monstrous.

She whimpered, spine arching, and looked up with gold-tinged eyes. "Yes, Sir."

He reached for her, long-fingered hands stroking her cheek. The nails were claws, black and curved, but Brie leaned into the touch as if it was a lover's caress.

I tried to shout. I tried to break the chains, to lunge between them, but I couldn't move. The shadow pressed closer, lips at her ear. "Good girl," he crooned, and she shuddered, thighs pressed tight together.

A voice hissed behind me, cold and amused: "All you can do is watch."

The shadow bent Brie forward, palming the back of her neck, and spread her knees. She moaned, not in fear, but in desperate, shivering want. He stroked between her thighs, found her already wet, and dragged two claws through her slickness.

"Look how ready you are," he said, voice rumbling with cruel delight. "Always so ready for your Sir. Such a good, good girl." He raised his fingers to show me the wetness there; a sick smile on his monstrous lips as he licked them clean.

Still looking at me he taunted. "I may not be able to take her from you physically, but I don't need to do I? I can have her whenever I want her, right here. And doesn't she taste sweet?"

She whimpered. "Please…"

He lifted her up and spun her around. He pressed his hand so that she bent; his hand flat against her ass. He parted her with a single, brutal motion, and lined up his cock with her pussy. It wasn't my cock. It was huge, twisted ridged, purple-black, with veins that glowed like embers in the half-light. She gasped, hips grinding back, hungry for it.

"You want this, don't you, little slut?" he asked, pushing just the head in.

She nodded, drool running down her chin, eyes glazed with need. "Please, Sir. Please, I'll be good—"

He thrust forward, splitting her wide. Brie screamed, head thrown back, but she didn't resist—she fucking took it, the way she always did with me, and I saw her body quake with pleasure.

He started to fuck her, slow at first, then building in tempo, hips slamming against her ass with punishing force. Each time he bottomed out, she clawed at the stone, raw and feral, begging for more.

"See how she loves it?" said the voice at my ear. "See what she really is?"

I was screaming through our bond: *Brie, that's not me! Resist him!*

All at once, she turned to me her eyes wide. I heard her voice: *No! No! You're not Finn! Stop!*

Together we fought to get away from this nightmare.

I ground my teeth so hard I tasted blood.

The shadow leaned forward, biting her shoulder, drawing a thin line of red that beaded and ran down her back. He licked it, savoring every drop as he continued to pound into her while she moaned.

I kept calling out in my mind, using the mate bond like a flare: *Brie, this isn't real. Fight him. Please, baby, fight...*

She blinked, eyes clearing for a second. "Finn?"

The shadow jerked her back, fangs bared, and for a split second his face was clear: Maltraz, demon king, eyes burning with hellfire.

"You'll never win," he sneered, and then everything went black.

I woke to screaming—my own and hers, so loud it rattled the windows.

Brie was thrashing in the sheets, fighting invisible hands. I grabbed her, hauled her onto my lap, cradled her as she sobbed and clawed at her own skin.

"It's okay," I kept saying, "you're here, I'm here; it's just a dream."

But I knew it wasn't. I knew Maltraz was in her head, using her, using us both. I knew that next time, maybe I wouldn't be able to pull her back.

I held her until the screaming died, until her body stopped shaking, and the only sound left was the wet hitch of her breath against my chest.

When she finally fell asleep, I sat there for a long time, staring at the dark.

If that demon wanted my mate, he was going to have to go through me.

I'd kill him, even if it meant dragging us both to hell.

CHAPTER 19

BRIE

By the time the sunrise found its way through our bedroom blinds, I was already awake—if you could call it that. Most of me was still locked in a dream somewhere else, or maybe a nightmare, and the only thing keeping me tethered to this bed, this house, was Finn's hand around my wrist.

He was watching me, eyes wide open, barely blinking. There was something sharp in his gaze—worry, hunger, the residual charge of a night spent fighting things you couldn't see. I tried to roll over, but my body didn't want to cooperate. Every muscle was sore, like I'd run a marathon or spent all night at the gallery hanging drywall by myself.

"Morning." My voice was hoarse, like I'd been screaming.

Finn's grip on my wrist loosened, but he didn't let go. "You okay, Maverick?"

"No, but give me a minute and I'll fake it."

He cracked a smile—tight, but real. His hair was wild, sticking up at weird angles, and he was moving slowly.

I sat up and immediately regretted it. The room spun, and a bolt of nausea twisted through my gut. "Shit," I whispered, pressing the heel of my hand to my forehead.

He was back with a glass of water, which I drained in two gulps. Then he stood and started pacing, which was never a good sign. "Last night. The dream. Do you remember any of it?"

I closed my eyes, tried to drag up anything besides the taste of blood and the feeling of suffocating. "Not really. Just like all the other times. Just know when I woke up, you were also screaming. Because you were there too. I tried to hold on to it, but it just faded and I fell back to sleep."

Finn stopped, raked a hand through his hair, and muttered something under his breath.

"What about you?" I was still a little freaked out that he was somehow having the same dream.

He stared out the window, shoulders hunched. "Just darkness and a shadow." He shivered, the movement violent. "It wasn't just a dream, Brie. I could feel it."

He sat back on the edge of the bed, hands balled into fists. For a second, I thought he was going to punch the mattress, but instead he picked up the notepad on the nightstand. There were notes scrawled there.

"What's all that?"

"It's what I wrote down last night right after." He fumbled with the pages.. "Before I forgot the details. It's not much. It's like everything started to disappear right after I woke up."

His eyes squinted like he were trying to decipher what he'd written in his haste to get every memory down before it had vanished.

After a minute, he read the list he'd made. "Here's all I got: *stone room? chains? Brie on knees? voices/mine, not mine? shadow monster/man? man touching Brie? not me? claws? NOT REAL?? can't help her? DEMON???* Clearly all questions and what seems like nonsense."

"That's fucked up." My voice couldn't help but shake.

He nodded. "I know."

We sat in silence, the list between us. My skin prickled; I remembered a little of the dream now. The stone, the heat, the way my body wouldn't cooperate, wouldn't even try to fight back.

I hated it. Hated how it made me feel—weak, exposed, helpless. I'd spent my whole life building armor, and now I felt like a kid again, naked and afraid of the dark.

Finn touched my hand, so gentle I almost missed it. "I'll figure this out, Brie. I swear."

"I know you will." I squeezed his fingers, tried to ignore the tremor in my own. "But what if it happens again?"

He hesitated. "Then we get help. Juliet, Aspen, Aspen's father, I'll call in every favor I have."

The wolf in him was still fighting to get out. I could see it in the set of his jaw, the way his shoulders were squared for a fight that hadn't even started yet.

He took my face in his hands. "We're Iron Valor. We don't back down from a fight. And we don't lose. Do not forget that." Then he kissed me like he were sealing a vow.

We sat in silence for a long moment, letting his words settle.

When we finally tried to stand, I felt a little stiff, like I'd been stretched in unfamiliar ways as I made my way to the bathroom. Finn made coffee in the kitchen, slamming the mug on the counter so hard I thought he'd break it.

I joined him at the table, arms wrapped around myself. The morning was bright, too bright, and the world felt wrong, like it was a dupe of an original.

He handed me the mug. "Drink this. You'll feel better."

I did, and he was right. The caffeine cut through the fog, just enough to make the world seem solid again.

He watched me, his expression unreadable. "You remember any more?"

I shook my head. "Not really. Just... it felt like we were being watched. Or judged. Like the dream wanted us to do something, but I couldn't figure out what."

He tapped his finger on the table, thinking. "It's not normal for people to share dreams. That means it's not just in your head. Someone—or something—put it there."

"Maltraz," I said. The name tasted like battery acid.

He nodded. "He's the only one with that kind of pull."

I finished the coffee, set the mug down, and looked at Finn. "So what do we do?"

He smiled, and for a second he was my Finn again, not the haunted version. "We go see Aspen. She'll know what to do."

I laughed, a little unsteady. "You think a bakery witch is going to fix us?"

He grinned. "Sweetheart, she's not just a 'bakery witch.' She's got the blood of an Immortal in her veins. When you're the daughter of the Angel King, you can consider yourself a bit extra. And if she can't, at least she'll feed us enough sugar to put us in a coma. It's a win either way."

"Shit. I forgot who her father was. Yeah, she's who we need to ask for help."

I felt better, just a little. Enough to stand up straight, enough to think I could make it through the day.

We dressed, gathering our armor for the world outside. I wore leggings, tall boots, a t-shirt, scarves tied around my waist, leather bracelets and chokers. Yep, my mother would be appalled at my bohemian style. Perfect. Finn looked sexy as hell. Cinch jeans and a black pearl snap, boots and a black cowboy hat. Say what you want, but give me my cowboy all day long.

He slipped his arm around me and pulled me close. "You ready?"

"Fuck yeah. I'm Iron Valor." I thought if I said it with confidence it would make it so.

He grinned as we stepped outside, into the light, into whatever came next.

Buttercream & Blessings smelled like heaven on the second day. It was only 9:07 a.m., but Aspen already had the ovens blasting and the pastry case lined with glossy cinnamon rolls, warm scones, and croissants the size of baby footballs. The place was as bright as a dental lab—sun pouring through the big windows, white tile everywhere, and a wall of coffee mugs painted with cutesy animals. The morning rush had run its course, so there was only one customer seated in the dining area, and she was an Iron Valor wolf.

Aspen was behind the counter, her dark hair wound into a glossy braid and her apron dusted in flour. She saw us and immediately went on high alert, which for Aspen meant pressing her hands flat on the counter and going completely still, as if bracing for a tidal wave. In the open window between the kitchen and counter area, Oscar, the world's most dignified prairie dog, popped up and squinted at us like a fussy schoolmaster.

"Mornin'! Look at you two; the original 'match made in heaven' couple." Aspen crooned, but her sweet southern voice held a slight edge. "Y'all look amazing, if not a tad tired."

I sidled up to the counter. "Just the usual terrifying shared dream with your mate scenario. You know, nothing out of the ordinary." I bent down to Oscar's level and did my best British accent: "Lovely mornin' init?"

Oscar's nose twitched. "Well, I've kept the shenanigans to a minimum so far today. But you're here now, so..." He gave me a small prairie dog wink.

Finn smothered a laugh, then jerked his chin at Aspen. "You got a second, A? We need to talk."

She glanced around, clocked that the only other customer was Papa's retired aunt (deep in her crossword and not listening), and motioned us toward the little table by the window. "Give me one sec. I'll bring your order."

Oscar scurried after her, tail up like a feather duster.

I perched on a stool, legs bouncing. My hands wouldn't stop fidgeting. Finn's presence was a low hum next to me, every muscle wound tight. He looked out the window, scanning Main Street for threats that probably didn't exist. In another life, he could have worked as a bomb-sniffing dog.

Aspen brought over a tray loaded with pastries and coffee—she remembered exactly how I liked mine, which made my heart squeeze in an embarrassing way. Oscar leaped onto the table and started preening, whiskers twitching.

Aspen sat down and immediately took my hand. "What happened?"

I swallowed, picked at a croissant flake, and told her everything. The dreams, the feeling that it wasn't just a regular nightmare. I didn't hold back—if anyone would believe me; it was Aspen.

Finn added, "We were both in the dream together. That's not supposed to happen, right?"

Aspen's eyes went wide. "No, sir. Not unless there's actual magic involved. Did you see anything else? Any... colors, or smells?"

I blinked. "That's the thing. Most of the dream vanished when we woke up. I only remember darkness and shadows. But Finn was smart enough to write down what he remembered right after we woke up."

Finn pulled out the little notepad and read off his disjointed notes.

Oscar gave a small, sympathetic look. "Demonic signatures can present thusly." Information rolled off his tongue as if he were reading from a textbook. "The important thing is not to let it fester. My lady, I believe you have the tome to remedy their situation."

Aspen straightened, all business. "I've got my mom's grimoire in the back. I could look up a dream suppressor spell. Or maybe a charm—something to block the intrusion at the source."

Finn looked skeptical, but didn't argue. "Would it work?"

Aspen nodded. "If I get the recipe right, it should stop the dreams. At least for a while."

I felt a wave of relief, followed immediately by guilt. "If you can just get me through the gallery opening that would be incredibly helpful. But you don't have to do this, Aspen. I know how busy the bakery has gotten."

She squeezed my hand. "Honey, you're family. This is what we do." Then, softer: "My mom always said, there's no harm a fresh cinnamon roll can't mend. But if there is, you add more magic."

Oscar beamed, which for a prairie dog looked like baring two long incisors. "Precisely. You see, Miss Lawson, you are in the safest paws in Dairyville."

I giggled and instantly felt better. I inhaled a cinnamon roll, the sugar and spice grounding me, making the nightmare seem less real. Finn had two black coffees, and a scone gone before I even noticed.

Aspen took notes on a little pad. "Just to be clear: you both had the same dream?"

Finn nodded. "At the same time. I just remember a flash of seeing Brie chained." He stopped, eyes going flinty. "I think she was hurt. It was like somebody else was pretending to be me. At least that's what the notes I scribbled down right after seemed to indicate."

Aspen wrote this down, her lips tight.

Oscar chimed in, "If you require additional security, I can stand guard while you sleep."

Finn actually smiled. "I'd take you over half the pack, Oscar."

I reached for another roll, then remembered my actual reason for being up early. "Aspen, can I get a box of these? I want to pay Lysander and Inez for working so hard to finish the gallery install on time."

Aspen boxed up half a dozen, adding a few extras "for creative fuel." She labeled the box in pink marker: For the artists, love Aspen.

I stood to leave, suddenly aware that I'd been holding Aspen's hand the whole time. I squeezed it once more. "Thank you, A. You're the best."

She blushed, waved it off. "You just focus on your show. I'll have something ready for you this afternoon."

Oscar bowed from the table. "Be vigilant, Miss Lawson. And try to get some actual sleep, if you can."

Finn and I stepped out into the brightness of the street, the scent of the bakery still clinging to our clothes.

He leaned in and kissed my forehead. "You good?"

I nodded, the pastry and coffee working their magic. "Yeah. For now."

He looked like he wanted to say more, but instead pulled me in for a long, solid hug. "I'm going to head over to the clubhouse. Bronc wants a full security run-through before tomorrow. You'll be okay at the gallery?"

"Please. Compared to last night, the gallery's nothing." I grinned, surprising myself with how normal it sounded.

Finn stroked my cheek with his thumb. "If you need me, you call. No matter what."

"I will."

We stood like that for a minute, neither of us wanting to break the spell. But life didn't wait, and I had work to do.

He peeled off, boots thudding down the sidewalk, already on the phone with the club. I watched him go, a pang of longing settling behind my ribs, then squared my shoulders and turned toward the gallery.

The day was young; the sun was hot, and I had cinnamon rolls to deliver.

If the darkness wanted me, it would have to wait in line.

By the time I got to the gallery, the air was thick with the smell of drying paint, overpriced espresso, and Lysander's cologne, which today was something between a forest fire and an absinthe hallucination. The entire main floor was chaos: almost finished temporary walls, extension cords snaking across the raw floorboards, Inez up on a ladder in paint-splattered overalls, swearing in what I was fairly certain was a mix of Spanish, Italian, and direct invocations of the Virgin.

I dumped the pastry box on the reception counter and called, "Breakfast, if you don't want to die before lunch!" It got their attention immediately. Inez clambered down the ladder, wiped her hands on her thighs, and snatched the box as if it might grow legs and run off. Lysander, who'd been in the back office, glided out, his phone tucked between shoulder and jaw, gesturing at me with his free hand.

"Darling, you have saved our lives," he mouthed, then into the phone: "No, not you, Bruce, the actual artist, yes—" and vanished into the makeshift office.

Inez broke a cinnamon roll in half and offered me the gooier side. "You look tired," she said, which was her way of being polite about the bags under my eyes.

I shrugged, mouth full of pastry. "Didn't sleep. Too much on my brain."

She rolled her eyes. "Don't let Lysander boss you around. He gets dramatic when he is hungry. Like a child, that one."

I laughed, and for a minute, it was almost like last year, before the universe decided to treat me like a chew toy.

We took our breakfast onto the metal benches in front of the gallery. It was early, not yet hot, and the pale light made the whole place look softer. Inez told me about her latest commission (a mural for a yoga studio in Santa Fe), then pressed: "Really, Brie. Are you okay?"

I looked at her, at the paint still clinging to her hands, and decided to just say it. "I'm having nightmares. Bad ones. Finn too. And they're getting worse."

She frowned, then crossed herself—a gesture she usually reserved for hospital dramas and horror movies. "Mal de ojo," she muttered, then in English: "You need to break the curse, no?"

I snorted. "If you have a recipe, I'll try anything."

She leaned in suddenly solemn. "If you want, I'll make you a protection candle. My abuela taught me."

It was so sincere, I almost cried. "Thank you, Inez. Maybe after the install, we can do a whole exorcism."

She grinned. "I'll bring tequila. That's how you get rid of all evil spirits."

We finished the rolls and went back inside; the sugar made the next hour blur. Lysander ran logistics like a cruise director on speed, organizing everything: lighting, installation order, photographer schedule, even the catering walk-through. He was a machine, and I let myself get swept up in the forward momentum of it all.

At eleven, we broke for coffee and regrouped in the office. Lysander sprawled on the couch, legs crossed at the knee, while Inez perched on the window ledge, feet swinging. I collapsed onto the couch next to him, letting the caffeine do battle with the exhaustion.

"Alright, darling," Lysander said, voice soft for once. "Are you ready for the good news, or should we do bad news first?"

I stretched, feeling the ache in my back. "Let's get the bad out of the way."

He waggled a finger. "Cynicism, my dear! I love it. Okay. The bad news is, the main gallery floor still smells like industrial glue, and we might need to open a few windows and pray it airs out before tomorrow."

I snorted. "Noted. And the good news?"

He sat up, and suddenly he was closer than I expected, eyes very blue and very, very serious. "The good news is, you're going to sell every piece you hang. Maybe more. I got an email this morning—there are buyers flying in from Boston and Santa Fe. Not for Inez, for *you*."

My jaw dropped. "That's—what? How?"

He beamed. "Because I am a genius, darling, and because your work is honest. People can smell the blood and the sweat. You're not trying to impress them, and that's why they want it."

I blinked. "Wow."

Inez whooped, then hugged me from behind, nearly choking me. "Brie, this is amazing! See? You make something real, and people feel it."

For a minute, I was speechless. I thought about all those years of trying to be someone else, trying to make something worth being seen, and it was almost funny that the thing people wanted was the mess I'd always tried to hide.

Lysander watched me, hands folded, smile softer now. "You okay?"

I nodded, tears pricking the corners of my eyes. "Yeah. Yeah, I'm good. Just..." I swallowed. "Thank you."

He leaned forward, brushing a hair off my cheek. "You deserve it, darling. All of it."

Inez left to call her abuela about the candle, so I was alone with Lysander. He moved closer to me, close enough that our knees touched.

His voice dropped. "Can I say something strange?"

I raised an eyebrow. "When have you ever not?"

He smiled, then bit his lip. "I know we joke about it, but I really do care about you, Brie. I'm not just your rep, you know?"

I looked away, embarrassed. "I know."

He took my hand, held it just a second longer than a friend would. "Promise me you'll let someone take care of you, okay? You don't have to do this alone."

The words gutted me a little, but I managed a nod. "I promise."

He pulled me into a tight hug. I'd never felt the slightest bit awkward with Lysander's touches, but this one felt... different. More personal somehow. As he let go, I caught a whiff of a familiar scent, but I couldn't place it. Before I could think about it, he pulled away, suddenly shy. "Okay, enough of that. Let's go make you famous."

We finished up the rest of the install by three. The floors were swept, the lighting perfect, the walls pristine. The transformation was almost supernatural—like the gallery had finally woken up and realized what it was supposed to be.

I was hanging the last label when Aspen walked in, carrying a canvas tote and looking like she'd run the entire way from the bakery. Her cheeks were flushed, and Oscar was peeking from her bag, his head swiveling on a tiny neck.

"Hi!" she called, and even Lysander looked happy to see her.

I jogged over and pulled her into a hug. "Did you come to save us from glue poisoning?"

She laughed. "No, but I brought you something." She rummaged in her tote, then produced a little pouch tied with a yellow ribbon.

"Protection charms," she whispered, glancing around as if someone might overhear. "You're supposed to put them under your pillow, but you can carry them in your purse if you need to. They should block out anything trying to get into your head."

I took the pouch, nearly crying again. "Thank you, Aspen. You are the best."

Oscar made a tiny cough, then bowed. "I contributed sage advice, as is my duty," he said, and for a second I thought maybe Lysander heard him, because his eyes flicked to Oscar, then back to Aspen, face unreadable. Which was odd, since only supernaturals could see Oscar.

Aspen glanced at Lysander, then whispered: "If anything changes, call me. I'll do more research tonight."

I nodded, squeezing her hand.

After she left, Lysander saw the pouch and pulled it from my hand. "Ooh, let me see!" He emptied the two charms into his hand. They sparkled under the installation lights. "These are beautiful, Brie! I didn't know Aspen also made jewelry."

I was so stunned that he had pulled the pouch from my hand that I was almost speechless. I quickly took the charms and placed them back in the pouch and stuffed it in my pocket for safekeeping. "Hey, Mr. Grabby Hands! Yes, she dabbles and doesn't really want the word to get out since she's just started playing around. So please keep it to yourself." I lied.

We walked the gallery floor one last time. He seemed different—quieter, more thoughtful. I wondered if maybe he'd seen something in Aspen that he couldn't explain, or maybe he just wanted to protect me the way I always protected everyone else.

Either way, I felt lighter. Ready.

At five, Finn pulled up outside in his fancy pickup truck waiting for me, window rolled down. I saw him, and my heart did that stupid somersault again.

Lysander walked me to the door, then, with a sudden rush of bravado, pulled me into another extended hug. He held me tight, then kissed my cheek, his lips lingering just long enough to make my skin tingle.

He and Inez trailed out after we turned out all the lights. I gave one last look at the gallery. We were ready as we'd ever be.

"Knock 'em dead tomorrow, darling." He waved as he and Inez reached their rental car. She gave me a big smile as they drove away.

I climbed into the truck, the weight of the day lifting with every step. Finn reached over and tucked a strand of hair behind my ear.

"You ready for a real night's sleep?" he asked.

I smiled, the protection pouch warm in my pocket. "I think I am."

For the first time in weeks, I wasn't afraid of what waited in the dark.

If the nightmares wanted me, they'd have to get through a bakery witch, a prairie dog, a small army of cinnamon rolls, and the two best men I'd ever known.

I liked my odds.

CHAPTER 20

GUNNER

Brie didn't have a nightmare all night. That was the first miracle. The second was that we both woke up just after sunrise, tangled up in each other, not shivering, not clutching at the bedsheets for dear life, but just... at peace. Aspen's little charm bag still sat on Brie's nightstand, the yellow ribbon laid out like a canary feather, and whether it was the magic of the charms under our pillows or just the power of suggestion, I didn't care. I'd have placed a hundred charms under the mattress if it meant I got more mornings like this.

She stretched long and catlike before blinking over at me. "Did you sleep?" she asked.

"Like the dead," I said, and meant it.

She smiled—maybe the first real one in days—and sat up; the sheets falling to her waist. I watched her for a second, just memorizing how the soft morning light painted her skin gold. Then, she did the thing that always melted me: she went from goddess to gremlin in a split second, sticking her tongue out and making a little goblin noise as she fished for her phone on the nightstand.

"Don't take pictures of my morning face," I warned, rolling onto my side.

"Too late." She snapped one anyway. Then she climbed out of bed, stark naked, and did a little victory lap around the room while she scrolled through her notifications. If she cared that I was openly staring at her, she didn't let on. Honestly, at this point in our lives, the only person who could make her self-conscious was her own mother.

Brie's morning routine was a war zone of accessories and last-minute inspiration. She started with the wardrobe: ripped black jeans, her lucky vintage cowboy boots with the cracked turquoise leather, and a shirt that looked like it had been cut from a 1970s grandma's curtain. Over that, she layered on scarves, a vest, and then picked her way through a mess of necklaces on the dresser. She selected three: one made of glass beads, one with a silver wolf pendant, and the last—a choker of braided leather with a big chunk of amethyst. She wore them all, like a shield.

Her hair, wild from sleep, took her less than a minute to tame. She ran her fingers through the dark brown waves, tousled with blue-dyed streaks. Mascara went on in a single pass. No blush, and her lips wore just a little tinted lip balm in dark plum. She looked like she was about to knock over a train, or at least steal the hearts of every art critic in the Texas panhandle.

"You nervous?" I asked, sipping my coffee at the kitchen table.

She slumped into the chair across from me and made a face. "If I stop moving, I'll start puking."

"Then don't stop."

She took a deep breath, then gave me a look. "Will you come with me, or do I have to brave the gallery alone?"

I finished my coffee, then grinned at her. "I'll drive. You can choose the playlist, but I am not starting my day with more Johnny Cash."

"Sacrilege," she muttered, but her hands were already on my forearm, squeezing tight.

She ducked back into the bedroom to grab her statement dress—because, as she explained to me last night, every artist needs a statement piece for the opening. She'd gone with a floor-length gown in a sage green that set off her eyes, with bursts of violet in random panels and some kind of mesh overlay that made it shimmer like grass after a rain. She'd hung it in one of those plastic garment bags like it was the Hope Diamond.

Today was a day for pulling the King Ranch out of the garage. My mate deserved to arrive in style on this occasion.

"Wow, I *do* feel special getting to ride in the lap of luxury today. You know how to make a girl feel treasured, cowboy." She gave me a cute wink when I got her strapped into her seatbelt.

"You're precious cargo, Maverick. Gotta be sure everybody sees I know how to treat a lady."

I loaded her dress and tote bag full of whatever else she had packed up for the day. We spoke little on the drive, both of us half-lost in our own heads, but it was a comfortable silence. The kind you only get with your mate, or someone you've spent a thousand hours beside on a tractor or in a foxhole.

Dairyville was still mostly asleep at seven. The bakery was just turning on its 'Open' sign as we passed, and the only movement on Main was a stray dog trotting down the sidewalk. The gallery stood out on the block; its fresh new facade and awning looked modern and inviting. I could see Lysander's rental pulled in behind us, and park a few spots down. It idled there while we got out.

She bit her lip when I helped her out. "Stay until they get the signage up?"

"As long as you want."

She leaned up, kissed my cheek, then pressed her forehead to mine. "I love you."

"Back at you, Maverick."

She grinned, then headed for the door. I watched her strut up the front steps—scarf blowing, boots clomping, every inch the artist she'd always wanted to be. She stopped at the door, fumbling for keys, then glanced back and gave me a thumbs-up.

I caught movement in the corner of my eye—Lysander and Inez walked up, all smiles. Lysander's platinum hair was runway coiffed, and he looked dressed like he was making a pit stop at a fashion runway before they got started for the day. Inez, for her part, was wearing a paint-stained jumpsuit and carrying a dress bag and tote that likely carried her shoes and other items to prep for this evening.

The two of them approached Brie, and Lysander immediately placed a hand on her shoulder, the way you might steady someone on a balance beam. My jaw tightened. I had no real reason to dislike the man, except that he was too smooth by half, and every interaction he had with Brie seemed one inch closer to crossing a line.

I made myself unclench. This was Brie's world today, not mine.

I made my way down the sidewalk with Brie's things in tow; hat pulled down close to my eyes, while I kept watch. Bronc always said you could spot a threat a mile off if you looked for the one person acting like he didn't belong. I watched the sidewalk, the street, the gallery windows, counting the seconds until I saw Brie's silhouette pass behind the glass.

It took ten minutes for the crews of workers to show up. The contractor came in for finishing touches. Next came the florist with tall vases of wildflowers. They reminded me of Brie so much I caught myself smiling.

Harper blew into her studio to help Big Papa set up the tables for Aspen, and the food. Then the company hired to install the sign backed a big truck up to the curb. They unloaded a blue scissor lift, the backup alarm beeping incessantly. I watched it all, running silent mental notes. No one acted suspicious, no one lingered where they shouldn't. Lysander took charge, charming the install crew and flirting shamelessly with the florist, who was at least thirty years his senior and blushing like a schoolgirl. Inez painted set pieces on the sidewalk with a five-year-old's sense of decorum. It was all normal, all above board, and yet, every time I saw Lysander's hand brush Brie's arm or back, I felt a jolt of something like static up my spine.

That was my problem to fix, not hers.

When the gallery sign went up, Brie ran outside and did a little spin under the awning, arms flung wide, not caring who saw. I snapped a picture of her as I leaned against my truck, then set it as my phone's background, because fuck it, I was soft like that.

She saw me, grinned, and mouthed, "It's beautiful."

I nodded and whispered, "Not as beautiful as you."

Then, I blew her a kiss, got in the truck, and started the engine. As I pulled away, I checked the rearview. Lysander was still watching her, but there was something different in his face this time—something almost admiring.

I told myself it was fine. Everything was under control. She *should* be admired. She was fucking magnificent, and even a man who preferred males for sexual partners couldn't deny her appeal.

Still, I made a note to come back at lunch, just to check the perimeter. Some habits died hard.

The new Iron Valor clubhouse was much improved over the one that had been blown to hell by the Greenbriar pack several months ago. Juliet was a hell of a Luna and had been raised as New York royalty; old money. So she brought a sense of style and a tiny touch of class to the joint. But thank fuck she had become more Iron Valor than any East Coast hoity-toity rich girl, so the clubhouse was warm and inviting. The building was three stories if you counted the basement. A pretty front porch ran the length of the building, and the great room was warm and inviting for family gatherings. The basement was where the adults did their thing; strictly a kid-free zone. Our officer meeting room was down there. It was as no-nonsense as Bronc. But Wrecker had decked it out with all the tech we'd ever need. Wide screens were mounted on the walls for video conferencing and watching surveillance cams. Network hubs were on every wall. We were set for any emergency.

I let myself in through the kitchen entrance and followed the sound of raised voices to the meeting room.

The air was thick with the smell of fresh biscuits and sausage gravy, plus a percussive undercurrent of dark roast that could probably eat a hole in your stomach lining. Ms. Pearl always cooked for the officers on big days; she'd made enough food to feed a cavalry platoon, which was about right for our crew.

The men were already at the long table. Bronc at the head, back straight, eyes alert, the man born to lead. Arsenal and Wrecker had their hands wrapped around mugs like they'd just come in from a blizzard. Big Papa was quietly demolishing a mountain of eggs while Doc was picking apart a fruit bowl and watching the room over the rim of his glasses.

As I sat, Arsenal nodded to me. "You're just in time, Gunner. Bronc was about to make us say grace."

Bronc gave him the finger, then looked at me. "How's Brie?"

"She's good. Real good," I said, meaning it. "Ate breakfast, dressed up like a peacock, ready to conquer the world."

Wrecker snorted. "I saw her Instagram post. She looks like an acid trip in human form."

"She looks happy," said Big Papa, his voice as big as the rest of him. "That's all that matters."

Doc offered a rare smile, then forked another piece of melon. "She and Gunner both look better than last week."

"Thanks for noticing," I muttered.

Bronc rapped the table. "Let's get started. We got three priorities today: security, logistics, and making sure the pack looks good in front of a shitload of humans."

He looked at me. "First up—report."

I set my fork down and folded my hands. "The nightmares are gone, for now. Aspen's charms worked. But before that, Brie and I had a... situation."

Arsenal leaned forward, elbows on the table. "Define 'situation.'"

"The last nightmare she had was really bad. 'Cept this time I was also having the same dream at the same time. I saw what was happening to her, but I couldn't speak, couldn't move. At least that's what I gathered from the notes I jotted down when I woke up. Based on those; it wasn't something I'd want to remember. But I *do* vaguely remember a shadow, and I caught a glimpse of who I thought could be Maltraz. It seemed like he was making Brie think he was me. Again, my notes were sketchy. My memory, even more so. We both woke up screaming."

The details of the dream and that name sucked the oxygen out of the room.

Wrecker didn't flinch. "Fuck, you sure?"

I nodded. "It was more than just a dream—it was like he was using us to test something out."

Doc went full clinical. "Any aftereffects? Physical symptoms?"

I shrugged. "Tired, sore. Like we'd been fighting in our sleep. Brie couldn't remember most of it, but she felt it, too."

Bronc drummed his fingers. "He's clearly got something up his fucking sleeve."

I nodded my tired head. "I agree. But I think he's waiting. He wants us to know he can get to us, even if it isn't actually physical yet. He's just fucking with us right now. He's still got a hard-on for Iron Valor, but I don't get it. He's a fucking king of a realm. Why does he care about a pack of wolves?"

Big Papa put his fork down, expression grave. "We've beat him several times. He clearly doesn't like losing. Iron Valor has his number, and he can't have that. Hopefully, that will make him sloppy, causing him to slip up."

Wrecker caught my eye. "Aspen's charm is a temporary fix. If he wants in, he'll get in eventually."

Bronc's jaw set. "After the gallery opening, we take that fucker down. No more waiting for him to make the first move. Menace and Savannah land in an hour. I'll discuss Maltraz with him; see if he's noticed any weirder behavior from him with the Council than usual. Then we'll act on our own. It would be helpful if we had Council help. Lucia had mentioned it would take more than wolves to bring him down. We'll need more firepower. After the opening, we'll find out what she meant."

There was a silent round of agreement. If anyone could kill a demon king, it was these men. Or, these men and the people we were associated with.

Bronc gestured to Wrecker. "Back to the gallery opening. Security?"

Wrecker wiped his mouth with a napkin, then slid a folder down the table. "I've got micro-cameras up in both venues, with cloud storage. We'll monitor everything from Harper's office, and Arsenal will run physical sweeps. We've got prospects on rotating perimeter shifts, disguised as gallery staff. Two plainclothes at the front door, three more handling the parking lots. We want all hands on site in case anything goes down."

Arsenal added, "I got local police to stand down. Iron Valor has security on lockdown."

Bronc shifted to Doc. "What about medical?"

Doc took a gulp of his coffee and then set his mug down. "I got EMTs on standby, plus me. Low chance of violence, but better safe than sorry. There will be as many human patrons as supernatural. Need both on hand."

Bronc asked me about logistics.

"Harper's dance studio is the reception and food area. Temporary walls, fabric drapes, floral installations. Brie wanted it to look like a fairy tale. Prospects will set up tables that Papa didn't get to this morning. That and chairs should be done by noon."

Big Papa smiled, proud. "Harper did all the prep herself. She's proud of what she and Brie have accomplished."

"And she deserves it," I said, not bothering to hide my affection for my new sister-in-law.

Arsenal passed me a page. "Aspen's got the food. I saw the menu. She's going full Southern. Delivery starts at three, set up by five. Big Papa is helping her set up the cake."

I looked down at the sheet, suddenly overwhelmed by the precision and the planning. Every angle, every risk, accounted for.

Wrecker caught my hesitation and grinned. "Don't worry, Finn. We won't let anything happen to her."

I looked around the table. These men had literally saved my life before. They were the reason I'd survived battles, the reason I could wake up next to Brie every morning. For a second, I couldn't talk. My throat locked up, and I had to take a deep breath to steady myself.

Big Papa noticed. "It's okay to let them see you care, son. That's the difference between us and them."

Bronc nodded. "We're a pack for a reason."

I drained my coffee, then stood. "Thank you. All of you."

There was a round of grunts and nods, the men's version of a group hug.

Bronc finished his biscuit, then clapped me on the shoulder. "Get out there, Gunner. Make us look good."

I grinned, heading for the door, the weight in my chest replaced by something light and warm.

The world might be full of monsters, but I had the best crew in Texas backing me up.

Let them come.

The trick with a Tom Ford suit is to act like you wear it every day, not like you just took it out of the dry cleaner's plastic and spent half an hour watching YouTube videos on how to tie a "semi-formal" tie. The truth was, I felt like a fraud in that suit, but Brie had asked for it, and there wasn't a man alive who could say no to her when she turned those turquoise eyes on you and said, "I want you to look like a million bucks tonight."

So I showered, used the expensive aftershave she loved, and tried not to think about how many ways this night could go off the rails. By the time I pulled into the lot across the street, I'd gotten my nerves down to a dull roar and convinced myself the real reason I was sweating had nothing to do with the suit.

Harper's space didn't even look like itself. The front windows glowed with soft light; every inch of glass was lined with string lights, trailing like a river of stars through the foyer and into the big studio. The floors shone, and there was this smell of fresh-cut flowers, buttercream, and lemon polish. Tables were set with white linens, little gold-trimmed flyers, and arrangements of wildflowers in mismatched vases. Someone had even managed to get a soft jazz playlist going, which made the whole place feel more like a speakeasy than a dance studio for little girls. I knew that Brie had hired a string quartet that would arrive and start playing soon. She thought they'd "class the place up" just right.

The main attraction on the food side was the cake Aspen had delivered. It was four tiers, stacked in a way I'd never seen before: instead of circles, each layer was a triangle, the edges lined with gold leaf; the surfaces paint-ed with delicate brushstrokes of color that mirrored the gallery's palette. There were sugar flowers in the same purple and green as Brie's dress, and a big, abstract wolf made of blown sugar crowning the top tier. Aspen stood off to the side, hands folded, watching the cake like it might try to escape. And she was her own cute little work of art dressed in a flowing hot pink dress with a high waist, big white daisy appliques and a scoop neck. Her hair was in its signature high ponytail, and her green eyes almost glowed.

I caught a glimpse of Oscar when his head popped out from under the tablecloth on the floor. He gave me a little salute and disappeared.

I stopped at the table and grinned. "That's a work of art, Asp."

She smiled, cheeks pink, then shushed me. "Don't make me cry. If I cry, I'll mess up my eyeliner, and Juliet will kill me."

"Where is everyone?"

"Gallery's locked down for final touches. Most folks are changing or doing last-minute stuff at home. Harper and Parker are upstairs trying to pin Juliet into her dress. Brie's in her office, probably having a panic attack."

Aspen reached out, straightened my tie, and gave a little nod. "You look nice, Finn. Very... grown up."

I rolled my eyes. "That's the meanest thing anyone's said to me all day."

"Just wait," she said, then drifted off to talk to the florist.

I wandered through the space, hands in my pockets, just absorbing the vibe. It was weird—seeing the whole pack's work in one room, knowing how many of them had bled or fought or nearly died for the privilege of eating canapés under a string of twinkle lights. I thought about the nightmares, about the weight of Maltraz's attention, but right now, it was like all that darkness belonged to someone else.

I made a circuit of the room, chatting with prospects as they set up chairs and rearranged hi-top tables, checking the perimeter out of habit. Nothing felt off. Even the air was calm.

Then I wandered over to the gallery side. There she was at the top of the staircase that led down from the gallery's mezzanine office.

Brie.

She stood there, both hands on the rail, her dress flowing behind her like she were riding a breeze no one else could see. The sage green was lighter than it looked in her closet, almost silver in the artificial light, and the flashes of purple were like violet lightning every time she moved. The neckline plunged, and every inch of skin was dusted with a shimmer that made her look unearthly. Her hair was up in a twist, with the blue streaks fanned out like flames at the nape of her neck. Around her throat were three necklaces, each more complicated than the last, and she'd gone heavy on the eye makeup, smoky and smudged and just a little wild. The effect was somewhere between debutante and bandit queen.

My breath left me like I'd taken a punch.

She didn't walk—she floated down the stairs, pausing halfway to look out over the room. People actually stopped talking to watch her. Even the servers. I wasn't the only one slack-jawed.

At the bottom, she hesitated, then caught my eye. That grin—mischief and relief in one package—broke the spell, and she ran the last few steps to me, nearly slipping in her boots.

I caught her, arms around her waist. She pressed her face into my shoulder, then whispered, "Don't say anything. Just hold me."

"Gladly," I said, squeezing her tight. "You okay?"

She leaned back, eyes shining. "Not even a little. But I will be."

"You look—" I tried to find the words, but nothing fit. "—like you."

She smiled, then pecked my cheek, careful not to get her lipstick on me. "You look pretty damn good yourself, cowboy. I don't know whether to kiss you or frisk you for weapons."

"Why not both?" I muttered, earning another laugh.

She laced her fingers through mine and pulled me toward the cake. "Look at this. Aspen's a genius."

"I know. I already told her."

"I'm going to get so fat. I want to eat every bite."

"I'll roll you home," I said. "Or just carry you."

She squeezed my hand, and for a minute, everything felt like it was supposed to.

Then I heard Lysander's laugh, sharp as a knife, from the entryway.

He swept in with Inez on his arm, both of them done up to the nines. Lysander had on a suit that probably cost more than my truck, navy with black velvet lapels, and he moved like he owned every molecule in the room. Inez was in a short, spangly number, her hair in an elaborate updo, makeup flawless. They looked like they'd walked off a runway.

Lysander made a show of noticing us, then glided over, a glass of champagne already in hand.

"My, my, you make a striking figure all cleaned up, Mr. Walsh," he said, his eyes roving up and down the length of me, then lingering on Brie. "And as for you, darling—there are no words."

Brie grinned, basking in the attention. "Thanks, Sander. You look expensive."

He belted out a laugh, then turned back to me, voice dropping into something a little too intimate. "I was hoping we'd get a moment alone tonight. There are things we should discuss with regard to Brie's art. About... the next phase."

Something in the way he said it made my skin crawl.

I stepped forward, a hand at the small of Brie's back. "Nice to see you, Lysander. Everything looks great."

He smirked, like he knew exactly what I was doing, then tipped his glass to me. "You're a lucky man, Finn. Don't ever forget it."

Brie rolled her eyes, then elbowed me in the ribs. "I need to go say hi to Harper and Juliet before the crowd gets here. You gonna be okay without me?"

"I can handle myself," I said.

She squeezed my arm, then drifted off into the crowd.

Lysander watched her go, then leaned in. "If you hurt her, I'll have to kill you," he said, not quite joking.

I stared him down. "Odd threat seeing as how you barely know her. And right back at you, *buddy*."

He grinned. "Touché, cowboy."

Then, he and Inez vanished into a group of buyers, who'd started arriving, laughing and air-kissing like it was what they were born to do.

I stood by the cake, feeling like the last man standing at a wedding reception. I wandered to the bar and asked for a finger of whisky, tried to blend in, and kept an eye on the door.

I never wanted to punch anyone in the face more than that guy. It was going to be a long night. But at least for now, I could see my mate in the middle of the crowd, shining so bright even the darkness took a bow.

Chapter 21

Brie

It wasn't real until I stood smack in the center of my own gallery, breathless in the hush between violin notes and the low, bubbling talk of a crowd that now belonged to me.

Wildbrush Gallery was filled with who's-who of Dairyville, and art buyers from Amarillo, Santa Fe, and throughout Texas. The core of the Iron Valor pack surrounded me with warmth and a sense of family. The storm that had howled through the panhandle last night left the glass storefront so clean it looked newly minted. The light—that impossible Texas sunset light—came in gold and lavender rays through the windows, lighting up the whitewashed walls like a movie set.

My paintings hung around the perimeter, circling the beautiful exhibition we'd curated of Inez's paintings. Every frame was aligned, every piece perfectly spot-lit so you couldn't see a single flaw. The gallery temperature was perfect, not just from the air conditioning, but from the glow of bodies in dresses and jackets and boots; some that still carried a dusting of pasture on the heels. People stood in small groups and lines, clutching crystal flutes of champagne, glasses of whiskey and even a margarita or two from the cash bar. They were tilting their heads at my work, making appreciative "hmmm" sounds and talking about "color story" and "emotional depth"

like it was all perfectly normal and not the result of two years spent scrab-
bling in obscurity with a paintbrush and a chip on my shoulder.

I was honestly shocked. I thought all eyes would be too focused on
Inez's breathtaking canvases to have bothered with the paintings displayed
against the bricks. Deep down I knew my pieces were good. But it's not a
thought I'd ever allowed myself to speak aloud. But since this gallery was
mine, I figured no one would balk at the display of my own work. I'll be
damned if strangers didn't agree with my assessment and think my painting
had merit. Good on me. I smiled to myself as I strolled along listening to
strangers' assessments of my use of light and how my brushstrokes "capture
the movement of the wind on the wildflowers."

Through the open doors of the connecting archway to Harper's dance
studio, I saw happy people enjoying Aspen's delicious food. The sounds
of the string quartet drifted through, contributing to the comfortable atmosphere. It wasn't stuffy or pretentious. It was just comfortable; peaceful
somehow.

I continued to drift between paintings, trailing my fingers over the air
like a ghost afraid to touch the living. I watched as people posed with my
art—selfies, group shots, even a few "serious" patrons trying to look more
profound than they probably were. I caught my mother, Nanette, in the
act of straightening one of my business cards on the reception table, her
face a brittle mask of pride that looked more like a disbelieving joy, but I
knew her well enough to understand. She'd spent years telling herself I'd
outgrow my rebellion. Now here she was, standing in a room built by that
same stubbornness, and the only thing left was to feel it.

It was overwhelming, almost suffocating. I'd spent so long in the
trenches, painting as an escape, attending art school as we hid from wicked
men, that being here—seen, appreciated, respected—felt obscene.

That's when Gunner appeared at my side.

He was in his finest: black Tom Ford suit, crisp white shirt and black
silk tie. His auburn curls wrangled into something tamer than usual. The

suit clung to his shoulders, all business from the neck down, but his eyes still held the wildness of a man who'd rather be out on the range, or naked in a bed, than under gallery lighting.

He leaned down, his breath warm at my ear. "Look at you, Maverick. You built this."

I tried to laugh, but the emotion caught in my throat. "I just hung the paintings."

"Don't do that." He squeezed my hand. "Don't undersell yourself. I've never been prouder of anyone in my life."

I shook my head, blinking fast. "Don't say that. I'll start crying and ruin my makeup."

He grinned. "Then I'll have to carry you out of here, won't I?"

"God, you're such a caveman."

He kissed my cheek, and the heat of it stayed with me long after he pulled back. "Stay close tonight." His voice had gone low and tight. "Want you near me."

I nodded, too grateful for words.

We did a slow lap of the gallery, taking in the spectacle. Nanette caught sight of us and beamed, straight-up beamed, as if she'd never once doubted her wild, artsy daughter would amount to something. She flagged us over with an urgent wave.

"Oh, Brie, darling, I'd like you to meet the McCulloughs from the Amarillo Museum!" Nanette was on a cloud. "This is my daughter; she owns this gallery! And her paintings are the ones along the walls in the gallery."

I managed a smile, shook their hands, and endured a round of soft-voiced compliments that bordered on embarrassing. Nanette squeezed my arm, and for a heartbeat I thought she'd actually cry, but she didn't. She just looked at me like I was the answer to every prayer she'd never had the nerve to ask for.

Across the room, Lysander was holding court.

He'd dressed for the occasion. The velvet lapels of his suit wouldn't have worked on anyone but him. And with his platinum hair styled just messy enough to look deliberate, he was impossible not to notice. He moved through the clusters of guests like an eel, magnetic and always just a little out of reach. He laughed at the right moments, touched arms and shoulders, drew people into his orbit, and when he talked about my art, he made it sound as if I'd invented painting from scratch.

I watched as he drew two older women and a banker from the city over to the big triptych in the far corner. He set up the group, hands gesturing, describing my brushwork, then paused so the others could step up and stare. He caught my eye across the room and winked.

I flushed, but this time it wasn't embarrassment; it was gratitude.

At the edge of the crowd, I caught Harper in a pale blue sheath dress, hair up, her arm through Arsenal's. He looked quite dapper in a navy suit that included a vest. She caught my gaze and grinned, her eyes shining with pride.

This was what I'd always wanted: not fame, not money, but a moment where I could see, with my own eyes, that I belonged somewhere.

I glanced at Gunner, who was deep in conversation with Big Papa and Wrecker near the front door. He looked up, caught my gaze, and gave a chin nod. It was enough.

The noise rose and fell, conversations orbiting Inez's paintings, people moving from wall to wall, some even making notes on the little cards Lysander had supplied. The wine flowed, the food disappeared, and as the sun went down, the world inside the gallery became its own universe, untethered from the rest of Dairyville.

I let myself bask in it.

For once, I didn't feel like an impostor.

I felt real.

I felt seen.

And that feeling, that impossible, intoxicating feeling, was worth every sleepless night, every hour spent doubting if I'd ever get here.

I let myself believe it.

I let myself belong.

And as the evening stretched out, the storm still rumbling somewhere far off, I stood in the middle of it all and thought: let them come.

I'm ready.

It was Aspen who started the clinking. From there, it rippled through the room as glasses of champagne were passed around. The quick hush of the crowd signaled that they were ready for the show. Someone dimmed the lights just a touch, and the faces around me turned toward the far end of the gallery. For a second, I considered ducking into the bathroom, just to kill time until someone else started the toasts, but Gunner's hand slipped around my waist and pinned me in place.

"You've got this." His steady confidence lifted me up.

I squared my shoulders, stepped into the little pool of light, and watched as the crowd stilled, all those sharp, hungry, hopeful eyes tracking my every move.

I'd written my speech three times and torn it up twice. Now, holding the champagne flute, my hands shook so badly the bubbles spilled over the rim.

"Hi," I said, a little too loud.

The laughter that followed made it easier, and I let the next breath out slow. "Thank you for coming. Seriously, I didn't think even half this many people would show up, and if I'd known I'd have made Aspen bake twice as many cakes."

A soft murmur of approval rippled from the bakery contingent.

"There are a lot of people I want to thank, and I'll keep it quick because I hate speeches almost as much as I hate attention, which is ironic considering I'm standing up here with every single person I know staring at me. So, uh, first—thank you, Inez Chavez, for choosing Wildbrush Gallery for your first ever exhibition. I'm so proud that I'll be able to say, 'I knew her when…'. I'm honored and thankful you allowed me to hang my work alongside yours. When I first saw your work and learned my gallery had the opportunity to host your first show, I couldn't believe how very lucky I'd gotten. So, thank you."

Inez raised her glass, eyes glassy.

"Harper, for being the best big sister and role model I could ever have. If you hadn't believed in me—even when I didn't—I wouldn't be here. And thank you for not kicking my ass when I stole your boots in high school. And your sweaters, and earrings…" I trailed off. The crowd laughed, and Harper dabbed at her eyes.

"My mom." I looked at Nanette; her face lit up with a pride that made my chest ache. "You pushed me to be better every day, even when I didn't want to hear it. You showed me what real grace looks like, even in the most difficult situations, and tonight I hope I made you proud."

Nanette's hand covered her mouth, but her tears had already escaped.

"Juliet and Bronc, for making me feel like a part of this family from the day I set foot in Dairyville. Your support, your faith… I never thought I'd find that feeling of family. You proved me wrong. Thank you."

Bronc nodded, face stern but eyes soft. Juliet had one hand on her very large belly as she gave me a reassuring smile that said, "You've got this."

"Gunner—Finn. For being my biggest fan, my anchor, and for loving me even when I'm insufferable. There's no one I'd rather share a life, or disasters, with." I glanced back at him, and the way he looked at me nearly broke my composure.

"And finally, Lysander Hale. I never imagined a stranger from Boston would bring me the chance to host a successful gallery exhibition and opening, much less show my own work. You believed in me, in my art, even when I didn't see the point. Thank you for putting Wildbrush on the map."

He bowed his head with a little flourish, grinning.

"And thank you, Dairyville. For showing up. For giving me a home." I raised my glass. "To everyone here. To the weirdos, the dreamers, the people who think maybe—just maybe—they can make something out of nothing. Tonight is for us."

The room erupted.

There were howls, claps, a dozen voices cheering in unison, and for a second, the air shimmered with something beyond sound, something physical and bright that landed right in the hollow of my chest and stayed there.

Harper ran up and hugged me, nearly knocking me off my shoes. Nanette followed, and it was a rare and glorious moment when my mother's arms wrapped around me and she whispered, "You are perfect, Annabelle Brie. Always have been."

Even Juliet, radiant and round as a moon, waddled over and kissed my cheek. "You were always Iron Valor, darling. You just needed to see it." Bronc's handshake was brief but crushing, his grin wide and proud.

When I turned, Finn was waiting. He kissed my forehead, held me for a heartbeat longer than anyone else. "That's my girl." His pride radiated from him, fierce and unbreakable.

The crowd settled as Lysander drifted into the light, glass in hand. He didn't raise it until the room was fully silent.

"When I first reached out to Wildbrush Gallery, I expected to find potential," he began, his voice floating just above the hush. "I did not expect to find brilliance." He swept his gaze over the crowd, but landed on me. "Brie Lawson is... luminous. Not simply as an artist, but as a soul. She reminded me *why* art matters. Why *connection* matters. Why beauty—in all its forms—deserves a home. Tonight, I gained not just a client... but a friend I hope to keep for life."

There was a sigh, a collective melting in the room. Nanette glowed, Harper wiped her eyes again, and even Gunner, stiff at the edge of the light, couldn't stop a grudging smile.

"Raise your glasses, to Brie Lawson, and to the Wildbrush. May it never be tamed."

The echo of it—Wildbrush, never tamed—rolled through the crowd, a wave of joy and belonging. Glasses clinked, people called my name, and for a second I felt like the universe was built for me, by me, and nothing could ever knock me off center again.

The strings started up, laughter filled the gaps, and for the next half hour I floated through the room, hugging people, answering questions, signing programs, even posing for a few pictures with Inez in front of our shared mural. There were more speeches, some silly, some serious.

Finn stayed close, never quite letting go of my hand or waist. He steered me through the crowd with gentle nudges and soft words, always grounding me, always reminding me where I came from.

It was perfect, all of it. The kind of night you build your whole life around. The kind of night you hope will never end.

And for a while, I believed it could last forever.

****

The crowd didn't thin so much as it began to swirl—people drifting between the gallery and Harper's studio, the air dense with music and the faint tang of lemon buttercream. I made my rounds, thanked everyone who so much as looked my way, then gave myself permission to slip upstairs for five blessed minutes. I needed to breathe, and, okay, maybe to double-check the little box I'd wrapped for Inez as a surprise thank-you.

I slipped away, telling Finn I had to use the "real bathroom" in my office. He let me go, but his eyes tracked me the whole way, green and intent, promising protection..

The stairs to the mezzanine were long metal steps each one echoing over the noise below. My dress—floor-length sage with lavender insets and ridiculous clusters of handmade flowers—snagged on the rail as I hurried up. I laughed at myself, half-drunk on joy, half on the flute of champagne still in my hand.

My office at the top had the door barely ajar. Inside, everything was just as I'd left it: the old wood dining table desk, the battered easel in the corner, the half-finished painting I was pretending not to be obsessed with. The window looked down over the whole gallery, and for a second I stood there, hidden, just watching the world.

The little box was right where I'd stashed it—behind a row of paint thinner jars. I pulled it out, checked the ribbon, then let myself spin around once in a moment of pure, giddy pride.

That's when Lysander knocked.

"Darling?" he called through the crack. "You okay?"

I opened the door wider. "Yeah—just had to get this." I held up the box. "It's for Inez. But I needed a minute to, uh, reassemble my face. I am a mess."

He laughed, leaning in the doorway, arms crossed. "If I looked like you, I'd stare at myself all night. They're all obsessed with you, you know."

"Shut up." I smiled. "You want to take this down to Inez? I could use a minute to—"

"Are you kidding? Let her see it's from you." He stepped into the room and closed the door gently behind him. "You deserve the moment."

His voice had gone soft, stripped of all irony. I looked at him, really looked at him, and for the first time all night saw something tired in his eyes. The mask was slipping, just a touch. Maybe it had been a long week for him too.

He reached out, palms up. "Come here, you brilliant thing. Let me hug you before I combust from envy."

It was so un-Lysander I laughed. But I stepped forward, letting him wrap me up in a tight, platonic embrace. He was warm, lean, smelled like salt and citrus. For a moment, I let myself lean into it, just bask in the weird siblinghood of two outsiders making good.

Then I tried to pull away, and couldn't.

His arms had gone steel-hard around my waist, pinning me tight. At first, I thought he was making a joke, some elaborate bit, but when I looked up, his face was just inches from mine, smiling in a way I'd never seen. There was nothing in his eyes—no shine, no affection, no warmth. Just empty, bottomless black.

"Told you we'd be lifelong friends," he whispered.

My mouth opened, but no sound came out.

The world tilted.

His face was changing. The skin shimmered, stretched, warped. In the blink of an eye, it was still Lysander—but layered over something else, something ancient and wrong. I saw the shadow of horns, the glint of razor teeth, the slithering tail that flicked out behind him like a live wire.

I struggled against him, but it was no use. I felt his fingers move to my face, and I tried to scream, but the air caught in my throat. I was disoriented as he muttered words I didn't understand. But then he turned his head, just slightly, and stared straight into the security camera mounted in the corner. He smiled a slow, deliberate, evil smile and said something that sounded like: "Come find me."

Then Finn was in the room.

His anguished face was the last thing I saw. I squeaked out the only words I could say. "I'm sorry."

There was a sound, not quite a pop, not quite a crack—a snap of cold, of nothing, and the world went empty. The next instant, the room vanished.

All that was left was the little box, rolling in a lazy circle on the desk, and the echo of my name in the void.

CHAPTER 22

GUNNER

There's a unique flavor to a crowd just before a storm. The gallery's air was thick with perfume, cologne, paint fumes, and anticipation. People milled around, drifting from canvas to canvas, pretending to admire the art while searching for someone more important to notice them doing it. I'd posted up by the bar, careful to nurse a single whiskey so nobody would talk my ear off and ask who the hell I was supposed to be. In the corner, Harper fielded questions from a woman in a pantsuit who looked like she sold more real estate than God. Juliet—eight months pregnant and radiant as the full moon—was locked in a deep, animated conversation with Ms. Pearl and half the Dairyville Chamber of Commerce. Wrecker hovered up in Harper's office, his "civilian" shirt straining against his biceps, scanning for threats with all the subtlety of a gun turret.

I should have felt invincible. Instead, I was pacing inside my own skin, hands jammed deep in my pockets, doing math in my head. I watched Brie as she spun through the room, a comet in that sage-green dress, the blue streaks in her hair catching the spotlights every time she turned her head. She was in her element, and the mate bond hummed low and content through the marrow of my bones. Every time I checked, there she was—sometimes talking to a buyer, sometimes holding court with Inez and Lysander, sometimes just drifting with a glass of champagne and that proud, nervous smile. Nothing out of the ordinary, just the slow orbit of a woman finally seeing her dreams catch up.

The string quartet shifted into something baroque and odd, and the crowd started to migrate toward this room for the "curated bites." She had told me she needed to head up to her private restroom for a moment. It was the first time all night she'd been out of my sight. A few minutes later, I glanced over to see Lysander heading up the stairs toward Brie's office behind her. I felt a tingle up my spine telling me something was off. The situation just seemed wrong. I set my whiskey glass on a table and made my way across the gallery. A local woman stopped me as I was making my way to Brie. She wanted to ask about beef prices. I gently told her I was only there tonight to support Brie and not talk shop. She graciously said she understood and hurried away. One more step and I felt the bond flare white-hot, so suddenly my knees almost buckled.

The wolf in me roared awake. It was pain, raw and unfiltered, not physical but somewhere between a panic attack and being struck by lightning. My whole body went rigid, and the only thing I could see—burned into the backs of my eyes—was the image of Brie upstairs, terrified, her breath coming in silent, shallow gasps. The world snapped into a new kind of focus. I looked up and saw through the smoked glass wall of the mezzanine office, two silhouettes locked together.

I froze just for a moment when Lysander's form shifted and I saw a hint of something unnatural.

I moved quickly to the stairs with what could be described as inhuman speed.

I shouldered past a pack mom without even registering the yelp. I took the stairs two at a time, boots skidding across the landing. I could see through the glass door the two of them in a tight embrace; Brie struggling against Lysander, who had her pinned tight. His face was turned, blocking hers, but the way he held her was all wrong. Not like a lover or friend, but like a snake coiling for the kill.

My palms hit the door, but it didn't budge. The handle was locked, so I braced a shoulder and slammed into it. The cheap hardware popped, and the door flew open with a crack.

"Let her go!" My voice was a snarl, thick with wolf.

Lysander didn't even look up. His hands were on either side of Brie's face, thumbs pressed to her cheeks. Brie's eyes were rolling, her legs kicking out blindly. I saw then, in a split second, that Lysander's lips were moving. He was whispering something, words slick and venomous. Her fingers clawed at his suit, desperate to pry him off.

I barreled forward, but Lysander whirled, dragging Brie's body in front of him as a human shield. He smiled at me, and for the first time that night, there was nothing pretty about him. His eyes were black, not blue, and his skin rippled as if something inside him wanted out.

He tsked, his fingers tightening until Brie whimpered. Then, impossibly, Lysander's features began to unravel. His skin grayed, his lips curled back, and his smile went wider, then wider still, until it split the whole bottom half of his face in a leering crescent. Horns pushed out through his platinum hair, curving around his skull like a ram. The suit tore as his body swelled, stretching into something inhuman and terrible, but the hands—those beautiful, manicured hands—never let Brie go.

Brie gasped, found my eyes, and mouthed, "Finn, I'm sorry—"

Lysander jerked her head back, baring her throat.

"You won't find us," the demon hissed, voice now a rasp of old coal and fire. "But by all means, try."

I dove for him, claws out, but the demon king had already started to fade, his whole outline collapsing in on itself like a dying star. There was a shockwave of pressure—heat, the smell of sulfur and burnt roses—and then Lysander, Brie, and every trace of their struggle vanished into thin air.

I hit the floor where they'd been, hands grasping at nothing. I bellowed, a howl so full of pain and rage it rattled the walls. The office was sound-proof, but the wolves below heard my cry. Arsenal was already on his way.

I stood shaking, the mate bond a ragged, torn string in my chest. I'd lost her. Not to a rival, not to a bullet, but to a fucking nightmare that wore a pretty boy's face.

I wanted to run after him, but there was nothing left to chase.

My hands curled into fists. I saw on the desk, Brie's little box—her gift for Inez, wrapped so neat and perfect. I seized it, hurled it at the wall, and watched it burst open in a cloud of ribbon and shredded cardboard.

Somewhere behind me, footsteps pounded up the stairs. Arsenal, Bronc closing in, their voices tumbling over each other.

But I barely heard them. All I could hear was the echo of the demon's promise: You won't find us.

I planted my fist through the drywall, splintering it to the stud, and let the pain burn the rage down to something I could use.

She was alive. The bond still throbbed, faint and far, but unbroken.

So long as she breathed, I would find her.

Even if it meant following the bastard straight into hell.

I was halfway down the stairs, hands slick with drywall dust and the tang of my own blood, when my wolf tried to rise up. My vision tunneled gold and black. The world slowed—every sound, every motion warped by that predatory clarity that only came when a shift was right behind your ribs. I heard my boots hitting hardwood, the string quartet below playing on, and somewhere behind it all, the thin, echoing voice of Parker.

"He got her, he took her!" Her voice was a saw blade, chewing through the hush like a coyote through bone.

I kept my head down so no humans would notice my blazing gold lupine eyes as I all but staggard over to the security office on Harper's side. My mind couldn't let go of what I'd just seen. His demon claws on my mate. Touching her. I wanted to rage, to destroy everything in my path. It was the worst time to be surrounded by humans.

I zeroed in on the security booth. Wrecker was hunched over the monitors, his face ghost-pale, sweat dripping down his neck even though he never sweated in the worst firefights. His fingers hammered the keyboard with a precision I'd never seen, his eyes flicking back and forth between feeds as he muttered, "Gotta save this, gotta save this, he'll try to nuke it from the inside, fuck—" He didn't look up when I came up behind him, but Parker did. Her face was bloodless, lips drawn back in a snarl that would have been funny if I weren't seconds from tearing someone's throat out.

"Gunner," she panted, "it's all over the screens. Maltraz, he just...he just..." She gulped air, shaking.

Wrecker cut her off, still not looking. "She's alive, Finn. I had eyes on her for three more seconds after the blink. But then the camera goes dead. Black. Nothing."

I leaned in, every muscle shaking, and watched the replay. It was clear, the angle from the corner, but there it was—Brie's body going limp as Lysander's face opened up and the horns split out from his skull. The air shimmered, the glass warped, and then both of them blinked out, leaving a shimmer of smoke and a little rolling box on the desk.

Wrecker saved the two minutes to four different flash drives, shoving one into his pocket, another into the lining of his laptop bag, then a third to Parker with a curt, "Go." She snatched it and ran, already dialing her phone as she sprinted to her car.

I dropped to my hands and knees, crippled by the loss of my mate and the press of my wolf. I fought it, teeth grinding, the taste of iron thick on my tongue.

Then a pair of hands seized my shoulders. Not rough, but heavy as a mountain. Bronc.

He leaned down, putting his mouth right at my ear. "Look at me."

I snarled, twisting, but his grip didn't budge. "Look at me, Finn."

I looked. Bronc's blue eyes were ice, and the wolf in him was so close to the surface I could smell the danger, the authority. He locked my gaze, his Alpha voice rolling out in a wave that crashed over the chaos and rooted me to the floor.

"You will not shift here," he said, every word a weight. "Not with civilians. Not with the Council's eyes on us. You hold it together, right now. Do you hear me?"

The command dropped like a sledgehammer. I felt my wolf stop, stunned. My body settled. My vision cleared just enough to see the smears of blood I'd left across the table.

Bronc didn't let up. "We will find her. But I need you in control. If you go full animal, you lose her for good."

I forced air into my lungs. His Alpha command stopped me dead in my tracks. Subdued me. I felt more human than animal instantly.

Wrecker finished a last keystroke, then whirled his chair to face me, his eyes gone flat and feral. "We need the Angel King. Now. Only he's gonna have the juice to track Maltraz in whatever hellhole he just crawled into."

Bronc nodded. "Get Aspen. Call her father. Tell him it's a pack matter and a Council matter both."

Wrecker leaned out the door and yelled for Papa who was directing the other wolves to handle interference with the humans. He told him to have Aspen see if she could get ahold of Archon and get him here as soon as possible. Bronc gave my shoulder another squeeze, then let go. "You ready, Gunner?"

I gritted my teeth.

"Ready," I said, and meant it.

We weren't going to wait.

We were going to rip the world apart until we got her back.

If you want to see a pack's true colors, kick it square in the teeth.

The moment Maltraz took Brie, Iron Valor snapped into formation like a fire team on D-Day. The patrons had started to thin as the night had worn on. The only people left were serious buyers.

Maddie managed to calm Inez down and explain that Lysander would call her as soon as he had things sorted. She was content to go back to Amarillo with the large contingent of family who'd come to see her big debut. She was leaving for Santa Fe in the morning and told Maddie to tell Lysander she sends her love.

"Everyone, I am so sorry," Ms. Pearl called, her Southern drawl smooth and comforting as a glass of sweet tea. "We're experiencing a small emergency upstairs, so the evening is going to be cut short by a few minutes. If y'all would kindly follow us toward the studio side, you can grab additional treats on your way out." She smiled at every face, and somehow it worked; people automatically wanted to follow her lead. And people were content as long as Aspen's sweets were still available. Juliet, round as a planet happily directed people to the exits.

On the far side, Arsenal and Big Papa ran perimeter, blocking the fire exit and the back door—nothing obvious, just enough presence that nobody thought about sneaking off. Wrecker disappeared into the utility room. Parker who'd just come back in was on his heels, both of them talking so fast and so low only wolves could have heard. Every member of Iron Valor not nailed to a chair found their station. Orders were barked, decisions made, and every second bought us time.

Nannette who'd only a while ago beamed with well-deserved pride now slumped in a chair, one hand white-knuckled around a mug of coffee, the other clutching Harper's; both their faces stricken with utter disbelief in what had transpired.

I stood in the middle of the chaos, useless as a scarecrow. I wanted to do something; anything but watch. But Bronc had posted up a few feet away, and the look in his eyes was clear: Hold. Don't crack. This is how we win.

Menace was the first to break from the inner circle. He buttoned his suit jacket and ducked out onto the sidewalk, phone already pressed to his ear. He wasn't just calling anyone—he was calling Rafe Mayfield, King of the Southwest Wolves, the only man with enough muscle to call an emergency Council session on a Saturday night.

Menace never wasted a syllable. "Rafe. It's urgent. Maltraz just snatched a mated female out of Iron Valor territory. Yes, that's correct. I have video footage. It happened in full view, public venue, no regard for covertness. I need the Council assembled in two hours or less. No, I don't care if it's midnight their time. They'd better goddamn well come together or shit is gonna fly. We can do it by video conference. Wrecker can facilitate."

He hung up, looked at me through the window, and nodded once.

Inside, Aspen already had her phone in her hand. She looked smaller than usual, her hands shaking as she scanned her contacts. Oscar perched on her shoulder, whispering in her ear, his prairie dog voice high and anxious.

She pressed the icon for her father: "Dad? We've got a big issue. It's bad. There will be a fight. Gunner's mate. Maltraz took her. Yes, in front of everyone. We need help."

A hush fell over the room as every supernatural in the building felt the shift in the air. Something old and holy had been called, and even the civilians picked up on it even if they had no idea what just happened. They'd started to clear out, one by one, until only the immediate pack and a handful of stragglers remained.

Meanwhile, Juliet worked the crowd with the kind of poise that came from surviving a hundred black-tie events. A woman in pearls cornered her, voice pitched high with concern: "Is everything alright? Where's Ms. Lawson? She was supposed to speak again, I think—"

Juliet gave her a look, warm and a little regretful. "I'm so sorry. Lysander Hale received a call from his mother. There was an accident back East, and he and Brie are trying to reach her by phone now. It's family business." She touched the woman's arm, an anchor in the confusion. "I promise you can direct any questions about the art or purchases to me or Ms. Pearl." She smiled, and it worked. The woman softened, letting herself be led out.

Juliet reconciled the other buyers' purchases, taking Venmo payments and handing out receipts. Several other members of the Iron Valor team were carefully wrapping paintings for people to take home.

Within twenty minutes, the gallery was empty except for us.

Then the dam broke.

I bounded back up the stairs, not caring if I knocked another hole in the drywall. I burst through the mezzanine door, eyes wild and searching. I caught the scent of Brie still hanging in the air.

The office was a wreck. Her papers and paintbrushes scattered across the floor, her chair knocked sideways, the half-finished painting on the easel torn through the middle. I paced the room, nose hunting for anything—sweat, blood, the perfume she wore just for me. It was all faint being overwhelmed by the hot ozone stink of Maltraz's magic and the weak, desperate trace of her fear.

I flipped the desk, slammed the drawers open, shredded the little rolling box that had been left behind. For a second, I saw it: a single strand of Brie's hair, blue-dyed and perfect, curled around the handle of her favorite palette knife. I pressed it to my face and howled.

I felt like my heart was being ripped from my chest, like I couldn't remember how to breathe. My body felt wrong, as though someone had reached inside of me and removed a crucial organ, one that was meant to keep me alive.

And then the air changed.

It went from hot and electric to cold and weightless, like a door opening in the middle of winter. The shadows deepened, and the edges of the room filled with white light that pulsed with every breath. When I looked up, Archon was there, standing in the doorway.

He was taller than I remembered. Seven feet if he was an inch, hair like a river of spun silver falling down his back. He wore a white suit, too, but it didn't look like any human tailoring—each seam shone, each button glinted like a star. His eyes weren't gold; they were every color at once, swirling and shifting.

He walked to me, slow and solemn, and knelt until our faces were level.

"Finn Walsh," he said, his voice the song of every river I'd ever heard rushing by. "Your mate is alive."

I couldn't speak. I just nodded, the hair still clutched in my fist.

"She is frightened, but she is not alone. The demon king has taken her, but she is not lost to you."

He reached out, two fingers extended, and pressed them to my forehead.

"You must not lose yourself. She needs you whole."

I stood up, wiped my face, and looked down at the security camera that still blinked red from the corner.

I stared into the lens, every cell in my body burning with a new promise.

"I'm coming for you, baby," I said, voice low and steady. "I swear it."

The world outside was already moving—phones ringing, engines starting, the war machine of Iron Valor gearing up for the biggest fight we'd ever faced.

But right now, it was just me, her, and the echo of a vow.

The next time Maltraz saw me, there would be hell to pay.

CHAPTER 23

BRIE

I woke up in pain, which was getting to be a pattern with me, but this time the pain was more honest about itself. No headaches, no sense of drowning. Just the raw, white-hot throb of my shoulders being wrenched nearly out of their sockets, and the stinging ache where cold iron dug into the thin skin of my wrists.

I hung suspended, toes barely scraping the slimy rock below, and for a minute I didn't know if I was dreaming, dead, or in one of those fucked up movie scenes where they put you in a meat locker to cool off before the real torture starts.

The smell was the first clue: dank, fetid, with an undercurrent of something sweet and rotten. The air was cold but not freezing, the darkness close and thick, broken only by occasional flickers of blue lightning that skittered along the chains. My dress—the one Gunner had called "statement worthy"—was in shreds, the skirt hung loose at my ankles, the wide lavender wrap-around belt was tattered. My skin was streaked with grime and sweat, my legs undoubtedly spattered with dried blood from where the manacles had pinched. I didn't even want to know what my hair looked like, but judging by the lock that hung in my face, the streaked blue was as filthy as the rest of me. He must have dragged me by my arm through Lord knows what to get me here.

My first thought was, *"Well, this sucks."*

My second was, *"I can feel Finn."*

Somewhere out in the darkness, far away but real, the mate bond hummed. It was a sickly, thin thread compared to the roar of it back home, but it was there. Not enough to speak across, but enough to remind me that my life—my real life—hadn't ended. It made something in my chest clench tight and hot, and suddenly, the fear was second place to the anger.

I would not be a victim. Not again.

I forced myself to scan the room, eyes adjusting to the deep dark the best I could. It was a cave or a cell, with walls so rough and ancient they could have belonged to a volcano. The only "decoration" was a rusted iron ring set into the stone, the chain snaking from it up to the manacles that held me. I flexed my wrists, testing for weakness, but the cuffs were solid, heavier than anything I'd ever seen. He hadn't intended on me getting out.

Footsteps echoed from the left—a soft, deliberate scuff, followed by a second, heavier stride. I froze, and the chains clinked softly.

Two figures came into view. One was unmistakable: Maltraz, demon king, in his demon form. He stood every bit of seven feet tall, his skin a translucent gray color; smooth and matte. His face was sharp angles and shadows; his cheekbones high with a nose like a blade, ridges from bridge to nostrils pierced with three gold rings. His hair was jet black and shaved on the sides with a long braid that started at the top of his head and ran mid-back. His eyes glowed red, but not like wolfs; the irises were vertical; monster eyes that shimmered when they caught the light. His mouth was wide and full of sharp teeth. His hands were massive and tipped with black, lacquered claws.

He wore a leather coat over what looked like a bulletproof vest, and he carried himself like a bodyguard, but his eyes flicked up to mine with an intelligence that said "Don't underestimate me." I did not.

Maltraz surveyed me where I hung with theatrical boredom, then focused on me, his lips curling into a smile that made my skin crawl.

"Ah, the artist awakes." His voice was as warm as antifreeze.

"Can't say I love what you've done with the place." I was horse but my voice was steady.

He grinned. "It's temporary. You'll be moving soon. But it suits you, doesn't it? The chains, the dirt, the little stage lighting?"

I looked him in the eye. "How'd you do it? Become Lysander Hale, I mean? I know they did background checks on you...or him."

His laughter boomed around me.

Maltraz leaned against the obsidian wall, a cruel smile playing on lips that had once smiled at me with Lysander Hale's warmth. "The real Lysander Hale," he began, his voice a velvet nightmare, "died screaming in a Venice alley three months ago. I've worn his skin—his memories, his credentials, his entire existence—since."

I remembered Wrecker's thorough background checks—the bank records, the gallery certifications, even the childhood photos. All flawless. Maltraz chuckled. "Demons excel at forgery, little curator. We *invent* truths. When your tech genius dug, he found only Lysander's impeccable history."

The horror coiled in my stomach. Those three weeks flooded back: Lysander bringing me coffee during late-night cataloging, laughing with me over terrible modern art, confiding about his "boyfriend." All lies. I was a damn fool.

"Every shared secret," Maltraz purred, "every vulnerable moment you gifted me—was a stitch in the net to trap you." He stepped closer, shadows clinging to him like loyal hounds. "I needed your trust to lower your wards. To make you *want* me to follow you up to your office opening night."

I squeezed my eyes shut, remembering his speech—the beautiful things he'd said about me. The last thing I'd seen before darkness took me was Lysander's concerned face melting into Maltraz's triumphant grin. I remembered Gunner's devastated look as I disappeared. Now, iron cuffs bit into my wrists. My dear friend had been the demon king, weaving my chains stitch by stitch, and I'd handed him the thread with a trusting smile.

"You should be very proud. You played me perfectly." I hung my head. I may have appeared sad, but I was furious.

"Aren't you so pitiful now, bestie?"

I didn't answer. I was too busy cataloguing everything I could about the room, the chains, and the men. Any clue. Any weakness.

Maltraz turned to the other demon. "Adramal, what did I tell you about Iron Valor? Every time you think you've crushed them, they get back up."

Adramal grunted, unimpressed. "You said they were like cockroaches. Hard to kill."

"Harder, even." He moved closer, hands in his pockets, as if he'd just strolled into an art opening and was about to critique the drapes. "Did you know, Brie, that your little pack nearly cost me a year's worth of planning in the past several months? And then, last night, you made it all worth it."

I rolled my eyes. "Sorry if I don't share your joy. Seems like a pretty shitty experience to me. Zero stars. Do not recommend."

Adramal snorted. "You let her talk to you like that?"

Maltraz chuckled, never breaking his gaze. "It's delightful. You should have seen the look on Finn's face when I took her. I'll replay that memory every night for a decade."

Something inside me twisted, but I wouldn't let him see it. I spat blood onto the floor and glared. "So what's the play, Maltraz? You gonna drag me into the underworld and make me your hell bride, or is there some actual plan here?"

He leaned in, close enough that I could smell the sulfur of his magic and the rot of his real self beneath it. "I could. But what would be the fun? You see, I've spent the last ten years building a network in your world. Money, power, influence. I made a bet on the right wolf, and then your Iron Valor bastards went and burned it all down."

He pulled a gold coin from his pocket and rolled it along his fingers. "So now, I do what humans have always done with valuables that won't stay put: I auction them off."

For a second, I didn't get it. Then it hit me, and my stomach lurched.

"I'd heard that you traffic women. It's a bit cliché, isn't it? It's about the most heinous thing you can do outside of messing with children. In Paris, Steiner mentioned he was sending me to you. I hoped that the operation had been shut down. Guess it's hard to stop evil." I don't know why I was poking the bear. Or demon or whatever. Maybe because he was Lysander, and I still felt like I knew him.

"Oh, *little girl*, you are naïve."

I winced at that term. "So, *that's* the plan? You're going to sell me?" I laughed, partly because it was insane, partly because it was the only way not to start crying. "To who? The highest bidder gets to what, hang me on the wall? Make me paint for them?"

Maltraz's eyes sparkled. "Not paint. I'm thinking more of a trophy. A warning to every wolf and every rebel who ever thought they could cross me and walk away. There's a buyer already, actually. The Vampire King of the West is quite taken with you, and he hates Iron Valor almost as much as I do. There are others too. You'd be surprised how many people want to own you, Brie."

Adramal looked skeptical. "She's not an alpha. She's not even that strong. Why bother?"

Maltraz never looked away from me. "Because it's not about what she is. It's about what she means. Take her, and you rip Gunner Walsh apart. You rip apart the heart of Iron Valor. The Council will scramble, the alliances will fracture, and then—when the world is nice and weak—I swoop in and collect the pieces."

I didn't want to give him the satisfaction, but I couldn't help it: I bared my teeth and snapped, "He's coming for me, you know. You think you're ready, but you're not."

Maltraz placed the coin on his tongue, let it melt into smoke, then grinned. "I hope he does. It'll make the final act so much sweeter."

He turned to go, but paused and looked back. "Don't worry, darling. I won't touch you. I'm not interested in that. I only touched you in your dreams to weaken your mate. Now I'm saving you for someone who will truly appreciate what you are."

He gestured to Adramal, and the big demon stepped forward. For a second, I thought he was going to hit me, but instead he produced a battered water bottle and held it up to my lips. I drank; most of it ran down my chin, but the cold felt good.

When he was done, he wiped my mouth with his thumb, his touch unexpectedly gentle. He looked me in the eye and spoke barely loud enough to hear. "Don't let him win. He loves that."

I nodded just once, and then he stepped back.

Maltraz sauntered to the door, then stopped again. He turned, strode across the room, and bent so our faces were inches apart. He smelled like smoke and death.

He ran a claw along my jaw, tipping my chin up. "You hang on to that anger, Brie. King Otero will drain it out of you, slow and sweet. That's his style. I wonder how long you'll last."

I spat in his face, and he laughed, a big, joyous, evil sound that echoed through the cave like a thunderclap.

He stood, brushed off his jacket, and walked away, whistling a little tune that I recognized from somewhere, but couldn't place.

Adramal lingered, glancing back at me, then followed his boss out.

I hung there, arms burning, blood running down to pool in my shoulders. But I wasn't scared anymore.

Finn was coming.

And Maltraz was about to find out just how much trouble one wolf girl could cause.

It was hard to tell how much time had passed since Maltraz had left. Down here, the air didn't move, and the only way to measure minutes was in the slow, aching pulse of blood through your hands. I'd been chained to a metal chair that was bolted to the floor. I must have dozed off, because the next thing I heard was a new set of voices, arguing in low, furious whispers from somewhere just out of sight.

I held my breath and listened.

"You idiot. You absolute glory-drunk idiot." The voice was sharp, nasal, with a lisp around the s's. I recognized it instantly—Nazek, the other demon from Maltraz's inner circle. He'd always been the sidekick, the note-taker, the one who stood two feet behind and two IQ points below the action.

"Maltraz does what he wants. We serve. That's the order," rumbled Adramal. He sounded less like a demon now and more like an exhausted middle manager.

"You heard what he did. In front of all those wolves. In front of a King's goddamn daughter. There were humans there! If you think the Council is going to look the other way..."

A heavy thud, like someone punching a wall. "I'm not paid to think."

Nazek hissed, "You're not paid at all. If this goes sideways, they'll wipe you out first. They always do. The King is obsessed with his precious rules. You know who was in that room? Archon's spawn. And the Angel King himself was in Dairyville not twenty-four hours ago."

There was a pause, then the soft clink of chains. I could picture Adramal pacing back and forth, jaw clenched, hands curled into clubs.

"Maltraz said this was supposed to be a snatch-and-grab. Not a fucking production. Now, every wolf in the south will come for us. Iron Valor will burn the world to the ground."

"Don't forget, fucking Menace Hardin that new fucking Midwest King is former Iron Valor too. You think he won't bring an army also?" Nazek was in full panic mode. "If they can find us." His voice trembled a little less certain now. "Maybe we kill the girl before they get close. Maybe we blame it on Otero."

Adramal snorted. "You kill the mate, and Maltraz will use your bones to pick his teeth."

"He'll use my bones no matter what," Nazek snapped, and for a second there was real fear in his voice. "You think he cares what happens to us?"

Another thud, louder this time. "He cares about the Plan. We make the Plan happen. Or we die."

Nazek fell silent, then spat a glob of phlegm onto the floor. "I'm going to see if the perimeter is holding. If not, we run. If he asks, you say I was here the whole time."

There was the scrape of feet on stone, then Nazek's shape flickered across the edge of my vision as he slunk away, hunched and muttering. Adramal lingered, standing just inside the doorway, arms folded. Even in the dark, I could feel him watching me.

I let my head hang forward, hair covering my face, and tried to look as limp and broken as possible. But every sense was dialed to the max. They were scared—really scared. Not just of Maltraz, but of the bigger, scarier things waiting above him. If the Council found out what they'd done, there would be no hiding, no deals, no mercy. It was the same way my old art teachers talked about the "gallery system"—all power at the top, everyone else just fodder for the grinder.

I rotated my wrists in the cuffs, feeling for play. The metal was too tight, but I thought I could maybe, just maybe, slip the right wrist out if I broke my thumb first. I'd need a distraction, or maybe to catch Adramal in a good mood. I filed that away for later.

For now, I listened.

Adramal sighed, a noise so human it made my skin crawl. "You shouldn't have mouthed off to Maltraz," he said, not to me, but to the empty room.

I kept my mouth shut, but when he didn't leave, I risked it.

"What's it like?" I whispered. "Working for a guy who'd take your soul to make a point?"

He looked at me, those black eyes bottomless. "Is it different for you? You follow your Alpha. You fight his battles. When he loses, you die."

I shook my head, ignoring the lurch of pain. "We choose our Alpha. If he fucks up, we can challenge him if we think we're strong enough to take him out."

Adramal considered this. "We're not wolves. There is no choice. Just power. Just survival."

I nodded, then flexed my wrists again, hard enough that one of them bled fresh. "Yeah, well, wolves bite back."

He snorted, then pushed off the door and walked over. His boots splashed through a shallow puddle and stopped an arm's length away.

"Maltraz will keep you alive as long as you're useful. If you want to survive, you'd better figure out what that means. Fast."

He turned and stomped out; the door slamming so hard it rattled the chair I was sitting in.

I waited until the echoes died, then set my jaw and twisted my right hand, pushing my thumb down and in until the bone strained. The pain was blinding, but it was better than doing nothing. If I could get free, even for a second, I could run. Or fight. Or at least die on my feet.

Out in the corridor, I heard Adramal's voice, low and urgent, talking to someone else. I caught the name "Otero," and then a phrase that made my blood run cold:

"If he can't kill the mate, he'll break her instead."

My vision went red for a second, but I made myself focus. Breaking was a wolf thing. You couldn't break someone who was already in pieces. I'd been broken and glued myself together so many times, I barely noticed the cracks.

So I waited, and I listened, and I learned.

When the rescue came—and it would come—I would be ready.

Let them try to break me.

I was Iron Valor now.

And I wasn't going down easy.

CHAPTER 24

GUNNER

I didn't know how many times I could replay the abduction in my head before it burned itself out, but I knew I'd never forget a single second of it. Wrecker had pulled the security cam files from every angle in the gallery, then triple-encrypted them on a hard drive locked in the Iron Valor safe. We'd all watched it—once, twice, a dozen times—until even the new kids who'd never seen a demon king in action understood just how outmatched we were.

It had barely been two hours since Brie had been ripped away from me. I was in the basement meeting room with the other officers and Ms. Pearl, waiting for the Supreme Council session to start. Wrecker's laptop was already bristling with cables, the big screens on the walls waiting for the video conference meeting to blink to life. Bronc paced the length of the conference table, boots thudding on hardwood. Arsenal and Big Papa flanked the door, arms crossed and faces stone-set. Doc leaned against the wall like he were holding it up. Ms. Pearl moved like a ghost between us, a coffee mug in each hand, making sure nobody bled out from lack of caffeine.

I sat at the end, hands wrapped around the biggest mug she had, waiting for the signal. Every muscle in my body twitched like it was waiting to pounce. My fingernails pressed into the ceramic so hard, the knuckles ached. I could feel my wolf just behind my ribs, howling and clawing to break free.

"Easy, Gunner," Bronc said. He slid into the chair beside me, closer than usual, a steady hand anchoring my shoulder. "We need your head, not your teeth. Let the Council see we're in control."

I nodded, jaw locked, and took a breath so deep it rattled the mug. "I'm good," I lied.

He grunted. "You will be."

Wrecker finished wiring the screens, then called over his shoulder. "Sixty seconds, boys. Everyone ready to meet these fuckers?"

A collective exhale from the room. Even Big Papa let out a grunt, flexing his hands like he'd just split a log. The tension was a living thing, crawling up the walls and hiding in every corner.

Ms. Pearl put a hand on my forearm, her touch cool and soft. "They're rattled too, sugar," she murmured, eyes locked on mine. "Don't let them see anything but fire."

I swallowed and nodded. "Yes, Ma'am."

The video conference tone echoed through the room, and the screen flickered to life.

First up was Rafe Mayfield—King of the Southern Wolves, seated in a leather chair that barely fit his frame. His black hair was slicked back, full beard trimmed sharp, but it was the eyes that killed. They pinned the camera with a predator's focus, like he was about to reach through and wring a confession out of whoever looked back.

Next to him, the king of the Midwest; our own Menace, who looked more like a hitman than a king, with his mate Savannah on his lap, one hand stroking her hair and the other flicking a knife open and closed. We'd set him up in Juliet's office just off the meeting room. Menace was deadly. Guess he'd put Savannah on his lap to make him less threatening. The knife ruined the effect.

The East wolves were represented by the newest king, Savannah's youngest brother Griffin, pressed into duty when her father was executed for stabbing (and killing) Menace after the battle to keep her as a mate. Of course, Archon saw to it that Menace was still alive. And the Southwest shifter king Slade Stewart looked alert and tuned in.

Three witch covens were also represented. Shahsta Tierney was dressed in fiery reds as her role as High Flame Caller must demand, her hair in tight braids around her head. Starweaver Fallon of the Astral Spire Coven was draped in purple and black lace with a silver shawl draped over her shoulders. Her blonde hair was in a high ponytail that highlighted her washed-out face and plum-colored lips. The oddest by far was the Mistress of Shadows from the Gloamreach Coven. I always wondered whether they wore their clothing as a costume or if it gave them power. Her hair was a tangle of curls and feathers; her pale face was pretty but made to look so fucking weird with one eye lined with thick black eyeliner and the other with no makeup at all. She wore some kind of loose black robe and sat in a feathered chair.

On the other screens were non-wolf delegates: Otero, Vampire King of the West, beautiful but with a weasel-like air that made you want to punch him in his face. His silver hair spilled over his collar, eyes like black oil, and his mouth never lost the little hint of a smile. Next to him, Archon looked radiant and almost holy. He radiated light even in digital form; his golden gaze somehow made the whole room smell like light and lilies. I'd never seen anyone make Bronc nervous before, but Archon did it with a tilt of his head and a gentle blink. We'd set him up in an empty apartment next to Arsenal's on the second floor.

Rounding out the group was Kazimir Kozlov, the Eastern Vampire King; the most ancient of all the supernaturals. His black hair hung like a satin curtain over his shoulder. He sat relaxed on a large golden throne and wore what looked like a red and black satin smoking jacket. Next to him sat his beautiful daughter, Lucia. Black curls framed her delicate face;

large dark eyes and full red lips held a slight smile. Lucia always looked like she knew a secret she could share but kept to herself.

Wrecker turned the camera on us, and I felt the weight of every gaze. Rafe nodded once, slow and deliberate.

The Council Chairwoman called the meeting to order and handed it over to Rafe. He got right to it, his voice low but carrying. "We are here in the matter of The Demon Maltraz's many violations of Supernatural Law. The evidence submitted by Iron Valor is... significant. But I want to hear it from you, Bronc. No theatrics. Just the truth."

Bronc didn't stand, didn't shift his weight. He just leaned in, hands folded, and spoke in the voice he used for deployments and funerals.

"Earlier this evening," he began, "Brie Lawson—fated mate of Finn 'Gunner' Walsh—was abducted by Maltraz, demon king, in the presence of no fewer than fifty witnesses; including humans. He was using an assumed identity: Lysander Hale, a Boston art rep, and had established a relationship with Brie over several weeks. The abduction occurred during her gallery opening. He took her from our territory and left no trace."

He nodded at Wrecker, who piped up. "We have video evidence. Maltraz's disguise drops at the moment of abduction. There's a visible shift—horns, skin, eyes, the whole thing. I can play the file at your request."

Rafe grunted. "We'll get to that." He glanced at the top row of screens. "King Menace, you've been tracking Maltraz for months. Did you suspect this?"

Menace's face flickered with a smile. "I'd heard he was back in the trafficking game, but no, I didn't think he'd get bold enough to snatch a mated wolf within sight of a standing-room only crowd. I was there at the time. He deliberately put our world in jeopardy. This is beyond breaking human law."

Otero, Vampire King, leaned forward, fingers steepled. "And if the video is fabricated? Iron Valor has a long history of... creative editing when it comes to demon activity. I remind you all of the tainted water issue." His voice oozed disdain.

Archon's gaze cut through him. "There is no fabrication here. I was in Dairyville not long after Brie was taken. I felt the taint. Maltraz's signature is unmistakable."

Kazimir nodded. "I want to see file," he said, his Russian accent slight but heard. "Play it."

Wrecker clicked play.

On the wall, the video started, first from the mezzanine camera. Brie stood at her desk, hugging Lysander Hale. He held her for a second, then his hands flashed up to her face. The skin rippled; the camera caught the moment the horns burst out, and the face collapsed inward. Brie's body flailed as Maltraz spoke to her. Then, I rushed into the room, and in a flash of black and red, both were gone—smoke and nothing left but my grasping at air and falling to the floor.

Lucia's face showed her anger and concern as the footage played; by the time Maltraz vanished with Brie, her hands were white-knuckled on the arm of her father's throne.

There was dead silence. Even the witches stopped whispering to each other.

Wrecker changed angles, showing the main gallery cam: the abduction happened so fast, the only hint was the slight sound of my wails through the soundproof room. My own face flashed on screen, twisted and feral, as I barreled after them. Then the video cut to black.

Rafe was first to break the silence. "There you have it. Otero?"

Otero didn't even blink. "Could be staged. Demonic illusions are child's play for his kind. I've seen Finn Walsh's file—decorated soldier, PTSD, excellent liar when the cause is right. Maybe this is an Iron Valor bid to pin their missing member on an enemy."

I felt my hands snap my coffee mug in two. Scalding liquid poured over my hand, and I didn't even twitch.

Slade Stewart who almost had nothing to say took exception to this fucker. "Otero, why don't you go fuck yourself. That kind of accusation has no place in a situation where a man has lost his fated mate."

Otero had at least the false decency to look contrite as he must have remembered that Slade had lost his fated mate only a year ago in a horrific accident, and he apologized.

"My apologies, King. I had forgotten about your loss. I was simply trying to remind everyone that Iron Valor is not a pack beyond reproach."

Bronc was ice. "You can't fake that signature, Otero. Archon just confirmed it."

Otero's smile was pure shark. "If the Angel King wants war, he can say so directly. But I don't buy this. Maltraz may be many things, but he's not a fool. He'd never abduct a wolf in public unless he wanted us to hunt him. And why? For this Lawson girl? I see no motive."

Archon interjected, voice calm and musical. "The Council has always protected the balance. Maltraz crossed the line when he targeted a mated female in front of humans. I have already erased the memories of every mortal witness, but the stain remains."

Shasta Tierney still seemed worried. "Can you guarantee that, Archon? There's no risk of exposure?"

"I guarantee it," said Archon. "But I will not do so again if the Council does not act."

She followed up. "We lost a sister to trafficking last year," her voice flat. "If Maltraz is involved, we want his head. But we also want assurances this isn't just a wolf turf war."

"Agreed," said Rafe, glancing at us. "Iron Valor, I know what you say is the absolute truth, but for those who may doubt; do you swear this is unvarnished? That you haven't doctored the record or omitted any facts?"

I stood before I could stop myself. My voice didn't even sound like my own.

"I swear," I said, "on the mate bond and my Alpha's name. We didn't touch a thing. If you want to see the raw files, Wrecker will send you the drive."

Rafe eyed me, gaze softening just a hair. "Understood, Gunner. Sit."

I did, only to realize that I'd cracked the corner of the wood of the table. Bronc squeezed my shoulder, and Ms. Pearl silently handed me a new, unbroken mug. The burn finally started to throb, but I ignored it.

Otero wasn't done. "Assume it's true. What's your solution? Last I checked, Maltraz has the ability to burn an entire pack to the ground. You want to risk that?"

Menace shrugged. "We have numbers. And a motive. If we let him get away with this, no wolf is safe. Fuck, no witch or any of us is safe. What happens when he grabs a Luna, or a queen?"

Otero's smile lasted all of three seconds before the venom leaked through.

"This is all very dramatic," the Vampire King said, lips barely moving. "But anyone who knows Iron Valor history will see this for what it is—a desperate attempt to paint Maltraz as the devil. It's your brand, isn't it?" He let the dig hang, then turned to the rest of the Council. "Does no one find it convenient that the only footage comes from their own systems? That the only so-called witnesses are wolves and their dependents? Please."

I saw Wrecker's knuckles go white on the edge of the laptop. Even Bronc's pulse ticked at his jaw.

Rafe cut in, tone harder than rebar. "Enough, Varic. The footage is clear. The signature is there. Archon himself testified."

Otero leaned back, steepling his fingers. "Archon is not above bias. His daughter is Iron Valor. He has a stake in this little melodrama."

A hush fell over the call, and for a moment it was just the faint buzz of a thousand-mile connection, the tick of a grandfather clock somewhere on Rafe's end. Then Archon spoke, voice calm and absolute.

"I am beyond bias, King Otero. I was present. I examined the site. There is no fabrication here. The only question is whether the Council will stand for what is right, or allow the whims of the undead to sway justice." His eyes locked on Otero's, and the screen itself seemed to shiver.

Rafe nodded to the Council Chairwoman, drawing every gaze to his corner of the world. "You heard the testimony. I call for a formal vote."

The Council Chairwoman agreed. "All in favor of removing Maltraz from the Council, raise your hand."

Hands went up. The witches, the wolf kings, Kazimir. Even Otero's own hand twitched, but he left it on the table, staring straight ahead. Archon, of course, did not vote—he just watched, waiting.

"Majority carries," Rafe said, voice dropping the gavel. "Maltraz is rogue."

Otero leaned forward, not even hiding the hate in his eyes. "If this goes bad, the next wolf the Council buries will be yours, Rafe. Don't forget who really runs this continent."

"You done?" Bronc said, not looking at the camera.

"Quite," Otero said, pushing his chair back, a sour look on his face.

Then the witches chimed in, their voices weirdly harmonious. "We need to contain the fallout. If Maltraz retaliates, it could spill over into human territory. I propose a task force. Wolves and witches. We're closest to the human community."

Menace nodded, eyes darting to Bronc. "We can coordinate. But we don't do anything until Brie is home."

The Council Chairwoman agreed. "But there must be a chain of command. Rafe, you take point. Slade and Menace, joint field leads. Witches, please supply support for the pack borders."

Rafe looked at Bronc, then at me. "Iron Valor?"

Bronc glanced at me, eyebrows raised: Your call.

I didn't think. I just felt it burning up my throat. "We don't wait. We hunt. The longer Brie's out there, the more likely Maltraz kills her—or worse. We take every able body, every resource, and we hit him now."

A couple of the other screens flickered with muted agreement. Nikki Caufield, the Gloamreach coven leader, actually smiled, tight and small.

Menace was next. "That's my boy. But we gotta do it right. I'm not having you lose your mate to Maltraz's games."

I was about to agree, but then one of the witches piped up, "What about diplomacy? Should we at least attempt to negotiate for the hostage's release?"

Something in me snapped. I shot out of my chair, sending it crashing into the wall. "Negotiate? With a demon king? He'll rip her apart the second he hears there's a chance the Council is considering ruling against him!"

Bronc was already moving, hitting the MUTE button on the laptop and holding up a hand to block the camera's view. I felt the wolf surge, my teeth snapping, vision tunneling yellow at the edges. I heard myself breathing like I was running a hundred-yard dash.

Arsenal and Big Papa moved fast, creating a wall between me and the screen, just in case I lost it and went full animal in front of every supernatural leader on the Council.

Bronc turned me toward him, speaking in the low tone that cut through any kind of noise. "Listen. Otero's playing a part. He wants you to go off, make us look weak, unstable. But now Maltraz is off the Council, Otero's alone. He won't help Maltraz, not at the cost of his own seat. He'll stay out of the fight. That means we can hit Maltraz with everything. Do you understand?"

I forced myself to breathe, to relax my fists, even as the claws wanted to push out. "Yeah. I get it."

He slapped my shoulder, hard. "Good. Now, get back in your chair, clean up, and let's finish this."

I nodded. Ms. Pearl handed me a towel, then wiped the sweat off my brow like I was a little kid. It didn't even embarrass me, just made the fire settle into something steadier, something I could use.

Bronc unmuted the feed.

"Apologies for the commotion," he said, sliding back into his seat. "You know how wolves get. Being violently separated from his fated mate is upsetting, as you can understand."

Menace smiled a little. "Don't apologize, Bronc. When this very Council tried to separate Savannah from me, I almost burned the whole place down." He pulled her into a heated kiss. Leaving her breathless. "Remember that, Red?"

She looked right into the camera, the fire of that shitshow still burning in her eyes. "How could I forget?"

Rafe was all business. "Yes, well…we have consensus. The task force is formed. Menace, Bronc, assemble your teams get a solid plan, and move out. Wrecker, coordinate with Archon for surveillance—anything unusual, any spike in demonic activity, report instantly."

Archon nodded once, but his eyes were on me, gentle and strong. "Brie is alive, Finn. I can feel her. She's as angry as she is scared. Hold that bond. You are the anchor."

I tried to push encouragement and confidence through our bond. "Thank you," I managed.

Rafe closed it out. "If there are any packs or factions willing to stand with us, contact me directly. We will coordinate the assault and ensure no one gets left behind." His eyes flashed, then softened. "We're going to bring her home, Gunner."

I believed him.

The meeting blinked off. The room was silent except for the faint pop of joints as Arsenal cracked his knuckles and Big Papa's chair scraping across the floor.

I looked up as Harper touched my hand. I hadn't even realized she was in the room. I caught her gaze and nodded, refusing to put off anything but that we were getting Brie back. "Go get my sister, Finn."

Wrecker closed his laptop, then looked over at Parker. "Looks like we gotta a fight on our hands, Wren."

She was quickly packing things into her bag. "Let's go get that girl, Eli."

Bronc nodded, eyes shining. "Let's go get her."

Arsenal grinned. "So what's the move, boss?"

Bronc looked at me. "We hunt."

Doc walked up more raring for a fight than I'd seen him in a while. "I'm sick of this motherfucker. Let's go take out a demon."

Archon glided into the room and looked me straight in the face. "I think I've got a fix on the demon's location. Let's go find your mate and bring her home."

Every muscle in my body sang with the need to run, to tear across the plains and find her. But for the first time since this started, I felt something else, too—a cold, bright clarity. I wasn't alone. I had my pack, and for once, the whole damn world at my back.

We'd bring Brie home, or die trying.

Either way, Maltraz was fucked.

CHAPTER 25

GUNNER

After the Council call, the Iron Valor war room snapped to life. I blinked against the LED glare as Arsenal, Wrecker, and Doc closed in from three sides, their boots loud on the hardwood, their faces fixed with urgency. I was still seeing the after-images of the Council—every king, every witch, cold-eyed stare of the vampires with their perfect poker faces—and then suddenly I was in the middle of a live-fire drill with all the grown-ups barking orders and making plans. I couldn't remember when I'd last slept or even taken a full breath. My hands shook so bad I dropped the fresh mug Ms. Pearl had just handed me.

Arsenal was first. "Gunner, we gotta talk now." His grip was iron as he steered me away from the others, voice pitched low, clipped and businesslike. "Menace just said that Rafe's sending his witch—the one who shielded us in Paris. You saw her when we got off the plane. Remember her?"

"Gwen," I said, though the name barely made a ripple in my memory.

"Right. She got hit twice by a Renault sniper while we were getting Harper and Brie off the bridge. Should have bled out. She kept the shield up the whole time. And when we went in for the warehouse raid, she was in the hospital, still running magical over-watch for our team."

Wrecker cut in, tone flat but with a nervous undertow. "Even patched in remote, she was enough to keep us shielded from view of humans. Never seen anything like it."

Doc folded his arms. Never been keen on witches besides Aspen, but Rafe wants her on-site, and I gotta say, she's the shit."

I tried to picture Gwen. I remember seeing a fancy woman get off the plane after the Paris job, sure. White-blonde hair, fitted suit. What I remembered most was that she never flinched, not once, even wounded I felt the power coming off of her.

"Rafe trusts her?"

Arsenal barked a dry laugh. "She's on Rafe's jet, along with his enforcers. ETA four hours to our landing strip. That's wheels down, assuming no Council fuckery in airspace."

I glanced at the clock. Four hours. I looked down at my hands, flexing them open and closed. My left pinky was still sore with the ghost of a bruise from where I'd tumbled to the floor trying to grab Brie as she vanished. I pressed at it with my thumb, just to feel something, to erase the hours between now and when I'd see her again.

"Where do they want us?" I asked. I could hear how tired my voice sounded.

"Here, for now. We assemble everyone at the compound. Menace and Savannah are up in the family room; the other teams are en route. Bronc wants a full headcount by dawn," said Arsenal. "And we've got to prep for the witches, too. They're coming in from three covens, and each group needs a safe landing. They don't want to waste energy on travel; they're saving every ounce for the actual fight."

Wrecker tugged me aside, his voice dropping to a hush. "They're bringing in Griffin Calloway and the entire East pack royal guard. Kazimir's got his best four plus Lucia. Slade Stewart's running point for the West wolves. Everybody's showing up for this."

My mouth felt dry as sand. I couldn't believe everyone in the country was showing up for my mate.

Wrecker asked if I could feel Brie through the bond.

"It's faint, but I don't get an overwhelming feeling of injury. I think she's hurting, don't get me wrong, but things just feel hazy. Maybe it's because she's on another plane. Maybe she's asleep, or maybe she's pretending to be. If Maltraz wanted her dead, he'd have done it already." Just saying that made me want to vomit.

We turned back toward the main room, where Bronc had assembled a huddle of the key players: Ms. Pearl, Juliet (waddling, massive, still the Luna even with a baby due in a few weeks), Big Papa, and the rest of the officer corps. The mood was pure trench warfare: no jokes, no nervous tics, just the kind of grim efficiency you get when the only options are win or die.

Bronc spoke, voice low and steady, the way a big dog calms a whole kennel with nothing but a growl. "We're on the clock. Menace's team is wheels up. Rafe's bringing his best, landing in four hours. The witches are split—each coven leader with a team. Kazimir and Lucia will be bringing their private jet straight here. Slade Stewart and his team will also fly directly here, ETA three to four hours. We're gonna make this happen tomorrow. Eh..." he looked at his watch. "Well, shit, actually today at dusk."

He scanned the table. "Nobody gets in or out unless we say so. Wrecker, double the guards on the compound perimeter. Arsenal, make sure Juliet, Harper, and Maddie are locked down. Pearl, you're in charge of all incoming teams. Doc, set up triage in the garage. Assume worst-case scenarios."

Then he looked at me. Just me.

"Gunner, you hang tight. Brie's alive, and she needs you sharp. You're no good to her if you run yourself into the dirt."

It should have been a comfort. But the words just made my skin itch.

"I need to do something," I said, and heard the desperation in it.

Ms. Pearl moved over, her hand gentle on my shoulder. "You are doing something, honey. You're holding it together. Sometimes that's the hardest job there is."

Juliet slid a mug across the table toward me, but I barely noticed.

Everything started to blur—voices, faces, even my own thoughts. I watched Arsenal hand Wrecker some document; couldn't make out what it even was. I saw Doc pulling supplies from a duffel, his movements precise and surgical. Ms. Pearl poured coffee, but her eyes never left the entryway, scanning for threats I couldn't even imagine.

And still, all I could see was Brie, in the dark, alone, waiting for someone to come through.

I drifted to the window and looked out at the compound. Trucks and bikes lined the drive, headlights cutting through the deep night. Even from inside, I could smell the pack: hot oil, sweat, a trace of wildflowers and diesel. Above it all was the tang of wolf, sharp and bitter. That was the scent of fear, and it had taken up residence in every corner.

I felt like I was sleepwalking. The emotions of the previous hours and lack of sleep had finally caught up with me. I must have looked like a corpse with a broken leg, because Bronc didn't even bother with the keys—he just picked me up by the armpits and half-carried, half-walked me across the compound to his house. The screen door creaked, the smell of baking bread and lemon cleaner hit me, and suddenly we were inside, the noise of the war room swapped for something softer, closer to human.

Juliet was already in the kitchen. Eight months pregnant and still on her feet, belly round as a pumpkin under a blue cotton dress. She had her hair twisted up in a knot, apron tied over her midsection like a flag of surrender. When she saw me, she smiled, genuine, as if the world hadn't just fallen to pieces.

"Sit, Finn," she said, and her Luna voice was so gentle I sat before my knees even had time to argue.

She put the kettle on, moving with slow, deliberate grace. Her feet were bare, her toenails painted a glittery purple, and I stared at them, grateful for the ordinary detail. I could feel her aura—a warmth that radiated through the room, smoothing out the jagged edges in my skull. For the first time in hours, I felt my hands unclench.

Bronc went to the fridge, poured himself a glass of water, then settled at the table opposite me, elbows wide, the top button of his shirt popped. He looked at me for a long minute, then said, "You holding up?"

"Not really," I said, but the words tasted less raw than before.

Juliet brought over a mug and set it in front of me. Chamomile, heavy on the honey. "Drink," she said. "It'll help."

I did as I was told. The tea was hot and sweet and tasted like memory, like something my mother would have made me. Shit, my parents. I hadn't even told them what was happening. It was just as well. I didn't need them in the middle of this. Just more people to worry about. Juliet put a hand on my wrist, cool and dry, and gave a squeeze. She didn't say anything else, just let the contact do the work.

"Come on in here." She led me to the great room and sat me on the large sofa. Her eyes held mine. "I know you want to be in the fight this minute," she said after a while. "But right now, you need to let others work. You can't help Brie if you're falling apart."

I nodded, not trusting myself to speak.

She smiled, soft and sad. "I used to think I was weak for needing people. That the only way to survive was to handle everything on my own. Turns out, the opposite is true. The strongest thing you can do is let someone else help."

I tried to think of how she might have been before Bronc; a little scared, a little proud, still finding her place in the world.

"Thanks, Jules," I said. My voice cracked on her name.

Bronc reached over and squeezed the back of my neck. It was a big, brotherly gesture, and I felt the pressure go straight to my spine, holding me together.

We sat like that for a few minutes, drinking tea and not talking. The world outside was still on fire, but in here, there was just the hum of the fridge and the clatter of a spoon as Juliet stirred her tea.

Then, as if the air itself shifted, Archon appeared in the doorway. He filled the room—seven feet of white-suited angel, hair like a spill of moonlight down his back. He moved without a sound, but when he put a hand on my shoulder, it felt like the touch of sunlight on bare skin.

"May I sit?" he asked, his voice gentler than I'd ever heard it.

I nodded.

He took a seat next to me, folding himself down with impossible grace. For a long moment, he just looked at me—into me, really—and I realized he was seeing things I couldn't even name.

"Your mate is strong," he said at last. "She is resting, as best she can. The demon king is clever, but so is she."

Something unknotted in my chest, just for a heartbeat.

"She's... okay?" I managed.

Archon nodded. "I sense she is whole. But she will need you when the time comes."

He stood over me, and for a second; the world turned gold and soft. I felt warmth run through my veins, sweet and heavy, and all the noise and pain drained out of me.

"Rest now," he said, his lips curving in a small, secret smile. "You will be needed soon."

He brushed his palm across my head, and I felt the drag of his power—a gentle, insistent pull, like the tide pulling a swimmer out to sea. My eyelids went leaden, my head dropped over to the arm of the couch, and the last thing I heard was Archon's voice, low and musical.

"He will wake when it is time, Juliet. Until then, Brie will hold on. But she will need him alert, and whole, when the breach comes."

Juliet's reply was a soft hush, almost a lullaby: "Thank you."

I let the magic take me, grateful to finally let go, if only for a few minutes.

The last thing I thought before I slipped away was that someone, somewhere, had finally made me rest.

And for Brie, for us, I would give them anything they asked.

When I awoke, it was like waking from the best sleep of my life, but with the creeping guilt of a man who knows he's about to be late for his own execution. My face was mashed into a pillow that still smelled faintly of Juliet's shampoo and cinnamon rolls. There was a quilt over me, thick and absurdly soft, and as I sat up, it slipped to the floor with a hiss. The light outside the window was now deep blue, clearly heading for dusk, and for a second I wondered if I'd slept through the whole war.

My first thought was for Brie. The bond was there—still a faint, fluttering line, more a shadow of her heartbeat than the real thing. But it was steady, not fading. I let myself feel it for a second, then shook it off and checked my watch.

Four hours, almost to the minute.

I ran a hand over my face. My regular scratchy stubble met me, but I felt no sore muscles. Whatever Archon had done, it worked better than any drug or medical protocol I'd ever seen.

The house was alive with noise. Somewhere to my left, Bronc barked orders in a voice like a rifle crack. Down the hall, I heard the rolling, singsong voices of witches as they chanted in unison, their words foreign but oddly familiar. In the kitchen, someone laughed—a short, sharp sound, immediately hushed. I rolled off the couch, feet hitting the rug, and staggered into the hall.

Kazimir Kozlov was standing in the entryway, looking like weapons-grade royalty backlit by the glow of porch lights. His black hair spilled over his shoulders, immaculate, and his suit jacket looked like the softest plum leather with a high velvet collar. His pants were black soft wool silk tucked into tall, soft leather boots belted with a gold buckle. He had obsidian daggers strapped to his sides. His hands were covered in fingerless gloves, and I wondered just how many other weapons were hidden on his body. Next to him, Lucia whispered rapidly in Russian, her lips barely moving. He responded with a nod, then turned those icy blue eyes on me.

"You awake, Finn Walsh?" he said, his accent just thick enough to make my name sound like a threat. "Good. We will need you."

Lucia winked at me, then drifted down the hall, her black lycra body-suit undoubtedly reinforced with spells and sigils, her own obsidian knives strapped to her thighs. Her red-soled sneakers made no noise at all on the hardwood. I didn't know how vampires did that, but it never failed to unsettle me.

I moved to the kitchen, where Maddie was pouring coffee into a tray of mismatched mugs. She handed one off to Big Papa, who had the faraway look of a man praying for peace and expecting a fight instead. At the far end of the room, Juliet sat in a rocking chair, one hand on her belly, the other holding a phone to her ear.

I nodded to them, then headed for the dining room, following the unmistakable scent of magic and power.

The table was the center of gravity in the room. Around it stood a collection of beings I never thought I'd see together outside of a Council photo op: the shifter kings—Menace, Rafe, Griffin, Slade—each with their own retinue of stone-faced betas. The witches were there, three coven leaders flanked by their seconds, all in variations of black or midnight blue.

There was even a warlock or two, I think, their faces hidden under shadowy hoods.

Then the vampires: Kazimir and Lucia, plus two others who stood so still I wondered if they were actual statues.

The room was alive with tension, but nobody spoke. Instead, all eyes were on the map spread out across the table—a massive, glossy printout of the Texas Panhandle, with Palo Duro Canyon circled in red multiple times, as if someone wanted to burn a hole through the paper.

I drifted to the edge of the table, taking it in.

Menace noticed me first. He raised a brow and grinned. "Well, if it isn't the man of the hour. Ready for showtime, Gunner?"

"Always," I said, my voice steadier than I felt.

Doc materialized at my shoulder, some kind of smoothie in hand. "Nice of you to join us. The witches want a blood sample before we go." He produced a tiny kit, already loaded with a fresh needle.

"Now?" I asked, but held out my arm.

"Now," he confirmed. "They need to tune the ritual to your signature. Makes it easier to breach the veil without frying your brain."

I looked away as he drew blood, focusing instead on the witches. One of them—a sharp-featured woman with silver braids—was painting sigils on the map with a brush dipped in what I hoped was just ink. She didn't look up as she worked, but her hand was rock steady.

"Is that going to work?" I asked nobody in particular.

"Best shot we've got," said Wrecker, who was manning a laptop patched into the kitchen Wi-Fi, monitoring satellite images and comms from the compound perimeter. "This particular witch can breach a shielded safe house from five miles out. It's good to have us all accounted for."

There was a sudden silence, and then the room seemed to chill as if Jack Frost had blown by.

Archon entered, flanked by four enforcers.

They didn't look like the angels in stained glass: no wings bared, no halos. Instead, they wore immaculate white suits, their hair cut close, eyes a shade of gold that seemed to pierce everything they landed on. Their movements were synchronized, fluid, and more than a little terrifying.

Doc nearly spat out his smoothie. "Jesus Christ."

Menace whistled, low and impressed. "Didn't know we rated the full Seraph response."

Archon smiled, and it was both kind and deadly. "The Council requests observance, but the Dominion requires enforcement. When a demon king crosses the line, we attend personally."

I stared at the four enforcers. "Holy shit."

Archon turned to me. "Nah, it's just ordinary." He winked.

That was enough to break the tension for a moment, and laughs carried through the room.

Rafe looked up from the map, his dark eyes gleaming. "So, what's the plan?"

Bronc leaned forward, spreading his hands over the table. "According to the angel, Maltraz is most reachable at the canyon. The witches will protect the entrance to the gate after Archon commands its opening. The wolves will form the vanguard. Vampires on flanks. Angels will then provide oversight and keep the humans away. Dominion Law prohibits their entrance to any hellscape. We fight our way through, locate Brie and extract fast."

Menace added, "No heroics. If it gets hairy, fall back. Our primary objective is Brie. Secondary is to fuck up Maltraz's operation as much as possible."

Wrecker clicked through a set of maps, highlighting choke points and cover. "We'll have drone eyes over the Canyon, and Parker's running point from here. Any movement, any weirdness, we'll know."

Aspen slipped into the room, wearing a battered leather jacket, a black tunic, and black leggings. She looked more witch than baker today, her hair up in a high pony, a silver chain around her neck. Oscar the prairie dog was nowhere to be seen, but I had a feeling he was lurking in a pocket somewhere.

She caught my eye and smiled tentatively, but brave. "Hey, Gunner. You good?"

I nodded. "Thanks to you. And Archon."

She stood beside me, arms crossed. "We're going to get our girl. I believe that." She set her hand over mine. "I'll be right behind you. I promise."

I swallowed hard, felt the fire settle into my bones. "Okay," I said, then louder, "Okay."

I tried to say thank you, but my voice didn't want to cooperate.

Instead, I looked back at the table.

The map was a mess of colored lines and sigils, but the focus was clear: Palo Duro Canyon, the "thinnest" spot in the veil between worlds. It was where the local tribes had said the spirits walked. Where the early settlers went mad with visions. Where tonight, we'd make our stand.

Archon lifted a hand, and all eyes turned to him.

"Maltraz is clever, but he cannot defeat unity," he said, his voice echoing in the silent house. "There is power in purpose. In loyalty. In love. Let that be your shield."

For a second, nobody spoke.

Then Bronc said, "Let's do this."

I took one last look at the map, tracing the red circle with my finger.

Brie, I thought. I'm coming.

The whole house moved at once, a living thing. Wolves loped out the door, witches whispered their last incantations, vampires melted into the dark. The angels followed, silent and certain.

I trailed after them, heart thumping, head clear and clean.

Menace grabbed my arm. "You see Maltraz, you don't try to kill him. You can't—not in that space. You focus on the target."

Archon nodded. "If you linger, you risk more than your own soul. The longer you're inside, the more the hellspace bends reality. That's how Maltraz wins."

Kazimir finally spoke, his accent rolling out smooth as silk. "You are brave, Gunner. But don't let it blind you. Sometimes the deadliest traps are the ones that look most like home."

I looked at him, and for the first time, saw the flicker of respect in those old, ancient eyes.

At dusk, the entire compound blurred into motion. Wolves and witches and the occasional vampire swept across the grounds with a purpose and an urgency I hadn't seen since we moved against Greenbriar. I watched it all from the front porch, the last sliver of sun catching the glass in Bronc's hand as he barked out orders. I could taste the battle in the air; copper and grit and the old, cold tang of fear dressed up as adrenaline.

The plan was simple, as all good suicide runs were: Get in. Get Brie. Get out before Maltraz realized we'd come to burn down his house. Bronc and Wrecker would drive the lead vehicle; I'd ride with them, Menace too, because apparently if you're going to run headlong into hell, you might as well do it with royalty at your back. Doc and Big Papa took the second truck, with Arsenal and Aspen in their back seat. The rest followed. Juliet, Harper, Maddie, and Ms. Pearl stayed behind to manage the fallback.

Parker and Savannah were everywhere and nowhere, tailing the convoy in the tech van controlling the comms. Savannah drove while Parker parked her ass in the back of the van, where she was already streaming live feeds from several drones back to the house and to their location. Everyone had been given instructions to watch the screens for anything out of the ordinary. "I don't care if it's a naked angel, or a tornado made out of bees. You report it," Parker instructed.

I loaded up in the back of the Expedition, the seat already stinking of Wolf and sweat and gun oil. Wrecker sat in front of me, arms folded over his chest like he was riding to a picnic. Menace was next to me. His white-blonde hair spiked up, glowed in the dying light, and I caught a flicker of the scar on his jaw when he glanced over at me.

"You ready, Gunner?" he said, voice calm and lethal.

"I'm fucking getting my mate back," I replied.

He smiled, sharp and clean. "That's the spirit."

Bronc led the convoy, his truck's engine growling so loud it made my bones itch. In the mirror, I saw Arsenal's truck, the man himself barely visible behind the wheel. Aspen sat in the back with Big Papa a look of pure murder on her face. I wondered what it would feel like to have two kinds of magic burning through your blood, but mostly I was grateful she'd be on our side when the gate opened.

We hit the highway hard; the sun melting down behind us and the road stretching flat and endless ahead. Every few miles, I saw another car, another piece of normal, and wondered if any of the humans had the slightest clue that monsters were at war just beyond the reach of their headlights.

The Palo Duro Canyon cut through the plains like an axe wound, the road falling away to a lip of orange and blood-red rock. I'd been here as a kid, back when my grandfather used to hunt jackrabbits and tell stories about "the old ones" who still walked the cliffs at night. Now the parking lot at the rim was empty except for our trucks, the air cold and sharp with the promise of a coming storm.

Bronc called a halt at the lot. I climbed out, boots crunching gravel, and took in the gathering. Everyone was already in position: Wrecker sweeping the perimeter with his eyes and his Glock; Arsenal and Aspen heads together, arguing over a battered duffel full of charms and medical gear; Doc hunched over the hood of the truck, loading magazines with iron-tipped rounds while Big Papa said a prayer over the open box. Aspen and Oscar pressed sigils on the boxes of ammo so that should they hit their demonic targets only a gooey mess will be left. Disgusting, but effective.

Rafe pulled up in a midnight-blue Escalade that looked like it had never been dusted in its life. He brought with him a woman I recognized instantly as Gwen—pack witch, sorceress, and the only human alive who'd ever gotten Rafe to shut up for more than a minute. She walked in Arsenal's shadow, eyes steady, lips pursed, the air around her faintly crackling with the promise of something arcane and deadly.

The angelic contingent made their entrance without a sound. Archon and his four Seraphim stepped from nothing onto the sand. They wore robes that seemed iridescent in the fading light, their faces so perfect it hurt to look at them for long. They stood at the edge of the parking lot, eyes turned to the canyon, hands folded as if waiting for a train. Their wings were folded, no flaming swords in sight; just presence. The kind that made everything else in the world seem a little less real.

They moved everyone to the mouth of the canyon. Archon spoke first, his voice rolling out like a choir in a stone cathedral. "This is as far as we go," he said, raising his chin toward Bronc. "Dominion Law forbids us from crossing into hellspace unless the Creator specifically commands it. We will open the path and hold it, but what happens inside is your fight alone."

Bronc nodded, grave. "We're ready."

Archon's gold eyes fell on me. "Are you?"

I swallowed, felt the answer rise up from somewhere below my ribs. "Yes."

He smiled. "Then attend." He raised his hands, palms outward, and the Seraphim mirrored him. The air went electric; the hair on my arms and the back of my neck stood up like it wanted to run away. The wind died, replaced by a low, humming vibration that crawled up my spine and settled behind my eyes.

"She is on the other side," Archon said. "There are wards—old ones, deep as the bones of the world. They will try to confuse you. To turn you against each other. To make you doubt." He swept his gaze over the gathered army. "Demons don't conquer by blade alone. Their greatest target is an unguarded heart and mind."

I looked at Menace, saw the grim set of his mouth, then at Big Papa, who'd taken Aspen's hand and wasn't letting go for anything.

Archon continued, "When you feel the cold, that is their breath. When you hear voices, ignore them. When you see things that cannot be, remember your purpose." He smiled, eyes suddenly full of wild, brilliant humor. "You're wolves. You know how to hold the line."

Doc snorted. "Can you give us anything stronger than a pep talk, Boss?"

Archon grinned. "You already have everything you need. But if you survive, I'll buy the first round."

Even the Seraphim cracked a smile at that.

I stepped closer to the rim of the canyon, the mate bond pulling me forward like a chain around my heart. The air was thick, heavy, and tasted of lemon and frost. I remembered what Maltraz had said. "Come find us." I intended to.

The others lined up behind me: Bronc and Wrecker, then Rafe, then Menace, then Arsenal and Aspen, then Doc and Big Papa. Gwen hovered just behind Rafe, her hand on his sleeve, her other hand clutching a bundle of dried herbs and bone.

Lucia and Kazimir had hung back, but as Archon started the ritual, they stepped up to the edge, vampire eyes gone full black. I was glad they were here, and that they had our backs.

Aspen leaned in and whispered, "When you see her, don't hesitate. The longer you wait, the more it eats away at you."

I nodded. "I'll bring her back. Promise."

She squeezed my arm. "See that you do."

Archon raised his hands higher, the hum swelling into a physical force that made the rocks at our feet vibrate. He began to sing—not in words, but in notes, long and deep and ancient. The sound bounced off the canyon walls, set the world spinning just a little slower, made the moon seem bigger and brighter overhead.

The wind stopped. The sky went utterly still. For a heartbeat, every single thing on earth seemed to listen.

The stones at the rim of the canyon began to glow, first gold, then white-hot. The glow crept along the dust and grass, crawling toward the center of the overlook where Archon and the Seraphim stood. As it reached them, the air split—not with a bang, but a soft, insistent tearing, like silk being ripped by careful hands.

The witches held hands and quietly chanted something low and ancient.

A shimmer appeared in the open space above the canyon, wavering and flickering, then resolving into a perfect oval of blackness. Beyond it, the world was inverted—sky below, canyon above, and something like stars burning in the void.

Archon's voice cut through the hum, clear and final. "Go! Run as one. Do not falter. Do not hesitate. Unity is your armor. Your purpose is your shield. Let no demon claim what is not theirs!"

For half a breath, no one moved.

Then Bronc nodded, and we all ran.

I heard boots hitting gravel, heard Wrecker's voice counting off in my ear, heard Rafe bellow a war cry that made the canyon echo like a thousand wolves had come to the party. I heard Aspen's feet behind me, heard the click of Arsenal's magazine, heard the rush of blood in my own ears.

The veil shimmered, and then we were through.

For a second, I thought nothing had changed. The ground was the same, the air cold, the canyon walls red and sharp in the night. But the sky was wrong. Too dark, too close. The stars were different—jagged, moving, alive. The canyon floor below boiled with shadows, things moving in the dark that had no shape or sense. I felt the mate bond in my chest, a white-hot wire tugging me forward, down, into the abyss.

Behind us, the gate glowed low and dark. A slit in reality, waiting for us to finish our mission and return.

The world was silent except for the pounding of my heart.

I looked at Menace, who grinned, feral. "Showtime, cowboy."

We moved as one, down the trail, into the screaming dark, into the jaws of hell.

For the first time since this started, I didn't feel fear.

I felt home.

Brie was close. I could feel her. The closer I got, the stronger it pulled, until there was nothing else—no doubts, no pain, no memory of a life before this.

Just the promise.

Just the hunt.

Just the sure, unbreakable knowledge that nothing in this world—or the next—would stop me from finding her.

I grinned into the dark, and let the wolf have the reins.

Hell had never met Iron Valor before.

They were in for a surprise.

CHAPTER 26

BRIE

Hell wasn't the word I would have chosen. It was too poetic, too mythic—suggested fire and brimstone and all the cartoonish trappings of damnation, instead of what it actually was: rot, and rock, and the kind of darkness that stains even the thoughts in your head. Of course, this wasn't hell. Not really. Not hell proper. It was a facsimile, like that bastard Maltraz. He wasn't the devil. He was just the devil-lite; a minion of his, if you will.

I was chained to a chair so heavy the metal had worn a groove into the volcanic stone beneath it. The chair wasn't bolted; it was the chains that did the work, crossing my chest, cinching my wrists to the arms and my ankles to the legs so tight I couldn't even lean forward far enough to touch my knees together. There was no light except for the phosphorescent ooze running down the wall in greenish streaks, and the only sound—aside from the perpetual drip—was the low, scratchy rasp of Nazek and Adramal arguing somewhere just out of sight.

I'd stopped trying to keep track of time. It was impossible, even if you cared. Sometimes the cell was freezing cold, so much that the condensation on the stone froze in fractal patterns I would have found beautiful if I could see them without shivering myself into a seizure. Other times it was so hot the air itself turned syrupy, thick enough to choke. Right now, it was both:

my feet had gone numb, but sweat kept dripping down the small of my back and pooling under my ass.

My dress was ruined. I'd lost count of how many times I'd wished for sweatpants, for literally any outfit that didn't broadcast "victim of a demon gala kidnapping." Sage green had been such a pretty color on the mannequin. Now it looked more like something a swamp threw up and left to ferment. My skin was raw where the manacles bit, my lips were split, and I was so thirsty that even the mold on the wall looked tempting.

But I was alive.

Barely.

I could feel Finn, even now. It wasn't a voice, not a presence, just a tug—an itch deep in my chest that no amount of screaming, cursing, or yanking at the chains could dull. I clung to it. I let it lull me into hallucinations when the thirst got bad, let it replace my fear with anger when my mind started to slip. It had only been a day.

They hadn't broken me yet. And if there was one thing I'd learned from the last two years of hell, it was that the world only breaks you if you let it.

A scraping sound, then a thud. I twisted my head just enough to see the flicker of movement in the gloom. Adramal, the demon with the face of a boxer and the attitude of a divorce attorney, was dragging Nazek by the collar, shoving him up against the wall. Their voices were low, urgent, barely above a hiss.

"She's not worth it," Nazek spat, baring teeth that were just a little too human. "Let them take her, Adramal. The Council's going to level this place in twelve hours—less if Maltraz keeps drawing attention."

"She's worth everything," Adramal shot back, his voice all gravel. "You know what happens if the king fails."

"We're not loyal to him. He's already lost. We should run. Take what we can and—"

A slap, loud and sharp enough to echo. Nazek staggered, clutching his cheek, then reeled back to spit blood on the floor.

"I plan to set myself up to take his place," Adramal growled. "Let's prove our worth to the Council when they finish with Maltraz."

Nazek snarled, but didn't argue. He shot me a look—equal parts greed and pure, reptilian loathing—then stalked off into the dark.

Adramal lingered, watching me. His eyes were old, bruised with centuries of seemingly having it all; then having nothing. For a second, he looked almost sad.

"You could make this easier," he said.

I gave him the best "fuck you," smile my parched lips could manage. "You want easy? You should've picked a different team."

He huffed a laugh, then melted back into shadow.

I didn't know whether to feel vindicated or scared shitless. Probably both.

Time passed, or maybe it just circled the drain, and eventually the cell door opened again. This time it was a lesser demon, one I hadn't seen before. He was built like a man, but his skin was the slick, pebbled black of an alligator, and his jaw looked like it could bite through bone. He carried a glass vial in one hand, and a wickedly sharp knife in the other.

He crouched beside me, set the vial down, and pressed the blade to my throat.

"Open," he said, his voice a hiss.

I bared my teeth. "No, thank you."

He pressed the knife in just enough to nick the skin. I could feel the heat of my blood as it ran down to my collarbone.

"Open. Or I will open it for you."

I considered spitting in his face, but my mouth was so dry there was no spit to spit. I opened my mouth, and he dumped the contents of the vial straight down my throat. It tasted like bleach and old pennies, and

I immediately convulsed, gagging it back up. He held my head steady, forcing my jaw shut until I had to swallow or choke.

As soon as he let go, I puked a stream of bile onto the floor. It burned all the way up, leaving me retching until nothing came out but a dribble of saliva.

The demon made a disappointed sound, then licked the blood from his knife. "Ruining the product is not wise," I rasped. I was gonna kill that fucker when Finn got here.

He laughed, then turned and left without another word.

I slumped in the chair, shaking, wiping the vomit from my chin. My wolf healing fought to keep up with my inquiries, but I think these iron manacles slowed it down. I wanted to scream, but my vocal cords felt like sandpaper, and even the thought of making noise seemed too exhausting. Instead, I let my head loll back and watched the flicker of green slime on the ceiling. I tried to save up energy.

If I closed my eyes, I could almost imagine Finn. The way he held me after those nightmares, his arms so solid and safe even when the world went sideways. His smell—leather, sweat, the faintest tang of cattle. His voice, deep and low, telling me to "hang on, Maverick." Sometimes I let myself believe it was real, that he was already on his way.

Sometimes I just wanted to die and be done with it.

I was dozing—drifting in and out—when Adramal crept back in. He waited until the door had swung shut, then knelt beside me, just out of reach.

The next time the cell door opened, it didn't creak or groan or scrape; it rattled like an announcement; the handle twisted hard enough to snap. I braced myself, spine straight, hands limp in my lap, like a dignitary awaiting the gallows.

He entered in shadows, his shape too tall and too still for a normal man. His face was as I remembered it: Lysander's sharp jaw, the unruly white-blond hair, the navy three-piece suit like something off a GQ cover.

He moved with a dancer's grace, and when he smiled, it was perfect—so convincing, for a second, I almost believed it was him.

"Bestie," he said, voice soft and sweet as Turkish delight.

The word hit harder than the knife earlier. Every humiliation, every moment of stupidity and hope, bunched together and clawed up my throat until it burned. I forced myself not to look away, not to show him what it did to me.

"Maltraz," I managed, making the name a curse.

He placed a hand over his heart, feigning hurt. "You wound me. After all we've shared?"

He drifted closer, feet gliding across the floor. There was a kind of beauty to it, the way he stole all the light from the room and used it to frame himself. Even in this pit, even after everything, I couldn't look away.

He leaned down, putting his face inches from mine. His breath was warm, sweet, and cold all at once.

"Did you really think Finn would save you?" he whispered, the words sliding over my skin like oil. "Did you imagine a rescue? A knight in shining fur?"

I felt my insides twist, but I clamped down on the feeling. I wouldn't give him the pleasure.

He switched tactics, morphing his face in subtle, horrifying ways. First, it was Finn's face: the wild eyes, the sun-baked freckles, the smile that could still my heart. He leaned in, voice deeper, familiar.

"Brie," he said, and for a split second, my heart stuttered. "It seems Otero is suddenly not interested in you, little girl."

I wanted to scream, but I wouldn't.

He grinned wider; the mask slipping as horns curled out from his hairline and his teeth lengthened, turning the Finn I loved into a cartoon monster.

I laughed, a dry bark that surprised even me. "Guess your network isn't as big as you made out, huh?"

His face fell, just for a heartbeat. The power in the room shifted. I'd seen this before; the moment when the predator realized the prey could bite back.

He straightened, eyes glowing. "You're clever," he said, the words ice cold now. "But cleverness won't save you."

He snapped his fingers, and the alligator-skinned demon from before scuttled in, bowing his head low. Maltraz drew a single claw along the demon's scalp, splitting it open from crown to eyebrow. The black ichor that spilled out hissed as it hit the stone.

"Failure," Maltraz crooned, slicing the demon's throat in one swift motion. The body toppled, writhing, but he was already moving on. Another demon in the hall tried to run; Maltraz lashed out, catching it by the ankle and dashing it against the wall until the bones exploded out through the skin.

Blood and gore painted the cell, spattering my legs and the ruined hem of my dress. I fought the urge to vomit, settling instead for a withering glare.

Maltraz turned back to me, his face now fully his own—smooth, inhuman, the eyes black as a collapsed star.

"You matter, Brie," he said, the words flat. "If you didn't, I wouldn't have wasted my time grooming you. I wouldn't have killed for you."

He crouched again, lowering himself until our eyes were level.

"You're not going to die, *little girl*. But you'll wish you were dead by the time your buyer is done with you. And by the time I've made every wolf in Texas pay for what they've done to me."

I wanted to ask why. I wanted to understand the madness. But I knew better than to invite a monologue.

Instead, I locked eyes with him and said, "Then do it. Stop pretending you have a plan."

The words hit. Maltraz's face twisted, and for a moment, I thought he'd rip my heart out right then.

But a voice from the hall interrupted. "She's right, Sire. We need to move her now, or the shipment will be compromised."

Adramal. Unflappable, untouchable, always showing up at the worst possible moment.

Maltraz straightened, shaking off the rage like a bad coat. "Who's the buyer?" he said.

"Foreign. Asian. Paid triple the normal rate. Wants her shipped with the others in the next shipment."

He considered this, then glanced back at me. "See? You're special."

He touched a finger to my cheek, leaving a smear of black blood.

"We leave tomorrow at midnight," he said. "If you're a very good girl, you may even get a window seat."

He turned, the tails of his suit flicking blood onto the wall, and left the cell.

Adramal lingered, his face unreadable.

"That was risky," he said, voice low. "He could have killed you."

I managed a laugh, weak but real. "He could kill me anytime. So could you. But you haven't. Why not?"

He didn't answer. He just looked at me, silent and watchful, as if trying to solve a riddle he didn't understand.

After a moment, he said, "You'd better eat if you want to have any strength."

He tossed a chunk of stale bread onto my lap, then closed the door with a finality that made my stomach drop.

I stared at the bread, not sure whether to eat it or use it to mop up the blood.

Outside the door, I heard Maltraz scream at someone, the sound so loud it shook the whole hallway.

I closed my eyes, counting the seconds between screams, and tried to focus on the mate bond. It was weak, stretched thin, but still there. Still real.

I wouldn't die here. Not like this.

I owed it to Finn.

If you've ever seen a haunted house at closing time, you know the vibe: all the performers are tired; the lights are flickering, and nobody really wants to be there. That's what Maltraz's fortress felt like now. The door to my room hung open, the dungeons half-abandoned. I could hear demons packing up, bickering in the hallways, ready to bolt at the first sign of a lost cause.

Adramal and Nazek were the only ones who stuck around. Nazek had a nervous habit of counting something in his head—tapping his fingers against his thigh, muttering numbers under his breath. Adramal stood watch by the door, arms crossed, eyes never leaving me.

I took inventory: two guards, both distracted, chains still loose on my ankle. I waited until Nazek drifted to the far end of the hall before I whispered, "You know they'll kill you if you stay. Finn doesn't do mercy."

Adramal didn't flinch. "If I run, Maltraz will catch me. If I stay, your mate might. I pick the lesser death."

I leaned forward, ignoring the ache in my shoulders. "Help me, and I'll vouch for you. My Alpha will listen. Finn might even let you live."

He stared at me, unblinking. "Why would you bargain for a demon?"

"Because you could have killed me, but you didn't. That has to count for something."

Nazek crept back, eyeing Adramal with suspicion. "What's she saying?"

Adramal shrugged. "She wants to make a deal."

Nazek snorted, spitting a gob onto the stone floor. "She'll promise you heaven, then sell you to the first wolf who asks. Don't be a fool."

But Adramal kept looking at me. "You mean it?"

I nodded, once, as serious as I'd ever been in my life. "You help me. I help you."

He seemed to consider this, then stepped away as if the conversation was over.

I didn't have time to worry about whether he'd go for it.

Because right then, the whole world shook.

It started as a low rumble, barely enough to rattle the chains. Then the ground heaved, and a sheet of dust fell from the ceiling, coating everything in fine gray powder. The torches along the hall guttered, sending the whole dungeon into a flickering, strobe-lit chaos.

Nazek let out a shriek, running for the stairs. Adramal went still, eyes wide.

From somewhere far above, I heard the first howl. It was low, long, and beautiful—pure wolf, full of anger and promise.

The mate bond exploded in my chest, white-hot and impossible to ignore.

"They're coming," I breathed, more to myself than anyone.

Adramal spun on his heel, unlocking my wrists and ankles with a key he'd hidden in his belt. He pressed a finger to his lips, then jerked his head toward the door.

"If you want to live, you stay put. If you run, you'll get caught in the fighting and die."

I rubbed my raw wrists, every muscle screaming to run anyway.

"Why?" I whispered.

His face was stone. "Because I gave my word. And because Maltraz will kill us both if we're caught."

The footsteps on the stairs got louder—boot heels and claws, shouts in languages I didn't recognize. The walls trembled with the weight of violence.

Adramal shoved me back into the chair, looping the chain around my leg so it looked like I was still locked down. He stood behind me, arms folded, projecting the air of a bodyguard on loan to a very unpopular VIP.

I heard Nazek scream. The sound cut short by a heavy, wet crack. Then another howl, closer this time, echoing off the stone.

Adramal's hands tightened on my shoulders. "Don't move until you see Finn. Not before."

The power in his voice was old, older than anything I'd felt from a wolf. For the first time, I wondered if Adramal had ever been anything else.

I nodded, silent.

We waited, the air thick with blood and fear and the sweet, electric promise of rescue.

And somewhere in that chaos, I knew Finn was coming.

All I had to do was hold on.

Hell came apart from the top down.

The first sign was the shift in sound—a roar, then silence, then a higher-pitched shriek that didn't sound like anything human or animal. It was the kind of noise that made the stone sweat, that made every cell in your body want to curl up and quit. It rolled through the dungeon in waves, loosening centuries of dust and rust, setting every chain and bar to humming.

Adramal, for all his calm, looked rattled. He knelt at my feet, slipping the chain off my ankle with hands that trembled only a little. "Hang on," he muttered, not meeting my eye. "The way is not clear."

But every instinct in me screamed *GO*.

Another shockwave hit—closer this time. The torches along the wall blew out, plunging us into strobing darkness as emergency magic fizzled and guttered. I could smell blood now—thick and clotted, layered over the rotten citrus of demon sweat.

I heard Nazek scream again, this time from the far end of the hall. Something big and fast hit the door, hard enough to buckle the iron, then the hinges gave out, and it crashed inward. Demons were running away.

In the flickering gloom, I saw a shape—a blur of black hair and high, elegant cheekbones. Lucia. She was beautiful, even when she was covered in blood up to the elbows and her lips were curled back in a snarl.

She moved with inhuman speed, cutting down the first demon she saw with a knife so sharp it barely left a mark before the head dropped off. She moved to the next, a downward slash opening the chest like a zipper. The bodies barely had time to fall before she was on the third, shoving the blade up under the chin and out the top of the skull.

Behind her, the hallway filled with screams, crashes, and the wet, meaty thud of violence.

The knot in my chest immediately loosened, and I threw off the chains.

From somewhere above, I heard a voice—Wrecker, I realized, cussing a blue streak as he fought his way down the stairwell.

"Come on, you ugly fuckers! That's right, line up! This monster has got a present for everyone of you!"

The sounds of claws against stone, of flesh tearing, of bones breaking were everywhere.

It should have scared me. It did, but the fear was laced with a wild, desperate hope.

They were here. My pack. My family.

I pulled myself up by the bars on the chair, using every muscle left. I was on my feet, my legs finding their strength. Suddenly a rush of demons slammed through the cell door—four, maybe five, their eyes all lit up with panic, not hate.

They didn't attack. They ran. Past me, past Adramal, straight for the back wall, where a tunnel sloped away into blackness.

Lucia followed, stepping over bodies without even glancing down. She saw me, and for a moment, our eyes locked. She bared her bloody teeth in what I decided to interpret as a smile.She made eye contact with me. "Hold on little wolf. Your Finn comes." Then she blurred after the fleeing demons.

Then the stairwell exploded, and Finn was there.

He came out of the smoke, his eyes so green they hurt to look at. He was bleeding from a cut on his forehead, but he didn't seem to notice. He ran straight for me, leaping bodies in a way that would have looked ridiculous if it wasn't so beautiful.

He caught me, one arm around my waist, the other tangling in my filthy hair.

Wrecker burst through, half-shifted, his hands claws and his teeth elongated just enough to give his threats extra weight. He was covered in blood and demon goo, his shirt torn to ribbons, his jeans black with demon goo.

He saw me and gave a manic grin. "You look like shit, Brie. Good to see ya."

I opened my mouth to thank him, but the sound that came out was pure animal—some kind of mix between a sob and a howl.

Behind him, the hallway filled with more wolves—Arsenal, eyes wild and teeth flashing; Big Papa, his bulk blocking the entire passage; Doc, glasses gone, eyes glowing like embers.

They barely registered Adramal. He held up his hands, stepping aside.

Finn hauled me into his arms, tears in his eyes. "Sorry it took so long."

I kissed him. "I'm just glad you're here. I knew you'd come. Please tell me you have some kind of a weapon for me."

"If I had my way I'd carry you, but I knew that would be too much to ask." He said while he reached behind his back and pulled out the compact 9mm with a double-stack mag I practice with at the ranch, and handed it to me. "I only have two extra mags in my pocket, and that's it so aim well, Maverick."

"I'll do my best cowboy. Now please get me out of here."

He grabbed my hand, and we headed for the stairs with me glued to his back. On the first landing, the ceiling above started to collapse. Chunks of rock and molten metal rained down, burning holes in the floor.

He barely flinched as he put his arm around me and pulled me along.

At the top, the world was chaos.

I'd always thought rescue would feel like freedom. Instead, it felt like a sprint through the world's goriest funhouse, with every step a gamble and every breath a brush with dying.

I noticed Finn was holding his side as we ran. His shirt was shredded and bloody. Someone had clawed him up pretty good, but he hadn't let go of me. Not for a second.

The staircase out of the dungeon was a choke point, and the demons made the most of it. They were packed in so tight it was hard to see where one body ended and another began—claws, fangs, and eyes like hot coals. Lucky for me, it was pretty much like shooting demons caught in the world's worst cattle chute. They hit the walls and the floor and didn't get back up. I was just thankful Maltraz hadn't taken my boots off as we walked over their corpses.

Behind us, Menace and Wrecker kept the pressure on. Every time I looked back, it was a blur of teeth and claws, blood splattering the rock in arcs that would haunt my dreams if I lived long enough to have any.

Lucia was everywhere at once—sometimes behind, sometimes ahead, moving so fast she was just a smear of hair and knives. Kazimir followed, cool and collected, his gaze alone enough to snap a demon's neck or fling it into the abyss that had opened up below the stairs.

At the top of the stairs, we broke out into a half-destroyed chamber. Bronc was in the thick of it, his wolf half out, muscles bunching under a shirt that was more blood than fabric. He was fighting three demons at once and winning, but just barely.

Finn stopped when we hit the main room at the top of the stairs.

"Stay here," he said, but I didn't want to. I didn't want to be alone. I grabbed his hand and didn't let go.

"I don't think so, cowboy."

Maltraz waited at the far end of the room, in front of the only visible exit. He was less human now, more a fusion of every nightmare I'd ever had—horns curling out like antlers, eyes burning with hate, body radiating power so thick it made the air shiver.

He saw us and howled, "None of you are leaving! The girl is mine!"

He turned to Adramal and Nazek, who'd followed us up the stairs, and bellowed, "Defend your king! Now!"

Adramal looked at me, then at Finn, and just... stepped aside.

Nazek did the same. They both melted into the shadows, unwilling to die for a lost cause.

Maltraz's face went from furious to desperate in a heartbeat. He hurled a lance of black fire at Finn, but it fizzled out before it reached him. I looked over and saw Aspen at the far side of the chamber, hands raised, her hair floating around her face like she was underwater. Oscar perched on her shoulder, squeaking out a prairie dog war cry.

The next volley from Maltraz—spinning daggers made of pure magic—hit an invisible shield. Aspen caught them with her hands and spun them right back, three at once, hitting Maltraz in the chest and knocking him back a good ten feet.

He screamed, clawing at the wounds, but they didn't bleed. Instead, blue smoke poured out, the essence of his power burning away with every breath.

Lucia was at his side in an instant, her blade at his throat.

But instead of begging, Maltraz smiled.

"You think you've won," he spat. "I haven't even begun to lose."

He twisted out of Lucia's grip, burning himself in the process, and tumbled backward into the darkness beyond the chamber. There was a hiss, then silence.

Kazimir stepped up, eyes still fixed on the place Maltraz had vanished. "He'll run," he said. "He always does."

Finn looked at me, his face wild and beautiful and alive. "You okay?"

I nodded, tears leaking out despite everything. "You came for me," I said, voice shaky.

He pulled me in tight against his chest, and kissed my hair. "Always," he whispered. "Always, Maverick."

Behind us, the world started collapsing again. Chunks of ceiling dropped, setting off cascades of debris that drove us toward the exit.

Bronc shouted, "Move! Now!" We did, the whole crew—wolves, witches, vampires, and one prairie dog—pouring into the narrow corridor that led to the surface.

It was pure chaos. Every corridor seemed to want to collapse, the one was jammed with more bodies, every corner a trap. But with the pack at my side, I felt invincible.

At the very end, where the air turned from hot and toxic to cool and real, Archon was waiting, his robes as white and perfect as ever, wings rising open slightly.

His hands were still raised.

"Go," he said, voice echoing in my bones. "I'll hold the breach until all are clear."

Finn and I were the first through, then Aspen and Lucia, then the rest. I saw Adramal and Nazek trailing behind, neither looking back.

As soon as we cleared the tunnel, we rounded the corner to find a clear spot. The moon and the stars illuminated the entire area around us. I collapsed onto Finn's lap, and for a second, I couldn't breathe.

His hands were everywhere as though he were making sure I was real. He kept muttering, "You're safe, you're safe, you're safe."

I tried to answer, but my throat closed up and all I could do was sob.

Other people continued to stumble out, one by one, and collapsed on the surrounding rocks. Bronc slumped down, bleeding from a dozen wounds. Wrecker and Menace were both missing pieces of shirt and probably a few pints of blood.

Aspen and Big Papa staggered over together. She knelt beside me and pressed her cool hands to my face. "We did it," she said, voice choked. "We got you out."

Oscar hopped onto my shoulder, patted my cheek with a tiny paw, and squeaked something that sounded suspiciously like "Foolishness."

I laughed, the sound high and broken, but real.

Finn wiped the tears from my face, his own eyes red and wet.

"I thought I'd lost you," he said. "I thought…"

I put a finger to his lips. "You didn't. I'm here."

He kissed me, dirty faces, mouths, and it was everything.

For the first time in my life, I felt it—not just the mate bond, not just the adrenaline rush, but real belonging. A place. A purpose. A home.

And as the moon rose higher over the canyon, painting everything silver and perfect, I realized I wasn't just rescued.

I was found.

After a few moments, we heard a commotion. Kazimir was gliding towards us carrying someone in his arms, with a large trail of blood pouring behind him.

It was clearly one of us who'd been injured, but who? Then I heard the voice—deep, raw, and unmistakable.

"Shit, shit, shit! They got him!"

Wrecker, his voice breaking on every word.

Kazimir carried Doc in his arms, bridal style, but there was nothing romantic about it. Doc's leg was pumping blood with every heartbeat, a dark, arterial spray that painted the sand behind them.

The group was stunned for a second—then everyone snapped into action.

Aspen screamed, "Set him down here, right here!" and Kazimir laid Doc out on a flat boulder. His face was ghost-pale, sweat soaking his hair, glasses gone and eyes rolling in their sockets.

I saw the wound just above the back of his knee. The muscle had been torn open, and blood was pouring out in surges, pooling under him, soaking into the stone.

Finn grabbed at his own shirt, ripping it off in one motion trying to fashion it into a tourniquet, but the blood just soaked through, hot and fast.

Wrecker dropped next to Doc's head, cupping his face. "Stay with me, man. You hear me? Stay with me."

Doc managed a smile. "Wouldn't dream of missing the afterparty."

His words slurred, eyes drifting.

Aspen was already working her magic, muttering spells, hands glowing green as she tried to slow the bleeding. But it wasn't enough. Nothing was.

"Where's Archon?" I shouted, scanning the crowd. "He can heal—he has to—"

But Archon was still at the breach, holding it open. I saw his outline in the glow, huge and impossibly bright, arms upraised and wings spread wide, his whole body straining to keep the gate open.

"He can't come!" Bronc yelled, voice tight. "Not until everyone's out. It's Dominion Law—he breaks the line, the rest are lost."

I looked back at Doc. His pulse was fading under Finn's fingers. His lips had turned blue.

I wanted to scream, but all I could do was stare.

"No, no, no!"

The world, which had seemed so bright and beautiful just minutes before, narrowed to the spot of blood growing larger and larger on the ground.

Aspen was crying now, her voice shaking as she whispered the spells. "Don't you dare go. Don't you fucking dare. We need you!"

Kazimir tried to help, but even his hands shook. "The artery is gone," he muttered, voice flat. "He cannot last."

Doc looked up at me, his eyes oddly clear for a second.

"It's okay," he said. "You made it. That's what matters."

And then he was gone—eyes rolling back, body going slack.

The silence that followed was the worst thing I'd ever heard.

Wrecker let out a howl, part wolf and part human, so full of grief it tore holes in the world.

Finn let go of the wound and wrapped me in his arms, but I barely felt it.

I just kept staring at Doc, at the blood, at the place where hope had been.

We'd made it out.

But not all of us would make it home.

EPILOGUE
DOC

The first thing I noticed was the cold. Not the stabbing, shocking kind you get from a chest tube or a February wind off the canyon, but the kind that starts in your feet and radiates up, hollowing you out from the inside until there's nothing left to shiver with. I remembered reading once that when people freeze to death; they take off their clothes at the end. Paradoxical undressing. The body gets so desperate it tricks itself into feeling heat, and you strip down naked, lie down in the snow, and that's it. Game over.

I wasn't naked. Not unless someone decided to take my pants off in the interim, which would be both unprofessional and highly concerning. My last memory was being carried by Kazimir Kozlov, his hands cold even compared to my own, and then the ground coming up to meet me like a cold wet towel. Someone said my name, I think. Maybe it was Wrecker, or maybe it was Brie. The voices blurred. What I knew, with the crystalline certainty of a dying man, was that I was bleeding out. Bronc's anguished voice had told me he knew. He knew I was gone. He had been my brother, and I had left him. I felt like crying, but I couldn't make any tears.

The rest of the sounds bled together. It was a symphony of voices, but there wasn't any harmony. Wails didn't waste time trying to find resonance.

They just came from the guts of the people who loved the dying. The people who loved me.

Wrecker's curses tore through me like shrapnel—each word a raw, ragged thing that carried the weight of his helpless fury. I could feel Arsenal's growl vibrating in my own bones, his pleas for me to "stop being a pussy" rough-edged but trembling with a fear he'd never admit aloud. Gunner's voice shattered me worst of all; grief and guilt bled into every syllable, and I ached to tell him none of this was his fault. But how could words reach a soul drowning in blame when the true evil lay far beyond any of us? Beside me, Papa wept openly, his tears falling hot against my skin, while Bronc—no, Alpha now—commanded me to fight with a voice that cracked under the strain of command. Their voices, desperate and shattered, pinned me to that moment. I wanted to give them what they begged for... but the darkness was swallowing me whole. My brothers' love became the last thing I felt—a crushing, beautiful weight—as I realized I had nothing left, not even breath, to fight with.

They say you don't actually feel yourself die. That's bullshit.

The pain was monumental, and then it was just... gone. The last thing I felt was the pressure of Finn's hands on my thigh, the torn artery pulsing against his palm, the blood bubbling up hot and then cold and then nothing at all. I wanted to say something—classic last words, something pithy like "Tell my ex-wife I never missed her"—but the words wouldn't come, and I didn't have an ex-wife, anyway. Maybe I'd already said them. Or maybe my synapses had just gone on strike.

After that, there was nothing but the dark.

Not that I'd ever expected a parade of angels or a warm golden light or any of that crap, but it seemed like, I don't know, maybe a transition would have been nice. I'd been a combat medic. I'd stitched up more bodies than I could count, cracked more ribs than the Dairyville BBQ joint. When people died on you, even if it was ugly, there was always a moment. A shift. Something. Here, there was only the dark. I waited for the light at the end of the tunnel, but all I got was a long, echoing silence, the kind that fills up an ER waiting room at three a.m. after a code black.

This is how it ends? Not with a bang, not with a wolf howl, but with my ass in the dirt and a hole in my leg? Great.

My thoughts were running, but they kept tripping over themselves, derailing into dead ends and weird loops. Was this what dying was? An endless run of shitty reruns and half-remembered dreams? I tried to focus, but everything slipped away like a suture in greasy gloves.

For a while, I was convinced I'd hallucinated the last few minutes. Maybe there had never been a demon war. Maybe Brie wasn't even real. Maybe I was just some loser in Amarillo, half-mad from too many surgeries, finally losing the plot for good. My brain rolled through every highlight of my career: the time I set a broken tibia with nothing but a tire iron and duct tape, the time I stitched up Bronc's scalp in the back of a moving F-150, the time I saved my own damn life by yanking a knife out of my own shoulder. Not a single one of those stories would impress anyone on the other side. There probably wasn't even another side.

After a while, the cold went away. Not because I was warm, but because I was gone. I floated above the ground, a spectator in my own post-mortem, and watched the others with a kind of disinterested awe. Finn was holding my hand, but it looked like he was holding a dead fish. Aspen was crying. The prairie dog was, for some reason, flipping me off. Kazimir was talking, but it was all white noise, like a news anchor with the sound muted.

I wanted to scream at them: I'm not done! Put me back! There's still work to do. But the words evaporated.

There was supposed to be a bright light. There's always a light, right? I'd watched a million hospital dramas. There was always a tunnel, a golden glow, a choir. I waited for it. I waited for a soft voice, a memory of my mother, maybe the sound of rain. But all I got was a static buzz and the echo of my own voice, bitching about the lack of amenities.

Seriously. Does everything always have to be fucked up? I killed a bunch of demons, then tore my femoral artery on a jagged edge of a fucking rock, and I don't even get the courtesy of a proper afterlife? Kill me. Oh, wait. Guess it did.

I waited some more. Time doesn't mean much when you're a ghost or whatever I was, but it felt like hours. Maybe minutes. Maybe it was just one long, stretched-out second. I was no longer watching the scene. I was just here. In the dark. Waiting for what, I didn't know.

Then I heard the voice.

It came from somewhere above, or maybe inside my skull. Female, the vowels rounded and old-world. There was a smile in it, the kind that meant trouble.

"Wake up, Ryder Lowrey. I'm not finished with you yet."

I'd recognize that accent anywhere, even if you stuck me in a sensory deprivation tank and force-fed me cold borscht for a month. Russian, but the kind of Russian that got you thrown out of St. Petersburg for being too beautiful and too deadly for polite society.

Lucia Kozlov.

I'd been dodging her for years. Not that it was personal, exactly. It was just that wolves and vampires didn't mix, not in a way that ended well for anyone involved. Sure, the MC did business with her family, and I'd played at her father's club from time to time, but that didn't mean you had to get cozy. But here she was, cutting through the darkness with a few syllables.

I tried to ignore her. Maybe if I pretended to be a better corpse, she'd go away.

Instead, I felt the air shift—sharp, like booze, or the moment before you take a really good punch to the face. There was a pressure, a hand on my chest, and for a moment I thought she was trying to crush my ribs in.

"Come on, Ryder. Don't make me force you."

That was definitely Lucia. Nobody else called me by my first name unless they wanted something, and Lucia always wanted something.

I tried to answer, but my mouth wouldn't work. There was no mouth. There was no body. I was just the sum total of all my bitching and moaning, drifting like smoke.

"You are not dead, not yet. Do you hear me?"

No, I wanted to say. I do not hear you. Fuck off. Let me die in peace.

She laughed, a quick bark. "If you die, you will make it too easy for them. You are not coward, Ryder. I have seen you fight."

I wanted to protest, but she was right. I hated losing, and I hated quitting. But what was I supposed to do? Will my arteries back together? Rub some dirt on it? Walk it off?

"Try harder," she said, and I could swear there was a smile in her voice.

Suddenly, I felt the cold again, but this time it was mixed with heat. Liquid fire surged up my thigh and into my chest, setting every nerve ending alight. The pain was so real, so raw, I almost wanted the darkness back. Then the pain faded, replaced by a slow, steady thumping.

My heart. It was still beating.

How the fuck...

Voices, louder now. The others. Finn, somewhere close, called my name. I sensed them: Bronc pacing, Wrecker and Arsenal just staring down at me, with an "Oh shit" escaping Wrecker's lips. Big Papa and Aspen were praying I think. Even the prairie dog was in on it, squeaking like a deranged CPR instructor.

And over it all, Lucia. Was she straddling me?

"Drink, Ryder, now. Or I will make you."

Drink what? There was nothing left to drink. Did I even have a mouth? My blood was on the rocks, painting a masterpiece for the local vultures.

She leaned over me, so close I could smell the faint trace of rose and cold iron. "Do not make me repeat myself."

There was a lot they didn't tell you in medical school. Like how to handle the moment when a vampire is trying to force-feed you her own blood while your femoral artery still sprays out little decorative splatters onto the Texas sand. Maybe that was covered in some prestigious European program, but my instructors were more about the hands-on approach: figure it out, or die trying.

"Drink," Lucia said again. I somehow sensed her face right above mine, lips already glossy with the stuff she was trying to pour down my throat. The compulsion in her voice was more than just the usual vampiric charm; it hit me like an anesthesia mask clamped too tight, filling up every available space in my mind with one simple command.

Do what, now? Yeah, that's a no-go.

I'd sooner drown in my own blood than take orders from a vampire, even one who looked like she could have run Paris Fashion Week with one flick of her eyebrow. But my body disagreed. My jaw went slack, and the next thing I knew, she had her wrist pressed to my lips, the skin already split and leaking thick, arterial red.

The taste was not what I expected. It wasn't altogether unpleasant—just iron, salt, and a bitter edge; but the idea of it made me want to retch. I coughed, tried to spit it out, but she was ready for that. She clamped her free hand over my nose, pinched it shut, and when I tried to gasp for air, all I got was her blood, filling my mouth, burning down my throat. For a moment I panicked, tried to bite her, but the flesh was as unyielding as steel cable.

"Good," she crooned, her accent making it sound like "goot," and pressed her wrist harder. "You must drink, or you die. Is simple, yes?"

I tried to tell her where she could stick her "goot," but the words got drowned in the rush of blood. My stomach lurched, and for a split second, I thought I'd puke it all back up. But then the warmth hit, spreading from my core outward, flooding my arteries with fire.

That's when the healing started.

I could feel my leg—my actual, ruined leg—start to pulse. It wasn't like regular wolf healing, slow and steady, bone knitting over hours. This was accelerated, frantic, like every cell was a soldier in retreat, falling back to the heart and regrouping in a panic. The muscle twitched, spasmed, then began to pull itself together, fiber by fiber, like time-lapse footage played at insane speed. I could almost hear the wet squelch as the artery zipped shut, the flesh knitting over it, the skin sealing so fast it left no scar.

All of this while Lucia still had her wrist in my mouth, pouring more of her blood in.

I should have been revolted. I *was* revolted. But I was also alive, and as the blood took hold, the world started to look less like a bad fever dream and more like an actual place again. The night was sharp, every sound clear as a bell, the smell of blood and sand and spent gunpowder so intense I thought I'd drown in it.

I sensed my brothers around me. I didn't care.

My body wanted more. A lot more.

I didn't want to admit it, but the taste—now that I wasn't dying—was addictive. *She* was addictive. All those years I'd wanted her and run the other way, gone and now I was consuming her. Like the first cigarette after a fifteen-hour shift, or the exact burn of a good rye on a shit-cold day. My hands, which had been limp and useless, clamped onto Lucia's arm and pulled her closer, fangs breaking through my gums and slicing into her skin.

I heard her moan, low and throaty, and the sound sent a bolt of something electric right through my spine.

What the actual fuck? I wanted to let go, but I also didn't want to let go. I drank, and drank, and with every swallow I felt myself getting stronger, the world coming into focus; the pain replaced with a kind of furious energy that made me want to run, to fight, to rip the goddamn moon out of the sky.

Her hand reached out and touched my cheek, and fuck if I didn't lean into it.

I'll just have a little more, I told myself. Just enough to make sure the bleeding's stopped. Strictly survival.

Bullshit.

Every instinct in my body screamed for more. I drank until the world spun, until my heartbeat was a drum in my ears and the colors around me went too bright, too sharp, almost painful.

Then Lucia pulled away, tearing her wrist free with a flick of her hand. I spat blood, coughed, tried to clear my head. My vision swam, and for a second all I saw was her—her face flushed, eyes dilated, lips parted in something that was almost hunger.

She knelt over me, her mouth stained red, and stared down like I were the most fascinating thing in the world.

"You are stubborn," she said, voice low. "But soon we will see how stubborn."

I tried to curse her, but the words got lost in a new wave of sensation. My leg burned, then froze, then burned again. My teeth ached, my bones creaked, my skin prickled like it was crawling with ants. I groaned, doubled up, and hit the ground so hard I bit through my lip. The blood tasted different now—my own blood, but laced with something new, something ancient and hungry.

"Shit," I whispered, pressing my hand to my face. My fingers came away covered in red, but I didn't feel weak anymore. If anything, I felt like I could run a marathon, or tear a car in half with my bare hands. My heart hammered, not wolf-fast, but something in between. A predator's heart.

I looked at Lucia, and for the first time, I really saw her. Not just the stunning surface, but the power underneath. She looked back, her eyes glowing in the dark, and I saw approval there. Maybe even pride.

"Did you—did you just—" I couldn't finish the question.

She smiled, all teeth. "You are not dead, Ryder. Not really."

I tried to stand. My legs worked, but I was shaky, light-headed, like I'd just sprinted a mile at high altitude. The others were staring—Bronc, Wrecker, Finn, Arsenal, Menace, Brie, Aspen, even the damn prairie dog. They looked at me like I'd grown a second head. Maybe I had.

Kazimir raised an eyebrow at me.

I ran my tongue over my teeth. They felt normal. Human. My skin, too. No burns, no wounds. Even the scar on my left hand—a souvenir from a childhood dare gone wrong—was gone.

Fuck. Fuck. Fuck.

What had Lucia Kozlov done to me?

THANKS FOR READING

Thank you so much for taking this journey with Gunner and Brie. Truly—thank you.

Writing *Gunner* meant stepping into the quiet strength of a man who carries more than he shows, who loves deeply, protects fiercely, and stands steady even when the world around him gets loud. Watching him find the one person who sees straight through the armor was one of those stories that settles into the bones while it's being written. I hope it settled into yours while you read.

The Wolves of Iron Valor MC has always been about courage, brotherhood, loyalty, and the kind of love that doesn't flinch when things get hard. Gunner's story leans into that truth in its own way—sometimes softer, sometimes sharper—but always with heart.

If you enjoyed this book, I'd be incredibly grateful if you'd consider leaving a review. Reviews help more than you know, especially for independent authors, and they help new readers find their way to the wolves.

And now, as I dust myself off (and stock up on more tissues), I'm gearing up to write Doc, our grumpy, stoic healer's story next. And what a story it promises to be now that he is inexplicably tied to the vampire princess Lucia Kozlov. And as they will no doubt make one final stand against Maltraz, that damn slippery demon who keeps insisting on being like that pebble in your shoe that drives you crazy. Except this pebble can possess your soul and drag you to hell. If you thought Gunner was a bit of a crazy ride... brace yourself.

Thank you, from the depths of my ink-stained soul, for reading. For feeling. For staying.

With endless gratitude,
Dex

P.S. If you ever need to debrief after this emotional rollercoaster (or demand more details about the wolves and their mates), find me on my socials: Facebook (www.facebook.com/dexhavenauthor) Instagram (@authordexhaven) or Tiktok (@authordexhaven), or haunt my website (dexhavenauthor.com) for previews, deals, and confessions I can't make anywhere else. You can even email me dex@dexhavenauthor.com

ABOUT THE AUTHOR

I'm Dex Haven, a romance author nestled in a tiny town in central Texas in a 1901 Victorian money pit. I've been married a hot minute to my Mean Man (since 1986). I know how important it is to keep those fires burning when life bogs you down. I write the kind of spice that's for you. For everyone who's spent their day juggling kids, work, house chores, and a never-ending to-do list. For the people who feel like their spark has been buried under "all the things" — this is for you. My books are your escape. Your reminder that you're still that sexy, powerful, wild creature with so much to offer. And trust me, your partner definitely notices.

I'm so glad you've found your way to my books. I hope my stories remind you to fight for your magic and, just maybe, give you a reason to stay up way too late reading "just one more chapter."

ALSO BY DEX

If you loved Gunner and somehow missed the other books in the Wolves of Iron Valor MC series, you need to read them all! There will be seven when the series is completed.

Bronc- Book 1, Menace- Book 2, Wrecker- Book 3, Big Papa- Book 4, and Arsenal- Book 5

And if you're a fan of romantasy, my first series is a fun tale of an orphan from Texas who realizes she's actually not so much from Texas as she is from an entirely different realm. She's tasked with saving the realm from destruction by a power-hungry goddess. Along the way she meets her mate, a dreamy shadow-wielding vampire king, as well as a host of other fabulous creatures, including dragons, of course. Read the completed hot and steamy Kingdoms of Eldoria series **Claiming Starlight, Starlight & Luna Rising, and Starlight & Fire**, where you'll meet Olivia and Cade as well as the Dragonia and group of wonderful friends and family she comes to know and love. You'll find yourself on the edge of your seat with the heart-stopping action and needing a fan to cool yourself off as the steam heats up between several couples.